IRON MAIDEN

by

Glenn L. Goettel

ISBN: 1-5600-2791-6
ISBN-13: 9781560027911

Dedication

For Rebecca

1

It was a midwinter's afternoon in Salem, white and blue and certainly cold, since the window glass was frigid to the touch. Little commas of frost by the lattice corners; cold inside a little, cold outside for real.

Linda Bloom liked to sit on the window ledge of the apse in their top-floor apartment. With her legs crossed, nice and cozy, she'd read her paperback novels. She kept the curtain drawn just so, to see and not be seen. She'd wait for her husband, and read. Or just read.

And look. No neighbors in sight—not even a dog. The families across the way had their curtains drawn, like that might keep the cold out. The two-family houses were closed up like prisons, guarded by bare black elms. So bare and black, so gnarled and old. Yet they made the street a claret-colored dreamworld in the fall, and they gave the street its name all year.

Samara Street.

There was a silver BMW parked in front of their building. Its hood was open. Linda's husband bent over the engine, fixing it or something. The driver, a petite brunette, was hovering nearby, like she wanted to see what was wrong with her car but was scared that she'd jinx him by getting too close. She wore black boots and a stylish beige coat and looked snug and svelte as a sachet. She probably thought Samara Street was some ghetto hood. She hugged herself against the cold and flashed glamorous smiles, *How silly of me to break down, of all things.* She was probably late for her board meeting, or whatever.

Linda's husband stood back, glanced up at the house—at the apse window—*oh God, he's looking right at* me. Linda touched the curtain but then knew she shouldn't draw it; that would seem like getting caught, spying possibly. Linda was wearing only the petticoat that went with her jumpers, like it was a nightie or arguably a slip-dress. It was fine around the house, even outside on summer evenings, since their backyard had a wooden fence. But she didn't need some rich, successful twit to catch her spying, like she didn't get dressed all day but just read books and spied. A yuppie who drove BMWs wouldn't understand, that some of us work second shift and veg around the house all day. But now it was too late to hide—Derrick looked at her.

Linda meekly waved her fingers: a chord on the piano, *oh hello.*

He answered with a nod, mischievously minimal: *Just fixing something, why what did you think?*

Linda returned a quick, tart smile: *Fix or flirt, you're mine.*

She imagined, rather jealously, how Derrick might look to a stranger. With that army jacket, those gloves, kind of rough. With those hard, slender legs in tight jeans—prime evil man. Which was ever her conceit—Little Miss Muffet with blue-collar stud, So who is she really. And of course, he looked ten years younger than his actual thirty. Thin face; large, serious eyes, and his auburn hair in spikes over his collar. A Japanimation action hero—the All-American Boy, seen from an exotic perspective. She imagined the *real* exotic view, how he seemed to other men: like a kid until he spoke and moved with masculine authority and grace, Well pardon *me.*

He was talking to the woman, now—explaining something about her car, no doubt. Beige Miss brightened, blushed and tittered; car fixed and charm poured on, no extra cost. *Der, you know I'm watching.*

He glanced up again, like he'd heard his wife's thoughts. She moved her bunched black curls from her shoulder, then reached the same hand to draw the curtain *some,* looking up to make sure she didn't pull on a snag. That would be a show-stopper, all right—pulling the curtain rod down on her head. It would be like holding up a big sign: STOP FLIRTING WITH MY HUSBAND, YOU BRIE-EATING RAT!

The curtain didn't fall on her. She stared up at it sternly, just in case it got some funny ideas, then sighed and read her book.

Outside, the woman got back in her car. Derrick lectured her about something; she thumped her forehead, like she'd already forgotten something he told her. Final amenities a tad too warm, then Derrick watched her pull out onto Lafayette. (Linda sighed at her page, And *stay* out.) Derrick nodded to himself, another good deed done, then turned and strolled up the walk.

Shit. Linda needed to double check, make sure all the signs of sin were removed. Hands fanned to fly, she froze—a ballet pose, bedeviled. Her legs were long and the sill was packed with her sun-loving herbs. She pulled in her heels and spun on her tush—dismount complete and not a petal stirred. She stood and glanced about—what first?

The den was okay—she hadn't done anything wicked in here. All neat and sweet, her pride and joy, even though it was the most intimate room in the apartment. So much for Madam Laptop, thinking she was some dark, dirty thing who spied on hapless motorists from her ghetto sun room.

The den was her sewing room, his workshop. A large oak

table, with a Shetland lace spread, was burdened with the Singer and her other stuff, fabrics and patterns and pins and threads, along with all his crazy tools. There was a rocking chair draped with a "Black-eyed Susan" throw, its busy-bee colors belying its indolent use. She had seven different ways of sitting on, under or with that throw, and lots of variations on each theme. The wallpaper was her triumph—ivory rosa veilchenblau. She'd told him that it made the room, though she knew he'd never understand. (He obligingly told her she was half right.)

The doorway, in from the hall, was hung with an odd portieré: a rich, resplendent curtain, scarlet jacquard toward the hall and purple satin in the den. She found it in a "second-hand shop," one of those permanent tag sales found throughout Greater Boston. She'd fallen in love with the fabric, feel and scent—closed her eyes and sensed the ion-tang of gaslight. So they had a novelty for a door, like they were still living in a college dorm—who cared?

She slipped through the portieré, passed the bathroom on her left, glanced into the bedroom on her right. A gracious compromise, his Yankee utility with her artful disarray. His bike and barbells hid behind her Victorian dressing screen—faded florals, ensembles on black. Space savers, loaded with his technical books and tools—no problem. She'd covered them with tassled needlepoint spreads. Unidentified Flowery Objects. On top, she'd put her potted caladium, her porcelain owl with a lampshade on its head (not trying to be wise; you turned it on). And of course the bed was made; the heavy quilt, no-nonsense pink with stitched-relief carnations, set square and covered with her toys and laced pillows in their proper tableau. She never let him make the bed—he thought he could just throw everything back on, like each doll and Disney icon would be happy upside-down. Anyway, she hadn't been bulimic in the bedroom. She hadn't profaned King David's bed. The thought made her shudder—he would have *known*. His eyes would have delved into her own, tasting the sin-fragrant pool of her heart. True virgin of Israel, she'd have confessed.

Though, her mail was still on the vanity. Placed there, an offering to her vanity—Lovely One, open thy mail. Since she felt, if the address wasn't handwritten, she could simply choose to leave it unopened and truthfully say she'd not received it. Anything even pseudo-official gave her absolute nightmares. A letter from a collection agency was like a wasp in the bedroom—his job to dispose of, quietly. Since he would not, she snatched the letters—careful not to look—and stuffed them in the vanity's bottom drawer. Just to make sure, she put her curling iron, in its box, on top of them. He'd never mess with her curling iron, nor anything else in her vanity drawers—all Girl Stuff, taboo.

7

Looking at his (the window) side of the bed, she saw his attaché case, open on the floor. He'd been surreptitiously working in bed, early in the morning while she slept, and that was sin. Now she felt less guilty about eating a few thousand Oreo's. She came and looked in the case, feeling like Bluebeard's wife. Yes, the case was stuffed with the pre-natal substance of his master's thesis: *Puritan Influence on Nineteenth Century American Lit.* His brow was always darkened by its fetal stirrings; he worked on it in his sleep. He'd bore her stiff over breakfast, trying to infect her with his wonder, that something as sensual as *Rapuccini's Daughter* had its spiritual roots in Cotton Mather. Then he'd go to the Salem Library, take his accustomed seat like a chronic drunk, his bar stool—focused and resigned.

Well anyway, the bedroom was secure. On to the front parlor. *That* was where she might have been mesmerized by *All My Children* and left a crumb or two. But no, it was her showcase, all Dust-Bustered perfection: the light-contoured chair and sofa, dark navy with aster pattern. The door-side wall, all bookshelves and electronics: TV, stereo system, PC, WP, VCR et al; no one here stupid enough to leave black-and-white crumbs. The lacquered coffee table was set squarely on the margin of an Oriental rug, the one she saw advertised on the back of the paper's TV guide (*This price is* NOT A PRINTING MISTAKE!!); machine print on synthetic wool, but so far it held its colors. On the table were two picture books: *At the Roof Of The World*, a travelogue of Tibet, and *Tasha Tudor's Garden*. Consciously or not, his and her: adventure lies at the end of the earth, but wonder dwells on your windowsill.

His "living room," her parlor; *I want to be rich, Oh you mean we're not?* and finally, her statement to the world: *I'm the elegant ethnic wife of a working-class white stud; my Victorian clutter's all in back and all for his eyes only.*

She went and stood, her back to the front door. Arms crossed under her bosom, she looked; she closed her eyes and listened; she felt for a gestalt.

Modest elegance, a warm blend of her genteel poverty with all his boyish aspirations. Smells of nutmeg potpourri and the cat's pervasive musk, last week's spilled milk and the freckled Lenten roses he brought her on Friday. Softly from the bedroom, sound: Tracy Chapman, on CD.

The apartment was nothing but home. Where the heart is; where bulimia is naughty, not a crime.

She heard him at the bottom of the stairs, opening their mailbox. Quiet, as he stood there—*looking at the mail*. It awed her no end, that he could do that—stand and calmly open abusive ultimatums from important people. Open and *read* them, like they were plain old letters—calm as a SWAT team specialist, defusing a bomb. She wondered what he could possibly be made

8

of.

Now she heard him coming up the steps.

She put her hand to her mouth, then flew down the hall—quietly, on the balls of her feet, lifting the hem of her petticoat. Quickly, she perched on her window ledge. Crossed her legs, caught her breath and read like she'd been living *Heiress To The Tide* for hours.

Whoops!—forgot the cat. It was sphinx-like on the ottoman, alert to its mistress' capers. She clicked her tongue and patted her thigh, the cat came to her lap. She had a way of *molding* it, like a furry lump of dough—instant sleeping cat, proof positive she hadn't stirred from the window ledge.

The apartment door opened to a solemn " . . . says me"; he knew she was always afraid, it might be Some Guy Off The Street. She heard him go into the bedroom. Yank stuff out of his attaché, jam some other things in. She always wondered, Why didn't he just get a knapsack?

(*She* had a knapsack, thought nothing of lugging it all over town: a twenty-something earth mother, with wild black curls and long calico dresses. She wore sandals, with wool socks in winter. She didn't shave her underarms or legs because Hey, the body's beautiful, right?

(She still had Moody Blues lp's on vinyl.)

Her husband came into the den. He presented himself with a rather macabre grin, like some Welsh actor: *I made it, unscathed, through another desperate sortie into the cold, cruel jungle.*

She lowered her book to her lap, returned a Mona Lisa smile. *My, and aren't we proud.*

Then softly said "Hello, Derrick."

She carefully put the cat aside. Limp, it was a both-handsful, and her brows knit in reproof—a quick, sharp frown she appointed to all Life's impossibilities. She stood and came to her husband, a tall and gentle, slender girl.

He moved her inky curls from her cheek, took a moment to study her face. She never could dream what he saw.

(Large, dark eyes, studying his own. Like a bird that looks stern but is only alert: a timid girl with a serious expression. Her childish lips, impassive. Her warm, sweet scent: she was caramel.

(He'd mentioned all this, but she always forgot. She thought, instead, he was like her father: studying her face to see if she'd done something wrong.)

She held his shoulders and stood on her toes, though she was nearly as tall as her husband. She fondly gazed, then kissed, like a careful cat deciding to nip.

She warmly said, "I see you have a woman-friend. You know I'm very happy with that." (Shadow of her pillow-talk; a masochist/romantic, and she meant it like she hoped to die.) She raised a schoolmarm finger: "I did not say *girlfriend*. So the J-

9

word can remain in verbal limbo."

His smoothest-whisky murmur, "Well to be quite frank, my damsel, I don't find white girls appealing."

"Oh. All right, I'll remember that, the next time you're 'not paying any attention' to a Toni Braxton video."

His smile, her timid show of teeth: delighted with each other. Another kiss, her listless arms around his neck. A taste of tongue to let him know, the genie could get loose at any time.

He held her waist and said, "Can't stay. Got called in early."

She twisted her mouth, resigned; it wouldn't break her heart this once, not that she'd ever approve.

He brightened, said, "I made it to the Y, already."—he'd beaten the system. Like an energetic boy, he was easily enthused. There weren't enough hours in the day to do it all—but he'd scored the goal of jumping in the pool.

She lowered her eyes, feeling a moment's sadness.

Before she met Derrick, she'd know little about men, whom she still called "boys"—being, herself, still something of a girl. She loved the innocence, enthusiasm, the strength and joy of being male. She herself was Tinkerbell, but still loved Peter Pan; she sighed, a weary mother, knowing boys will be.

He asked, "What's the matter?", happy to find marvels under the sun—since he could never see how anything could be wrong. If shit didn't happen, Derrick wasn't sad—a law of nature unto himself.

She softly bumped his thigh with hers—a light *bug off*, requesting a gentler connection. She murmured, "I think it's my allergies. Things are too loud. I want the time to go slower."

"We don't have a chronostat; I can't adjust the time for you."

As silly girls are always told, she told him, "Oh, just stop."

"I have a minute. I'd like to make your lunch for you. Soup or something."

She absently swiveled her hips, a daughter's impatience: give me something nice or let me go. "Nnn. . . no. Super-something: I don't want it."

He held her hips, stilling her. He kissed her forehead. She was certain he could read her vital signs, like some wonderful yogi or Jedi knight. He knew that when she was skittish like this, she'd go away if he was too direct. She *liked* to think he knew she'd hurled, even though she'd brushed and gargled and chewed cinnamon. She *liked* to think there was no secret guilt. Love is thicker than hot fudge sauce—she craved that acceptance.

For a public school jock from South Boston, he was usually pretty sensitive.

She said, "I've got that game hen thawing for dinner. I clipped rosemary today."

He said, "She didn't mind, I hope?"—Rosemary, whom she'd

10

clipped.

She gasped; it was all too much. "Oh, she hates my guts now. I denuded her completely. I guess I'll have to make a potpourri."

"Start cooking smells again."

While he was so in tune, she bared her heart. "A draft got in. I keep walking into these, like, cold spaces. They wait for me where I don't expect."

"How would you describe your mood right now?"

Her eyes softened from focus—a sensuous ditz who would give it her best shot. She felt sweet and drippy, kind of fuzzy—but she was allergic to peaches. "Apricots."

"Then the homeopathic solution would be to buy and feed you apricots."

"If you buy me, you have to feed me; yes."—cued into her submissive dreamworld of quadroon balls and passion under the Spanish moss. "But only fresh, not canned. Is there such a thing?—as fresh apricots."

"Hell no. They grow in cans off trees. Ask any apricot farmer—there's gotta be lots of aluminum in the soil. That's why, sometimes, you pick up an unripe can at the store: the label's faint, you can barely read it—"

She stuck her tongue at him, went back to her window ledge. Resumed her timeless profile, cross-legged with her book. Though she slid him a sly and meaningful glance: plenty more mischief where that came from.

Derrick went to get ready—his elaborate scientology of departure; it involved steeping killer tea (with enough caffeine to stamped a herd of buffaloes), balancing their checkbook, donning the most minimal but weather-proof garments and filling his pockets with every little gadget and tool he might have use of. While he was in the bedroom, the phone rang. A minute later, he reported into the den: "Mommy, on the phone."

Linda rolled her eyes, murmuring to Her Unseen, "Oh why didn't you adopt someone else." She told her husband, "Just what I need," but then hurried, like it was. She sat cross-legged on the bed, cast a rueful glance at the hallway—*Mommy* indeed, and he'd probably eavesdrop. She picked up the phone and said, "Hm."

And heard, of course, her mother's voice. Champagne soprano, magically unchanged—a voice from eternal childhood. As though at the other end of the line, there was still no bike-riding after dark. "Hello? Is someone there?"

"Mom, I said hello."

"Oh.—we must have a bad connection; all I heard was, *hm*. Well, regardless: I'm in town." By town, she always meant Boston. "I'm arranging a Conference seminar, and naturally residing at the Radisson." That last, a doleful note: not that money was an issue. But Shelley—Linda's mom—had a perfectly good domicile, and here she was, paying for another.

(She had odd ideas of frugality; her parents had been European. Her father had achieved meteoric success as a freelance marketing consultant, before he and her mother both perished in a plane crash, out in Idaho. Shelley had grown up, largely, in private boarding schools—an orphan ere her parents even died.)

Duly sympathetic, Linda said, "Oh, Mom."

Shelley said, "Oh, *well*."—the Radisson was not without its pleasures. "So merely to inform, I'll eventually brighten your doorstep and I'm sure you're simply thrilled . . . ?" —sweetness frothing over, like a no-cal fountain drink: convinced her daughter hated her.

(She had an odd personality. Linda explained it, once, to her husband: "Her parents didn't love her. Or they did but she didn't love them, so she didn't experience their love. Or like she says, they were *emotionally distant*—I'm not real sure what that is. But like, when they died, she wasn't sad. It just made her how she is."—a comic book heroine's origin, explained; sound-bite wisdom and greeting-card compassion, in lieu of lassos and power-beams.)

Linda tiredly said, "Mom, our door is always open. Anyway, you—"

She caught herself; it was a secret from her husband. She hugged the phone and whispered, "—*have a key*."

"But I'm fearful of intruding. Is the thing."

"Mom, it's not intruding." *Especially if we're going shopping and you're buying/lending/prompting me to spend.*

"It's dear of you to say that. But don't expect any wild shopping sprees."

Linda made a witchy face. *Just for that, stay at the Radisson.* "Mom, I'm not a spoiled brat. I mean, I'm twenty-nine? Hello?"

Derrick, with his coat and keys, checked into the bedroom. "Call you later." Silent-mouthed: *Hellacious phone sex.*

Yoga-postured on the bed, Linda had the princess extension on her shoulder. She had the file and polish and her toe-nails to be done. She returned a proud and feline gaze: Camped out with Mom, who needs men. Then solemnly winked: Lovers are aces-high, don't forget. Derrick flashed two fingers, V, he'd be victorious—he left, to go to work.

2

Derrick Bloom worked in juvenile corrections. He was assistant supervisor of the evening shift at a lockup in Lynn, the City of Sin (You can't get out the way you came in). He also took classes at Salem State.

Derrick grew up in South Boston. His parents were originally from New York. They were stolid lower-middle class: Irish-German, Lutheran, their vices few and harmless. His father was senior QC inspector at a large foundry. Having once been deeply down on his luck, he'd relocated to Boston to seize an opportunity through family connections. Derrick's mother dabbled in children's literature—shorts, mostly, for scholastic magazines, though she was perpetually at work on a book.

(The book—which she both wrote and illustrated—was about fanciful creatures called *plins*. A plin looked like an eyebrow on stick legs. She'd taken early drafts to different publishers, who'd treated her ungallantly—jabbed their fingers at the plin and shouted *What the hell is* this?! like it was a horrifying thing from space or, worse, like they'd never opened a children's book.)

In keeping with their background—honest burghers in measured pursuit of the American Dream—she listed her vocation, when asked, that of "housewife."

Derrick grew up in a neighborhood quite like the one he lived in now: two-family walk-ups with little square yards behind retaining walls. No elms, though. Just urban-jungle landscape: lots of sumac. It was poorer. There was always home improvement going on. Cars out back that needed work, tools that had been lent and needed to be retrieved. There were big, extended families, like Buick-driving, pizza-eating tribes. Any male older or taller than you was your boss.

(On her fist visit, Linda was enchanted. "Oh, it's like *All In The Family*—you know, in the beginning, driving down the street? Will Daddy call me 'little girl'?"

("Nah, he's not that kind of meathead.")

Derrick's father wanted him to follow the blazed trail: into the foundry. Right into the Union, like a secular bar mitzvah. The nine-to-five path to progress up the ladder, slow as it was sure. Derrick said he'd pass. He wanted to go to college. He wanted to be a teacher.

He wanted to split from the lower-middle class.

You can do that, in America. You just have to run a little gauntlet of abuse, until you have your ticket in your hand.

Derrick saved two thousand bucks. It was a ticket to *some*where, at least. From thereon in, the American working class backed its own. Keep those grades up, apply to those schools—nag nag nag like it was Pop's idea to begin with.

Derrick worked his way through Salem State, got his BA in English, then served two years in the Army. He did his hitch stateside, but for one rapid shuttle through the Pacific; worked towards a specialization in logistics planning which he fell short of achieving, then was honorably discharged. Back in the Boston area, he needed more school and so needed work. He found it, bulling wayward youths back onto the straight and narrow. Along the way, quite incidentally, he met a girl, and fell in love.

Lars and Shelley Bauer lived in Merrill, a small rural township west of Springfield. He was a doctor of Semitic languages, active in Lutheran missions. She held a master's degree in pastoral counseling, and was also active in the Lutheran Church. Their home was a late mock-Tudor, of honey-colored Cotswold stone. The three-acre lawn, mostly given over to violets, sloped down in back to a wooded stream. Behind the stream, a neighbor's dairy pasture rose rather steeply to a spruce-and-maple woodline. Down in front, the house overlooked a wooded slope, beyond which were the fairways of the Devon Valley Golf Club. On a clear day, the blue of the near Berkshires filled the view over the valley.

The house was a fairly recent addition to a long-settled area. Long stretches of woods divided deep meadows of hay, and some apple orchards. (Cortlands.) The houses, generally far between, were storied cottages, built in the mid 1800's.

The Bauers had near neighbors, though. A short path through the woods led to an apple orchard and a backyard, belonging to a couple named Binette. They didn't mind when children used the path and orchard for short cuts.

The Bauers' address reflected a Yankee past, when things were called what they were: 26 Longmeadow Road.

They'd wanted a child, but were unable to conceive. They decided, at last, to adopt through a nationwide agency. They agreed they wanted a girl. Their search united them with a seven-week-old baby, held in state custody in Baton Rouge, Louisiana. The mother had been a distraught child, a Puerto Rican girl of seventeen.

The Family Services workers never learned Marcelina's last name. She said the name on the birth certificate—Blanco—was "blank, like a white lie." The kind of Spanish damsel who'd protect her family's honor—sign plain Juana, last name blank, and leave her *addicione* never mentioned. The Bauers felt for this poor girl, asked not to hear her story—let her loss be private to her. She'd given up a daughter of misfortune to be blessed.

Thus, a point of no consequence, just of passing interest:
The Family Services people felt that Marcelina's manner was distinctly Puerto Rican upper-class. She was recalled as a dark, lovely girl with a serious, intelligent expression of her eyes. She wore a black leotard, jeans with no belt, like her curves were enough. She sat with her feet up on her chair, like a contemplative pose from interpretive dance; the interviewer marveled that it all fit in the chair. Also noticed Marcelina's feet: white stockings and black velvet slippers.

She said *We have the best ballet in the States, you know. —in San Juan, where I studied.*

She spoke so very softly they kept asking she speak up; anyway she didn't like her interviewer's Spanish. Said her own was *from the castle,* and *Does someone here speak French?* Batting zero in Baton Rouge—no one present, that night, did.

Poor Marcelina.

She said the baby's father was *the prettiest boy. He plays the piano. Don't write, he is black—my papa will be mad with me.*

The baby had been christened Linda. *Since she is so pretty, like the one who plays piano. She's baptized in Church already. I told the priest her name. Can I stipulate or something, they keep bringing her to Catholic?*

The interviewer sadly shook his head—You give her up, *finis.*

Some of the Family Services people thought she was "ambivalent" about giving up her baby; others thought she was very upset, but reserved. She cooed and kissed the baby before handing her over, but didn't cry. She went quietly, childless, back into the night.

So much for Marcelina. In connection with her baby, she was never seen again.

Lars felt it was Shelley's decision, seeing she'd already made it—she held the baby, beautiful in ecstasy of love. They gave her the middle name Meredith, after Lars' mother.

Linda grew, from a quiet baby to a docile toddler. Then she was a gentle, pretty girl.

She was shy and very timid, though playful and affectionate with people she knew well.

The public grade school, there in Merrill, was tried but it wasn't for Linda. Large groups were no-go; she was invisible at school, hysterical at home, precociously complaining of "stress." An unsympathetic male teacher perceived "daydreaming" and "attention-getting fits," in fact he was really her nemesis.

15

Declaiming in meetings that Linda was "dirty, dingy, passive-aggressive and really just a precious little brat." He demanded that a psychologist be seen. This was done. The explanation of the "fits" was simple: Linda had *petit mal* seizures. She was epileptic.

The psychologist said further, "Her fear of strangers is actually good; otherwise, she'd be at risk. She's very interactive, and also very passive. She doesn't try to impress her will on others; she wants people to come to her, with rules she likes to follow. She's really fun to work with. But this environment, here—boys shouting and wrestling—no. You have to get her out."

Her parents then sent her to Coleman, a small Christian school in nearby Pittsfield. When the chartered bus came back that afternoon, Linda was asleep and the driver woke her up. Shelley said, this meant Coleman was good, someplace Linda liked.

Linda did okay in school, though homework was often a problem. Working alone under pressure wasn't something she was good at. She gave up on arithmetic. As an adult, she would need a calculator to figure anything out.

She did all right in the small school's limited curriculum of girls' sports, until she played field hockey goalie. A girl on the other team said, *"Get out of the way!"* and Linda meekly complied—letting the other team score. She then became afraid of some girls in the locker room, whom she described to her mother as a "gang." Evidently there was teasing and pestering, which Linda couldn't deal with. No more gym class. The school had an indoor pool, where she languidly swam laps all by herself.

This didn't endear her to the gang, who still teased her whenever they saw her, saying she was "sissy exempt."

Shelley encouraged her by buying her a two-piece turquoise bathing suit—a decidedly "adult" gift.

At home, Linda liked quiet times, one-on-one with a friend. Talking, listening to records, in her room. She was interested in nature—bird walks with her dad—and fond of collecting things. She took up dolls—*antique* dolls, which she made quite clear was an adult pursuit.

In her senior year, she said she wanted to be a social worker. Her parents were a little skeptical. They said it meant being outgoing, taking charge of peoples' lives. Her mother said plainly, "You're not a leader."

Linda answered evenly, "I know."

They viewed her more as a private person, most at home with crafts and hobbies.

Linda answered, less evenly: "No one gets paid to listen to records."

She applied to a small Christian college in upstate Vermont, and was accepted. The dorm life was more fun than Linda ever dreamed of. This sweet, funny, astonishingly innocent girl was the apple of everyone's eye. The fun, of course, was making popcorn at two a.m., or having pillow fights in the hallway. Kids who are into White Zombie and crystal meth don't generally end up in Christian colleges.

The whole four years she was there, Linda went steady with a young man who aimed at the missions field. He was quiet and serious with people in general, but playful and witty with her. They took weekend trips—skiing in the winter, canoeing in the autumn and spring—, invariably with another couple.

Linda *told* people she skied and canoed; she really shied back from the actual sport, preferring long walks with the other girl, or shopping in nearby towns. The latter was first choice. Linda had a fear of meeting "wild dogs," convinced the Green Mountains were full of dangerous animals.

Her boyfriend was a gentle man. No worries there, at all. Though his feeling for Linda was real, even deep; he wrote poetry, to and about her. Himself as young as she, he didn't understand what it meant to fan the flames of a young woman's heart. His decision to go overseas, after their graduation, was a terrible trauma for her. She'd been wearing his "pre-engagement" ring for three years. They'd spent countless evenings at the Pewter Pot, having endless talks about devotion and purity over their bottomless cups of decaf. Now, at last, she realized that the devotion and purity he meant all this time was towards the Lord, not her. She'd get over her loss, she'd love again. It just wouldn't happen at the Pewter Pot.

Shelley waxed sublime. "He loves you, but his duty calls; you're part of something wonderful."

She said, "I want to be part of *him*," got off the phone in tears.

Linda's friends gave comfort: "You learned a lot about men. You learned how to cope in a relationship. When the real one comes, you'll be that much stronger for your experience." She liked happy endings, stories that closed with the moral spelled out. She didn't like the idea that she had to be strong to have a boyfriend, like it was the Olympics or something. But she got on with her life.

She looked for work near Boston, rooming with two girlfriends. Lately dorm-mates, they called themselves "the Class of '88." They shared a flat on a block in Malden, noted for its brisk trade in crack—three girls who thought *Three's Company* risqué. Whose idea of a "blow-out" was Ben and Jerry's *with hot fudge*. While dealers got shot and pedestrians got mugged, no one so much as leaned on their cars. As one of them explained to a neighbor downstairs: "If you believe in stuff like Noah's Ark, you can take angels pretty much for granted."

The job search went slowly, and Linda needed income. She

applied to a company that supplied substitute staff to human service agencies. Gentle, caring people would find assignments where Linda could acquire hands-on skill in a flexible, supportive environment. Her first job was at a home on Cabot Circle, up in Danvers.

The street was well-shaded, lawns dark under sycamores and maples. Then there'd evidently been a mistake in her directions.

44 Cabot Circle was a cubical brown cottage, surrounded by a knee-high lawn. A mock-up house, like a target for missiles, suspended in waving-green stasis. No lawn furniture, no children's toys. No curtains, no door mat.

She guessed that meant she couldn't go in.

She'd been told to look for a VW Rabbit, parked behind a brand-new Ford Aerostar. She'd not been told who these cars, respectively, belonged to: a guy just out of the Army who worked for DYS, and an autistic fellow who put everyone he saw in the hospital.

She parked behind the Rabbit.

It was late afternoon, late August, and unseasonably cool. A dark-green day that felt like spring, since changing seasons reminded her—not of the last such season—but of the last such change.

Purse in hand, she walked to the door, mentally rehearsing her little speech. *Good afternoon. I'm Linda Bauer, from Options Associates*—a company with offices, letterhead, prestige. *Have I the honor of addressing—?*—oh right, like this was Victorian England. *Are you—?*—oh *shit*, she couldn't remember who she was supposed to report to! Somebody *Bloom*. Eric or Daryl or possibly Dirk . . .

She just hoped he would be nice.

She'd been sheltered, not secluded; she knew about Gender Inequality In The Workplace. Patronization, harassment. She read women's magazines, though not devilish ones like Cosmo.

But this wasn't Corporate America. This was human services. And of course he would be *nice*, for heaven's sake. She envisioned Alan Alda, minus the sarcasm. Or better yet, an older guy—a teddy bear with a beard. She wasn't looking for love—she just didn't want anything bad to happen.

She stood on the doorstep, clutching her purse. She looked at different things in front of her—the door itself, the shingled siding, a juniper bush. Half a dozen newspapers, scattered like a seer's sheep bones, left to biodegrade inside their plastic sleeves. She eventually realized what she was doing—waiting for someone to open the door, without her having to ring the bell.

She looked down at herself. Never really a fashion plate, she wore one of her mother's Sunday dresses. Floral-print organza, peach blossoms on sky blue. Low-cut neck with mid-length sleeves, classy and demure. *Hi, I'm Lin Bauer from Options Associates*—a brave and cheerful woman like her mom. She rang the bell and plunged into the unknown.

The unknown answered dreamily: "Come in, it isn't locked."

Linda walked in and froze. She didn't drop her jaw or purse or pee her pantyhose, but she almost did all three at once.

The living room was a gruesome study in off-white—an astonishing palette of varied shades, mismatched monochrome. She was soon to learn that everything in the house—furniture, fixtures, appliances—was bought at Unnamed Discount Store. Everything was bottom-rung, fall-apart-first-time-you-use-it cheap, and all brand new. The decor was, in fact, Early Aversive Therapy—but no one could have told her that. She wouldn't have known what it was.

On the off-white sofa, with its foam-filled cushions and candied pinewood frame, a young man lay with his feet up. He was the handsomest, happiest, most mysterious man in the world. He'd be star of the show, he'd do whatever he liked and she'd follow, heart and soul—a little black poodle, yapping to jump through his hoop. *What if he's some kind of scumbag?!*—but her exit key was jammed. She could still be shy and run away—after her eight-hour shift.

He wore those army pants with pockets—camouflage or whatever, and a long-sleeved shirt of pale blue silk. She later learned it was from a school of Chinese martial arts in Boston. It had a green praying mantis, surrounded by Chinese ideographs. As it happened—she later learned, just *happened*, through a completely unrelated incident—he *had* a praying mantis, sitting on his hand. He was petting it, like it was a hamster. He looked at Linda.

He slowly realized awesome things by phrases and degrees. The insect boxed his finger and he gently touched it, Quit. He stood and gave his bug its freedom, came to Linda, nodded—his confusion, like her fear, set in sterling frames of wonder. "Well, hello."

"Um . . . hi! I'm Lin Adoptions from Bauer Associates and maybe I'm late? Or—?" She gestured her hands, These are my hands, the ones I wring when I'm nervous, I'm not going to do that now. "Is this HCG?"

"I'm afraid it is."

Admitted, then: a fraternity of fear. She stared at him wide-eyed, shrugged: We're both sissies, what's the deal here?

He said, "There's been a mistake . . ."

She gave him her hand. Not hello; he took her hand, she stepped close, I'm with you. His surprise was chivalrous, a dreamy shake of his head: he'd never heard of a grown woman doing this, but who was he to question. They exchanged looks, she smiled: I'm trying not to blush. He led her to the sofa. She asked him, "Is it gone?"

He was pleasantly befuddled. "What might it be?"

"The . . ."—oh, no: *praying mantis* was a stuttering extravaganza, waiting in the wings. "Bug."

He answered softly, parting veils of wonder: his life, just then, was a symphony of terror, in which the praying mantis played a definite, if infinitesimal, note. "I think it flew."

She let go of his hand, looked around. Now accepted, part of the scene—little sister had opinions. "There's so much *empty space*. Why's everything off-white, with these . . . *pink smudges?*"

He said, "Oh. These Impressionistic smudges are obviously . . ." Old blood stains; Linda realized this, and gasped. " . . . ketchup. Here, please be seated." She sat for him, quick as he pleased.

He stood quite relaxed, his hands in his pockets. "Look: I'll paint the picture. You decide if you should stay."

Her heart dropped—she felt it. It bounced on the bottom of her tummy then shot up into her throat, like one of those Superballs you can bounce over a house (supposedly. Hers had always just gotten lost, somewhere). This pronouncement was doom. It was like being late for class the first day of semester. She'd never been able to endure even the thought of an instructor's distracted pause, of herself framed in the doorway, prey to the contemptuous stares of the punctual majority. For someone who wilted from even the most positive attention, it was something like her ultimate nightmare. Yet her mother's hand was on her still. *Oh hon, it's like watching a Chia Pet grow. Don't just sit—say* something.

"No?"

"Uh . . . I'll paint the picture *first*. I do need to ask you a question. Ms. Bauer." He smiled. A cool, strict lady. Ms. Bauer she was not. "Are you, by some odd chance . . . a lot different from how you appear?" A guilty girl's denial—she shook her head *yes*. "Are you, perchance, some high-powered behavioral psychologist? Are the bangs and church dress some cutting-edge fashion statement—grunge cuteness, maybe? Are you really a tough street chick in lamb's clothing? What, are you a karate expert?"

She stared at him, entranced—his favorite kind of person was none of the above. She remembered to answer his question. "Uh . . . not really. I know how to kick, but I learned it in ballet."

He adoringly echoed, "Ballet."

"Not a real lot, I stopped going. It hurt to stay up on the balls of my feet. The barre was like torture. The teacher was an ogress. She yelled and called me names."

The guy, Derrick—how did she forget?—couldn't speak.

Faced with riches of delight, he didn't know where to begin.

At last he said, "Your experience. You work primarily with . . . ?"

She jumped in, eager to finish. "My degree's in Human Services. My minor was Special Ed."

The house just seemed to swallow this, We are not impressed. Everything looked minimal and generic, like the set of some psycho-drama. The lights were too harsh and white and something, somewhere, buzzed like the electrical wiring was too complex and strong. There was a weird smell—something electrical, burned, and the pukey-sweet smell of new vinyl, and/or puke itself. She felt exposed, outside of herself, like she was having her picture taken at the airport.

Derrick didn't seem like he belonged here—anymore than she did, according to him. He was a friendly, boyish actor who'd strolled onto the set of the wrong show. With his baggy pants, Bohemian air and all-the-answers attitude, he seemed like an unchallenged grad student—one who'd been in a bar fight, except he didn't smell like booze. He smelled like British Sterling, which she liked—her father used it. Like her father, he would explain what was going on, to help her decide if this was what she wanted. As he started talking, she took a pad and pen from her purse—uncertainly, so he could see what she was doing and correct her, if it was wrong. Charmed, not distracted, he said it wasn't necessary. She softly said, "All right," calmly put the things back in her purse. Since she'd only meant to show him, *I'm a lady, I will honor men. I'll write down what you say, since it's important.*

But it turned out more intense. Like tales of deep and wicked things that go on in a prison. She sometimes widened her eyes at him, but never so much as parted her lips.

He said that Options Associates was a *social services protection racket. Christine vs. State* meant that sociopathic violence was a disability. The *Equity Decree* meant the cure was to throw money. HCG was a *pirate agency clear for the pass. Exploratory staffing* meant you harried jails and detox centers and hired people over the phone. An *emergency clause* was how *ships' doctors*—the men who ran HCG—forced the State to provide staffing, even guys like Derrick, like sending the National Guard into a disaster area. The guy upstairs was *Martin Bennedetto*. Had Linda seen *Rain Man*. (It was just out and she shook her head, no.) Well, forget Dustin Hoffman, think Sly Stallone. Beating himself in the face all his life, so he has a knob of scar tissue on his forehead, so he looks—and pretty much acts—like the Venusian Ymir in *Twenty Million Miles To Earth*. (Linda said "I don't like sci-fi," both to clarify her frame of reference and in case Derrick ever asked her out.) He gave her a long description of some kind of insane robot, or rogue elephant,

21

or insane rogue elephant and she realized he meant Martin, the guy upstairs. There were weird directions that sounded like fixing a computer. If he hit himself, you went to Mars. ("That's *Manually Assisted Restoration*. I know you don't like sci-fi.") There were bizarre and ferocious responses to Martin saying "suitcase." There were descriptions of rough, kinky sex which she realized—paling—were pro-active interventions. Dog collars, hands and knees. Wax on, wax off, sight of blood then take him down to count of twenty-thousand. ("That's one-one thousand, two-one thousand"—"Yes I know," she said.) Then he told her, he'd been through seven co-workers in the last three days. Their stories, run together, were like casualty lists of some war. The last was surreal comic relief, however all-too-true: some guy in a Mercedes, the son of the deposed President of Ghana. At a Chinese restaurant, he told Martin to cut his steamed dumpling.

Linda asked, "What's a steamed dumpling?"

Derrick said, "It's sort of like ravioli."

Linda said, "Oh." She'd grown up eating canned ravioli like everyone else in America so yes, that was clear enough.

A description of some real bad kung fu movie; she realized he meant, the waiters jumped in. When Martin turned the tables, no metaphor intended. The guy from Ghana tendered his resignation by requesting separate checks. Derrick's tale was done.

Linda said in sum, "I don't like science fiction."

Derrick told her gently, "You don't have to stay."

When Linda was nine, she was riding her bike through the grounds of Merrill High School, looking for a shortcut home from her friends'. That was plenty daring by itself, but the High School was forbidding: vast, deserted, impersonal. She knew she'd never go there, since she had *special needs*. Since she *missed things*, and got upset when boys were loud or angry.

Now she whizzed through the empty parking lot, a fearless explorer. School was out for summer, the sun was going down. The treeless grounds were bordered by woods and houses beyond, their yellow squares of light just coming on. She imagined she was in Africa, exploring a jungle clearing, and the forest all around was full of native people with their firelit huts and colorful clothes.

She heard a noise and looked. Make-believe and feeling brave all vanished in a wink. There were four big boys, playing basketball. They were big as men and lean as lions. Because it was warm (*or to scare me?!*), they had their shirts off—something only boys were allowed to do. Since they had real muscles, like heroes on TV. They were leaping and bounding and shouting words no caped crusader ever used, and no grown-ups were there to make them behave. Linda knew boys could be dangerous.

They knew how to fix cars and run big machines—like Daddy, except they weren't nice; they were tuned into the dark side of the Force. She knew that boys could get money and guns, take drugs and go around shooting people. Maybe these four did, when they weren't playing basketball. She kept to the margin of the blacktop, keeping them under surveillance. She didn't see when she went off the blacktop and hit a rut in the ground. She spilled off her bike, sat up with a frightened gasp. She must be hurt and now these boys would finish her off, like wild dogs in Africa, eating the baby wildebeest the moment it was born.

She yelped in fear when two hands grabbed her, under her arms. In fact she panicked, squirmed to be free. Yet he picked her up like she was a stuffed toy and for a second, her feet were off the ground.

She found herself standing, looking up at a powerful, black-haired youth. He had a Catholic medallion on his brown, sculpted chest, so she thought he was Italian and not even from Merrill but from some evil metropolis like Springfield.

He thought it was funny, the way she'd wiped out. *What, you don't talk? Whaddaya, scared?* She nodded, yes—he was scary.

He picked up her doll. (Shelley got her adopted daughter a Latina Barbie.) He put it on her speckled-purple handlebars, almost the way she'd had it before. Like he knew it was important to her and should be treated as a real, eight-inch-tall woman. She remembered his hand, lightly touching her chin-cheek-hair, a careless inventory of where little girls want to be touched. Then he said *Go on home, get lost* like he had little sisters, and took care of them whenever they were around, and talked to them like they were tough little boys, and that was all anyone got.

She said, "You've been here three days. Seventy-two hours, and you've been alone since last night. You've been physically fighting with this guy who could kill you. I would be in some crisis center or hospital and you're still on the clock. I can't imagine why on earth you don't call HCG."

Derrick grimly smirked. "In a cluster-frag like this, they take their phones off the hook. For me, it's like a tractor-trailer: I can't just leave it jack-knifed on the highway. You know the program's technically abandoned. Martin is alone upstairs, that's not supposed to happen. He could be hitting himself while we speak. He could be saying 'Suitcase, suitcase,' over and over with impunity. Anyway, give me your time card. I'll put you down for half a shift, say we didn't need the coverage."

Linda said, "But it's my first job. It's what I went to school for. I can't get off to a bad start."

Derrick said, "Hon, you already have. Cut your loss and go start over somewhere else." He seemed actually happy for her.

She could walk away, do something else—lucky her, she really could.

She replied, smooth and cool as coffee ice cream, "I'm not 'hon.' Before you said 'Ms. Bauer' and I feel that's more appropriate."—but it really felt like a crime: Impersonating Your Mother.

Violent chaos from above—pounding feet. Derrick softly said "Stand up." It wasn't an order from a supervisor; it was more like a moment in a black church service. *The Spirit is upon you, sister, stand up and proclaim.* Linda stood, holding slack of her skirt like she'd curtsy or flee but whatever the case, be a woman and act. She looked left, at the door. Then she turned right, went and stood at Derrick's side. Her world of paperback romance, of red and pink water-color splashed beneath gilded script, left no other option: the Lady stands by Her Man. The Man, with tender pity, said, "Oh baby, real bad choice," as Martin thundered down the stairs.

During her eight-hour shift, Ms. Bauer—who later said "Linda is fine"—wrote brief, spidery entries in a log book. She did a load of Martin's laundry. She said "Hello" to Martin. She even tried to chat. She cut cucumbers for a salad, washed a skillet, and checked a closet for a pillowcase. She swept up the pieces of a shattered plate, and put iodine and a band-aid over Derrick's forearm, after he got rug-burned in a fight.

That was all she did, in the course of an eight-hour shift.

She remembered not doing, only watching—Locked Inside of Linda, helpless to assist. Yet in years to come, Derrick would recall the things "we" did, like she'd been this lively, dynamic presence.

She remembered disbelieving that he'd just been here three days. He seemed, instead, like some founding father; he and Martin seemed to have this ancient, deep rapport. A mystic understanding of these strange and terrible rules. Derrick cheerfully showed him the right way to set silverware. Martin blinked, then calmly assayed to remove Derrick's head with a punch that *whoosh*ed like a tomahawk. Timeless as a Roman fresco, modern as Mike Tyson; Linda tossed her head, a pretty pony, stirred by this. Derrick weaved under the blur, looked humble and harried and focused; he did his job the best he could and hoped he did it right. She remembered his move, like a football player's tackle, and Martin's winded, dispassionate "Shit."

Derrick remembered how Linda looked when Martin threw the plate at her—when it just missed her, and shattered on the wall. He remembered how she held her hands up, standing away—the lady of the manor, distancing herself from an unpleasant scene.

24

Linda didn't remember that part—her dainty pose and noble disregard. She just remembered *smash*, then getting a broom and dustpan.

The final conflict happened in the living room. Linda watched from the kitchen. Insanely, she'd earlier given him a hankie from her purse when he was bleeding; now it swished, tucked to his belt, like he was Lancelot. She knew this whole thing was behavior modification, that calm men with trimmed beards detailed all this in papers to the psychiatric journals, that it was an *Over-Corrective Intervention*, but it looked like Wide World Wrestling. *Master Karnov's up from the mat, Gorgeous George is going for the cobra clutch, unbelievable, in twenty years at ringside I've never seen such fury—*

Derrick stood up from the floor. Martin stood as well. Derrick said, "Let's go get ready for bed, old chum," in the most casual and friendly tone conceivable.

Martin said "Okay," in his Marlon Brando whisper.

Two tired workers punching the clock.

While Martin brushed his teeth, Derrick and Linda stood outside the bathroom, in the darkened hallway. Derrick, mellow and reflective, shared his whispered impressions of the experience they'd just shared. *"It's the habilitative academic's fault, is what I'm saying. Bureaucracy's eternal, it's the ethical milieu—the theory itself, the . . ."*

It astonished her to learn it was all about this. She'd thought they were trying to get along with a big man, in a small house, who hurt himself and others for no apparent reason. *"I guess my education's just a sheepskin with an attitude."*

This froze his lecture on his lips. Perhaps he wondered how any kind of parchment could display a mental state.

She said, *"Inside, I'm someone different. I'm the one who'd make real good decisions. Kind ones. Not that you're unkind."* He blinked, a bit confused—thought his kindness was a given. *"But I can't be who I want, because I'm locked in by my fear. I'm trapped inside of this."* She motioned her hand down the length of her hip and thigh, like her form was an obvious prison of shame. *"It's like, I'd make a really good* man. *Though of course, all women feel this way."* He tilted his head; he'd been completely unaware of this. *"But someday I'll be a pro. Trust me—Girl Scout's honor."* That left her uncommitted, since she'd only made Brownie.

"Linda."

"My friends call me Lin."

"Lin. If we make it out of here, you know, alive . . ." She giggled, girlish fashion, her hands over her mouth. He nodded, Yeah, you're right. *" . . .I mean, if we get out tonight—you will; I might be stuck here still—I'd like to, um . . . have coffee with you,*

25

somewhere."

He solemnly studied the fire alarm. Red light blinking, very good.

She looked at him, her dark eyes serious under her bangs. *Oh no way are you shy.*

"*Since you're new to the field, thought you'd like some feedback, or . . . I've expressed myself poorly. I'd like to try again.*"

A gentleman's modest request. She nodded *Yes you may*, finding that she was in turn a lady.

"*When you entered the house, I rose to my feet. Moved and dismayed?—you bet. A beautiful woman commands that response. Now you've taught me what a woman is made of, inside, and I simply . . . want to learn more. From you. About you. If you're not busy after, I'd be honored by some moments of your company.*"

She cuddled against the wall—at home, as though in her college dormitory. Toying with a stray curl, she touched it to her lips. Her gentle eyes spelled girl-games, maybe even mischief. *So far, all right; let's hear your offer.*

"*I'd like to buy you coffee, somewhere quiet. Somewhere nice.*"

(Martin was brushing his teeth; it took him quite a while. A somber meditation, possibly leading to the conclusion that someone had to die. He was flossing, now.)

She decided, and said, "*As long as it's not Pewter Pot.*"

"*I can meet you on that: I don't know what a 'Pewter Pot' is.*"

She said, "*There's one in Allenborough.*" She added, "*That's in Vermont.*" She shared a private passion: "*I'm never going back.*"

He said, "*There's a Friendly's on Main Street.*" His eyes were a poignant plea. They served apple pie, they were happy to. She crinkled her nose, I accept.

He said, "*I understand about the Pewter Pot. I got shut down at Bess Eaton, once.*"

Hand to her mouth . . . not just a threat. He made her giggle. He honestly did. He nodded, warm approval. If she had the laughter, he had the mirth—enough for the rest of their lives.

At eleven-fifteen, "Area Director" Tom Masotti arrived, in his Porsche, with a hefty goon as bodyguard.

Derrick and Linda watched them from the dormer window in the upstairs hall. Since Martin was in bed, the hall was dark. The upstairs hallway's dormer window was, of course, a fixture of New England houses—the Puritans spied on their bosses, late at night.

Derrick hadn't called in twelve hours, and at last HCG had gotten nervous. They could handle a wrongful death lawsuit, perhaps, but they weren't quite ready for *Sixty Minutes.*

The Porsche parked, its doors stayed closed—important men were getting ready. Derrick gave her a quick rundown on Masotti. A brilliant behavioral psychologist, his powers of deduction rivaled only by his nerves of steel. He walked into a scene of violent crisis, pushed buttons then stood by and blinked, observing what he made the madman do. Then knelt under fire of flying chairs to draft a contingency plan. Yet no legitimate agency would hire him as a janitor. He bragged of using DMR funds ("high five-figures") to buy his coke. He claimed he did "a hit" for a company not in the phone book. Now, he'd doubtless been rousted from what he blandly termed his "recreation"—sorties east of Tremont Street with a Smith and Wesson .38 and, naturally, his beeper. Linda asked, "What's east of Tremont Street?"

"Um . . . ladies too kind with their favors."

"*Eew*."

Two men got out of the Porsche. An officious little yuppie in a rumpled grey suit, though he sported a pretty cool beard. A young man, obviously a weight-lifter, with shaved head and handlebar mustache, like a circus strongman. He wore black pants (they looked like tights) and tank top. So HCG really was a sort of Impossible Missions Bureau, complete with covert contracts and enforcers. Linda whispered, "*What is it?*"

Derrick said, "*A fairy.*"

They rang the bell, and Derrick went down. Masotti got right in his face. "I'm told you hit the panic switch. What failed?"

Derrick was too disciplined to disrespect a superior, even if that "superior" was a coitus. He said, "I just pulled fifty-six hours emergency OT; you can read the log, like everyone else." He noted the Amazing Igor's hostile, bewildered stare: "Nice scalp." He went out on the porch, to take the cool night air.

Masotti passed Linda on the stairs. He smiled, brave assurance. The head Ghostbuster was on the scene; everything would be okay. "Well. An un-met colleague."

Linda stared, a wily mouse. More in awe, more curious: *What's the secret code word that will get me out of Wonderland?* "The nicest one you ever never met." She wandered from the house she'd been afraid of, out into the night to find her friend.

The restaurant closed at midnight; the only other customer was an elderly man, perhaps a local insomniac. A recovering alcosaurus who told tired dames in pinafores the sins he once confessed to men with shakers and bow ties. Derrick and Linda took a booth in back. They ordered decafs, joyful—the Squeaky Cleans are here! Linda was a happy fruitcake, free at last from fear. She talked all about Friendly's—how her mother used to take her there each Sunday, after church. How nice and clean it always was "and well, so *friendly!* Like it says so on the sign, and so they really are? Won't Heaven be that way, you think?—the sign says *love,* they give it? They have it, here—my own true love. Reese's Pieces Sundae Cups."

Derrick said, "I'll buy you one."—happiness was simple.

Linda stared, in shock. She'd been borderline bulimic and he might as well have asked if he could buy her lingerie. Thrill hushed her voice. "But it's not even Sunday."

She shivered. *"Whew!"*—life was too exciting, all her romance books come true. "That house was a bunny trap. I never sweat so much in my life! I . . . oh." She curled her lip: *you know, stink.* She wanted to run into the ladies' room, take her dress off her shoulders and douse herself with Halston's. That was of a mother's repertoire, dark as masturbation: *Never give this to yourself.* "French shower."

He gazed with interest, never said, You spoke something aloud.

She realized it herself. "You didn't hear that. Women. Secret."

"Lin, we've been closer than this all night."

She blinked, curious. Was it like gym, at school?—sweat was okay? With *men?*—she just didn't know. She'd had so few men in her life, other than her dad and a childhood friend. She'd never hung with mixed groups, mainly since her *fille amie* of choice was another shy, fem girl who didn't have male friends either. It was like a co-dependency: sissy-exempt from male friendship.

She'd never been comfortable chatting with, say, the boys on the football team. Boys-plural was impossible per se; she'd look around for another girl to mediate on her behalf. In her junior year at Coleman, she had one date with the varsity captain. For a few bright days of heaven, she held her head high—the dizzy wallflower with hopeless hair, magically made equal in the company of girls. He never called her again, was cool and snide when they met in the halls. Her mother consoled her: "His expectation of you wasn't noble." For years she wondered what this meant. She thought it was something really deep, touching Elysian meadows of Christian ethology. She thought he'd wanted her to be something good but less than truly noble, that the fault was hidden somewhere deep in spiritual esthetic. She was nineteen when someone finally told her, "He just liked your tits."

Her romance with Brian, her college beau, had been a romance on his terms: platonic and in retrospect, a pious rip-off. There was always Jared, her childhood friend—always just her childhood friend. Once someone put a Creepy Crawler in your Slurpee—even in pure jest—romance was simply precluded. Some nights, in her Malden apartment, she'd hugged her pillow and fantasized, how sweet it would be to meet Jared again and just cry on his shoulder, telling him how lonely she was. (She'd done that, once or twice, in their teens.) But he hadn't been in touch with her since Christmas break. He was living in Springfield, last she heard. Sculpting day and night, no time for any social life. She somehow drove men to monastic seclusion.

It sounded maiden-auntish, but she didn't know how else to ask: "I'll bet you've got lots of girlfriends."

(The restaurant staff were flickering the lights. She followed Derrick's lead: lights flickered had some meaning, but who knew?)

He said, "I've had women friends. I've never made commitment." She looked at him, entranced. He was calm and confident; all the women's magazines were wrong. Noncommittal was a virtue: he sought the Holy Grail.

A peculiar thing, they later shared: each reminded the other of earlier same-sex friends. The way she told him, "Yeah, I'll bet," the quizzical tilt of his head, brought warm puzzles of remembrance: *Just like Kenny/Exactly like Pris.*

He was busy, these days, rebuilding his VW Rabbit (again). She caught his subtle meaning, *I am poor but righteous.* Rich and insecure, she *pif fed* at her Tercel. "Bought with Daddy's Gold Card, I confess." *Oh no that sounds like bragging* "I'm a spoiled little rich girl." *That sounds antagonistic—dear God no* "I'm adopted." *Oh wonderful: self-pity.* "It's really not like *Falcon Crest.* Derrick, it's like nothing's really yours. You feel special and helpless. I mean, *I* do."

She watched his face, her own eyes wide—*I completely blew my turn; you assess the damage.* "Linda. Lin. More people are poor than not. If poverty imparts some sort of moral nobility, then Jamaica Plain's the safest part of town. Everyone gets mugged on Beacon Hill."

This confused her. "Are you poor?" That confused him. "I don't care." She was going for strike three when the manager came, flatly informed them the restaurant was closed. Derrick blinked, enlightened—*that's* what all that light-flashing meant.

He drove her back to her car. Hell House was now darkened, a dinosaur refrozen that could do no further harm. An outlaw syndicate's penalty box was just an ugly house. Her Tercel was in the driveway, Smile Face decal triumphant. He made a date for dinner, she smiled at him, radiant. Victoria took all the marbles home.

She pulled away with her window down. The crisp cranberry sea-chill of a North Shore summer night. Her radio on, she looked in her rearview. He stood under a streetlight, watching like a brother; he knew she saw, he winked. Michael Jackson told her it was only *Human Nature.* She sighed with joy and turned left onto High Street.

In the weeks that followed, Linda had it bad. She lay in bed for hours, hugged her pillow til it smelled like love. She imagined Derrick's neighborhood—a busy Gasoline Alley, run down yet full of life, and paradoxically verdant. She imagined Derrick's youthful days—endless summer afternoons. Fixing cars, playing hoop, drinking Mountain Dew and going fishing. (Her imagination put a creek in the center of South Boston, where her Tarzan also swam.) A world of joy and vigor, native virtue, honest sweat. All that she could never be, all she truly was inside. She'd have him or she'd die.

They decided to go steady on their second date. In late October, they toured New Hampshire's mountains. An oddly hectic, modern trip: all cars and rain and ATMs, the forests just a view. Outside a roadhouse, late at night, they flirted with their darker sides and gave in to a fight. He was harder than she could believe. She was fiercer than he could accept. "Just dump me then, I'll hitch-hike home. Just break my heart. *Just kill me!*" Derrick was so right on so many different levels, it amazed him just how right he really was. He preached, professed, berated til she doubted, then despaired. Til she cried like a child for her father. Til he knelt, and asked her hand.

She looked to heaven, full of grace, blessed among women and unworthy of her truth: Everything you want is yours if you know how to scream.

The Bauers were mainly concerned about their daughter's planned step down the financial ladder. Derrick was at perfect peace; righteousness persuades. He even went to his knee—proposed to Shelley too. However Fate treated him, Linda would have his best. The Bauers gave their blessing. Their only hope for Linda was her happiness. Their fear had been a man of dark glamour. Better a love that covers all sins than cruelty that spoils every treasure. Shelley's words. She said such things without even a twinkle in her eye. Her daughter married Derrick at the Bauers' church in Merrill on May 7th, 1990. On a day of spring so perfect it broke everybody's heart.

3

These days, Linda worked three to eleven, Sunday through Thursday, at a group home for adolescents with mental retardation.

(It was not officially acceptable to say "mentally retarded adolescents," since that was considered labeling.)

The home was called Pinski Place for good or ill, since that was the name of the street. The staff made it worse by calling it "Pinky Place," in imitation of one of the kids, who also called the residence a "boop home."

(It was not officially acceptable to call the boop home Pinky Place—period.)

Pinski Place was a towering, narrow, definitely ramshackle three-and-a-half floor monstrosity. It was built in 1850—like so many old houses in Salem, by an urban English architect determined to forget he had a continent of room. The house had gables, and a widow's walk under a polished-oak rose window, like it fronted a gilded study instead of a loft bedroom. The house was on a bluff above the city's harbor yard; it was on the same municipal power line and lost power nearly every day. It also had perfect acoustic alignment with the fog horn out on the breakwater. The house was tightly crammed between two others, with narrow strips of yard between. There was a postage-stamp backyard enclosed by rose bush, where they had their clambakes.

Inside, there was an unfortunate spiral stairway, where the residents and staff yelled up and down at one another, all the time.

Among the eight residents, aged sixteen to twenty, were a bright Downs Syndrome guy who worshiped Elvis; a happy, relentlessly annoying young woman who chronically repeated a dozen stock phrases; and a hyperactive, aggressive, "cute-looking" girl named Mindy.

("Cute-looking" was a caregiver's careful euphemism. Mindy was pretty as sin, except that she acted and talked like a nine-year-old and had snaggled teeth. Also, her female staff got even with her by giving her horrible haircuts.)

Mindy caused oceans of trouble. Her life was focused on her caregivers. She manipulated all the men and fought with all the women.

Housework was officially itemized in the job description as "incidental duties," like in order to feed, clothe and clean up after eight big kids you only needed to lift a finger now and then. Linda's specialty was laundry. She was always lugging baskets. She wore long, loose cotton dresses and her hair in a loose tail. When neighbors came to complain about noise, she said she was "just the housekeeper." Of course that wasn't true. She also did paperwork—compiled reams of data sheets to convince the powers-that-be that all sorts of wonderful progress was being made. Then there were the almost nightly "outings." These were everything from movies and outdoor concerts to elaborate festivities at the agency's social club. (This function was called "Friends Unlimited," assuming all retarded folk were kind and close, like Quakers. It was in fact held in a church.) The young staff were very dedicated. They put on gowns and clouds of perfume, like the socials were real balls. They spent half the evening standing together discussing how they looked, and how some of the male staff looked, just to make sure they were setting the best possible example. They took the kids to movies they themselves would want to see. They took the kids on trips to Martha's Vineyard and New Hampshire, responsible for big expense accounts and with no administrators there to help them. They cared so much about their jobs, the agency had them attend seminars on professionalism, so they would care even more.

Linda had been at Pinski Place for four years, now. She resisted all suggestions that she transfer to another program. She felt nowhere near burnt-out, though the agency said she was "going for an endurance record." She was part of the inner circle of full-time staff, "the family" at the center of a slowly swirling nebula of part-timers, subs and temps. There were three other women Linda's age, so of course they decided they were the Marsh sisters. (Everyone wanted to be Jo; Linda got stuck being Meg.) There was one older woman, a Polish matron, cantankerous as the Devil's ex and perpetually under allegations of abuse, though the kids adored her and called her "Mom" (which the agency abhorred). A relative newcomer, a girl just out of college, was House Manager. Lastly there was one man, a guy twenty-seven who was deeply into all "extreme" sports, named Steve Juraska. The only man in an otherwise female milieu, he behaved as the cock of the walk—a paid hedonist, disdaining all domestic duties and even insisting, at times, he was the program's "recreation specialist." But his main occupation was Mindy. Counseling, defusing and otherwise escaping from his nineteen-year-old nemesis. From the beaches of Martha's Vineyard to the aisles of Toys-R-Us and from the bottom of the spiral staircase clear up to the top: in its own strange way, a sort of long-term, sublimated romance. Mindy's fatal attraction to Steve—and his limitless patience with same—was considered the program's number one behavior problem. The agency monitored this relationship with a sort of placid fascination, ignoring the obvious solution of getting Steve out of there. Linda often worked with him which meant that, in effect, she had more "dates" with Steve than with her husband. Happily though, Mindy was a formidable chaperon. Linda was scared of her, not without reason—the girl was pretty strong and absolutely-insane jealous. The recipe for Hell was baiting Mindy, which Steve and Linda succumbed to under stress. "What, can't we sit close to each other?" "Mindy, I am married. Steven is engaged." "Min, Lin and I are gay."

In reality, of course, Linda and Steve were simply foxhole buddies. Things being as they are, people only human, there'd been some harmless flirtation. It had topped off—or bottomed out—two years before, at the cabin in North Conway. After the kids ("the clients") were in bed, Linda and Steve shared a bottle of chardonnay, then decided on a moonlight swim. The question of whether to "skinny-dip" was taken as the joke it was, but set the tone of the affair. In fairness to Steve, he didn't understand how frightening this was for her, partly since she was too scared to tell him. He could kiss her, she just didn't want his tongue; feel her nipples, but he had to leave her swimsuit straps alone. It just went on and on and she was frightfully embarrassed, glancing at the cabin when he let her up for air. She blandly said she'd slap him, finally demonstrated, *pat.* ("Steve, okay? I mean it.") Next morning, an innocent witness asked why Steve was "hurting" her, down by the lake. She had to gently explain this was "what mommy-daddy do in private"—adding, "Don't you dare tell Mindy." Humiliated and furious, Linda wrote a letter—a three-page treatise on adultery—which she delivered, without comment, with Steve's breakfast on a tray. For the next few weeks, Steve was as respectful as Linda was cold. But soon enough, their sibling love/hate balance was restored. They spent their shifts laughing and joking again. And Linda was telling her *other* co-workers what "Steve Jurassic" was up to. If nothing else, he was stalked and whipped by Mindy—a constant store of ammunition no one could resist.

All in all, Lin loved her job. The clients were the big, exuberant family she'd never had. She loved the riotous dinners, the three-ring circus getting everyone out the door. She loved the hyper bedtimes. And she loved being the centerpiece—the big sister, sometime mom, sometimes just plain silly one, the Linda everyone listened to and loved.

By working with children, she got to extend her own childhood. To go on a merry-go-round with friends her own age. To scream, scared for real, at the Witch Museum's moving mannequins. To have more souvenirs from the House of Seven Gables than anyone alive. And the night after her Oreo binge, the ravaging of rosemary and business-girl's free car repair, Linda got a big surprise she didn't like at all.

She wasn't going to Friends Unlimited tonight. Instead, Steve and Linette—the snide little witch who'd come in as House Manager—had taken all but one of the clients to the rented hall at Southside Presbyterian. Tonight's extravaganza was—O! Brainstorm!—a make-believe "Fifties Sock Hop"; it hadn't been done in nearly a month. They'd helped the clients dress up in V-neck sweaters and pleated skirts, with holiday frostings of hair-spray and gobs of Groom N' Clean. Linette had gone as young Liz Taylor, circa *National Velvet*—jerri-curled bangs, stuck-on lashes, the whole look. (Linda thought that Linette, with her pillowy thighs, could have gone as *Nineties* Liz Taylor too if she'd wanted.) In the four-girl bedroom, Lin's pal Michelle twirled round in her crepeline-flounced party dress and Linda whined "*I wanna go*" and not because it was fun. Because Linda was left behind, one-on-one, with Mindy.

Just as other girls her age had periods, or bad-hair days, Mindy had times when her behavior made her unpresentable. She'd *not earned* going to Friends Unlimited tonight; as Linette so artfully elaborated, she had not earned going *out with Steve* because *Linda* felt her attitude was awful. Mindy would therefore stay home with her (*rival, enemy, wicked stepsister*) "best friend in the whole wide *world!*"

Linda, in short, had been set up.

As she later learned, so passed another Monday night: Derrick tried to mediate a gang-related confrontation in the shower. While five miles north, as the Green Line rolls, Linda was cleaning up (self-induced) vomit while the Vomitress called her "a twatch." Derrick sat in the shift office, hearing two of his line staff accuse each other of disrespect in front of the youths ("You called me a *nigga*!" "You're smokin dust, I said *homeboy*!" "Front of these fools, it's the same damn thing!"). While Linda, Laundress Extraordinnaire, moved baskets of *badly* soiled stuff to find room to unload an unbalanced washer. Derrick investigated an alleged theft in Dorm Two, smiling skeptically at animated and biased "witnesses." While Linda got spat at by a nineteen-year-old woman who didn't want to take a shower. Who rushed at her half-naked, screaming, "*You're in love with him! You're a twatch I hate you and I hope you* ALWAYS DIE!" Derrick, alone in Dorm Three, was cautioned by three black youths, "Homes, you best step off our turf." While Linda sat like a child in front of her twenty-three-year-old "boss" (who took her station very seriously, roller-curled bangs and who-needs-mascara lashes notwithstanding), being told she should have "approached the shower issue with less of your own feelings at play." Derrick worked with a frightened and bellicose rookie, quelling an insurgency in Dorm One—telling the new guy

"Things will be cool, things will be good" like a TM guru teaching a mantra. While Linda made eight lunches for next day, and wrote down data that said how well each client made his or her own lunch, all per order of Linette.

At 10:45, it happened—as it often did—that Derrick and Linda were doing the exact same thing: sitting in a quiet place, he in a darkened dorm, she in an empty kitchen, both writing their shift notes. Both trying to state the facts, artistically redraw the truth to clear all parties, cover all bases, scratch all backs and appease all powers that be, making the whole of it enjoyable reading for the next shift, all the while listening for soft footfalls of midnight mayhem. Both happened to be sitting on the floor as they wrote—he, because there was no chair near his strategic vantage point; she, because she liked to emulate her husband's poses.

. . . *at that time, this worker replied, "Mindy, you should shower." She said, "Steve lets me skip sometimes," and this worker said how this was like the Indians who didn't own Manhattan, taking wampum for it from the Dutch. Since Steve is male staff and your shower is a female staff's concern. I told her, "I take mine each day. No one makes me either," and she called this worker a "b-tch." I said* EXCUSE ME?! *and she spat and called me other names and went into her room and slammed the door* (hard). *This worker strongly feels*

. . . *that the entire "colors" subterfuge has had its run on Broadway. Our politically sensitive counselors have deferred to this crap til now our angels are convinced they're gangsters. Tonight I impounded two red shirts out of Tim Curran's cubicle. He expressed, "Hey yo yo them my colors." I said I'm not a yo-yo and he'll wear a tutu if we really feel he should. Also in connection with the alleged theft of one (1) pair (2) Adidas high-tops from Mick Fagan's locker, I learned that this alleged (fake) occurrence was a scam to—*

Thump. He looked.
Click. She stopped writing.
He knelt upright, bracing his forearm on his knee.
She sat up on her heels, her hands on her thighs.
I'm the Man . . .
I'm the woman-in-charge . . .
I am the force that keeps things cool and . . .
If I have to, I'll be mean.
If it's Curran . . .
Mindy wouldn't dare . . .
Both sounds were nothing. Miles distant and worlds apart, Linda and her husband thought, *No problems on my shift.* They finished their writing, both hoping and praying, the other's night was better than their own.

She lay on the parlor sofa, Cleopatra in indigo dress. Dosed on the asp, she laxly reached her arm back, feeling for a Kleenex.

She'd started soon as he walked in the door—she wasn't cut out for this. For Life. He said, "Darling hold that thought," went into the kitchen. She lay and kept her moody peace til he came back with a glass of cranberry juice. She tried to explain what it meant. That "Little Miss Brown-Nose"—her boss, Linette—was still in a training bra when Linda started college. That Mindy was a retarded jerk who got treated like a princess. That loving a woman meant sharing her resentment. Derrick nodded, sympathetic. He held her concerns like a dainty china teapot, assuring her he really felt the tempest. At last he said, "I'll make us chow"—manly, cheerful and obtuse.

(There was seldom any question of who cooked. Derrick grew up caring for abusive, disabled grandparents; the Bauers had employed a full-time housekeeper. Derrick was a chef. Linda burned water.)

She remembered that the game hen didn't thaw. "I hope you can just" *take me away to a perfect world* "do something with it anyway."

He grinned. "Got you covered, babe." He was always optimistic. He could . . . her eyes roamed as she jealously imagined. Talk down a riot, or kick a knife out of a kid's hand, or counsel an addict in withdrawal, then come home hungry for dinner. "What else do you want?"

She said, "For you to be less than perfect, once. For me to be strong when you're weak or confused, so I could comfort you or—"

"I meant, for dinner."

"Oh." She gazed at the back of her hand, as though admiring her ring. Her look was of vacant enchantment.

(Linda's *petit mals* were seldom more than an endearing quirk, though she reported all sorts of overwhelming sensations. She'd *grand mal*'ed but once in her five years of marriage—out in front of the house on a warm autumn day, when she'd locked her keys inside her Tercel. Derrick sometimes wondered if this fascination with her hands was part of her epilepsy. Shelley said, "Oh, in love with her hands, you mean?—started when she was three." Linda never knew what either of them were talking about.)

She laid her hand on her tummy and sighed; she was all grown up, and her hands weren't magic anymore. "Possibly rice pilaf."

"That salad from last night's still good."

She clicked her tongue. "Is not. It's been in vinaigrette and I stay garlic. You should know."

"I should plant you so you'll grow." He stood, then noticed

her feet. "My, what fetish-worthy feet you have, Red Riding Hood." She wiggled her toes: Goodbye. "This little piggy got yelled at by her boss . . ." She whined, irate. Raised her chin, Come hither. He came to her, her prince. Sleeping Beauty, supine on her couch, she gazed up into his eyes. She gave him the balled-up Kleenex, sputtered goofy giggles as he tossed it. He sat and held her hand for real. She searched his eyes, a question on her heart.

"Would you still love me if I was white?"

"Then you'd be someone else. Wouldn't that be adultery?"

"You better be nice.—I mean, I wonder about your desires, what it is you feel. If you're only excited by brown-race girls, or—"

"Brown-rice girls exclusively, yes. Give me trail mix or give me my hand back—"

Playfully fierce, she hit him with a sofa pillow. "Just get—*quit* it! Out!"

Derrick went to the kitchen.

Linda found the clicker. She surfed by Leno and Letterman, came to rest on an old William Holden western. For whatever strange reason, vintage male-adventure flicks (the ones with no real violence) had a sedative effect on her. Daddy's on his horse and all is well. She liked how he stated the obvious, and his facial expressions always went with what he said. She lay sleepily, half-closing her eyes.

The phone rang. Derrick picked up in the kitchen. She knew exactly what went on. He got calls from former detainees—death threats, so he always picked up before the machine. He answered in funny voices—said "IBM" then "I am the Viper." Listened to the caller, then explained, "I vipes der vindows. Now I heffs mine vork." Or he was an Indian clerk at 7-Eleven who found the caller's language "most very unacceptable," and hung up. She sighed, wishing phones were not invented. She heard him in the kitchen. "Ah . . . *who dis?*" Some gang member, then, no doubt warned him not to walk the streets. "Ah . . . you make a mistake, dis *raundry!*" She twisted her mouth, disgusted. When would they stop harassing him? When would he grow up? Out in the kitchen, he raised his voice—an angry Chinaman. You bring ticket, I give laundry—Happy New Year, Blondie. The receiver slammed back on the cradle. Thank God.

"Darling, who called?"

He came into the parlor. "Just a friend from work."

"A girl?"

"Cindy Crawford. She works for DYS now; community service or something, I don't know."

"Derrick, I *hate* other girls. I wish there were none, anywhere."

"Well, the ones I work with all ride Harleys."

"Oh, right. Like that's chic now, I suppose."

He went back into the kitchen.

She watched TV. Big, bland men riding horses, stopping to talk, riding their horses somewhere else. Soon she was asleep.

and if you order now you'll also receive the Miracle Knife at no additional cost yes absolutely free see how it's seven knives in one it slices dices pares and peels shreds onions cheese and we all have to wear different hats Lin you're a caregiver housekeeper chauffer psychologist Lin you should be qualified to julienne carrots but I see you don't really know how here give me those you can set the table. Oh and see if your father wants to examine how the shower issue was addressed Lin that was so unprofessional Lin you're so unable dear you're such a baby.

So deep in the woods that it was always night, the snow was fallen before God loved the world. Even madness there was old, the red birds' feathers were forgotten flames. Iron statue in the snow, a tear fell from her empty eye. The white moth lighted, sipped the tear.

Baby Linda, wake up. Honeykins, dinner's ready.

His fingers brushed a curl from her cheek. She opened her eyes, sat up. Clutched his shoulders, said "My life. For me. If you could live it, then I'd go. Fly on the wall: no. Snowflake moth. Like a zillion others, falling. I can't find the statue."

He gazed into her eyes.

He was loving and obtuse. *Here you are, talking trash—a mystery to me.*

She squinted, perplexed. *But you can understand; you choose not to.*

He took her hand, led her. She toddled like a child, half asleep. He gave her plates and silverware. She looked at them as she took them to the table. Pfaltzgraf, "Oak Leaves" china. Much of what they had was from the Bauer house—nice, expensive things, like their Waterford "Herringbone" glassware, that Linda had grown up with, that her mom had since replaced.

Her husband served her plate. Half awake, her body followed a childhood script; arms crossed, she shook her head. Salad, no: she'd said she didn't want it.

Derrick started eating. Remarked, when he was young, when someone called 'Food,' you came running. Didn't matter if it was an old boot. Didn't even matter if you had an old boot for lunch. Linda wasn't in the mood. "You sound just like my father."

"Women marry their fathers—word from the ivory tower."

She looked at her game hen. Poor little bird. "Sounds incestuous.—I know: you don't believe the ivory tower. Anyway, I'm not your mom."

"No—my mother eats."

Linda said "Oh God"—every story had the same moral. She said "Your mother's blonde. She's cool-hearted, gabby and strict. I hate to say it, but she's so much exactly like *my* mom, it's almost—"

Derrick made a pained face. Took something from his mouth, touched it to the rim of his plate. "Watch out for bones."

She curled her lip. "That was pretty gross." It somehow tickled her, though. "Derry-dear, I'm revolted."

He pointed to her plate. "*Essen sie, bitte.*" She looked at a dubious sliver, captured on her fork. Cautiously nibbled the end. He said, "You can eat the whole thing. There's more."

"Der, you don't understand. Once I start eating, I finish. Tomorrow I'd have an enormous brunch, then stop at Dairy Queen on my way to work."

"Show up like the Fairy Queen, blessings in your hand."

"Wrong again. Bulimics never share. It's not a social experience, no. Not if it's vanilla. Soft swirls from the machine: you don't know vanilla. Like last fall, when I wanted that black body glove. Lost so much weight. At Emmanuel's fall bake-sale. Sheryl Heine had a sugar ghost on a stick. I stared. I asked if it was white chocolate, I mean, I hoped it was. She said No, vanilla. Der, I *scared* her. Soft, milky sugar on a stick. Her breasts—Der, that was *part* of it. That was the closest I ever came to being a man. The only way I could have been female was, a white wolf. With green eyes."

"Lin: you only *see yourself* as fat. I've done the research. You are underweight."

Frowning, she fussed with her napkin on her lap. Here were her thighs, before her eyes, and his incredible assurance. "Fine-boned. I should be, like, tiny . . ." She left the table, left her plate untouched. So much for continental dinners, when one worked second shift—when thoughts were left unfinished, and one never noticed things. She got a nearly empty pint of frozen yogurt from the freezer. Leaned her tush against the fridge, ate from the carton with a spoon, carelessly depraved. "Now, chocolate: this is me. Vanilla's my mom. She's spiritual temptation. I'm just plain old carnal sin. The calories. The tropical oil. What it does to your complexion. The alkaloid co-factor that makes you feel like you're in love. So you've got the stigma, the woman alone on Friday night with her Whitman Sampler." She frowned at her spoon, gave it a defiant lick. "It's saying, 'I want to be loved and fed and don't care if my thighs get huge.' Except I do. Despise my thighs. Legs should just be legs. They should just be straight, like yours."

"Linda."

"What-a."

"You didn't leave any for me."

"Then for boys, the answer's clean and honest. 'No second

39

helpings, run outside and play.' Girls do secret, shameful things. I mean, come on: 'purging' sounds like monks with whips." She remembered his complaint, spoke softly as a satin voice on FM after midnight. "Have some honey, then, on . . . something nice."

Their eyes met, warm and wanton; she licked the edge of her spoon. Something *really* nice—the secret lips so soft and wet, so kind of him to kiss. She stepped aside, her pose a dare, as he opened the fridge. He looked, and shook his head. "Mother Hubbard's cupboard."

"I know. Mother stayed in the shoe all day."

"Wrong rhyme. That was the old woman, who had so many kids . . ."

He took the bottle from the fridge. He held it, studied it, and she felt he was somewhat overdoing it, like he'd known the answers all his life and never been afraid, but now he didn't know, and now he was afraid. Though his face really had no expression . . .

She said, "Oh, stop. Remember Pazia?"

"Yeah. Girl my boss brought over for dinner last week." Derrick was a sport about it: "She was kind of tough." He put the bottle back in the fridge. "She was here? Must have been today. Dropped off a thank-you gift, or . . . Why didn't you mention it?"

Watching his eyes, she said, "I chose not to."

"Might I ask why not?"

"Only if you wish to be intrusive." The reason happened to be simple—it slipped her mind, since it wasn't important. Now she was concerned—what effected him, the gift or the giver?

"Lin, I don't want her here. She's a total freak, batteries included." Linda sighed, relieved. Nothing here more sinister, nor any less incorrigible, than her husband's working-class prejudice.

"Derrick, this is Salem. We're going to run into people who are quote-unquote 'seeking alternative spirituality.' We should be 'in the world, not of the flesh'; we need to love them."

He said he thought it was "odd." She made a face at "odd." Guests for dinner didn't mean pizza and beer. It didn't mean sitting out on the back porch, talking about car repairs and football scores. Guests for dinner meant RSVPs, carefully considered place settings, wine matched with the entrée, entrée before the appropriate centerpiece. Roses for beef, carnations for veal. Guests for dinner meant shopping with Mom, new clothes, perhaps new earrings. Playing the piano for Daddy's gentle cognac-sipping friends: a gracious home, a lovely daughter. Guests over, finally, meant thank-you notes and flowers via Western Union. Stopping by in person with a little homemade gift . . . well, it wasn't *odd*. It was possibly *bourgeois*. Her

40

mother always said, "Etiquette is only a guide, pointing the way to Kindness" which in turn was only Bunyonesque for *It's the thought that counts.*

"What did she say to you, anyway?"

Linda closed her eyes, Oh God give me strength. "Dear, *Pazia* said *nothing*. All right? She thanked us for having her over. I think she's lonely. She was very nice."

Derrick slowly nodded, this was Salem. Nothing stranger here than graffiti on an overpass. A multi-colored work of art, *Goddess Is Alive And Magick Is Afoot* and the black-on-grey retort that *Christ Is Lord.* "Sure she's lonely: she's a nut."

"And I'm sure the wine is perfectly wholesome. These wicca-wacks or whatever, you know they're so organic. It's probably better for us than the kind we buy in the store."

" 'If it grows from the ground, it can't hurt you.' "

She said, "Mm-hm," content; she accepted every Seventies truism *sans* critique.

Derrick said, "Tell that to Socrates."

She beckoned her finger, Give me your ear; she whispered something magic. "*She told me it's 'Pretty Girl' wine.*"

He gazed out the black kitchen window; dreaming darkly, wonder without joy. He softly said, "That means something . . ."

"*She said it will make us 'have eyes for each other' . . .*"

" . . . that means something, too."

She left him, walked towards the bedroom.

She paused, looked back, hinting at a pose—the glance down her shoulder, the curve of her hip. "Maybe you'll find out."

She went to the bedroom door. He stood in the kitchen, still staring out the window, searching the night for a riddle's solution.

He looked at her with longing, with peace enough for now; half the question was answered.

She slightly spread her hands—See me, be reminded. The hips on which he strove, seeking rest within her. The caramel breasts, for him alone to touch. The nectar between her legs, which only he should taste.

Black curls, white teeth, her soft, delighted whisper—"*Tomorrow's Valentine's.*"

She went into the bedroom, and softly closed the door.

The phone rang.

Alone in the bedroom, she wanted to faint—hand to her forehead, she fell on the bed. When would life be normal? But the longer he talked in the kitchen, *sotto voce*, the surer she knew it was Tony Biondo. That meant, change for bed and find a book—a long one.

Tony Biondo was Derrick's boss. He'd been at DYS for sixteen years—as an employee. He also grew up in the system.

41

Then was in and out of prison til he met the Lord, or something.
Yet his life story was this impossibly varied saga. Like, whenever
he wasn't in prison, he was a soldier in Vietnam or a hippie in
Haight-Ashbury or an outlaw biker at Altamont. Like he grabbed
the biggest slice of life he could, while he was out. He was now
a forty-seven-year-old adolescent, long-haired and tattoo'ed with
a smile like the glint of bar lights off a switchblade. He tried to
shock Linda with his right-wing, chauvinist views, but he only
made her laugh and once she even winked at him, We know
you're not so bad.

Linda picked up her princess extension—slowly, so it
wouldn't click on the line. For her, eavesdropping on men was
like being a child again—kneeling at the top of the stairs, trying
to decipher things that grown-ups talked about, so late at night.
A quick, confusing glimpse into this tough and hectic place
which she was sure could only sound and smell like the boys'
locker room, at school. Derrick said he called two boys into the
office, which made Tony mad. Since these *civil dignitaries* should
have been *Phantom-Zoned for the duration*, and the only thing
they needed *after lights* was an *office phone call*. And Derrick
said this *Hanoi Hilton shit* was for clowns, and Tony said then
fine, Put on your rubber wig and baggy pajamas, take a baseball
bat and go *secure your population*. And Derrick said that *day-
shift* plays the colors, *days* did that, not him. Then Tony said
Why you keep sayin my name? Who else is on the line? so Linda
pressed the breaker, slid the receiver down and read some of
Tasha Tudor's *First Poems of Childhood*. When she picked up
again, Derrick finished saying something about *the Commish* and
Tony said this subtle shift of emphasis was the kind of *co-
dependency shtick I get from the kids*. Then Derrick said he
didn't mean it that way, he just meant, how were things. Like,
the home front and the *woman*.

Tony said "*Woman*," like he'd heard of them but thought
they were a myth. Linda pressed her hand to her mouth so she
wouldn't laugh. Derrick said, "Pazia," and Tony said he called
that *entre-nous*. Asked why Derrick cared, which Linda thought
was a good question. Then Tony went off. "*Bloom. You even
think about cheating on that little doll-face of yours, I mean, you
even admit it to God in your prayers—don't think Him and me
ain't tight. Cause I'll show up at your door with a Bozo mask and
a chainsaw. You got oats to sow, you sow 'em in Dorm
Three—have I been clear, motherf—?*"

Linda hung up, almost yelping in shock at the expletive.
Then clenched her fist and pulled it in with a silent, ecstatic *Yes!*

Quietly reading, together in bed. The lamps on the two
nightstands were porcelain artichokes. The shades were ruffled,
Victorian florals, pastel-green azaleas. The bedroom looked like

the rest of the apartment: a woman's home where a man had been living. She could rearrange everything; as long as it didn't effect plumbing/electrical, he wouldn't even notice. He was reading a paperback history of aviation; it was, in some unknowable way, somehow more than just a book about airplanes. He solemnly nodded, like things he'd deduced on his own were found confirmed. She frowned, nibbling her pinky-nail as she read. At least her book had pictures, not photos of ugly machines. He asked why she never read adult books in bed, anymore. "Well, my romance books are private, dear."

After some time, he moved over and held her. She let him move in, not taking her eyes off the page. He cradled her; she shifted down, to get her head under his chin.

She tried to keep reading but he was focused on her, like an auburn-maned lion with intelligent eyes. At last she sighed, laid her book on her lap. Face to face, soul to soul, his deep-purring breath like a current through her body—they calmly studied each other's eyes. "Tell me a story, Daddy."

He laid her down, her head on the pillow. Kissed her forehead, then began. "Once upon a time there was a girl named Penny Pan. She had a very happy childhood. Helping Mommy bake and sew and cutting colored-paper leaves for school. And things like that. And Penny met a charming prince—" They shared the joke. *Oh really?* "—who thought Penny Pan was the neatest person ever. And she stayed a little girl . . . and lived happily, forever."

She frowned at him, concerned. "Is my story sad?" He lowered his eyes—he didn't know. "Der, I'll finish, then." Her finger lightly traced the contour of his cheekbone—his turn, not to be sad. "I do. Miss my childhood. So much it breaks my heart. I see little clips, like previews of Heaven. Only they're *post*-views, instead. Something I've lost and can never have back. And even the pictures are fading. I mean, I don't *remember*. I know what it is I'm sad for—I can hear it. Feel it, and some other sense I can't even describe . . . but I can't *remember*. And I think, if I stayed up all night for many days, if all it did was snow and snow so here-and-now was frozen, I might . . . find myself again."

She sighed, soft despair. He would always listen, patient; he would never understand. He frowned and she knew he was trying to recall when he hadn't let her buy things, or given her time alone. He was way too vital, here-and-now, to see what she was describing. At last he smiled—had his own idea how this, like any problem, could be solved. "Hon, soon I'll be a teacher.—No, I *do* understand, you don't mean material things. I'm saying, we'll finally be able to afford having a child. Because I think this . . ." He paused, searching for the term. " . . . *melancholy* of yours, maybe it's a woman-thing. What makes you want to have a child."

"To know her joys vicariously." She had to do that, every now and then—remind him that she was an intelligent adult, that she read the articles in Cosmo and, basically, knew what was going on.

He said, "And it's *coming*." He smiled, he was certain: gloom was doomed. "The house in the suburbs . . ."

Linda said, "Cows."

He corrected himself. "—in the country. With everything you want. Apple trees, a swing . . ."

She'd had enough, for now. "Oh why don't we just go live with my parents, then."

She got up on her knees to turn off the wall-switch. In the dark, he lightly touched her hip, the bare skin under her nightie. Telling her, this simple act—up on her knees to get the light—was a sudden provocation, igniting his mysterious and insatiable lust for her body.

She snuggled, close to him under the quilt. Then remembered to ask, "Are you done reading?"

"Well yeah, unless the sun comes up or I start seeing infrared."

She giggled, told him, "Stop."

He obligingly closed his eyes, well on the way to sleep.

She looked at him, curled on his side. Man-shaped strokes of brown, in the faint streetlight from the window.

She softly said, "I thought you wanted to play with me."

He murmured, "Oh yeah," his dreamy deferral—he'd do whatever she asked, someday. *Wait til we get to Heaven.*

She watched him, toying with a strand of her hair. Wrapped around her finger.

"Der, I *need* it . . . okay? I had a really stressful night. I mean, I'm feeling alone. I'm asking."

(She didn't sound plaintive or childlike. She sounded sensual and deep—Patti Smith, or some Beat queen of the cappucino scene.

She'd learned that after working with delinquents all night, childlike didn't grab his attention.)

"I mean, I need to be touched. Der, deep. Your manhood is the bow, caressing the strings of my heart. Oh baby, please. Lift my skirt and let me be your violin." *If that doesn't do it, I quit.*

He took her hand in the darkness.

His hand found her brow; her lashes flicked his palm.

They kissed, in no rush—Well, hello; hello, again.

She began to take his tongue in her lips, wanting more. His hand caressed her hip. The hem of her nightie, smoothed away. She asked, "What are you going to do to me?" breathless.

While they kissed, his finger didn't probe, just gently teased. Oh yes, *here's* where you live. Just behind the nub. The touch

44

went straight to her heart. Just knowing that he touched her, he wished her to be thrilled. *You'll always get your wish.* Soon they parted lips, he said, "*I think you're wet.*"

She wonderingly said, "*I am?*"

He covered her, slid in. She lay passive, holding his neck.

This was the slow part, for her. When he was in his stride, rolling like an engine, she longed to be a part of him but wasn't. She stared at the ceiling, felt hapless and exposed as a little girl waiting for the bus. With her lunchbox and corduroy book bag, waiting for him to slow down and stop.

He always told her, *It's all about you. Any way at all you want to be with me, to be yourself, a spoiled princess, wanton slut—I'll love it. I'll adore you* yet she always went away to her quiet place, instead. Her body wasn't *she.* She was free, she was . . .

. . . a bottle. Floating out on the swells of the tide. The ocean was strong, it did all the work. *It's deep and heavy, far and cold—I can sink, or even drown. But I'll only fall to the bottom, be part of my ocean that loves me.*

She sank to the bottom, stayed. Hollow metal statue, bright and perfect, filled with sand. Full of heavy wet sand, full of power, full of him. She began her fevered rhythm, her gentle belly dance. Moving her hips, turning her head, like a child having a bad dream.

O Baby yes, get off. O Mama, rise and rule, c'mon.

But Derrick it's all you. I want it to be you. She came loose inside, she let him in. The electric tingle, warmth, of letting all her inner parts be ruled by him, be still. Letting him come in, slip out, come and go at his pleasure. At last she surrendered, she was free to be his vessel, the vixen he demanded, she held him with her legs. He clinched her shoulders, soothing her with kisses, even as he pinned her to the bed. She held on, her cheek to his neck, as though he were consoling her, and something short of Heaven itself could ever fill her need.

She cried out from her soul, a woman's idolatrous passion: "Oh God, oh God, ohmy*God!* Oh *yes!*"

As they drifted off towards sleep, Linda lay still on her side. Derrick held her from behind, his hand on her hip. He lightly nuzzled, kissed her hair.

Early in their marriage, Derrick learned that Linda needed to be held after sex. If she wasn't held, she'd cry. She'd cry and cry, like a baby.

She tried to give a reason, which was hard at first, since she'd never made love to anyone else. She was new to this crying business, too. She said, "It's like when the merry-go-round stopped. When my father took me off. So sad, that it was over." Derrick's patient look said, he sort of hoped the reason wasn't over yet, either. She clarified, "I was five." She tried to explain what was over now. The time and place where those feelings were real. Childhood. Heaven.

Something like that.

She told him, "Girls are different. The sex is like, the warm-up. The holding is what's real." He gave her what she wanted. She'd lie on her side, staring off into space. Softly biting the knuckle of her thumb, something not too far removed from sucking it.

He asked, "Are you okay?"

She said, "Mm-hm." She was looking at her Tasha Tudor book, an oblique grey square on her nightstand. She imagined it was as she'd unwrapped it, Christmas morning the year before last—a treasure trove of wonder, not something she'd looked at a million times already.

He said, "Tomorrow's Valentine's."—something would be special.

She softly asked, "What should I wear?"

"What about your strapless gown?" In the dark, her lips formed the words, then he spoke them: "That's what it's called, right?"

She smiled, delighted by her psychic prowess. "Um . . . yes. A gown without straps is known to the avant-garde as a 'strapless gown'." Just to make sure: "The stardust blue one?"

Not knowing stardust from midnight, he affirmed, "That's the one."

"With the ruffled vee-seam, or . . .?"

"You're a cock-teaser, Lin. Anyone ever tell you that?"

"No. But I said it about myself, one time. To my guidance counselor at Coleman. At a *Christian school.* Because I got into an argument with this boy. About *wearing an earring.*"

"Linda Bloom."

"I thought it meant someone who causes a fuss. Like a farmboy who torments roosters. Ruffles all their feathers, or whatever. I was seventeen. Talking to *Ms. Jennings.* An old lady with glasses and her grey hair in a bun. I said, 'I'm just a cock-teaser'."

"Did they send you home?"

"I asked to go.—anyway, that dress is for parties."

"So we'll drink champagne and dance til dawn. A party of two."

I'll feel mildly silly. "Just promise you won't try to teach me fancy disco moves."

"Just sentimental classics. You can melt into my arms."

"With flowers and candlelight. Pretty Girl wine."

"You and I have a date."

He held her, and they slept.

4

She woke in mid-morning, alone in the bed. She sat up, poised still, holding the quilt to stay warm. Her large eyes, stern, slowly scanned the room—a dark, nervous woman, finding herself in a new day. Everything so quiet and still, minutes ticking by in suspense—the world outside, a dirty, cold machine.

She always woke up feeling like something bad would happen.

Her husband's footsteps, out in the hall—she looked that way, hopeful. He would be cheerful and brave, excited about the great things he would do. Nothing bad would happen today. Relaxing already, she stretched.

He came in with a tray. He set it over her lap, and her stretch became a pose—Oh my goodness, what a surprise.

Strangers who saw Linda Bloom on the street, tended to think she was a tough, sensual lady, probably an artist. They might have thought, if she bothered with breakfast, she would chase two Herbal XTCs with a tumbler of expresso.

Derrick brought her a big bowl of oatmeal with butter, milk and honey, and her Care Bears mug full of Strawberry Quick.

He kissed her cheek; she closed her eyes, Too perfect.

She opened her eyes and told him, "I'm so excited about tonight."

Linda came home at 11:15. She threw her purse onto the parlor sofa, trudged into the bedroom. She'd been tired all day, kind of achey; she had that itchy, tender dryness in her sinuses. They'd had an "in-house" night, catching up on the housekeeping and all the clients' programs—Pinski Place at its tedious worst. Now came the Special Evening. She felt her peculiar rich-girl's guilt: showered with gifts she didn't want, and fun that felt like work. She lifted her heart to the not-so-simple truth: *It will make me happy to make him happy, thinking he's making me happy.*

She undressed, stuffed all her clothes into the overflowing hamper. (The cobbler's children never have shoes—Linda did her own laundry as seldom as she possibly could. She feared getting caught by "Chatty Cathy"—Sonya Karpinski from downstairs, a large and chummy redhead who relished her ability to bore people dead. She, too, worked in human services—warmly assured everyone she met that she worked "in the nut house," meaning Danvers State Hospital. She always urged Linda to seek medical help for her infertility, as if *we choose not to have children yet* came over a scrambled wavelength.) She jammed the plastic lid down, almost getting it closed; she doubted whether the sight of her tangled pantyhose would heighten any romantic effect.

The front door opened; the sound always seemed some joyous exclamation, *I'm home!* She heard bags or something being shuffled on the floor. He was orchestrating one of his surprise miracles, while she stood naked in the bedroom. *Shit.* She sat at her vanity, combed out her ringlets with her bead-tipped brush, flounced her curls out over her shoulders. Picked a mascara clot from her lash. Fanned her hand over her bosom, like that would dry out a day's worth of sweat; decided to be real, used a dash of lilac talc. Makeup okay, she just freshened her lipstick. What was he *doing* out there?—well, she knew. A soldier of good fortune, making a silk purse from the sow's ear of his pocket cash. She got pantyhose from her drawer, and the damned dress he wanted from the closet. Now where the hell was—?

His intimate knock—light rap, once-pause-twice.

Her intimate response—"I'm dressing."

"Lin, I forgot all about tonight. Babe, I'm really sorry."

I'm not as dumb as I act, dear. "I'm still dressing." She pulled the gown's banded waist up. It made a soft, brown roll around her middle. *These are love handles—what, is he blind?* "Is there anything to eat?" No answer. "We have all those gourmet condiments in the fridge. We can mix them all together and call 911." She glanced round the room, her ballet-dropout pirouette. "Have you seen my strapless bra?"

"That stuff is like the wind, babe—it blows and I don't know where or from whence." The truth was even worse—he had to take her photo to Victoria's Secret, and leave his selection entirely up to the salesgirl. If her choice wasn't instantaneous, he went next door to Radio Shack. There was one possibility . . . she dragged the hamper out from the closet. There was her strapless bra—flattened on the floor, like a white tulip pressed between the pages of a book. *Oh I hope my mother doesn't have a crystal ball*—she shook the bra out, put it on. Dress zipped, back to the vanity. She parted her bangs down in front, held it with a tortoiseshell band. Her lipstick was claret, so she chose her mother's silver-set turquoise earrings. She stood and stepped back, determined to accept the mirror's verdict. The vee-seam pinched her waist and broadened her hips. *Ageing Puerto Rican housekeeper, dressed up to serve* hors d'oeuvres *at her employer's cocktail party.—God, if I was this mean to someone else . . .*

She went and opened the bedroom door. "I didn't have time

48

to—"

He stood in the hallway, rugged and slim. Hands in his pockets, he'd just strolled in. Weathered grey eyes in an eternal boy's face. Tight jeans, muscle pullover—he only needed to stay alive to be gorgeous, all his life.

She clasped her hands in front, stared blankly, her last resort—hoping he would like her, just because.

He said, "Oh wow," enthused—she was a monster truck. He touched her with his wand, and she was an Aegean goddess. Shy and timid, insecure—everything he cherished, just because.

"Lin, I better shower up. That place was a bucket of blood tonight." (His grandfather's term for a place where he *wouldn't go to watch a dog fight.*) "I'm a mess."

"I find you lovely. You did brave and manly things that made you sweat. Only girls need showers, since they just get *ick.*"

"Where do you learn this, Lin? Is there some secret class after school, when you're little?" He took her hand. "Come along, Ick." She followed up the hallway, til he stopped and let her wander on alone. She went softly, magic waiting in her parlor.

It was transformed. Two candles glowing amber in silver Seville stems. The coffee table laid with Anchini linen, the excess artfully tucked underneath. White carnations with ferns in a vase. Camelia-covered china plates—she'd seen them on her parents' table, since she was a baby. Her mother's old Gorham champagne flutes, and Pretty Girl wine in a handled serving basket.

The food was in crystal platters and bowls. Lots of small portions of sweet and pretty trimmings. He knew it was the color and variety that counted. Dinner, to Linda, was never about eating.

Where did the food come from? Sorcery, of course. If she asked, he'd say he cooked it when he got home. She wouldn't find boxes from . . . oh, Boston Market, maybe—even if she looked in the trash. They were gone from the apartment, like an Oreo bag after a binge.

She went into the parlor, was appalled to see a chair. He was going to sit *across* from her? "Oh, no! Do I have fleas?"

(When she was eleven, she came home from summer camp with a note from the nurse—addressed to her mother, which Linda dared not open—stating that Linda had body-lice. Linda's mother was sublimely tactful: *The nurse says you have body-lice.* Her father's droll advice that they get her a Hartz collar didn't help much, either.

(Her parents had been like that, all through her childhood—not cruel but sometimes insensitive. Casting funny coins into the bottomless well of her fear.)

He put a CD on the deck, thought to ask: "*Bare Trees*

49

okay?"

Linda darkly glanced, Sure is. Echoes of her liberal/Christian girlhood: what mommy-daddy listened to in private.

They sat together on the sofa.

Derrick uncorked the wine. Linda said, "You're supposed to sniff"; not knowing what to sniff for, he gave his wife the cork. She narrowed her eyes at him. *Wait till we get to Heaven*; she didn't like when anything was automatically her job.

(She vaguely believed that most feminist ideas came from somewhere in the Bible. She felt Judgment Day's first order of business would be a divine spanking for all chauvinists, even saved Christians; Heaven's order ever after would be Ladies First, amen.)

She sniffed the cork; she was thoughtful. "It smells . . ." *It was my idea he didn't want it* " . . . okay. Yeah: it's good." She turned to him, suddenly thirsty for acceptance. "Hon, I didn't shower. I'm coming down with a cold. I look . . ."

She stared at him, wide-eyed: *You tell me.*

He returned the look: blank, thoughts cleared, open to all impressions. "Like a . . . girl."

"Ew.—as in, 'You Tarzan'?"

"No, like that shirt dress I got you from Scribbles and Giggles. The lavender one: '*All Girl*'."

She acted touched, since the shirt was in her rag-bin.

She pointed at corn pudding, willfully naughty. "I like that. I want more." Soon she was appalled. "That's too much!"

They tasted the wine. She held her glass at arm's length, like it might bias her opinion. "It's very . . . unique. It's herbal. Not floral: it's piney." She'd grown up drinking wine with dinner; she knew Moselle from Rhine by taste. She'd never been drunk, any more than she'd ever used drugs. Derrick used alcohol like an Irish-German: as a social sedative. Though, married to Saint Linda, he'd virtually gone dry.

They ate for a while, she making her astute little comments. Pretentious fast-food was really American cuisine at its best. Tarragon was pointless unless fresh. "And these capers don't add *any*thing."

"Darling, that's a raisin."

She prettily ogled the ceiling, Donna Dimwits in evening blue. Left unsaid: *Duh.*

He poured more wine, the last of it. "Damn! Must be the MSG."

She said, "Boston Market doesn't *use MSG*," disdainful of the notion. In her trusting world view, nationally-known franchises must have passed some threshold of blamelessness.

Derrick said, "I know I . . ." and paused, so she knew he was trying to paraphrase. *Hugged a kid in heroin withdrawal while talking down an armed riot.* " . . . worked up a thirst tonight."

"Der, tell me about it. I did *six loads* of laundry. Oh—and Mindy was a jerk again. An even *worse* jerk. This thing with Steve—you know, her obsession: it just goes on and on, like the bunny with the drum. And he *feeds into it*, Derrick. He '*counsels*' her, which is like"—she sourly mimicked: "'*Oh Mindy, I like you too as a friend but that's all we can ever be, is friends*'—how can anyone not barf? Der, you wouldn't understand but, like . . . Steve is slightly above average in looks, okay? I mean, let's face it: if I was retarded, I'd chase him around all day too. He's *training* her that way—it actually inflates his ego. And Billy—you won't believe this; are you ready for this?—Billy *threw* all his *records* out his bedroom window. Because Mindy—who's at the bottom of everything—"

Derrick said, "Now, Mindy: she's sort of snaggle-toothed and noisy, but almost . . . young Goldie Hawn, that kind of goofy—"

"Oh just say she's pretty. Everyone at work does."—Sodom and Gomorrah couldn't shock her anymore. "Anyway, she told Billy that Elvis is dead, and he threw a model fit. As in: up in his room for *two hours* yelling 'Elvis isn't dead' at the *top* of his *lungs*. Der, the neighbors came over in person to *complain*. I answered the door and I almost *died*. They asked, 'Are you the person in charge?' and, well, guess what: Linette was out with Clara at her aerobics class. Steve was—major quote/unquote—'*defusing the situation*' by taking Mindy out to *Baskin-Robbins*. And hon, you know me—I'm never the 'one-in-charge'. I'm, like, looking over my shoulder to see who they're talking to. Der, you know what that kind of situation does to me." He indicated the ceiling—they had to peel her off; she hit his knee, since he knew she never shrieked or freaked except with him. "*Oh!*"—she remembered something else. Her eyes flared with girlish glee as she opened her mouth to tell Derrick.

She froze.

They both froze.

The wind didn't moan. The candles didn't dim. The curtains didn't stir, as if by unseen hands. And no more than a moment really passed.

They looked at each other, wet-eyed and revealed, like reluctant newlyweds or like she'd pee'ed while making love.

Derrick looked away. He said, "That wine's not good."

Linda said "No" like she was bored by that obvious fact. She gazed at the window, played with her hair. Blue moonlight filtered, azure beams, through the sheer curtain—a steep descent, midwinter's midnight angle. The candles' flames, two tiny globes of orange warmth. She saw both these things at once. She knew she hadn't given God or anyone else permission to do computer graphics with her parlor. Nice job, at least—it was beautiful. Its beauty would come get her if she kept looking. So she looked at

Derrick instead. But he was now enchanted too. Intriguing older actor. She wondered when this happened—when she married a screen idol, not knowing who he was.

She tried to look at nothing. Her feet up on the cushion, she slowly played with her hair. Purposefully, like she could somehow win. She lifted it straight, watched it fall. Scintillating through amber light, cascade of comma-ringlets. She saw that God had given her this crowning glory, like she was queen of angels. She wanted God to stop doing things like that.

She asked her husband, "Are we drunk?"

"Um . . . no but if we were, that wouldn't explain what just . . ."

She discovered her hand. Oh, *wow*. The hand of a dusky goddess, stretched over the wine-dark sea. "Derrick, I'm afraid."

Very calm, like he was too, he told her, "Well, come here." She came and burrowed into his arms. If she closed her eyes, it felt okay. There was nothing strange in her husband's embrace. Daddy's strong frame, solid and heavy within, silky to her touch. His faint/exciting lion-cage musk. The solemn, steady timbre of his breathing. What she'd loved and sought as a little girl and what she, as a woman, always craved. Calm enough, she tried to think. Dim ideas and lifeless terms a bored college girl once jotted down in class. *Effects of psychoactive drugs. Barbiturates. Reds. Speed. White. Add color-fast bleach if you . . . no: hallucinogens have the same effect, different chemical structures. LSD's an acid, mescaline's an alkaloid. That's like pH balance, or hard water, you should only do wool on cold cycle, you . . .*

can't stay on task can't focus my thoughts

We can always call 911. We didn't do this to ourselves. We're not druggies. Like Wendy Sloane at work—we're not. Maxed-out, or hammered, or trashed. *I don't have a bumper sticker* Only Users Lose Drugs. *I don't live over a bar on Webb Street—that's her. Oh God she has nipple rings how can I be on the same planet as her?*

"Lin, let's not drink homemade wine from people we hardly know, anymore. Okay?"

She felt his calm, and wanted it. He already held her like a daughter, like a lamb on his shepherd's bosom. *Yes, I'm your black lamb I'll always follow always trust Derrick never let me go.* She held even tighter, made sure he was real. He was—she opened her eyes. Bad move. While she'd had her eyes closed, the circus came to town. Everything was changing, turning colors, taking shapes. She saw what she wanted/feared/expected, not what was really there.

She closed her eyes again. *Derrick, as long as you're real. Let this be our covenant: I won't be afraid.*

She opened her eyes. "Derrick, what happened? In that moment when—?"

"—we couldn't move. I had some really weird symptom. You wanted to help me. You made some crazy suggestion."

"But I didn't speak. Neither of us spoke."

"Lin, we're . . . sick. I'm feeling sleepy. We should go lie down and rest, then I'll decide what we should do."

They stood, his arm around her waist. They went down the hall. She'd never known, before, that her hallway was this long and weary corridor. His arm around her waist was an actual help.

At the bedroom door, she stumbled. She caught the doorpost then sagged against her husband, muttered an "Excuse me" which seemed needless. He was her rock, her strength in time of weakness—that was his job, his part of the deal. She had her own—the faithful weaker vessel, no bed of roses either. He was there for her now in a way she found real useful—as a solid object to lean on.

He held her waist. He softly kissed her cheek, sought her lips; she demurred, he kissed her hair. She was his girl, forever his girl. He loved to kiss and lick her, rub her tummy, make her laugh. She knew this was his response to the Moment—what wasn't said as they couldn't move, staring into each other's eyes. Aside from that, the Moment's meaning was a shocked and wordless blank: she couldn't recall what wasn't said.

She peeled off his arms, trudged into the bedroom.

They didn't bother with the light. Everything was lit up with unholy, magic beauty. She started undressing. *Why?* Even now, at eternity's threshold, she would decently put on her nightie, fluff her pillow, set the alarm. Yes, she was out there, all right: *John 11:25—is that AM or PM?* "Dear, tonight at work . . . ?"

Derrick breathed, "Yeah, babe."—he was edging along the wall, trying to get to the bed.

"Did it feel to you, somehow special? Like people were saying goodbye? Like every nice thing you'd forgotten, came back one last time?"

He collapsed onto the bed, like he was mortally ill. Answered calmly, like he wasn't. "Nah. More like maximum shit detail. The sense of leaving, people saying goodbye . . . not until lights-out."

She knelt before him, sat, like she honored a dying priest. "Der, tell me. I need to know."

"After points meeting. Rest of the crew carded-out. Me and Tony. Standing out in the shift area. Told him. Had to, Lin. How you said you . . . didn't want to live your life."

"Derrick, I would never. Betray a confidence of yours like that. I shared my heart and you told *Tony.* God, what must he think?"

"Well, he . . . went real strange on this. Said 'You got a crazy problem'—me; I had the problem. He said, 'Here's my sick solution: then you're dead. She don't wanna live, you're dead.' Told me I was done. I was done for the night and done for good;

he 'fired' me. Like he has every other night for the last six years, but . . . this time it was real. Not official: real. I felt like a stranger, walking the quad out to the gate. Like those walls never knew me, I was someone who didn't belong there . . ."

"Darling, I never said I didn't want to *live my life*. I told you I didn't want *this*. Derrick, you *know* what I want." A tear ran down her nose; she wiped it off. "Christmas morning and sled rides. I want to build a snowman. I want Mommy to fix my breakfast. I wanna help Daddy gather pine cones for the fireplace. I wanna wear mittens, not gloves, when it snows. Derrick, I need you to understand. I love you more than Life itself but *I wanna go home*, I just . . ."

He lay on his side, his back to her.

She sniffled, and stood up. Walked towards her dresser, bumped her hip on the corner of her vanity. She whined, plaintive. Tottered back and noticed her reflection in the mirror. Proud and timid caramel girl, the self she knew so well. Little Linda Bauer from Longmeadow Road, yet she also looked like someone else. Some lady. Ink-splash ringlets, globes of breast; brown curves, her dark and knowing gaze. *That's not really me—I'm just a little kid.*

"Lin?"

She turned. He lay draped, clinched with the bed—his cheek pressed to the quilt, like he'd been knocked out. Like the subject of Surrealist painting, he alone was normal—everything else in the room was Fantasia. The nightstand glowed with breathtaking beauty. The alarm clock was some rare device of magic gears and crystals. He said, "I was going to propose tonight."

"Dear, we're already married. What should I put on, for bed?"

"Non . . . restrictive . . . clothing."

She chose her blue camisole nightie. It had always been his favorite. Ruffled neckline and adorably immodest; its laced-slit hem just touched her thighs. *It's not just an old joke. My mother actually told me, once, to always wear nice underthings in case I ever had to go to the hospital.*

She crawled into bed, lay facing her husband. There for him like a mother, just in case whatever. She drew up her knees and lay fetal. Her hand was at her mouth; she'd eventually nibble her knuckle.

Derrick sat up—he remembered some chore. He tried to crawl in reverse, but that didn't look like it would work. He tried to reach over her, groping for the princess extension on her nightstand. Even at death's doorstep, he was careful not to squash her.

But he couldn't reach the phone.

"Der, if you can't . . . then just . . ."

"I gotta . . . call the medics. Ask if they maybe wanna . . .

54

stop by, check us out." *Oh Der, please. I'll bet that's how your grandfather sounded, the day he died of a heart attack. Like he was still a soldier out in the Pacific.* "Sorry to bring you guys outta your way like this. Don't hook me to no fancy machine. Just gimme a cigarette. Hey, you guys ever been to New York? Ever see Times Square?"

She said, "You mean, call an ambulance?"

"Uh."

"Darling, who's sick?"—she couldn't remember.

He said, "We are, babe," and collapsed.

They lay face to face, his arm still holding her to him.

She studied his eyes, concerned. They were dark with only a spark, like he was far away and worried about her.

Oh God he's dying.

"Oh. Oh, no—You can't have him. No, You absolutely cannot have my husband.

"Derrick, I'll never let you go."

She searched his eyes. The spark was gone.

She followed it.

And followed. A single hope, a single thought that wouldn't change and wouldn't stop.

If I ask, you won't refuse me. If I'm empty, won't you fill me? If I'm good, if I wait, you'll come back I know you will.

bottle on the wave lift me dip me let me sink and fill me with your sand come back don't leave me!

Body. Tumbling clothes. Can't think, can't stop. Can't sleep, can't eat. It's called anorexia, dear. *Thoughts won't focus, mind won't work. Cold pill. Thoughts won't focus, mind won't work. Cold pill. Thoughts repeating endless cycle cold if you do wool. Oh no won't lycra stretch if the machine's unbalanced where can I find room with all these baskets ohmyGod I'm having auras—*

Lin you have to wear your med-alert.

Mommy, it is so humiliating.

Lin, you must. End of discussion.

Why not a tee shirt that says I'M EPILEPTIC?

AND ADOPTED?

Well, why not?

Mommy?

Mommy?

Derrick?

Who?—

5

Linda.
Linda?
Where was Linda?
"Where is Linda? Linda? *Where* is Linda. Where *is* Linda?
Linda. Oh, *Linda*."
She opened her eyes.
The woman was too beautiful. She was someone's mother,
and suddenly very happy. She sat by the bed, her hands clasped
anxiously, now rapturously, between her knees. She wore a snug
black turtleneck, a gold heart necklace. Her blonde hair cupped
her cheeks, was longer in back. Her soft brown eyes were liquid
with wisdom and warmth.
She pleaded now, with tears of joy. "Oh baby, please wake
up. Please, it's time to wake up."
Linda blinked; the woman confused her. She seemed to be
saying *Wake up, look: this is Life. I brought you here; I made
you. I love you.* Linda took her best guess. "God?"
The woman peered closer. Her eyes flashed softly, intrigued;
she'd drawn a rare response. She didn't deny she was God. She
just peered.
Linda was awake now, twice as confused. She knew the
woman well enough and couldn't guess what made the woman act
this way. *She called me 'baby'. Why?* Mouth dry, Linda
whispered. "Shelley?"
Shelley looked startled, but just for a moment; her love
conquered all. "Well, 'Mom' is preferred, but still." She wanted
to touch, was hesitant—a mother's regard for her adult child. She
couldn't help herself—she felt for fever, gently stroked her
daughter's cheek. Linda tried to sit up; her mother held her still.
"No, lie still. Lie still, *Linda*. Lin, lie *still!*" It was a funny
riddle: a child's verse that didn't rhyme. Shelley was happy.
Nothing could be wrong.
Linda gazed, calm and serious, up at her mother's radiant
face. Her own lips, dry, formed words: *Why are you calling
me . . . ?*
She looked around. A blinded window. Walls painted
chartreuse, their corners rounded, as though the plaster sagged. A
nightstand covered with flowers and cards. A pink plastic

pitcher, on which her focus stuck for a confused and terrified instant: *Why is it* pink? Dixie cups stacked, and a couple loose, next to the pitcher. A religious tract and a business card—things graciously accepted and left for the orderly's grey rolling bin. A green cloth screen on a mobile frame. A wooden door with a mirror on it. There was a crucifix over the door. Together with the concave chartreuse walls, it made the room seem like one in a convent—a quiet, boring cell for vernal rebirth. There was noise outside the room. Bleach smell. *Hospital.*

Shelley said, "Now, listen. 'Kay? I'm gonna explain what's happening." Linda blinked, that she understood. This was more the old Shelley. An open manner, both jaded and girlish; an innocently feline expression of the eyes. "You've been unconscious for twenty-four hours, plus . . . well, we don't know. Unconscious since I found you, yesterday afternoon. Needless to say, I've been right here." She rolled her eyes, confided, "I've been praying up a *storm.* Hon, I have been *scared . . .* to *death.*" She was holding Linda's fingers, squeezing with each emphasis. Linda stared, afraid, acknowledging connection and conveying how she felt: *Way too soft and little something's missing and I'm so afraid.* "For about an hour, this morning, you wouldn't stop seizing. You were seizing in your sleep, one right after another." Worried, Shelley studied Linda's eyes: *Surely you remember, unconscious or not?* "They wheeled in an EEG machine and *oh* my goodness, you'd have seen me half hysterical. The doctor told me to wait *downstairs.* Then he said you'd had a 'sustained flurry of *petit mals*'. Like, the same little bee in your bonnet, over and over again. But you're fine—oh Lin, thank God. They drew blood and tested your levels. Nothing's wrong, it's just the . . . well."

Linda slowly sat up; her mother moved a little, so she could. Linda sat on the edge of the bed, soft thighs draped over the lowered aluminum guard rail. She looked thoughtful—a gentle girl with a really serious problem. Hands daintily lifted, awareness—a natural, feminine pose. She saw her hands and was . . .

. . . fascinated. *Both* hands were really interesting. Because they didn't look like hers, they looked like—

She slowly brought her hands to her bosom, cupped her breasts. Her eyes went wide, dramatic, with horrified disbelief. She lifted a curl from her shoulder. Stared at her two fingers and thumb, holding a strand of her black hair. She let it go, watched it fall—bounce back into an inky curl on her brown bosom.

She put her hands to her cheeks, over-awed.

Frightened, she turned to her mother. "Shelley—"

" 'Mommy'."

Linda froze, stared blankly. At last she repeated, "Mommy?" like the thought somehow amazed her: girls have mothers and maybe, yes, she needed hers just now.

Shelley was amazed in turn. "Oh dear, you look like one of Titian's angels." A lovely gift she didn't want—Linda slightly shook her head. "It must be the . . . oh."—the reason wasn't yet to be discussed. "Lin, your life has changed. You need to be real strong now. Lin, know that Mommy loves you, and listen: Derrick isn't with us anymore. He's gone ahead and we'll meet him after." Linda stared; her mother had her full attention. "Do you understand? Linda, your husband has died. This is something you need to face. Mommy is right here."

Linda looked serious, calm. Like she'd face it, or she wouldn't, or she wasn't sure what facing meant. She crossed her arms and rubbed her naked shoulders, as if cold. Shelley asked her: "Are you cold?"

Linda answered, "Somewhat. Yes."

"Lin, that was the hardest part. Now we're starting the rest of your life." Linda looked serious, calmly rubbed her shoulders. "Lin, cry. Scream. Anything. Lin, it's *me*." So it was. Shelley sat with her back to the divider, a forest-green backdrop. She was star of the show. Outside the room, an elderly patient noisily complained. Asked someone if they knew what *lactose intolerant* meant. A cart rolled past the door. A young black woman's naughty quip to a friend, *apple juice in the urine sampler*, titter, the cart was past the door.

Linda asked, "Would you be terribly upset if I got up and looked in the mirror?"

Shelley softly said, "I'd be appalled . . . ?"—watched the question pass overhead, like a ball gone from the stadium.

Linda stood up. Hands at her hips in a gesture, why it's easy. She waited, as though to see if standing had any strange or terrible consequence. Plainly, it did not; she went to the mirror.

She stood, relaxed; she knew it was only a mirror. After a while she touched the glass, to see if it was really her reflection.

Shelley was smoothly detached. "Did you fall? At some point? You think you may have bruised your face, or . . . ?—I'm just trying to guess. What it is. That you're doing at the mirror."

Linda stared calmly; she wasn't surprised. She looked exactly the way she felt—no form or face was more familiar. It mimicked her expressions, mirrored her emotions, and that was nothing new either. The girl in the mirror was an old and dear companion—who'd suddenly turned malicious. Like a cruel, teasing sister, she wouldn't stop copying, even for a second. She squinted, widened her eyes in dismay, frowned sternly, went blank with awe. Will you stop?—*Will you stop?*

This behavior, of course, didn't go unremarked. "Okay, Lin? It's you. It's no one else. Your life has changed; you haven't."

Linda made a "pistol," shot herself in the head. She looked at her reflection the way Derrick looked at his wife when she was silly. She saw Linda, doing impressions of her husband. Her reflection wasn't at fault; it did whatever she wanted it to. It just wouldn't stop being Linda.

"Um . . ."

Linda looked at her mother, in reflection.

"Unless you're developing some autistic self-fascination, you should . . . you know, stop looking in the mirror."

Linda turned quickly, like the mirror was her private world.

Shelley was quite calm. Having a wild ditz of a daughter was hardly anything new. "What's wrong?"

Linda was solemn, searching for unlikely words. "Is it possible that I . . . just pee'ed into a diaper."

"Well . . . if you have a diaper on and you just pee'ed, it's almost certain.—it's like that time when you were sixteen."

"I'm supposed to understand."

"You should."

"I'm trying."

"That hot night at the drive-in. You and your friends at some devilish movie. It might even have been *Footloose*. You thought you were all the cat's meow, with your mattress and reading pillows on the bed of Sue Baker's pickup. You had a *grand mal*, then two more at home. Too much trouble changing you." Shelley added, irrelevantly: "The doctor thought it was caffeine, that time. Your friend Heidi said you drank most of a two-liter Mountain Dew." Shelley touched a tear from the corner of her eye. Those happy, innocent days.

Linda said, "Who diapered me. The doctor, here. A man."

Shelley said, "Your mom," blasé. A legitimate fear was unfounded; it was all in the family, all right.

Linda calmly blinked. It was normal that she stand and guard the bathroom door, My privacy, it's mine. It was normal that the day outside had mood, of tragic beauty. It was normal that Life held a stream of fear and she was moved by it, now this way, now that. She explained, "I need to go in here. Into the bathroom, and take this diaper off." Tense and upset, she softly, needlessly elaborated: "I'm twenty-nine, you know, I don't think women normally . . . whatever." She gestured her hands: Sorry, I'm eccentric, don't mind me. "It's wet. I want to take it off."

Shelley said, "No. You absolutely may not."

Linda was amazed, that her mother would joke. Then realized, *She only cares about me. Derrick was only her son-in-law.*

Linda went into the bathroom and turned on the light. The fluorescent buzz was so abrupt and its light so harsh, she almost shrieked. She realized, with horror, she'd do that—shriek, if she was scared.

She took the door, to close it. Shelley, sitting, watched her closely, unassuming; a daughter's business was her mother's, too.

Linda managed a smile. When she let her mouth go, the smile went with it. She closed the door.

The bathroom had no mirror—she gasped, inane relief. She looked down at herself, parting her black curls like a veil, so she could see. Her hair felt a little greasy. *I mentioned, Tuesday night, I hadn't showered. So I haven't washed my hair since Monday morning. But I was in a rush to go pick up those seeds I ordered from Jane's Herbs, so I might have skipped shampoo—which means I haven't washed my hair since Sunday. But can I recall which soap I used? Of course not. Regardless of the fact that I've an incomprehensible pharmacopoeia of soaps and I wouldn't know one from another.*

She realized what she was doing: thinking of proofs to convince Shelley. But they'd only work if Shelley believed her.

Linda looked down, saw some pretty blue satin-and-lace over two unimpressive mounds of flesh. Her skin had a warm, sweet-buttery smell. *Because I tasted the vinaigrette salad, that night—I stay garlic for days. Now, why the hell am I still wearing my* camisole? *Aren't there hospital regulations, or whatever? What, is it like human services—someone was just plain lazy?* Then she thought, it might have been a male nurse who didn't strip her. She didn't try to guess his motives. Men leaving her alone felt nice. Tender, righteous. A-okay.

The bathroom was a tiny, yellow closet. It was loud. No, that was her. Breathing deeply in her fear. Again, she held her shoulders, this time knowing why she did. *Frightened, I want to be held. I'm so scared God Mommy no I want Daddy I'm so scared.*

She looked at herself again. She saw her arms and breasts. She didn't see anything under her breasts.

They were in the way.

Duh?

She held herself in, bent slightly to see. No, wait . . . weak with fear, she slipped out of her camisole. She looked and gasped, anxiety/frustration *Oh for heaven's sake the damn* diaper. She picked at the adhesive strips, gave up and pulled the whole thing down. Stepped out. *Okay. Now let me see what—*

She lost her balance, squeaked sharply as she slapped her hands on the tile wall, caught herself from falling.

She hugged the wall, her hair completely in her face. Breathed deeply, trying to calm herself. Shelley was right there, on the other side of the door. "Linda, what on earth?"

Linda said, "I'm fine."

"What are you doing in there?"

"Shell . . . Mother, think for a moment, what you're asking me. I'm in a bathroom. All right?"

There was silence on the other side of the door, which Linda guessed was due to shock. That frightened her. Shelley was a

60

friend; who else did she have? Outside this hospital room, the world was full of strangers. "Mom, I'm *sorry!*" No answer. Linda softly whined, miserable with fear. She went and sat on the toilet. There, now she could see . . .

Tummy, thighs, knees. She extended her foot: it had toes, oh no. She wiggled them—hello down there. They wiggled back: hello. Belly-button, mat of adult hair between her legs. Her body so familiar, okay as an old shoe.

All of which was so wrong she did not know what to do.

She stood, felt lost and waiting, like the yellow bathroom was a gas chamber. *Did I do something I need to flush?*—she turned, her hand to her cheek. Oh. No, that wasn't what she was nervous about.

There was a soft rap at the door. Her feet actually left the floor; she clasped her hands to her bosom. Yelped "*Oh*myGod!" then frowned, confused—fear was a passion, all right.

A long, reproachful silence, then: "Linda?"

Frantic, she said, "*I'm okay!*"

"You sound frantic."

"Shell—no—Mommy! I'm okay!"

A pause and then, "You really need to yell?"

Linda stared at the door. *Why not? You said I could scream and cry.* Yet some plaintive note in her mother's voice burst floodgates of regret. Linda realized, all at once, the preciousness of being cared for. Wringing her hands, she said, "It's not just what you told me. Derrick's gone: not that. Something else is wrong with me."

Linda sniffled, rubbed her nose. Close to tears, she checked her palm for snot. Once she'd been a kid and now, she felt like one again. Shelley gently said, "I'd like you to come out of there," as if this bathroom stand-off was the problem, not a husband's death.

Linda opened the door, though only a little. Shelley, right there, asked, "What? This 'other thing,' what are you talking about?" There was a deep, soft intimacy, already in place. Mother and daughter were playmates of old—dramas of indecision staged in bathroom and boudoir.

Linda hid behind the door. Brows arched tragically, wanting to weep, she started to answer her mother's question but lost her nerve. "I'm . . ."

"You're . . . ?"

" . . . afraid to come out." Shelley sighed. They both looked at her naked hip and Lin, embarrassed, gently shut the door.

She put her camisole back on. Picked up the diaper—heavy, its white cotton yellow-stained and smelling of ammonia—and put it in the plastic bucket, with its thoughtful *Biohazard* sticker. She opened the door—again, just a little. Shelley stood waiting, patient as Lily Marlene under the lamp-post. Linda said, "What

61

I'm wearing . . ."

Shelley's piquant smirk, Oh well. "We'll get the nurse . . ."

"Mom, no."

"—we will *get the nurse,* and I'll ask for a smock. Now come sit. You were awful fresh, by the way. When I knocked."

Linda came out. Tall, willowy and dark, she felt wild/Amazonian before her mother. The parent-child relation seemed outgrown and never real. But of course, she'd been adopted. Maybe that could happen again—maybe Shelley could take complete control, explain all things and make her sane again. That would be great—if it could happen really quick. If it could happen, like, instantaneously. Shelley seemed assured that their rapport was quite in place—motioned at the bed, Now you sit here. Mother sat herself, instant-cozy in her chair. Pretty and unreadable, like Linda wasn't there and Shelley posed instead for TV viewers, far away. Outside the room, a tired, irate woman asked someone if 208's catheter bag was checked.—Not discolored; all right, good. Shelley blew a wisp of hair, baby-blonde, from near her eye. "Your move, kid."

Linda was puzzled. She'd woken to a metaphysical nightmare, hosted by Shelley. Who now told Linda the ball was in her court. Saying it was *her move,* like this terrible charade was a game of Parchesi. Linda said, "I don't understand. What it could be. 'My move'—I can't imagine."

If waiving her turn was unsporting somehow, Shelley showed no disappointment. She was light and sweet as vanilla ice milk, rouged lips for a cherry. "Darling, I meant it's your life. Oh, look—a box of Kleenex. On the nightstand, do you see?" Linda shook her head; she saw the Kleenex but not the point. Shelley explained, "You're pre-weepy." Linda took a Kleenex in a cloud of abstract wonder; she'd never been pre-weepy nor known anyone who had. Shelley watched, then shook her head—found her daughter's dabbing insufficient. Sent her back to the bathroom to wash her face. "Just soap."

Linda, standing lost in ozone, copied back, "Just soap."

Shelley said, "No makeup. They washed your face, I guess."

Linda forced a smile, brief. She went and washed her face, came back. There followed a long, tense, dreamy/unreal interlude. Shelley, watching closely, found weakness and need and fault. Was Linda still cold? Well, she *looked* cold. "Hon, cross your legs or something; anyone can come in. You can even use that blanket like an afghan for your lap. All right, don't."—a conflict developed and settled before Linda knew what it was about. So. Where did they begin?—well, all right; Shelley spoke with tender precision, closed-caption for the realization-impaired: Linda had *lost her husband.*

Linda felt the truth was obvious. "Derrick's gone? That's it?"

Shelley, put on the spot, rolled schoolgirl eyes at the ceiling. Well, that was . . . probably *enough*, didn't Linda think so too? What else would Shelley assume—that Linda had been having an affair, and this was all about life insurance? Linda calmly stared, like Shelley invented a game so complex she added new rules as she went along. Shelley wouldn't acknowledge the real problem. Instead, she would insist that a lot of other weird, little things were the matter. "Shelley—"

"*Shh.*"

Shh'ed and de-Shelleyed, Lin lowered her voice. "Mother, listen: I need to tell you something. I'm scared that you'll get mad."

Shelley gazed, her brown eyes gold—a gentle Persian cat who saw a sparrow. Delighted and mystified, mouthed the words silent: *scared that I'll get* . . .

"Lin, you've lost your husband. 'I'll get mad.' Lin, how? Let me see. Give me your best shot."

Linda couldn't speak. Her voice came out in disjointed titters, like Shelley Duvall in *The Shining.*

"Dear, I'm sorry. I didn't quite—"

" . . . that I'm not your daughter, or . . . ?"

They sat in the weak white light through the blinds. They looked at each other.

An ambulance wailed past, down on Laurel Street below; turned onto the Commons, and was gone.

"Lin . . . okay: I'll tell your favorite story. The fact that I didn't bear and birth you myself is irrelevant. I nursed you, Linda. A woman doesn't do that with a stranger's child, only with her own." Linda blinked, sedated by a puzzle: though not an expert on child-care, this didn't sound factually true. "When you opened your eyes and saw Mommy, that was me. When you toddled and spoke, you called 'Mommy'—me. I was the only one there."

"Mom, that's—" Linda spaced. What was it? Beautiful? True? Completely beside the point?

"Lin, you know you're being antagonistic—am I right? Here I am, to help and support and to drown you in love. Now, you've just made a rather vicious statement. You've said you're not my daughter. Which denies me as your mother. Linda, why was this said?"

"Shelley, I'm not Linda."

Shelley said, "Oh," slightly disappointed, like she'd glanced at the script and yes, of course, a line from a B-grade thriller came next.

"I'm Derrick. Shelley, I'm Derrick."

Shelley then remarked, "Okay . . . well, that's supposed to shock me. Linda drops her bombshell—end of chapter, turn the page."

Linda widened her eyes, not at mortal woman but at the unseen abyss—if her problem could just be dismissed like that, the fall down the rabbit hole was very, very far.

Shelley looked away. Hand to her forehead—dear, she was faint. "God, that gave me a chill. Hearing that, I just—" She shivered. "*Oh.* Don't know why, it just tingled my spine."

Linda reached out, alarmed. "Shelley—"

"Don't. Just . . . *ugh*, that chilled me so."

Linda picked up a corner of the nylon blanket. "Do you want . . . ?"—since Shelley was chilled.

Shelley softly snorted, humoring the absurd: no, she didn't need the hospital blanket for anything, thanks.

Linda was now terrified. She saw herself clearly: a frightened black-haired girl, sitting on a bed. And she saw, in a moment, all the world outside this room. A world of men. Men and machines. Trucks, jack-hammers, conveyor belts. Board meetings, facts and figures; cold, hard stats on cold, hard cash. A world she couldn't cope with. She was scared enough of her mom.

But then Shelley sighed. Her eyes flashed wet, her heart was broken. "Okay, so what does this mean—you're going to take up auto mechanics? Oh hon, what?—you've got a special friend? Another girl?"

Linda looked alert and stern—lost in anxious thoughts. "I don't know who I am right now. I don't think that I . . . like girls; no."

Shelley thought this over. "Well, then at least there's not an actual other person, compounding this dilemma. Oh, and if there ever was, you could forget about Thanksgiving and Christmas."

"I . . . don't like Thanksgiving either."

Shelley took interest. "*Linda* doesn't like Thanksgiving. I thought you said you were Derrick."

"I am. But I've become Linda." Shelley tilted her head, dreamy with wonder. "Mom, it's really simple. It's as simple as it sounds."

Shelley had her knees up on her seat. She nibbled the nail of her pinky, as her daughter often did. This was going to take a while.

She patiently said, "All right . . . something's been dissolved. Your marriage and so, in effect, your life. Leaving just a void. Your husband's personality still dominates you, so in effect you—"

Linda, patient too, explained. "No, not abstract; it's real. I mean the simple words I say, I'm not who I appear to be. I'm—" Her mother felt her forehead for fever. Linda touched her mother's hand, No take this away. Shelley held her daughter's fingers, No I'll touch; I'm in control. "No, listen, *please*: becoming someone else, it doesn't happen, but it did and you become that *whole person*, thinking and feeling just the way she

64

does but you *know*, you're . . ."

Shelley was merely fascinated, like her daughter's story was the synopsis of a morbid drama on TV. "How did it *happen*?"

"I honestly don't know. Something in the wine, we saw too deep into each other. She went into the light, I said, 'I'll never let you go.' It was her, she had the power, and her fear and weakness made her—"

Shelley dropped Linda's hand—All right then, you're fine.

"Well, that . . . must really suck! I mean, men—I guess; I assume; I suppose—would hate nothing worse than having to be women, so you must feel just miserable!"

"I see that you're skeptical, or—?"

"No, dear. 'Skeptical' involves a basis of non-assumption and I positively think it's the weirdest, stupidest thing you've ever told me." Blonde shrug, twitch of soft shoulder: so much for semantics.

Linda slowly said, "You . . . think this is a game I'm playing. Child's game. Let's make believe." And saying this, her heart became a stone. She hadn't made a point; she'd written her own epitaph.

Shelley said, "Well granted, you're grown up. But let's admit, I'm older." A truth not always plain—shag 'do, designer jeans and health-club bod, she could pass for thirty-five but for the sweet-old-lady shimmer in her eyes. Some magic of her alpine-Nordic genes. "And at my age, you find the years pass swiftly. It seems only yesterday you were seeing 'auras' on everyone. Being told by the doctor that you had them yourself was inadequate—they had to appear over everyone else. You talked to plants and they answered back."

"I'm Linda. Linda is a ditz."

"Um . . . the way we put it is, you've always tended to behave somewhat younger than you actually are." Linda was stunned. It was a wonderfully subtle turn of a phrase—could describe nearly anyone. Czarevna Anastasia. A girl with breasts who didn't like boys, and still wanted Barbie for Christmas. "So far as pretending to be someone else . . . well, there are plenty of people to choose from your own gender. Mary Baker Eddy reincarnate, perhaps."

Linda spoke with feeling—not as one who asserts a fact but rather, desperately avoids one. "I never said that."

"You implied it. You were seventeen, I think."

Linda gazed sadly at the floor.

"You were just becoming a woman. You hardly ate, you seldom slept; you lived on herb tea, burned candles in your room. You always wore black. Black leotards and skirts. And your gold cross necklace. Lin, that necklace—that was you. Linda, daughter of God. Reading the Bible, on your own. You felt you were near to discovering the truth. We had many long

65

talks. Because you were veering towards Christian Science. Had that icky friend from the health food store . . . Holly-Someone. She never flossed." Shelley's gaze was fond and dim; in the tragic present, connecting with the past.

Linda said, "*My life is so over.*"

"Ah, yes; we used to hear that, on the average, twice a month. Before it was 'so totally adolescent'; it's been a few years."

"But now it's *literally true.*"

"It always was."

"It hurts so much."

"It always did."

Outside the door, muted voices: . . . *hear them talking in there, so you can probably hold off on that another minute.*

. . . *can live with that call, doc; not like I don't have twenty million other things I'm trying to accomplish.*

. . . *so we can safely assume she's not, like, puking blood or—*

Stifled laughs, then loudly: . . . *why you even in this line of work, you gon be illin' even badder than the patients!*

Linda looked alertly at the door. Shelley held her daughter's hand, touched a curl back from her cheek, assurance so familiar that the words weren't even said: *The doctors and nurses won't hurt you, they're nice.*

"Mom, these things you're describing—I should remember them, right? I should be like, 'God, how was I ever so immature?' Instead, I don't know if I did them or not. Why is this true, do you think?"

"Dear, I'm awful with riddles. Why don't you just tell me."

"I can't remember things because I—"

Linda's fear wasn't like Derrick's. She never lost a battle with it. Because it was bigger than her, she never tried to fight it. "—have amnesia."

Shelley blinked and looked away, rather like a bored cat. Linda closed her eyes. Yes, of course. There was already a long history of exotic ploys and manipulations. Feigned illnesses, invented traumas. Moody internal exiles: the founder of Christian Science, reborn, and going to school in Pittsfield. And lastly a talent for blithe denial—if she honestly couldn't remember it, it truly hadn't happened. *Lin, when you were fourteen, did you have pet rocks? Not bought at Merrill's little psychedelic boutique but just rocks you found outside which you spontaneously empathized with? Which you arranged just so on your windowsill, so they'd harmonize vibrations?*

(A delighted gasp, then fond amazement): *Der, but that's so dim. Who have you been talking to—my mother?*

"Mother, listen. Please. When I was young, okay?—or maybe

66

in adolescence: did I ever have issues with my gender. Saying I wished I was a boy, or I wished I wasn't a girl? Is this what you think I'm doing now—is this why you won't believe me?"

Shelley said, "Oh!—you know, there used to be a standardized test? Given to psychiatric patients. All these true-or-false questions. One had two parts: 'A' to be answered if you were a man and 'B' if you were a woman. 'A' was: *I often wish I was female*. 'B' was: *I never wish I was male*. They counted as one question, since you only answered one. The answer *True* was pathological." Shelley winked. "If they ever give you the test, now you can cheat."

Linda gazed, alight with dawning panic. She barely found her voice. "Why would they give me the test."

"I said *if*. Dear, that was a joke. Anyway, you say you have amnesia. Honestly, I doubt it. You've had it so often, I'm sure you're immune. But luckily, this time we're in a hospital."

"But I don't want that."

Shelley said, "I . . . missed what was offered."

"To be com- . . ."

"-missioned. Compelled. Commiserated with. Lin, what?"

"Psychiatric hospital. Fine. Don't need it. Me."

Shelley gaped like she'd sat on a tack. She was one of those women who like that expression, because it likes them back—she was lovely as a girl. "Linda *Bloom*." If malice was denied, Linda was quick to agree—she touched her head and gestured, Where's my brain. "All I said was, we're already in a hospital. Where symptoms are checked out. I mean, amnesia's not healthy."

"Um . . . no. I mean, Mother, yes: you're right. Though you still haven't denied that it could happen. That a doctor could say, or—"

"Take your hand away from your eyes, please."

"-I'd be talked into signing something, then, you know . . ."

"Stop. You're imagining all sorts of terrible designs on you. Lin, there's no conspiracy. Okay?" But neither was there any unqualified assurance. Just these open-ended clauses, these sinister ambiguities. Then Shelley bluntly demanded, "Lin, what *happened*?"

Linda edged away. "Mom, you're scaring me."

"I hope so. Since I was scared shitless when I found you."

"You?"

"Uh-huh. I was downtown revising Conference memos. We'd planned to do Filene's, as we discussed on Monday over the phone. Lin, what are you trying to do to me? The Amnesia Game stinks. I quit."

Linda stared in fear, a silent-movie actress. Her voice went high, like Shelley was a villain. "*How on earth did you get in?*"

"Apartment keys work great for that. Even the one you gave me the week you moved in. Hello?"

Linda blanked. She wonderingly murmured, "That little bitch."

The two women looked at each other. Linda's hand drifted to her mouth.

"Lin, what are you feeling? Right now, at this moment."

The question didn't mean *Let's connect.* It meant *Let's start all over, on my terms.* The classic blonde in basic black, trimly curvaceous in Jordache Ladies' Fit. Master's in Pastoral Counseling from Harvard Divinity, '65; her question, softly dispassionate. Linda looked around the room. The nightstand, metal frame with faux-wood panels; a tray underneath, with a box of disposable latex gloves. A sympathy card from God-knows-who; winter sunrise, Yes there's hope. White carnations in a clear glass vase. *The same ones I bought at the florists, before—?!* —no, that was impossible. They couldn't have lived through that. No hope for carnations. A unit on a cord, for adjusting the bed, which someone had hung over the curtain rod, out of reach.

"The answer, Lin, is nowhere in this room. It is in your heart."

"If you're really interested in the truth, then: I feel like a man who is trapped in his wife's body."

Linda shrugged, the expression of her eyes rather poignant; it really wasn't any fun.

Shelley was sedate. After giving it due thought, she parted her lips to speak. There was much, very much, to be said in response to this outrageous statement. "Lin: okay. First of all, I—"

The door opened. The nurse came in. A large, black woman, about Linda's age; she eyed her patient dismally. She had, as she'd earlier declared, twenty million other things she was trying to accomplish. Life outside this room hadn't screeched to a halt. It hadn't even tapped its brakes.

Linda was simply blank. The thought hadn't really crossed her mind, that other people might come into this room and she'd be Linda, not Derrick. She didn't know how to talk to another young, black woman; she didn't know how to feel or behave. She didn't know who she was supposed to be. She simply hadn't a clue.

The nurse, bored and weary, said, "How we all doin'?"

Linda felt little and wimpy and dumb; she stared at the nurse like a sullen, suspicious child. She recalled reading somewhere that women don't like each other. She remembered to answer the question. "Sleepy. I feel somewhat tense." *I sound like a white girl. I sound like a white* girl.

The nurse said, "Mm-*hm*," which seemed the most perfectly neutral sound she could emit.

Linda sat, passive, while her BP was taken, her heart-rate

checked. Shelley stared haplessly into space, like her daughter wasn't worth all this trouble. "Open, hon."—a thermometer.

Shelley said, "Don't bite it."

Afraid of the nurse, Linda made an irate sound to show she wasn't pushed around by her mom. She couldn't say *I'm not biting it* without doing so. Shelley told the nurse, "She's just lost her husband."

The nurse intoned, "Oh my," like she wasn't about to jump into the middle of this.

After a minute, the thermometer beeped. The nurse took it from Linda's mouth, noted its reading without expression. Shelley said, "She has a fever."

"Mm . . . I read 98.4, to be real frank with you."

"She's very upset. Perhaps a sedative might . . . ?"

"That's the doctor's call, ma'am. Though with atropine toxicity, I doubt he'll order any kind of sedative.

"You feelin' upset?

"I said: Girl, you feel upset? Hon, you mad? You feelin' scared?"

Linda couldn't avoid the woman's question. She couldn't ignore the woman herself, who stood directly in front of her, while she sat—larger than herself, in authority and control, which made Linda feel even smaller. She looked up, into the nurse's eyes; the woman was not unkind, but fundamentally unconcerned. "Why? Wouldn't you be?"

"This ain't about me, hon. You say you're upset, you attempt to be still; your doctor will be in directly."

Linda asked, "Is he a man?"

Shelley had been sitting off to the side, passively attentive like a pretty young girl—the way she was with everyone on earth except her daughter. Now she didn't quite approve of Linda's question; she was passively attentive to the window.

The nurse said, "He a man indeed; I don't advise you worry. Ain't like you're gettin' a pelvic exam. You have a *systemic illness*. You ate the *funny flower*, okay?—what's causin' you these problems."

"I just asked if he was a man. Because I don't think I'm comfortable with . . . ?" *I thought women understood*—? "Can't I ask for a female doctor?"

"Girl, you're free to ask for the moon. Meanwhile, the man went to school and he knows how to practice medicine." The nurse glanced disdainfully at Linda's thighs. "Best get a smock on you, Ms. Bloom."

Linda said, "A smock?"

The nurse strolled from the room and shut the door.

Linda turned to her mother. "She said I was ugly and fat. She said, 'Ms. Bloom' like that was a joke, like Ms. Bloom is a lady and I'm not. But Ms. Bloom is my mother."

Shelley said, "Oh, stop."

The nurse came right back in with a smock. She sighed like she wanted Linda to know, this prompt service was less policy than luck. "Here now, this *should* fit." The nurse was very statuesque, quite black. Hair braided, tied at the back, framing an oval face. Lips full, sensual; almond eyes, complacently assertive. Linda saw that she was beautiful, even as she knew that *beautiful woman* had lost a world of meaning. It meant someone better than Linda; she couldn't remember what else.

The nurse began cleaning up the area, excusing herself with a muttered disparagement of the orderlies. Shelley said, "I'm sure they're awfully busy"; the nurse, a bona fide busy person, said they were busy in the store room, smoking dope. Linda went into the bathroom to change. She heard her mother say, "She's very shy."

The nurse said, "Well, to each her own way." Linda felt relieved that the nurse saw it too: Shelley's comments were absurd. Then it sounded like the nurse was gone.

Linda came out in her white smock, just as the doctor came in. She recoiled with a frightened squeak, then looked at him sternly. She'd never been a woman meeting a man, before.

The doctor regarded her blandly. He was slight of build and remarkably young; but for the trench-hardened look of his eyes, he appeared a bearded boy. He bothered with no greeting; just glanced at the bed, to suggest that Linda would be easier to examine if she stopped flying around the room, and sat.

She'd only been a woman twenty minutes. It seemed too personal an experience to share with Some Impatient Kid, MD. It felt like her only freedom was to squeak, then stare, then refuse to sit. So far, that was the plan.

She was startled again by Shelley—she sort of crept up from the side, took her daughter's hand like some chic freak in an alternative dance club. "Please excuse us." Linda was led into the bathroom. This felt so much better, just now—alone with the only person she could trust, in this humming yellow box which smelled of pine-scented Lysol. Shelley wasn't mad. She seemed a little manic but happy. "I came prepared for anything. For you to cry and go wild. I came prepared for *you* to do these things, okay? Don't tell the doctor you're Derrick. Oh, I really hope you don't!" *Saying she was Derrick* had been fully processed—filed under *Q* as a harmless but embarrassing *quirk*. "Lin, I'm happy." Shelley smiled, showed how much: *Curl-my-toes-and-shiver nice.* " 'Cause Lin, I didn't *know*. All the hours you lay, asleep—whether we'd ever talk with one another, face to face, again. To see you, not just rise like a phoenix, but take off like a bakuku bird, all dizzy into the stratosphere . . . I think you're just too cute." She held her daughter's head, planted a long, hard kiss. Staring wide-eyed at the tile floor, Linda knew for good or ill, *She really does love me, then.* Shelley held her daughter's shoulders, glanced stressed-but-ever-faithful at the door: daughter secured, now the world to contend with. They went back out and sat, together on the bed. The doctor hadn't moved, as though he'd been on *Pause.* Now he pulled up a chair.

Shelley sat close, her arm on Linda's back. She played with Linda's hair, held her cheek-to-cheek. Look at us, we love each other. Perhaps it was to soothe and still her timid girl. Also to let the doctor know, This is someone you have to be nice to.

The doctor asked how Linda felt, of course. Asked if she was having auras. She studied him, thoughtful. Aware of her silence, he looked up from his chart. He wanted her answer some time today. She said, "I have epilepsy. You're asking if I'm having auras now."

No time to repeat himself—skip, next question. She hadn't wanted this interview, so now it would be short.

There was none of the helplessness she'd felt with the nurse. There was something over-powerful, instead. Men were too awesome. She'd never seen anything like him; she didn't know what he was. An angel turned into a wolf. Light in his eyes like fire from the grave—she knew it was all about her. She wondered what he knew about her that she, herself, did not. She was only a bare-breasted maiden of Paradise, meeting an armored Spaniard on the beach. And of course she knew *exactly* what he was. He was God but in specific form: a man. *My whole body wants to kiss him*—she felt beautiful and proud. He was made to love and care for her—that was, like, his job. It meant she could finally lash back, show heaven how wounded she was. Act like it was all his fault; he'd failed to keep her happy. Except he was a spoilsport—he didn't like her either. He was no great lover of humanity, or something. He was even immune to a lost and lovely girl—his version of her statement, Where were you when I needed you. Shelley finally cut in. "What's her diagnosis?"

He was pleased to talk to Shelley; his manner shifted gears. Here was someone he could trust and respect—someone who understood adult speech. He spoke of Linda's bloodwork showing a "decrease to therapeutic levels" of atropine, like what Linda had experienced wasn't bad, in moderation. He added, "I wouldn't let her drive or operate heavy machinery for the next couple days."

"Doctor?"

He looked at her, blankly attentive. She stared grimly, while her mother's finger played with one of her curls. A spoiled French princess. He wasn't impressed. "You're not a veterinarian, or . . .?"

That rated no response; he awaited her complaint.

She explained, "I'm not a pet. I understand speech."

"That's wonderful, Mrs. Bloom. Uh . . . the levels I'm

describing don't normally impair receptive language skills. Or enhance them, if you mean this is something new . . . I don't understand."

"Why would I be operating heavy machinery? Like a bulldozer? Is that what you meant? Like, obviously I could never, so it's funny? Or PC, just over-inclusive?—I'm sort of confused."

"Not to the degree that would affect your driving, though. I just lost an elderly patient to cardiac arrest. I was making a joke."

"And it killed him?"

An obligatory smile. It reminded her, briefly, of Tony Biondo's great white grin. "I was joking with *you*."

Linda smiled back. She found she had an enchanting smile—it felt the way it had always looked. Her beauty somehow came from him—when he left, he'd take her coach-and-six. She'd show him how upset she was, before she turned back into a mousey pumpkin. "No, you were joking *about* me. I guess that's the epitome of med school humor: a line from a cold pill's caution label."

"You've chanced upon my actual meaning."—he was tired of this.

Shelley offered him a faint, alluring smile. *Play with me, I'm nicer.* She mouthed the words *She's traumatized.* The doctor chose to regard the wall. Maybe Shelley touched on something deep. He carved up human muscle like London broil, picked at viscera like a vulture, said *Trust me with your final breath* and later felt it on his face. Traumatized schmaumatized.—something like that. Shelley asked, "What about her eyes? Why is she so . . . oh."

He finished for her: "Beautiful." Not above mere mortal discernment; he even vouchsafed Lin a cordial nod. *You're beautiful. I still don't like you*—such exciting arrogance. Linda batted her lashes, to show she was impressed. "It's a classic symptom of the drug. That's why it was used by the ladies of Renaissance Italy." He spoke to Shelley; Linda probably thought *Renaissance Italy* was a salon, somewhere. "The master painters gave it to their subjects—hence, *belladonna*."

Linda found this conversation neat; she wanted to join it. "Before, I was one of Titian's angels."

"You've had an intriguing psychotropic voyage. I'm sure Carlos Castenada would be green."

Linda asked, "What else is wrong with me?"—she couldn't help but wonder. Her body felt the same as when Derrick held it in his arms; she couldn't understand how she'd become a dog with fleas.

He said, "You're going to be purging." She felt briefly startled—thought he meant her eating habits. "Your kidneys will be on overdrive."

"You mean I'll be . . ." Her sense of shame surprised her. " . . . running to the little girls' room a lot." *I think I would have blushed.*

"We prefer the term 'frequent urination'. Your BP's still elevated, you'll want to avoid salt. Whatever you do, don't take antihistamines." He arched his brows: May I go?

Linda asked, "How long? Until this is" *over. But I can't ask him that—he doesn't know what this is.* "out of me. Til I'm better."

He shrugged. "You know how you feel."

Linda completely spaced. She remembered being Derrick. His wife's cool hip and her warm whispers, in the dark. As Shelley rubbed her back her eyes were vacant, pools of sorrow. "*'Feels so good' . . .*"

"Mm-hm. But he means *inside* you, dear. Tell him how you feel."

"Okay . . ."

The doctor would accept that, no more questions asked. "Then your life is one sweet carousel. The police are on their way." He left and Linda, just a girl, put hands to her mouth in fear.

"Mom, I have to get out of here. I can't deal with men or police." She was squeaky-voiced with panic: "*They need someone to charge so they'll take me to jail oh Mommy help me* please . . .

"Lin, where did this *attitude* come from? Your husband's job, perhaps? All the rage to talk like some delinquent boy—not knowing *def* from Devo?" Some benign symbiosis was assumed. All men in blue were friends to all upper-class white (or adopted) females, who gratefully bestowed their total trust. "Lin, what are you—?"

"*Going to cry.*" She did.

Shelley held her daughter, kissed her hair. Whispered her syllables, sounds that meant love. Linda needed prompts to vocalize, make womanly sounds of loss. *Let me hear it, not that loud* and lastly, sure, *there, there.* Linda didn't realize, then, she was being taught to cry like a woman. Shelley didn't either; she'd been doing it all Linda's life.

Linda cried, she sobbed; it didn't matter. Girls were allowed, they had nothing to lose. Tears brought no release but only emptiness, instead. No matter what she thought or said, she was just a little girl—men would decide her fate, and she had to sit with her mother. Linda's sobs went high, a girl-child's wail, *I'm lost and unable, come find me.*

6

Shelley and Linda sat together on the bed. Linda was calm, red-eyed, all sniffles. Shelley still rubbed her daughter's back. *So warm and dark. So soft. My only daughter.* They sat surrounded by little clumps of used Kleenex. Linda recognized them—she'd seen plenty of them before, she'd just never made them herself. They were Linda-clumps, different from those made by other women: not mascara-smudged, and more abundant.

Shelley asked what she was feeling. Linda, miserable, whined something about her nose; Shelley *shh*'ed her. "Feelings, dear. Your heart."

"I really don't like myself." *Anymore.* "I feel little and messy and weak, like water. Like all I'm good for is peeing and crying."

"Nothing else?"

"Making used Kleenex."

"Dear, what about Derrick?—please don't sniffle into the back of your hand, that's utterly gross. Here." Yet another Kleenex. Linda, contemplative, blew her nose. She understood what was actually "gross": saying she was Derrick. "Linda, you're feeling a torment, a loss, unique to women. Your husband was Christ to you, Linda. He was God's imminence in your life. Your very own; personal to you."

"Somewhat feudal. Thanks for making me so liberal."

Shelley *pif*fed. "Oh, 'liberal' my foot. 'Liberal', to you, means skipping deodorant and being on Vienna time."—fifteen minutes late. "Lin, you grew up in the Church. We *know* a woman's shell is clay; you were she declaring that her soul within is fire. That you lived for your husband—his handmaid, his vessal. *He* was important, not you."

"But Derrick said it was me. He said he lived for me."

"But of course. For a husband to adore his wife, honor her above himself—that's the man's role. We're talking about you."

"I thought it was all about him."

"Lin, why don't I go? You can play *Alice In Wonderland* all by yourself."

She touched her mother's hand. "Please don't. I'll be good. I'll say things that you like."

Shelley looked at the divider, murmured, "Yeah, do that," as men walked through the door.

They were two Salem cops—an older white sergeant and a young Hispanic, probably a rookie. They looked ponderous and martial, with their boots and belts and accouterments. They seemed cold, like they came off the streets; hard, like they were going back out. The sergeant answered an electric voice from his belt: *On stand-by for that, willco*; switched it off, benignly viewed this room. A warm, soft, disturbing break from the action outside.

Linda sensed the tableau she and Shelley made. A classy-looking older blonde, perched up in her chair like some casual college chick. Can of Diet Pepsi on the floor beside her purse. Linda in her smock, red-eyed in baptismal romper, Venus of Detox on the half-shell bed, unmade. Mom and daughter down to the mats; they'd made this little alcove Fortress Bauer. Now it sweetly reeked of women and their nebulous concerns.

The cops asked Linda if she worked in a group home. Testing to see if she'd say, No—she was really her husband, and she worked in DYS. Of course, they only asked because they were familiar with the group home. Had responded to crank complaints from neighbors, things like that. They knew Derrick Bloom worked at lockup in Lynn, with which they were all-*too*-familiar. They hadn't come to bust a brother lawman's widow. When Linda offered to explain, they didn't need to hear it—sometimes things just happened, and no one was to blame. A real bad bottle of home-made wine—pretty much the story's end.

The younger cop spoke to her in Spanish.

Linda felt wonderfully odd—knowing exactly how her expressions looked, from living with herself five years. Head lowered, eyes serious under her bangs, like a proud, submissive daughter from a strict Spanish family. Which could only have been some mystifying coincidence, since she talked like any WASP cupcake. Since she understood no Spanish at all, just whitebread English and her mother's cradle-talk. She said, "That's Spanish, right? I don't speak it." She blinked. "I look Latina? Well, I'm . . . very assimilated. I went to private school." She turned to her mother. "Mom, didn't I *flunk* Spanish, once? I needed a tutor, or . . . ?"

Shelley, from the sidelines, remarked, "They're here about Derrick."

The rookie repeated his question in English. "Have you ever used illegal drugs."

Linda blinked again, confused. "Why'd you ask in Spanish?"

"Didn't want to embarrass you in front of my partner." He added with a chortle, "It's like being born on the bus—you don't want it on your tee shirt, nothin' like that." His tinted shades made him look like a sardonic clown. Linda studied eyes she couldn't see. She thought: *Asshole.* "You can incriminate yourself in Spanish too—watch out."

She said, "Oh. Well, until an hour ago, I was my husband. Is that incriminating?"

He answered her at length. He was animated, slightly and elaborately miming what he said. His voice was a clever, soft patter, like he came from Chelsea and would sell the Charlestown Bridge. "Hell no. We just tagged a guy engaging-in-pursuit down Route 1, Everett. Kept sailin' like the Eveready Rat. Like that won't put us 'hot' to cross town line. Chump ducked into a strip-joint like cops won't follow you into a pretty-bar.—Note that substitution, Nolan? Slick?—They checked ID, we checked his IQ. Doll up on the stage, to die for—more woman than human. Til homey hipified me, 'She's a boy'. Plastic surgery now, it's sick. Fact: fifty percent of the girls in the Zone. This guy"—the sergeant, unhappy with this—"knows the total score. Runnin' down Canal Street, knocked on every door. Said 'She had a baby, that's an XX-chromosome exclusive,' I said Dig. One-slice toaster installation is the fact behind the scar. Nah, you for real, *muchacha*—you *no hable Christanöl* like I drop dimes. When Science makes 'em sweet as you, we'll have an ATM on Pluto."

Linda softly asked the sergeant, "Can he wait outside?"

The sergeant only observed a moment's silence. Old Boston working-class genteel; Agreed, me lad's uncouth.

Shelley asked if her daughter would be charged with possession of narcotics. The sergeant said Belladonna, no; federal statutes restricting its commerce, basically it. Linda felt excluded. This was all about her, but her input wasn't really needed. She watched her finger press a curl straight down, along her bare shoulder. Took her finger off, it bounced back into a curl. She moved her lips: *boing.* The sergeant said, Otherwise it was like jimson weed—what kids at camp learn they must never put in their mouths. He told Linda, "Okay: we have the name of a suspect. Pazia, correct?"

"Mm-hm. I'm really, really sorry that she came into my life."

The cop said, "Yeah. We'll be in touch with Tony Biondo," like he and Tony were old chums and touched bases periodically. "You have my personal condolences." He presented his hand. For a moment, Linda just looked at it. Then she realized she wasn't supposed to do anything except give him hers, remaining seated. She let him hold her limp hand for a second. It engaged a magic circuit. He was her father and she, an adorable flower who'd never harm a fly. When he released her hand, it stopped. Weird.

She said, "You've been very sweet." Then fell thoughtful. Crystal-clear awareness: *Because I haven't been a woman, I'm naive about* men.

Shelley, gentlewoman from a distant green shire, coolly

76

thanked the Salem cops for their attention to this matter. The older cop caught his partner's eye, We're for the door. This had been light comedy—Mistress Mary, quite contrary, off in her own little garden. They left the room—bootheels clacking, accouterments swaying—returning to the streets.

Linda sadly gazed at the floor, arms crossed under her bosom. A tear dropped to the tile floor. She saw it, and knew: it was hers and hers alone.

Shelley touched her daughter's chin. "Poor little peony."

Linda, quite dispassionate, said, "Please don't call me that."

Betrayal. Shelley announced that she was going to Linda's apartment. *Why.* To get Linda's clothes. But wait. No. Why didn't she get them before? Shelley was astounded. "I wasn't about to leave your side." She left her daughter's side, got her purse from the chair, walked towards the door.

Linda, sitting on the bed, reached out. "Mom, don't leave me. Mother!" Her voice was deep; her tone, commanding. She sounded like a woman, speaking in a deep, commanding voice. Just Dorothy Gale, no matter what she did. Like her body, under her smock: mommy's thighs and bosom, mother's sex. She couldn't say All right I'm tired of this, and make them any different. She'd just be a tired woman, with the same old bumps and curves. Shelley turned, exasperated. "Lin, what more do you want of me?"

"Not to be abandoned. Stayed with. Support."

Shelley sagged—the weight of the final straw. "Lin, I am *getting* your *things.*" She raised her hand: God, look. "I raised a clinging vine and how it worked—you won't let go!" She left.

Linda kept vigil. She sat facing the divider. Lowered head, stern gaze—that divider wouldn't catch her unawares.

Being born-again, religiously, a portion of her thoughts were addressed to God. Not formal prayer—*Wouldst that Thou shouldst,* like God was especially keen on antique bad grammar; more like an on-going letter to Daddy. Having an awful time, wish You were here. She considered herself still His child. The shift from son to daughter was a lateral transfer only, though one she was really unhappy with.

At the least bit of sound which might have been someone about to come in, she flinched, but held her fixed stare.

Waiting, waiting. Waiting for what? Her fairy godmother to appear and wave a wand, change her back into Derrick? Wouldn't the opposite happen instead? Her fairy godmother was coming back with Linda's clothes.

She looked at the white carnations on the nightstand. Flowers for a woman. *Oh God they're for* me.

What was the connection, anyway? She didn't *feel* like a flower. She didn't feel pretty or delicate. She definitely didn't feel like a white carnation. If anything, a red rose—musty, dark and over-used. Maybe even wilted.

She *very* vaguely remembered. Being Derrick, holding . . . who she was now. Brief flashes of remembrance—a sensual kaleidoscope, but fleeting as a subliminal frame. *Soft light warm sweet precious.* Love-flash of her eyes in flesh-warm darkness. Velvet bow in her soft black hair. Sugar and spice and everything nice . . .

But the memories were very quickly fading. Becoming things she'd never tasted, musty-book ideals. Things your mom said to annoy you.

There was nothing magical about being female. You didn't come into the world with a pink-and-purple starburst, you came in as a kid—one who couldn't throw a ball right, or pee standing up. You didn't have storybook eyes, unless you saw something real awesome—a birthday cake, or a blank check endorsed by your father.

She wasn't a flower. Not a carnation.

Not even a crappy black-eyed susan.

Someone walked through the door.

Linda's heart raced. She calmly asked, "Who's there?"

"The Abandoner has returned."

Linda sagged her shoulders, rolled her eyes—relief, and also sort of an imitation of Shelley. Who came around the divider, radiant smiles, sunshine and love. Chic in her brown leather coat from Abercrombie & Fitch, rosy-cheeked from the cold outside. She'd brought a small suitcase and Linda's light coat, rolled up in a plastic bag. Attention to details, like all of this was fun. She set the things down, took off her own coat . . .

She noted Linda's interest. Offered the open coat, to be touched. The lining felt like some pliant, low-pile synthetic.

Shelley said, "Kangaroo."

Smiled.

. . . then sat on the bed next to Linda. *"Okay.* How are we holding up?" She sounded a little winded, like she'd taken the stairs. Linda gasped—she had to get out of here, *now.* Shelley took her hand, No gasping. "Now, this is what will happen. Tonight, we're going home . . ."

"You mean, you're dropping me off. At my apartment."

Shelley's gaze wandered, like Linda played some neat but unknown game. "No, I don't *think* so . . ."

So *home* meant 26 Longmeadow Road. The mansion of honey-colored Cotswold stone, looking out over the Berkshires. Beveled oak bannisters, crystal chandeliers. It meant Linda's childhood bedroom. It meant that, quite simply, her adulthood was revoked.

"For a while, at least. Yes, you'll be a child again. In our house. You won't be a guest. You'll be ours." Shelley's warmth was honest. "It will be all right."

78

All right seemed to mean, she wouldn't be stuck at the table til she ate her cold broccoli. Linda reluctantly nodded, Okay.

"Now, you know your father is in Jordan. We know he'll call as soon as he gets the news. What's wrong?—Dear, you always speak too softly, I didn't hear what—"

"I said, my father. I don't . . . would rather not. Talk to him."

Shelley waited, like she'd heard a joke but missed the punchline. None was given, so she delivered her own. "Light bulbs grow on Christmas trees. You don't want to speak to Dad." Linda tried her timid-woman smile, on/off: Just one of my little things; you know. But it was one of her little things Shelley never heard of. She said, "All right: because you lost your husband. You somehow lost your father."

"Don't try to psychoanalyze. I don't think you can."

"Can you give me hints?—I'm groping at answers. Lin, be a woman and speak your heart—I'm tired of holding your hand." For emphasis, she squeezed Linda's hand.

Linda resumed her sullen vigil of the divider.

She'd heard of sci-fi stories where men got turned into women against their will. They ran amok with rage. She'd been turned into a pretty wimpy woman then, she guessed. No urge to run out and shoot everybody with a machine gun. The awful, awful thing was that this *happened* to her, she wanted to cry and never stop and if she gave it any thought then yes, of course, she wanted *Daddy*. Whoever that was. She vaguely pictured Robert Redford. For someone to ruffle her hair, call her "princess," take her out for ice cream—that seemed pretty cool. In principle.

The problem was this particular relationship. When Linda was with her father, she acted seven years old. She played kitten, pleaded for favors and gifts. Bounced for joy when she got them, pouted when she did not. They talked baby-talk to each other. The most appalling thing Derrick witnessed was when Lars came back from a couple months overseas. He was standing in the Bauers' driveway when Derrick and Linda pulled up in Derrick's Rabbit. It was the hottest day all summer and Linda made the trip in a one-piece swimsuit, sandals. Lars was shouting at a neighbor—something ferociously obscure, about which he was enthused. *French-built turbines in a Euphrates hydroelectric dam.* Linda went to him and, while he shouted at the neighbor, she just . . . cuddled. Made herself held and went to sleep. Lars just held her, wasn't even distracted. *Stretched cables out to Tel Nabat and used jackhammers.*

"When your father calls, you'll talk to him. The alternative, Lin, does not appear. It's not right. It's not you. Lin, it sounds crazy—okay?"

Linda felt empty and crushed. She was no more shamed by womanhood than Derrick's wife had been, but that seemed to be surprisingly a lot. She murmured, "He'll be . . . nice to me, or . . . ?"

"Your father has always been *too* nice. He's never *not* been nice to you, no matter what you've done. It's been something of a problem, wouldn't you agree?—this getting away with murder? Always going from me to him, since you liked him so much better? Why even ask me, whether he'll be nice to you? Take it up with him."

"Mom, no. I . . . love you. Also. As much."

"Oh, Lin, I know. It's just that we parents are human. Jealousy is human. I remember how excited you'd get, every night when he came home. Down the stairs and right into his arms."

Linda grimaced sickly. "Til I was, what? Five or six?"

"More like, til your sophomore year at Coleman."

Linda closed her eyes.

Shelley busied herself with the contents of the suitcase. Explained how she'd take care of everything, all of Linda's affairs. She'd be back here tomorrow for more of Linda's things. "If worse comes to worse, you can wear some of mine. Oh, *thanks*." Linda wondered what for, then realized she'd made a face. "Miss Aquarius Boutique—I can only offer rags from Nordstrom's."

"Mother, we're whispering. Why are we whispering?"

"We're not, this is how people talk." Shelley motioned her finger, Thanks for the cue. "I spoke with your doctor as I was leaving. He admitted he's not a specialist and doesn't know your history, but he said you appear . . . well, these are his exact words: he said that you 'appear psychotic'."

"Well, he appeared to be a dick." Linda watched her mother's eyes and tried to smile. When her mother didn't smile too, she stopped.

Shelley smoothly played her hand. "I know *I'm* not amused by that." *Now* she smiled, fetchingly—Go fish. "I think I'll leave." She closed the suitcase, which she'd brought—leaving altogether.

Linda had a sudden vision, fact and frightful fancy, mixed. She was twenty-nine and Shelley had every right to walk out of her life. Leave her here in the hospital room. The doctor and black nurse would reappear, together. They would hate her, show no mercy—she was crazy and not even funny. She would pass through nightmare corridors of flaking yellow paint, grey-painted metal doors—psych ward, prison. Shower rooms, lesbian guards. Men with keys and dog-like grins. All because she chose—she, herself, decided—not to come home. A world of sunlight, caring, being loved—she'd just refused it. "Mom, no. I'll be good. Do better. Promise. Look." She opened the suitcase, took out the first thing that came to hand. A pouch of mauve silk duppioni with gold clasp. Something totally familiar; it belonged to Derrick's wife. She held it; it was hers. "You brought my makeup kit."

Another misstep. Linda skipped makeup a lot; Shelley saw her remark in that light. "Oh, I had some nerve. To think you'd leave here bravely, to begin the rest of your life."

An abrupt pause, a lull—John Carpenter's *Prince of Darkness* will return after this word from Snuggles Fabric Softener:

Altogether languid, Linda said, "I'm very upset at this time."

Docile, like a daughter not a mom, Shelley said, "I know that."

To begin the rest of your life . . .

I don't know what that means, Tony. Not even as a theoretical proposition, to 'live someone else's life for her', that's

in the Desk Reference for chrissake. No, keep it at 5 cc's. Nurse, will you secure that respirator? Atropine. *From* atropos. *Not turning. Not to be moved. Why don't you*

turn from thy sins and be healed saith thy Redeemer, lest I tell you to get lost. Derrick, your mother's calling you. Go see what she wants. Stay with her as long as she needs you, over there. I'm trying to patch a tire and you won't even

pack my Egyptian blanket. Beach blanket, you know which one. Oh, here—under the ice chest, good. Dear, I don't know why your father's upset. You stay here, with me. Help me unpack, but

"If you're going to stare at your kit like it's the disassembled components of a radar detector, I'll just—"

"No." Linda stayed her mother's hand. "It's mine." Her expression was calm as she opened the kit, began to desperately, cluelessly fish through its contents.

"Lin, why are you always like this? Frightened and tense, like you'll be yelled at or hit? We were never harsh with you . . ."

"Someone else, then. Teacher at school, or . . . okay: here's my": *it has a name come on you know* " . . . v-velour brush and my . . . little water-color paint set kids buy at K-Mart, no, it's shadow-something. For your eyes, it's *eye* shadow, and my grease pencil—no, it's . . ."

"Lin, I'm going to remain, and remain in control. If you scream and throw things, I'll be here. If you play an hysterical game—call your eyeliner a workman's tool because you're Derrick—I'll be here. I won't go away."

"I'll slash my wrists, or . . .?"

"I'll be here."

Looking at the folded clothes, Linda slightly shook her head, verging on fresh tears. Sitting on the bed, Shelley glowed, pure schoolgirl fun. "Um . . . what's *wrong*, 'Derrick'? Oh! . . . you don't know how to dress yourself in a woman's clothes! Did I

81

guess right?" Linda snatched the folded things, held them to herself, hopelessly defiant. "And the deodorant, dear."

Watching her mother distrustfully, Linda took the tube of Secret. Then paused. Serious, she asked, "Was that supposed to mean something?"

Shelley fluttered her lashes, surprised. "No, not a thing. You'd like a shower, but this isn't the Radisson and we have to make do. Oh, here." She took a tiny bottle from the suitcase. "Just a spray. You can even . . ." Circled finger: do your cleavage. "Don't go lavish." Linda stared, perplexed, like *lavish* was the newest thing from high-tech salons in Europe. "Like that time with my Eau de Charlotte. When I had to open windows in November. I thought it would never go away. Strawberry fields forever."

Linda couldn't believe this act, much less that she was blamed for it. "I was small. Very young." Unable to stand the suspense: "*All right I was fifteen!*"

Shelley stared, amazed; Linda stared back, fear-struck. She couldn't deny being Linda. She couldn't even deny going wild with perfume. "Mom, you're giving me Lin's . . . Halston's. Perfume. Why."

"Well, you're . . . an adult!" A funny little gesture went with that. It seemed to summon ruffled sleeves, a handkerchief of Windsor lace. "And all adults are different. You have an exquisitely soft, clear complexion and you . . . develop a body-scent sooner than someone fair-skinned, that's all!"

Linda faced her mom. Her expression might have seemed stern, almost accusing, but was just Linda's natural look. She'd been a silent baby in her stroller, staring grimly at fawning strangers. "You're saying, because I'm Latina, I smell."

She blinked: There, said.

Shelley beckoned: Come and sit. Linda came and sat.

Shelley held her daughter's arm. Tennis muscles, tendons in her wrist—it was a grip. She spoke in a quick sharp whisper; she didn't want this silly conversation overheard. "*Look, you picked the wrong kid to cop this attitude with, okay? I am your mother. I've carried you through your life, and it was almost too heavy for both of us. Your starvation diets: Lin, I saved your life. Water retention, you drank a pint of apple cider vinegar: ER. You cut your own hair and your father had to cancel a lecture to run home to a family crisis. And no, it was never your fault. You were beside yourself, helpless. Now I offer one word—one kind word—of advice and get this up-yours, Angela Davis bullcrap. Why not spit in my face, Lin. Say you never knew me.*"

Linda gazed calmly at her mother's eyes. Fascinated by their joy-light, amber and benign. Complete dissociation of self from speech. "Lin, you've been real hateful. Go get dressed."

"Mom, I love you."

"Just go."

Linda took her stuff into the bathroom. Closed the door, looked at what she'd been given. Her cinched-waist navy blue blouse, with its matching slit skirt. Linda mainly wore it to her staff meetings. Linda assumed—rightly or not—there was some logic to her mother's choice. Pantyhose, half-slip, bra. Her shoes. *If I were in your shoes. These are Linda's clothes.* The irrational thought: *Will she get mad?* Linda got dressed. There was no comedy of errors. Little clasps and stuff she wasn't used to, but things fit like she'd worn them for years, which she had. It seemed too quick and simple to be right; forgetful, she turned, looking for a mirror. It was scary to feel that she'd simply gotten dressed—that she was simply Linda, after all. *I don't have her memories and yet, of course I do—I remember everything she told me.* Oh when I was little, *talk talk talk talk talk—stored in my subconscious.*

Feeling more and more upset, she came out, closed the door. Shelley said, "Fix your skirt."

Wide-eyed, Linda softy said, "I'm sorry?"

"The slit. Pull it over to the side."

Linda did, protesting—close to tears—"I never learned these things. How am I supposed to know these things?"

"Did you spray?"

Linda sniffled bravely. "Yes."

"Where is it?"

"On my body, like you said."

"Lin, the *bottle.*"

She felt an oppressive weight. Herself a bubble of frailty, petty vice and weakness, in a room of lead walls, iron ceiling, godlike judgments. Her endemic low self-esteem, prey to every hint of disapproval. It felt so much worse than it ever looked, to another's eyes. She got the tiny bottle from the sink, where—death of shame—she'd left it. She came back out and gave the bottle to her mother, Here I'm helpless. Shelley put it in her daughter's purse—pausing to gaze, disturbed, into its depths. "Oh hon, no . . . for a professional, a career woman . . . this needs to be organized." Linda gestured weakly in despair. It was someone else's purse. A chipmunk's larder of unneeded receipts, uncapped Magic Markers, tampons, granola bar wrappers, greying peaches, wadded Kleenex, Q-tips, uncapped lipsticks, random esoterica. *She did it, not me.*

I have to get out of this room. She put on her coat, took her purse and faced her mother, I'm ready, let's go.

"No makeup, I guess."

"I don't use it."

"That was fresh. In times like these, the little things . . ."

"I just want to die. It's not my body, not my life—"

"You want to fall apart, and I won't let you."

Linda could endure no more. She narrowed her eyes, asked coldly: "If you're such a perfect iceberg, why's your daughter such a flake?"

Shelley peered, concerned. "He never said that to you, did he?"—maybe she meant Derrick. She waited for no answer, like she didn't want to know. Gave Linda a flat pink tube. *Clinique. rinse-off foaming cleanser.* Alice, holding the bottle that said *Drink me*, was no less sure what to do with something. Linda went into the bathroom, just so her mother wouldn't know that.

The tube was not an accessory to adventures underground. It was merchandise from Filene's. It told you to wash your face with the stuff. Linda did, and came back out. Tense, she murmured, "You want me to put on lipstick, too?"

"Linda, how delightful. You sound just like a boy. Icky girl-stuff: yes."

Linda stood at the mirror. Learned again, there was no sorority secret. Wax-based pigment, applied to soft surface. It tasted like the cherry from a birthday cake. She remembered to do that thing with her lips. Liner, mascara; she guessed that you applied the liner first. Eye shadow, very little, in case she had this all screwed up. For the barest moment, she was held by her reflection: furious, beautiful black-haired girl. She turned to her mom. "Okay?"

Shelley, plaintive, said "I guess"—whose arm had she twisted? Took something from her suitcase, handed: hair brush.

I would never have treated me like this. I fought with the punks all night, gave love like a big brother and took all their abuse, and when I came home, I just wanted someone to love. I didn't care how she looked. Or how she sniffled and whined. I only loved my Linda, just the way she was.

"Why are you hurting yourself?"

Linda turned from the mirror, confused. "Hurt . . . ?"

"You're standing there making a frightful face, pulling your hair out by the roots. Tears are streaming down your cheeks. No, you're absolutely fine. Lin, for God's sake."

She could only respond by offering her mother the brush, holding it out to be taken.

Shelley came to Linda. Her eyes glowed, they always did, a calm and eager snow-wolf; she was scariest when gentle. Fingertips on Linda's hips, like a delicate glass figurine, Please turn. She found herself turned, a music-box girl, back to her reflection. Shelley took the brush. "Like this. Dear, you've Mediterranean hair. These firm, black waves with ringlets on the fringe. Can be gorgeous, you just never . . ." She roughly but expertly combed out the snarls, then drew the brush in bold, round, loving contours of her daughter's face and neck. *Making me beautiful. This is how she sees me.* Shelley's voice went tender. Laying her baby down to sleep, speaking to her in her

84

bassinet. " . . . bother with it. Oh my goodness, what a waste . . . *erzählen Sie mir etwas Neues* though, hm? *Was ist mit das hübsche Mädchen los?*"

Linda, weeping, said, "Nothing. I'm not."

Shelley worked on her daughter's hair, fretfully murmured under her breath. The words were now soft as a baby's kiss. "Oh Lindakins, why is it hurting so much? *Where* does it hurt? Oh baby, why can't you tell me? Linda, why can't I find you? Where are you, Linda? Oh hon, where?"

Linda sobbed, gazing at her reflection in anguish.

Her mother waited a moment, then calmly continued brushing, while Linda quietly wept.

She said thinly, through tears, "I surrender. Mommy, I give up. I just want to be your little girl," but Linda still was gone, that was not the magic kiss. *Gone through the light.* She sobbed once more.

Shelley still spoke softly, vague and joyous wonder: "But that's all you ever were. That's all you'll ever be."

She *tsked*—of all the silly things to say; she made her daughter's hair bunch nicely at the back. Patted the bunched curls, they bounced. "Isn't that so much better? Aren't *you* my pretty little *girl* again! Yes, you really *are!*"

Linda shook her head, mouthed *No*, as tears dripped down her cheeks.

"Linda, your father and I . . . we know you're all grown up. That you went to college, and you drive a car, and . . . we know all this in our *minds*. Until something like this happens, and you need us. Then, we talk with you on the phone, we meet with you and see you, but we no longer see you as you actually are. We see a four-year-old child, standing by our bed in the dark. In her little cotton gown. 'Mommy, I don't feel good. Daddy, I'm sick.' That's who we see, Lin. That's who we hear, when you call us collect."

Linda wept, "*Please stop.*"

Please make it stop—Shelley held her shoulders. "All right, babe. Be brave now, we're leaving. We're going home."

Linda took a determined breath. She smoothed the flanks of her snug, black coat; it turned into a gesture, Look at me. How can I feel "brave"? Shelley winked, That's the spirit. She took the empty suitcase. They went out.

There were nurses and orderlies, med carts and gurneys and a single doddering, elderly patient—no doubt the one who'd been noisy earlier. He might have done great deeds in his life, terrible things in his youth. But because of his behavior, he was marked in Linda's mind—he was, forevermore, the Lactose-Intolerant Guy. The hospital hall felt like lock-up: spacious, echoing, hostile and abrupt. Linda was self-conscious of her walk, the indolent sway of her rump. She feared that men would look at her. At least, she knew she looked a way she didn't feel. Urban chic, in basic black—coat, curls, dilated eyes and Mommy's little time bomb didn't wish to be approached.

Shelley hustled, led the way. Spoke to a nurse and to an orderly. She seemed brisk and pleasant, like she'd arrived at a ski lodge and wanted the lift up the slope. Linda dared to glance around, saw that people were looking for real. Not lust so much as wonder. The tragic romance of Room 212 was passing into the hospital's store of legend. *A pretty girl was poisoned, and her husband came in DOA.* Now people looked away like they were satisfied—like they'd expected someone a little more glamorous. The doctor and nurse who'd attended her were standing by the head nurse's desk. While Shelley took prescriptions and had Linda sign forms, the two medics studiously ignored their patient. Their world was quite intense enough without any help from Linda Bloom. She told the doctor, "Please: if you have concerns about your patient, kindly address them to her. My mother does not have guardianship."

"Yes, Ms. Bloom, I'll do as you say. Enjoy your recuperation."

Doctor and nurse talked softly—once, she laughed—as Shelley and her daughter walked quietly to the elevator.

7

The garage was scary. It felt vast, cold and ominous. Linda felt tiny and vulnerable, walking up the graded drive beside her mom. Their footsteps echoed: *clack, clickety-clack, clack.* Men's shoes didn't do that. It felt like they were dressed only for some place that had carpet, and this automotive cave was out of bounds.

They arrived at Shelley's '94 Pontiac Sunbird. Linda saw the trunk lid in an existential light. Gold-speck finish, Armorall'ed. How could things be so the same and she be so much different?

They got in, Shelley turned the key. The engine revved, then the front end knocked and clattered. The Sunbird turned itself off.

Both women sat in silence, til Shelley said, "Just swell."

Linda waited, then ventured, "It's all right."

"Easy for you to say."—Linda wasn't paying the repair bill.

Linda pushed her luck. "I meant, it's no big deal. Could it be the fan belt?—I mean, it happened once. Derrick explained—"

"And now we're Little Miss Mechanic."

So that was it. Being unfeminine wasn't a fall from grace but just an uphill climb; you were ignored. "Mom, what if we walked to a store? An auto parts. Like Napa. I mean, if the belt just costs, like, eight or ten dollars . . ." *You put it on. We go.* " . . . then maybe the man there could explain . . . ?"

Shelley said, "Very amusing. I just hope I can find a pay phone."

Linda couldn't believe it. "You're calling Triple-A."

"I suppose you would recommend some local garage. Some knight in shining tow truck was nice to you, once; only charged you double, and charmed you out of your stockings. Said he was the man to trust and made a customer for life."

Linda flared her eyes, stunned by sheer non sequitur. The Linda she knew was not susceptible to mechanics, since she never interacted with mechanics and could not. *The Texaco Guy Who Sabotaged My Datsun* was her archetype of evil: Satan wore a name patch on his coveralls, *Ed.* All mechanics, everywhere, were Linda's natural enemies; they were snakes and she, a field mouse. Her mug shot was posted in every garage, over the caption *OUR VICTIM.* Whatever made guys want to work with cars, also made them abhor Linda Bloom. Anything to do with cars was Der's department, period. "Mom, you're going to *hire some guy to come replace your fan belt!*"

Shelley gently said, "You needn't be involved."

She got out of the car, walked back down the ramp. Linda sadly watched her go—her cool, assertive march. Any aspiring mugger would have a battle on his hands, all right. Confidence born of a saner, gentler time, when a woman with a loud voice and weighty purse could actually pose a deterrent. As for Triple-A, they'd refer whoever was closest. The guy would look at these two skirts, glance at Shelley's engine. That knocking, yes: your drive shaft. It scrambled your whole tranny.

Shelley returned after fifteen minutes. She got in the car, gave Linda the good news. "The man was very nice. He said he'd come himself, at once." Her eyes gleamed in the garage's yellow-bulb lit gloom: a dash through urban wilderness, survived. Chalk one up for Middle America.

Linda thinly said, "I hope so," looking out her window. That sounded right for her. *When the going gets tough, I stop paying attention.*

They sat for several minutes, waiting quietly.

Shelley then said, "When we were in Europe, last fall, we rented an Audi. It broke down outside of Dortmund. The truck was there in minutes. Lin, it was wonderful. The men worked fast like those pit-stop mechanics they have at car races. Just bing, bing, bing, you're all set. I mean, a whole different mentality. It's like, 'Things shouldn't break down.' "

Linda said, uncertain, "You were born there . . . right?"

"Well? My family moved from *Thuringia.* Our farm was in *Silesia.*"—she made them sound enchanted. Fairy kingdoms where flowers talked, and all the girls were lovely. "It might be part of Poland, now. How nice that we're getting to know each other!"—a light and giddy laugh, since her daughter was so silly. I forgot how to use makeup, I forgot where you were born—silly, silly, *silly!* "Anyway, the whole country's like that—very modern and efficient. But also very trashy and medieval. Everywhere you drive are these castles—you know, pretty ones, like in a storybook. White plaster with blue roofs, on forested hills—it's just the country's natural scenery. Everything's computerized and digital, except the lovely clocks but then the *people*—Lin, they're gross. As crass and rootless as we, without our conscience. The drinking and pornography—they're animals. And *dirty.* The women don't shave their body hair, and no one uses deodorant. And try to purchase pantyhose: they think that's 'French'. Too fancy. Since they never change their panties, so the nylon runs, of course. And their table manners—please. I mean, we eat—how? We cut up our food then eat it with our fork. One bite at a time, with our other hand in our lap, right? They saw and shovel both

88

at once, like the food's about to disappear. You can't be a woman in that country—talk like someone in *Beowulf* and drive a Mercedes, you can't. The autobahns are a bad trip anyway. They use headlights at night like we use high beams—switch them off when they see another car. Everyone drives at least a hundred miles an hour—it's perfectly normal and legal."

Linda blinked sadly, perplexed—it sounded okay. She said, "It sounds just awful. I'd never want to drive, there."

"Lin, you can't. Be type-A or get off the road; they get up right behind you, flash their lights and lay their horns on, all at once. It's not even considered rude. Then *you* get pulled over—for 'discourtesy'. It's really a post-civilized society."

Linda politely said, "I'm sure." She watched the dark ramp, below. She'd never felt so needlessly detained.

"The *amenities* are nice. The rest areas are like real parks. No one litters, since they really will arrest you. In the Schwarzwald, down south, the scenery's just awesome. God, I kept thinking of *The Vanishing.*—the foreign original. The American version's a spoof. Suspense is a lost art. If Alfred Hitchcock was alive right now, what would he be doing?"

Linda was confused—thought Shelley was still on *The Vanishing.* "Banging on the lid of his coffin?"

Shelley *tsk*ed. "Dear, he'd be suing everyone in Hollywood. What they did to *The Birds* was inexcusable. Oh, oh—look!" The tow truck arrived. Linda, unthinking, opened her door. Shelley was curious. "What are you doing?"

Linda closed the door, put her hands in her lap. Getting out of the car was wrong. "Nothing." *Think quick what would Linda say it doesn't have to make sense* "I got scared."

Shelley smiled, sympathetic; getting scared was all right. "He's just going to fix the engine, hon. You stay here, inside."

"Mom, it's the fan belt. You can say a man stopped by and told us—"

"That would be untrue and somewhat rude. Like telling the doctor what's wrong with you." Linda closed her eyes. She'd already been rude to a doctor; she wouldn't dare offend a mechanic. Shelley put the cap on a matter already settled: "I'm dealing with this." She got out, met the mechanic with laughing confidence—nobody's rube, this babe.

Linda's hands were in her lap. She looked at them. The guy was loud. She wished he would just fix the car, and not be loud and scary. When the hood was raised she looked up, wary as a newly caged sparrow.

Shelley said, "Just a crazy thought, but: how's my *fan belt*?"

"Your fan belt's fine. We replace them anyway, standard road maintenance . . . problem is your fuel pump. Sounded like it over the phone, so I've got it in my truck."

Shelley gushed, "That's super. I mean, as far as *we're*

concerned, this part of town could just as well be Harlem."

Linda sat serenely, picking at a loose thread on the hem of her skirt. She wasn't allowed to come out of the car; she didn't want to, anyway. Her job was to keep herself quiet and calm, while the man took care of their problem.

The sun set, a harsh orange disk, over the wooded slopes up ahead. Shelley flipped the sun visor up and down, murmuring, once, that she wished the road would make up its mind. Linda gazed out her window, watching the brown fields and leafless woods roll by. She was dimly aware that this was her heritage: a passenger in a silent, smooth-running car, being taken from one calm, comfortable place to another.

Shelley kept asking if her daughter was warm enough. Yes. Did she want to listen to the radio? No.—I'm sorry?—No thank you. Did she want a tape? Shelley had the Carpenters, Joan Baez. Peter, Paul and Mary. They were the background music of Linda's childhood. While huddled masses, far away, rocked to the Ramones, she'd chased Frisbees over summer lawns in a land called Honalee. Oh—no tape. No thank you.

"Lin, while I'm in Salem tomorrow, you'll have the house to yourself." A soft aside: "You'll be okay?"

Linda watched a dairy farm, went "Hn," a daughter's vacant *yes*.

"Lin, tomorrow: some men may come to re-caulk the patio tiles . . . you'll just need to let them in." Nonchalant: "Okay?"

Linda frowned at twilight fields, a proud adult with problems on her mind. "I could use some space from men. If that's all right."

Her mind had wandered when she remembered, Shelley's silences were decrees. No, it was *not* all right. Linda's man-shyness was a trait from her earliest childhood. It had long been indulged and even subtly reinforced. As she'd become a woman, grown fond of men other than her father, the problem had partly fixed itself. Her persistent fear of male strangers would still be tolerated, but not to the point where it interfered with anything. The patio would not be left unrecaulked because Linda was afraid to let the workmen in. She was twenty-nine, for chrissake. To insist on man-free environments was no longer an acceptable response. It was a guaranteed automatic *F*. It wasn't even the patio Shelley was worried about—it was the unrecaulkable fracture of her daughter's hard-won confidence. "And I haven't been shopping, so there isn't much food in the house." Latent there, too, was a world of shit awaiting resurface. Shelley had fought the anorexia wars and won. The rebel flag of self-starvation was never again to be unfurled. "There's tuna. Rice cakes. You'll find some things you like."

Derrick regarded those items as catfood and styrofoam,

respectively. Linda had lived on them. Her body still liked them. She envisioned tuna and rice cakes as she'd never imagined them before. Flaky fish on top of squeaky stuff. Her mouth watered. Shelley said, "Other than that . . . well, it's home. We haven't touched your room, except to clean. All the things you left behind—your records, books . . . your rollerskates . . ."

Derrick had been in that room, of course. Not once but several times. So this was Witto Winda's bedwoom. A decidedly adult kiss in the hallway, then back downstairs for a cocktail.

Did she really say "your rollerskates"?

" . . . assuming, too, you'll earn your keep. No lazy daisies at the Bauer home."

Linda thumped herself, lightly, on the head; she'd forgotten she was a flower.

She thought, *That felt so . . . bratty. Sissy. She's my mother.*

But I'm not her son. I'm her daughter. And I'm not supposed to seek her love. She's my model, I resent her. Since I have to become like her.

Linda brooded, watching the tall steeple of a white New England church as the Mass Pike neared some hamlet.

This is what it means to be a woman. To be hollow. An empty vessal, shell of desire, needing to be filled. Alone, I'm incomplete—an accessory with a soul. No: an anorexic's sudden fear—she was depleted. "Mom, I'm hungry."

Shelley asked, "So what would you like?" Her tone was nearly seductive. It was good to take heart and defy despair and besides, she was probably hungry too.

Linda didn't consciously consider. "Something with starch."

Shelley said, "Sure," languidly drawing out the sound; it could go wherever it wanted since it had a string attached. "Just, um . . . you know." They both knew: living on celery for a week, then eating half a gallon of toffee crunch with a jar of Jiff as sauce. If a word to the bulimic wasn't enough: " . . . the ladies' room. Visits are suspect when you come back to the table with wet eyes."

"If you're paying, I won't puke." Shelley laughed and Linda looked at her, wondering what was funny.

"Lin, Italian? Polly want some pasta?"

She was somewhat jarred by the genteel *pah*-sta; the *pisans* in South Boston called them *noodles*. She almost said *Cool*, but that would have been *imitating her husband*. She said, "That would be quite nice," which was cool: imitating the Duchess of York.

Her mind held a sensuous image; she couldn't define it. Her body wanted something. "Mom, is there such a thing as tuna lasagna?"

Shelley didn't answer right away. Perhaps she plumbed her mind. An impromptu gourmet, a wealthy man's wife, who'd seen—in the more obscure corners of Europe—people eating the strangest things. She answered, "No," then had a lovely notion. "*Domina's.*"

Linda liked the name, somehow. "Um . . . yeah; that's good."

"Then I'll turn off here, on 91."

A timeless, winding drive through outer suburbia. Queen Anne Revivals and rolling lawns, like compressed English countryside. It got dusky, then dark.

The restaurant was an art-deco villa with porticoed front. Pink stucco lit softly by pink lights behind pruned yews. Tall junipers, hiding a terrace; it overlooked a pond. The sign said *Domina's* in fluid script, with a butterfly dotting the *i*. It was framed by weeping cherry trees and porcelain flamingoes. Linda blinked, sorrowful. This had been part of her life, her world. "Mom, this is such a nice place."

"We've had nice times here; yes."

At the door, Linda asked, "Are we dressed all right, or . . . ?"

Shelley paused to look in her purse. "We're both fine, dear. This is Italian, not French . . . well here's my Visa, I just hope . . ." Linda stared. Her mother's purse was essential elegance. A Delorean to Linda's Love Bug. Laminated cards, accessories of gold-banded mahogany. She noticed her mother's perfume; orchids under stenciled glass.

There was a quiet lobby. Low blue carpet, potted palmettoes, a drystone wall enclosing a goldfish pond. There were pennies and quarters on the blue cement bottom.

Behind the pond, in a myrtle-trellised niche, was a marble Romanesque; a pretty lady.

All these magic colors, deep as feelings. Memories that aren't quite mine. Whose life was this?—I don't know. Didn't know you that well, Lin.

"Linda, don't start crying. Darling, please—not here."

She tottered slightly, as if drunk. Shelley held her, from behind. Held her wrists crossed, Linda cuddled, a giggling, helpless child. Shelley let her go, and they were two adults.

Linda knew she could do crazy things in public. It was like a wondrous talent which she seldom chose to reveal.

When she was nineteen, her mother took her and a friend to see Keith Green at the Christian Life Atheneum in Granby, CT. Linda wore a powder-violet summer dress, a lily corsage; every boy they passed, sighed. After the performance, Linda went up on the stage to speak with the singer, whom she idolized at the time. She basked in the dream-come-true radiance, a gentle virgin sharing her love for the Lord. With a young woman's single-heartedness, though, she'd confused the Lord with the man she was speaking to. Shelley, down in the front aisle, felt her daughter was being a pious flirt. Appalled, she frantically waved and mouthed that Linda needed to *come down* from the stage *this instant.* Linda freaked—screamed at her mother, "Allright—*Allright!*" A lighting technician thought someone had lost an earring, perhaps, and that someone had called for a *light*; he turned the spotlight on Linda. Thankfully, the Atheneum was small, and people were already leaving. No more than two hundred saw Linda shriek at her mother, "*Don't yank my leash, I'm sick of it—stop trying to run my life*" before she realized she was center stage, and fainted.

"Mom, I like this place. The statue. Pretty. See?"

"Yes, presh. *Shh.*"

A manager, a swarthy young man in black suit and bow tie, had been waiting for his cue. He looked at Linda, then at Shelley. "Uh . . . good evening, ladies. Will it be for two, tonight?" Linda assumed that he knew them; he seemed amused, like he'd caught friends in an unguarded moment. "You *like* the statue, hm?" It took her a moment to acknowledge him. Her smile, shy and brief—she remembered it looked proud and distant, Oh it's only you. "It's by Serpiatore—friend of my uncle's, he's big around Naples." She realized, then, he was a stranger; he'd never seen her or her mother before. He fascinated and scared her. She looked at the statue—ignoring him while staying on the subject he'd brought up. He talked to Shelley, then. "Oh, I'm sorry. That'll be for two?—then may I take your coats?" Shelley glanced meaningfully at her daughter: My, aren't we getting the treatment? Linda stared seriously at a bucolic mural. For all anyone knew, she was an art student or something. She wanted to be honored, left alone. Shelley touched her hand.

"Dear, your coat."

"Oh.—what about it?"

"The man would like to take it."

"I promise to give it back." She looked at him, thoughtful. He softly flashed his eyes, amused. Sure you can't ignore me. If nothing else, they both drank Ansel Light, watched *Friends* and were paying off college loans. She parted her lips like she'd tell him, *No I'm not Miss Lady of the Nineties.*

Shelley was playfully acerbic. "Oh Lin, give him your coat."

"Yeah, sure." A final glance at the mural. This wasn't what she was used to She'd grown up in South Boston, where the finer Italian restaurants have checkered cloth over the linoleum tables. Juke box playing Frank Sinatra. (They had a moody instrumental take on Mancini's *Moon River* here, very low.) This didn't seem like the kind of place where you hung out with your buddies til the owner said Here, take this calzone home to your dad; beat it. Well, maybe that was Sicilian, then. She started to slip her coat off.

The man took her shoulders, lightly. In sudden fear, she released her thoughts, let her shoulders be smooth. Slightly arched her back and there, he'd taken a lady's coat. He hadn't touched her, really. He took their coats to the coat room. Linda faced her mother, feeling tense. Shelley looked at the mural, as if trying to learn why it was so fascinating. Linda smoothed her skirt over her hips; she cleared her throat. She'd wanted to flee the hospital. Now she wanted to flee Domina's. She softly asked her mom, "Do we, like, know him?" Shelley scanned the lobby for a neighbor or friend. Linda motioned her fingers, No that fly that just buzzed by. "I mean him."

Shelley twisted her mouth; No friend or neighbor, shucks. "Oh. No, I don't think. They're a big family." It was a kiss-off answer anyway; her daughter felt accosted, every time any man spoke to her. Now she was twenty-nine, and it was time to cut the crap. Better yet, change the subject. "This got four stars last year. In the Boston Globe, no less."

The manager returned, quietly remarked, "We had critics up from New York, last week." Shelley was impressed. He walked them into the dining room, past an open lounge. Bauhaus chandelier, concentric rings of crystal; vinyl sofa, blue shag carpet. A wall hung with photos, autographed perhaps. A vintage RCA TV; the cabinet filled the center of the bottle shelf. Color tube installed; the Bruins played the Whalers, live from Hartford's Bushnell. Linda felt an urge, delirious and brief: to stop being female, go ask who was winning, sit and eat pretzels, drink beer. The manager asked, "Smoking or non-smoking?"

Shelley said, "Oh, non, please."—she'd never admit that her daughter sometimes smoked.

Linda fell behind a step, looked around uneasily. The dining room was spacious. *Faux*-pilastered walls, everything in milky blue. Linen-covered tables, all very 1930's. For a Thursday night, the place seemed packed. So far as Linda could see, every male diner had stopped eating—had in fact put down his silverware—to stare at her. She even tried, once, staring back but no, they really were. She vaguely understood that by glancing around, fearful, she looked pretty and preoccupied and so they stared more boldly. She stood near the dining room's center, was the center of attention. *Pretty women never stand around, alone, where everyone can see them.* She could accept that, now—that she was a pretty woman—since it was purely bad. Women stared at her too, and their faces were horrible. She was being hated, judged, dismissed. Her mind held the image of herself, like the effluvium of their thoughts: *dark dirty hair's a mess some artsy tramp oh get a look.* The men were diverse and she knew: *They all like my body, but some of them don't like* me. There were decent sorts who saw that she was uncomfortable, or aware of them, and stopped looking. She felt warmly grateful: *You can look, I don't mind.* Because there were also shining-eyed louts who gaped and wouldn't stop. What made it all so awful was that most of the men were scarcely more attractive than they would have seemed before. She felt locked in a cage full of powerful and perverted beasts. *They all want to get inside me. Deep up into my tummy, and* squirt. *It's like some Clive Barker story—they're all giant bees and they want to sting me, long and deep, again and again.* She felt this mass staring was an outrage, it might make *Hard Copy* and she might be on *Sally*—years from now, when she'd salvaged her life. The manager slowed a step, mindful of his other guest.

Linda was dismayed, because she knew nothing had happened. The manager was taking them to their table, Linda was dawdling behind, a sign framed by poinsettias said the special was prime rib and that was all the news. No one was staring at Linda.

She stood, locked eyes with the young manager. Yes, this *was* Hell and he was Lucifer Who Stared. But one-on-one, it was more about her. More personal, so maybe not as bad. He saw her dark and carnal, warm and tense and maybe she could trust her strange new feelings after all. *If I tell you—I'm uncomfortable, scared—you'll make it better? Somehow? Or . . . ?*

He was only the perfect waiter: a courteous silhouette. He made things happen by themselves—matched customers with tables. His manner stated—not *Well?* nor *Yes?*—but simply, *And . . . ?*

She had a funny way of talking in a crowded room: if her eyes were loud, someone could hear her murmur. The funny thing was that it worked. "Can we be somewhere there are less people?"

This saying pleased him, like he'd bet someone a drink this girl would say those words. His voice seemed to come from somewhere else, the table they were next to, perhaps. "Sure, I've just the place you'd like." She inclined her head, a slow-motion nod, accenting his *sure* and *like.* She held her hand, in jeopardy of wringing it; nervous doves knew only how to fly, you had to wring them. She looked at her mother, her mentor, only guide. Shelley avoided her eyes. Not coldly; she demured. Linda had done nothing wrong exactly but was skating near thin ice. She couldn't begin to imagine where she might have veered off-track. She just wanted to be alone with her mother. The manager led, then presented: *violà.* A blue-and-white appointed cove. Linen on the table, neatly folded milky blue. "It overlooks the terrace." Linda smiled, not at him. Cool colors for a February night. It felt insular and warm, like being buried in snow.

Putting no brake to the Old World charm, the manager pulled out Shelley's chair. Age and beauty before beauty alone. Shelley liked this touch and warmly murmured thanks as she was seated. He pulled out Linda's chair. She looked at it. Her consolation prize. Ignoring him, she sat. Did they want a cocktail?—Linda shook her head, Tell him, no. He told Shelley how the garden was built—mostly how much everything cost, and how it was imported from Naples. Shelley looked at her menu—even *she* was getting tired of him. The manager wished them a pleasant meal, and left.

Shelley said, "Calamari rings. With marinara, Lin: oh boy."

"Are you going to pressure me to start dating again?"

Shelley looked at her daughter. Crinkled her nose: All right, then let's be silly. "I'm sorry, Linda. What?"

She hurried to explain, "It was a question. Just a question."

"Apropos marinara."

"Mom, I was changing the subject. Like we do at home—you, me and Dad. Our minds are full of books. What did Joseph Conrad say?"

" 'The horror.' "—Shelley's clueless guess.

"No: what men find least appealing about womanhood. That it has so much to do with men."

"Lin, you do look warm. I'm persuaded that you're feverish."

"No: I'm fine. I'm strong. Here." She meant to lay her hand over her heart, but paused. She wondered what, if anything, her cleavage had to do with strength. Simply abstracted, at last, she toyed with a curl on her shoulder. Gazed wetly at her linen placemat.

Shelley said, "You should have wine tonight."

Softly, she wondered, "I should?"

"Are you having your period?"

Linda said, "No," without any thought. Derrick knew his wife's cycle.

Shelley said, "As for your question . . . darling, it's called *mourning.* You don't have to wear black for the next three years. But no, you don't have to start dating. My God."

Linda was relieved, so much she felt like crying again. She was free from the scary world of men. Free to be a nubile child. Free somehow to realize: *That's a reason why I married.* She said, "Well, I'm just . . . I don't know." Poked her finger in her cheek. *Simplemente Maria* in her navy blue blouse.

Shelley said, "Oh! Yes, Priscilla." Linda blinked and stared, open to enlightenment. "Nitwit, *Pris.* From Coleman. That's who you got that from."—ogling the ceiling, I'm a ditz. "You two spent more time up in your room, talking about boys, than most girls spend . . . well, dating. Then that business of 'camping out' in the backyard. Your freshman year, I recall. The first two wilderness explorers to pack in *Teen Rave* and candy-apple lip gloss. You called it, 'lip glops'. I remember that evening in August, you saw a snake on the lawn. Your father had to go bring in your stuff, next day."

Linda nodded, rather sternly. She went to Parnell High in Boston, not to private school. "I haven't heard. From Pris. Have you?"

Shelley said, "No. Though it's hardly unusual. I'd lost track of all my high school friends when I was your age. Oh!—did I tell you, they sold their house? Arnie—well, Mister Daigle to you—said he couldn't live with one more golf ball hitting his sliding door. Said, 'All these years, they've been aiming for the TV in the den—I trust the law of averages.' " Shelley shook her head. That old Arnie Daigle—whom Linda didn't know from a Lender's Bagel—was the same irrepressible card.

Linda said, "Priscilla's parents sold their house on the golf course."—it didn't take a psychic to make that deduction.

Shelley sighed, wistful—the passing of an era. She picked up the wine list. "According to today's *nouveau cuisine*, you can order sweet red with seafood. Viola delmonte but it's '92, yuck . . . Oh! let's get a chianti, you wanna? So nice with tomato-y things. Now he promised us a waiter, oh where . . . ?" Shelley peered out into the dining room, ready to happily wave at someone.

"Mom, what's tortellini?"

"Um . . . it's sort of like ravioli, dear." It seemed Linda's peculiar fate—always referred back to Chef Boy-R-Dee. Shelley ordered Florentine scallops. Linda asked for lasagna, not sure what the house specialties were like.

The manager, himself their waiter, said the chianti was out of stock. "We have some nice lambrusco, though—real smooth with the marinara." He spoke to Linda like she'd asked a question, confusing her. "Ours is from sun-dried tomatoes. Somewhat sharper than the more northern recipes."

Linda cautiously said, "Okay," wondering if that was some kind of problem.

He assured her, "The lambrusco's sweet." Smiled. It seemed some tease or challenge. Since her placemat didn't have puzzles or games—at least what he offered her was sweet. Not too funny, since she was cried-out and dressed for a staff meeting, and she really did have trouble figuring out how to clasp her bra. But her mom was right, she should have wine. Something deep and dark in a glass, to scatter her feelings like snowflakes. She looked out at the pond—a band of lunar highlights, blue-lit junipers. She murmured to her mother: Lambrusco, yeah; whatever.

He said, "How 'bout a salad? Nice antipasto; the basil's fresh."

She looked at him. A polite and pleasant ghost, he held his thin blue folder, pen. *Everything's so pretty, still—belladonna, in my eyes.* "I don't want a salad. No."

Shelley then mentioned how good the calamari was, last time. It seemed like she and Linda were playing Nice Girl/Bitch. Linda didn't like this game. She wondered how you quit. His remark on the seasonal vagaries of seafood: "Surf and turf, you never know which" and the melody of Shelley's laugh. He mentioned his wife's cooking, one pro critiquing another. "You measure oil. Wine, you dash. Her, she's got her ways." He stood relaxed, one hand in his pocket—a dandy in no hurry, finding the company pleasant. "Yeah, this past December in Naples—we go each year—town had a run on *angustines*. Brunch and dinner, sautéed and fried. On linguini with cilantro, little olive, that's . . . not *haute cuisine*. Home cooking. But it's nice. I smelled the sea and my tongue got hard." He smiled at Linda, lazily winked.

She nodded, understood. " '*Vidi mare et lamentum.*' "

He blinked, unassuming. "You 'saw the sea and wept.' "

"That's from Virgil, I think."

"It is." He scratched his nose. She'd made perfect Linda-sense; they were discussing her womanhood, she had her own view. Shelley carefully cleared her throat. The manager embraced this cue; Shelley was his idol, after all. She had her choice of angel hair pasta or polenta. She made a face: polenta, ick. Angel hair was fine. Linda got a choice, as well: salad (which she'd said she didn't want) or *soup de jour*.

Miserable with this, her role, she said, "What kind of soup?" and if she sounded like a guy, too bad. Swordfish consummé, with capons. She said, "No thanks," and gave him her menu. "I'm not into fish." So long as they were conversing in cryptograms, she might as well tell him she wasn't a lesbian. She added "Anymore" just to be completely honest. He jotted that, or something else, on his pad and went away. Linda sank her forehead into her palm.

Shelley said, "*Now . . . what?*" like Linda had embarrassed her to death. Linda shook her head. This was her tragedy, her soft-lit anguish in blue-and-white. She didn't have to explain anything.

At last she said, "Mother, that man was an animal. I felt threatened. He stared. He made personal comments. Mom, why are we still here?"

"You're not going to cry again."

She softly wept, "I'm not."

Shelley leaned forward, speaking softly across the table. "Lin, when did these things happen? Where was I?"

"Right here. You let it happen." All right then, she would cry, just like a little girl. "*You let it happen to me.*"

"Lin, nothing you described to me occurred. And you simply must calm down. You've been crying all day and your vocal cords are shot. You're squeaking like Marlo Thomas." Breathing through her mouth, Linda dabbed her eyes with her napkin. "For heaven's sake, that's not a Kleenex." Sub-vocal hiss: "*You're acting three years old.*"

"Mom, lots of women nowadays would feel that was assault."

Shelley was happy, unknowing. "Linda, he was flirting with you. Just a teeny bit, and it was harmless. How these people are. Just a way of being nice. Making you feel pretty and welcome." A coquettish little shrug. "He can flirt with me; *I* won't cry."

The manager came back with their wine and calamari. He poured Linda's wine. It felt so odd, sitting with her hands in her lap while a man served her. She slightly curled her lip. Shelley thanked him warmly, and he left.

"He saw that I've been crying. He knew it was his fault. He thought it was funny. Mom, how do you endure this? How do women—?"

"Lin, eat. Drink. Put something—*any*thing—in your mouth. Okay?"

The women sipped their wine.

Outside the little cove, a grey-haired man in an expensive black suit was bantering with some guests. Just as Linda prayed he wouldn't come to their table, he did. Delighted, he said, "Shelley! Doll, you look like a dream. How's everything tonight?"

Shelley, in her joyful turn, said, "Sal, *hi!*" Her son-in-law was dead, so she didn't say things were terrific. As Linda watched in horror, the man took Shelley's hand and kissed her cheek. Shelley warmed to the affection, her face angelic. They talked about her husband and his business overseas; the man laughingly referred to Lars as "Indiana Jones." Shelley roundly pooh-poohed that: "Oh, he's the most pedestrian excuse for 'Indiana Jones' I can possibly envision." There was mention of a catering to a party some years earlier. Talk of the man's daughter and reference to Linda in the third person. Linda stared at her wine glass, wondering when this would end.

Shelley said, "Lin, you remember Sal."

The man turned to Linda. "How could *I* ever forget." He approached her with his hands outspread. Linda squirmed in her seat. She didn't know what this was, and her eyes became a lovely plea, Please don't. His hands, huge and cold, clamped her cheeks. She was terrified. Her thoughts were of drunken grandfather, man with a belt, youth with a baseball bat. He was talking very quietly, barely asking her attention. His hands left her face but one now rested on her shoulder. Her hair. He was talking to her and *playing with her hair*. She looked at Shelley. Impossibly, Shelley smiled, benign indulgence. Oh Lin, you little attention-stealer. Linda looked at the man, held in his power, pressed into a corner. He still spoke softly. " . . . when you were the little bride's maid? Who gave you the *cannoli*, huh? Don't I remember whose little face that was with the *ricotta* on her lip.

Her lip like a little cherry. 'We've seen some pretty girls, but you . . .' I told you that, remember? Baby, you were eight years old. Who picked you up, that day?" Her fingers touched his hand. She was mesmerized by the connection, mesmerized by his kindness, wanted to hold the connection, was terrified, confused. " . . . for her birthday party. Shell, you were there. This little one asked why the cake was square and I told her it was a Sicilian birthday cake!"

Somewhere off in the distance, Shelley laughed, an accomplice fiend.

" . . . who spilled her little cup of cappucino? Who cleaned you up? Wasn't it the man who said he'd do anything for his little *bambina*. For the little angel in lilac. You were twelve years old. I bet you don't remember."

Gazing at him in awe, she cautiously said, "Please stop? Please leave."

The man's eyes flickered acknowledgment, and nothing more. He understood that women could be frightened, didn't need to know why.

Shelley said, "Inexcusable."

A long time seemed to pass while Linda looked into the man's eyes, and he looked back. He seemed to be telling her something. Some great store of information was flowing into her mind, like an instantaneous up-load of digital code, yet to be unscrambled and deciphered.

She wondered if everyone in the restaurant had stopped eating to turn around and look. They hadn't, of course. She heard the skuttle of plates and the clink of glasses, a woman's laughter, a man's cough. The good old boys in the lounge, cheerful traitors all, extolled the Hartford Whalers as the wonder of the age.

Linda said, "I'm sorry. I really am." The discussion of the Whalers seemed somehow more important than anything to do with her.

Shelley said, "Sal, Linda lost her husband yesterday."

The man broke free of whatever strange stasis had locked him with Linda. "Oh, Shell. Oh, Jesus and Mary. God, that's terrible."

Shelley said, "She hasn't been taking it well."

"Of course she hasn't, Shell. What is there to take?"

"There's no excuse for her behavior."

"How can there be fault with her. I'm the old fool who got in her face. Shell, your dinner's on the house."

"Oh no. I can't. I'd die of embarrassment."

"And I won't? Shell, the waiter lost your bill, *finito*."

Linda had been trying to speak. It didn't seem easy. She was the conversation's subject; she had some nerve wanting also to participate. At last, completely lost, she reached out and tugged the man's sleeve. Shelley saw this, closed her eyes, afraid of what

100

her daughter might do next. The man turned around, said, "Yeah, hon. Yes," as though she'd been a perfect angel, and he and Shelley discussed some other girl named Linda who told nice men to stop and leave.

She said, "I'm really sorry. You were nice, it wasn't you. It's me. Like Shelley says, it's me and only me and nothing else."

He said, "Linda, you don't understand yet. This pain makes you a woman."

She completely spaced on that. This taking away of all she'd been, leaving her a smooth-crotched doll, a grown-up child . . . was something people knew about? It happened, every now and then? Was there comfort and forgiveness for the victim, when it did? A cannoli with one little candle, aw girls are important too? She asked, "Is that what this is?"

Shelley breathed, "This was a big mistake."

Linda spaced out deeper. Being a miss was a mistake. Her father's Y-sperm missed, leaving her XX. Double-wrong, to be a girl. Her mother's fault. But now she could talk to a man, someone in charge. While Mommy could only needle and chide, Daddy had the power. He could make things better, if only she could tell him what was wrong. She knew she was confused and didn't care—logic came up lemons, ever since she woke up in the hospital. She told him, "I got scared. 'Cause women do. Feel helpless, like they . . . like we have no control. We act real weird, do hateful things, just because: you know." She swallowed, like she'd read a book report in school.

The old man looked at her sadly. She'd truly described a woman's heart—her own, at that moment. He was about sixty.

Linda said, "I have a problem I can't tell anyone about." He stroked her hair; she blinked, afraid of fear's return, it didn't and she told him, "Yet everyone seems to know so much about everything. Everyone seems to know what life is all about and what's going on, except me."

"I know. Baby, I see."

She told him, "I'm dark inside," wondering if he could fix it.

" 'If the light that is in you is darkness, how great then is the dark.' " He bent and kissed her forehead. "*Buona nata*, Lin."

He took his hand away; her fingertips slid off. She softly said "*Oh*," surprised to learn that he could say or do nothing more.

He walked into the dining room. Passing the young manager, he made a hand signal and jerked his thumb, they don't pay. The manager—perhaps his son—spread his hands, What did I do? The old man ignored him and both went about their business.

Alone again with Shelley. Leopard eyes and silken verdict. "Wasn't that just lovely."

"Mom, did you ever read *The Wonderful Land Of Oz*?"

Shelley might have sputtered, since this chord change messed her up; instead she smiled. "Sure." She winked. "I read it *to* you."

"Remember when Tip had to become a girl, at the end? And he didn't want to? And the Scarecrow said, 'It doesn't hurt'? That's such bullshit. L. Frank Baum was gay, or . . . ?"

Shelley had come here to eat; spooned calamari onto her plate. Linda looked at what was left. "That's really what they say it is."

Shelley gestured, fork and finger: Something in my mouth. Then "I . . . mm.—think you've by-passed denial and gone directly into rage. You're furious at Derrick for leaving you; you can't be mad at him and so you're mad at me. I '*let it happen to you*'." Linda shook her head, innocent of this. "Not another word. Not yet. No more free forgiveness, Lin. You have to start earning it."

"How?"

"Eat your calamari."

"That's how?"

Shelley dipped a morsel in her sauce and didn't answer. Linda looked at the serving plate.

I'm nothing like your mother.—No; my mother eats.

It seemed like some ominous sacrament. To feed this body and, so doing, admit it was her own. It seemed the final seal of fate.

Fried octopus?

The rings were delicate, rubbery; they were lightly browned, and smelled of the sea. Derrick's mind was ambivalent. Linda's body wanted it. She perched on her seat, a shy cat. She decided, took some. Looked at it, hands in her lap. Mother's patience, like God's mercies—constantly renewed. "Linda, you're not eating. Why?"

"Oh. I'm just not hungry." At once, her lovely eyes went wide with fear. "*Oh no!* Mom, not that! I'm not being anorexic. I don't want attention. I just don't want food."

"Lin, it's never a conscious design. That's the nature of your disorder."

Linda verged on anguish. "But it's *my body* . . ."

"I'm not afraid of a scene, Lin. *I'll* make a scene. I've had it. Linda Meredith, *eat*."

Linda sliced off a sliver with her knife. She dipped it in marinara. *Don't make me play Mother Robin.* A tear fell, ran along her nose as she daintily bit. *All of it. Into your mouth.* She closed her eyes and, silently weeping, chewed.

She lurched forward, hand to her mouth.

Shelley, melting, said "Darling, you're hopeless."

Linda, thinly through her tears, said, "*I don't like calamari.*"

102

8

"I swear you're the only person alive who throws passive-aggressive *tantrums*. —Lin, what on earth are you *doing*?"

"I'm spanking my octopus. *Bad* octopus."

"For pity's sake, use a knife."

Linda got up, stood picking at her blouse's lapel; a bread crumb, one of her own black hairs. "I have to use the *ladies'* room. I *have to* use the ladies' room." She took French leave, walked through the dining room. Let them stare. They were impotent, audited, overdrawn, HIV-positive, hellbound. Men Derrick wouldn't have been impressed with. She went out into the lobby, which seemed spacious and also cold, from people coming and going. The door to winter, opened and closed. The restrooms were near the cashier's counter. A notably odd affair. A manteled niche, like a 1930's radio cabinet. Within, a soft pink light over an amphora filled with blush-white cyclamen. The restroom doors were to the side, she guessed. The arched mantel had two symbols, men and women, really lights; *women* toned and lit up pink, meaning someone could go in. Like a Catholic confessional. The symbol *men* just stayed lit, blue. There were two women, apparently waiting. Linda never heard of this—waiting to use a restroom. An elegant brunette in taupe slip dress, a blonde in blouse and slacks. Each waiting patiently, an unassuming introvert; Linda felt part of something pretty and serene.

The brunette abruptly turned. "Here we go again, huh? Hours of our time. Should we file a class-action suit or what?"

Linda managed a ladylike smile, charming as it was brief.

The manager was behind the counter, talking on the phone. He didn't just not look at her; he positively didn't look. In fact, she realized he wasn't not-looking at *her*; he never looked at women who were waiting for the rest room. She'd never felt so not-there. She heard him talking on the phone, nothing about her.

'Action at the Bis last night': people throwing lasagna at each other. I don't know what you're referring to . . . I said Mom was 'ugly' towards me. No, I said she was la Donna de Milo. *Whenever these avalanche snowballs collide with the train, one of your misquotes is in the center of the wreckage . . . last pagan priestess*

at the Oaks of Avernus, she said 'Who bought all the chianti' . . .
*ready to weep like the fig. 'Laviana's been supplying me for
fifteen years, now who did you piss off'; usual thing, you know,
blaming the victim* . . . *Santino told me 'A la carte; we got it,
here's the price', so you treat that like the finale of* Figaro: *show's
over, everybody laugh* . . . *kid said his wife's cousin distributes.
Boat direct from Naples, right up the Connecticut River like the
morning milk. 'Backyard cows give yellow milk', he said he's got
eggplants in Springfield who show him more respect than this* . . .
*family sideline, nice. Mama's toenail polish on the bottom of the
cask, I said 'Lovely. What if it's mule piss?'* . . . *I don't know the
vintner, he's a* guido.—*You want I should draw you a diagram of
'guido'? Look in Webster's Dictionary, says 'Guido, noun, guy who
grows suave bola grapes in Naples.' Check your Thesaurus too,
under 'Stupid'* . . . *'Dinosaur'. Angelo. We're about to go New Wave
and serve celery juice, you're asking me about Barney* . . . *I love
you too; eat shit. Yeah,* ciao *on this.*

The pink light toned. Linda went into the ladies' room,
thinking *I haven't been in one of these since I was two, with my
mother.*

As it was, she'd picked a remarkable one to return to. The
ceiling was high, the room quite long and narrow. The walls were
faux-pilastered like those outside and (since the outer decor was
blue) naturally had to be imitation pink Italian marble. There was
a three-sink counter, likewise bogus marble, with mirrors over
each sink in lancet-arched fenestrae, like the bathroom was a
Roman *vomitorium* complete with shrines to Vanity. Amazing to
think that, by knocking out an attic floor and using a few
dollars' worth of speckled acrylic, they'd made this look like the
bathroom at the Italian Embassy.

The color scheme and the absence of urinals were the only
patently feminine aspects. Linda vaguely wondered what else
she'd expected.

There was a cloying smell—the juicy-sweet, green-grassy
fragrance peculiar to Hawaiian cannabis. Two women in their
early twenties, hanging out and talking. They might have been
out with parents, taking a Gen-X bonding break. One sat up on
the counter. She wore a leather skirt, white blouse, rose-tinted
glasses like getting stoned in public was a glamorous covert act.
Or worse, a camp nostalgia statement, like wearing a paisley
overall. She was telling her friend, it was literally a proven fact
that New York City bagels were better than those from anywhere
else. Something in the water which affected the yeast. Linda, in
passing, thought this was remarkable if true: God, at the close of
the Pleistocene, melted a glacier into a Westchester County
reservoir of the distant future, telling the angels Allright, in a
few thousand years there'll be millions of Jewish people down
there, let's do the little thing with trace phosphates now, or

whatever. Linda went into a stall. The pantyhose and skirt, which felt like being half-naked, now seemed to involve getting half-undressed to pee. Sitting, she found something wonderful: a confessional feel for real, a twilit sanctum of honesty before God, where evidently women sat looking at the coat hook, thinking Well I'm beautiful *inside*. Tinkle, tinkle little bat was sadly simple, and a lingering tingle brought strange grief: *I guess I need to wipe*. She finished up and went back out. The manager was in their little cove, talking to Shelley. He was sort of blocking her chair in; Linda tried to be nice. "Can I sit here, please?"

He said, "Why sure," just happy to have her back. Pulled her seat out, chivalry redux. "Here's Florentine scallops; lasagna for you."

Hands in her lap, she looked at her food. She asked him, "What's this green thing? I don't know what this is."

"A whole chive."

"All for me?"

He smiled, found that pretty cute. "Mm-hm; it's all for you."

Shelley glanced about; she was innocent of her daughter's behavior, as confused by it as anyone else. He asked if they'd like some more lambrusco, which Shelley promptly answered, No she thought they'd had enough. Linda said, "Oh. Well, just another glass for me, is all. And I ate all the bread. I'm the guilty one, not her. Can we get some more? More butter."

He said, "Wine and bread?"—the welcome mat of Neapolitan hospitality. Like asking for the air you breathe. Serious, she studied his eyes. *Latin, soft and soulful. I should like him, since mine are the same. I wonder why I married me, and not someone like him. Probably because I was adopted.*

I understand his poise—how fragile it can be. How easily I can spoil his interest. In fact—

She said, "I'm sorry if I was cold to you, before."

He glanced at Shelley. Only glanced. No puzzle or surprise to this. A pretty girl who said things just a little out of context, who didn't quite know how to do her hair or put on makeup. Shelley was her keeper and in fact she played the part—gazed at a vacant placemat, simply sad. He smiled, game, at Linda—she was still a pretty woman, even if she moved her lips while reading stop signs. "That's quite all right, Ms . . ."

"Bloom. Like a flower. *Mrs.*"

He said, "I'm sorry if I was . . ." She almost laughed, delighted—he searched a clear conscience, took a pure guess. "Insensitive."

"No, not at all. It's me." She saw her wine glass, close to the blue-and-white crocuses in their blue china vase. Softly lit by sconced faux-candle. She set her saffron garnish by the glass.

Still life. "I wanted someplace nice tonight. I didn't want people, so much." She lifted her chin, listening: the PA's muzak. A reflective piano take. "That's Bernstein's *Maria*, isn't it?"

"That's Bernstein himself; real old track. My mom selects and arranges all our music."

"Oh! I wasn't complaining."

He snorted, a gentle laugh. "I didn't take it that way."

"Anyway, just needing comfort: wine, fake candles, no one in your face . . . it's sort of like with God. You want Daddy to hold you but it doesn't mean you like Him, necessarily."

He observed, "We have our philosophical moments." He gazed into her eyes, fondly amused by what he saw. He liked her, who she was right now—whoever that might be. She didn't know herself. But he'd put her in the moment, made her someone real. And that was the final seal; now she was really only Linda, and she'd rattled no one's cage.

These games were sad and empty, and anyway she lost. Her new life was like an unknown child's doll: nothing in itself, unless somebody missed it. She gazed at vacant linen, absently wondering if she would cry. The manager addressed himself warmly to Shelley. "Enjoy your meal. The other things . . ."

Shelley instructed, "Just the bread."

The manager blinked languidly. A woman was tipsy, no one was embarrassed; Well done, madam. "Thank you." He left.

Shelley said, "I've always liked that outfit. From Lord and Taylor's, right?"

Linda shook her head. Derrick saw the bags his wife brought home. They had script logos so abstract, they could have been cuneiform: Sumerian for *Curse thy God and die.*

Except, in this one case, she knew; said "*Laura Ashley*" and broke down in tears.

As they were leaving through the front lobby, a woman asked how everything was, then joyfully recognized Shelley. She was about Shelley's age, but black-haired and dark like Linda. She wore a turquoise dress with lace-trim halter, puffed sleeves off the shoulder. She must have been proud of her naked shoulders, they were tanned and smooth and sculpted. She wore her hair loose, all over those magnificent shoulders, like she was young and had never been more beautiful. She *was* beautiful. She spoke loudly, gestured freely, had her fill of pride and joy. She enjoyed being herself—didn't everyone? She ruled the world, and laughed.

Linda looked at the statue behind the ornamental pond, and almost said *Wow!*, aloud. The woman was the real boss here, the heart and soul of the entire place. She was Domina. She turned and, mock-amazed, discovered Linda. "Lin, *hi!*" She waited, then smirked. "Oh what, you don't remember me?"

106

Linda didn't dare. "No, I'm just . . . It's nice to see you."

The woman answered sweetly, like the question had been asked: "Oh you know: I'm fine. Things *cosi-cosi*; so-so." Her eyes flared, like beauty was a magic force that knocked you through the wall. *"Did you start your own caterer's yet? You didn't?* After I taught you how to cook?" Scandalized, she gasped. She fascinated Linda and confused her. She was having fun with her life, assumed Linda was having fun with hers. She seemed like she could pull Linda from her nightmare, and they'd go do something fun. Music, food, wine, jokes—everything that Life was all about. Linda glanced at Shelley, a search for guidance that was becoming automatic. The black-haired woman touched Linda's hand: Look at me, not her. She took Linda into her counsel. "You should'a just come back into the kitchen. Lin, I had 'em make a veal cacciatore for *thirty people.* It was like something outta Medici Florence, I swear to the living *God.* We started with two whole gallons of fresh stock. Then I poured a whole fifth of rosé. Like a burnt offering, Linda. *Marone.*"

Though not really the happiest young woman on earth, Linda smiled. She wanted this woman as her mother. She wanted to go home with her, be hers. Home to a big family, a world of earthy jokes and wine and food. Where people understood about passion and beauty. As for this worrisome blonde, Linda cared nothing for her.

Why did Linda want to be an Italian? Wasn't that, like, strange?

No—that was *home.* Irish-Italian neighborhood. Wrought-iron patios. Old Cadillacs with refurbished interiors. Cast-iron fixtures of factories long gone. Old fogies reading newspapers in smoky barber shops. That was home.

The Hood, like all the mooleys say. Where you stand in the street and yell at an upstairs window. Spend the rainy morning in garages, looking for a certain part. That was Derrick's home.

Here was this woman, like Linda herself—twenty years older and impossibly triumphant over Life. Just by standing here so close, being who she was, she . . . reminded Linda who *she* really was. No: the truth was something stranger, more obscure, the woman stood shielding her from some pearly light that *kept her from remembering.*

Lock of hair on muscled neck. Warm hardness under cotton tee. A narrow staircase, pale green paint, and it smells of frying olive oil, Friday fish from Catholic folks downstairs. As long as she keeps talking, I can close my eyes and be myself. Be Derrick, and come home. Up the stairs, I'm almost at the landing. My ten speed, chained to the radiator. The door. Our door. *I hear Dad's voice. I'm almost there, I'm almost home, I'm opening the door and—*

"Lin?"

She opened her eyes. The woman peered, concerned. "You always cry. Anyone says 'Boo' to you, you cry. For a girl, you're an awful sissy—anyone ever tell you that, hon?"

Linda laughed a little, wiping a tear from her eye. "That's what people tell me, I just . . ."

"Did you get a load of Glamor Boy, in there?" Linda shook her head, blinked *yes*—she liked the words, whatever they meant. "My second-oldest son. He ran away and came back, now he's manager. *Thinks* he is. I needed olives, he ran away. A ten-kilo jar of Vesuvius olives, Linda—I had to climb up and get it. Me. Feel this, feel my forearm—go ahead." Linda hesitated, timid; the woman *tsk*ed, placed Linda's hand. Yep, hard—she wasn't strong like that, herself. "That's muscle, Linda. Who needs sons? You feed 'em, raise 'em, they run away. They run away and come *back*. Don't have sons, whatever you do. Have daughters, Linda; girls are cool." She noted Linda's tummy, flat. "What's up with this? Daddy holding out on you? What, you don't feed him right?" Linda lowered her eyes. Something she wanted that someone else gave her—a baby boy, from a man. *But no that's me that's who I am.* —totally confused. "Oh, okay—Lin's embarrassed. Better take her home, Shell." Linda turned and gestured, a child's explanation: That's my Mommy, over there. But the woman was already gone, drawn to other guests.

Linda felt alarm and sadness, that the woman went away. "Will you teach me how to cook? Again?"

The woman tossed a radiant smile—carelessly, over her shoulder, a bridal bouquet for whoever. "Have another party and call me at the caterer's." She winked, one happy-go-lucky girl to another. She was already talking to someone else, bid Linda bye-bye with her fingers. Linda watched the gesture, enchanted by sweet disregard, I love you too now run along.

Shelley touched her hand. Linda went along, lost in her thoughts. Things that ladies did and Linda, strangely, was involved: lip gloss put on, purses clasped, soft coats buttoned. Cold, wet wind. Walk in high heels, *click clack clack.* Shelley said, "We just needed to leave. You were very bad and silly." No malice, it was quite all right: Linda was a puppy who piddled, sometimes. The wind blew Shelley's hair across her face. She gaily answered *"Wooo!"* to the wind, no less a ditz herself. She was like a good sergeant over a squad of nincompoops: not mad at anyone, just wanting to get out alive.

The road up to Merrill was dark, but for the glare of far-spaced road lights. The night sky was overcast; Shelley used her wipers, on and off. The only visible landscape was the silhouette of wooded hills against the ochre glare of distant towns. Pittsfield was over there, somewhere. The hustle and grind of factories and warehouses, powering down for third shift. The world of men, all power and grit and complexity. It felt nicer to imagine that the light on the horizon was from a volcano, or something.

The road ran through pastures, the broad lawn of a distant church on the right. The golf course on the left. A dense stand of spruce, then the left up Longmeadow Road. Woods, a country store; a billboard out in front, such as often advertises COFFEE SANDWICHES. No Maxwell House on rye here, though: *Mesquite chips are in. Cappucino, Cold or Hot.* A fire station, more glimpses of the golf course through the open winter woods. *The Shops At Talcott Notch.* "Adrienne's, Lin. Where that velvet jacket broke your heart, last fall. You felt it was just worlds beyond your reach, in fact I teased you. 'Marrying for love beneath your station—romance has a price.' Well, it was . . . something you wanted to try."

Over a bridge, more woods. Shelley watched the road.

Linda said, "That took nerve."

Shelley drew a breath. "Yes, it did."

"You said so yourself, I've been crying all *day*."

"Because you have weird symptoms. And men are being mean to you. I haven't heard a woman's grief. I've seen a frightened child."

"Mom, that's terrible." She knew she was squeaking, like her mom had said, though she thought she sounded more like Sally Struthers. "If that was true. That he loved me so, and worked so hard, and always thought I loved him too, and he died and I didn't care. If I just went on, and lived my life, and . . . I'm going to cry again." Sorry, she assured her mother, "*Just a little bit.*"

"Oh Lin, you're widowed. Cry a lot," her mother offered dreamily—she'd drift along and drown in that same pool. This time, at last, her daughter's grief was contagious.

Linda put her hands to her face. She peeked through fairy-sparkle tears, saw a road sign, sudden yellow from the dark. A sign which Linda Bauer, growing up, must have seen every day, assuming—if she thought of it at all—that everyone in the world knew what a *Bridle Path* was.

"Lin, wake up. Baby, wake. We're home."

Linda opened her eyes, still full of magic nightshade; the front porch was an idyll out of Tennyson. Oak door under a stone arch, heavy-laden with clematis. Della Robbia fountains overgrown with English ivy. She softly said, "I like this place," remembered that was true.

They went in and passed from Tudor Brittany into the Nineties. White shag carpet; curtain of white Boussac damask, behind which were the sliding doors out to the balustraded porch. Cherrywood revolving bookcase; Easton Press Classics, complete, too pretty to read. The sunken den was floored with copper tile. A Chippendale sofa (white damask, too) and

Henredon leather chairs (white kid) around the central fireplace.

It was upscale, even chic. No way was it classy. Lars Bauer's shade presided: Well praise the Lord, I'm rich. It looked like the cocktail lounge of some snooty alpine resort.

The house had its familiar, pleasant smell. Old lemon-oiled wood, dark coal of fires past. But nothing echoed back and said *Oh yes, it's you; come in.* There was nothing Linda wanted in the fridge, no comfy couch she wanted to flop down on.

The house was not her home.

Shelley found herself blocked by the suitcase. "You're on your own now, kid. Same old place, same old rules. No maids here."

"No housekeeper."

"None of those, either"—a distinction drawn for Linda in her childhood, pointlessly restated. Shelley went into the kitchen. Linda began hearing voices. Answering machine.

She looked up at the spiraled, cedar-paneled staircase. Very woodsy. Ski chalet. The suitcase wasn't heavy, just seemed awkward with these strange, confining clothes. Child's upper body, mommy's bosom—*I'm not made for this.* Not maid enough, unless . . . she leaned a little, sort of used her hip. She was made to use her hip—exactly right. Took the suitcase to the landing, where she looked up at the hallway. *What you said was really hurtful. I'm not sure you should come up.*

nine miles to and from Star Market, pitch black on my bike
They're very pretty. I don't care. You really made me cry

Linda stared up at the hallway.

Those things were said, right here. I don't recall who said them and it didn't matter. She went up, dragged the suitcase to her room. Dark, and the smell of perfection: superfluous cleaning. She switched on the light.

Derrick had been in this room two months ago. Last Christmas. Linda in her long white challis dress, all goofy glee. *See, I do have Melanie. On 8-track.—Melodelic. How much eggnog have you had?*

The room was unchanged. Toys on the bed, all the more poignant for being unloved since her favorites were in their Salem apartment. Bedspread, curtains, Aquatones by Intent: Impressionistic swaths of pastel hues on white.

If they'd had The Lion King back then, I would've wanted it instead.

The green crepe pom-pom pinned to the bedpost.

'Sup with this, were you a cheerleader?—Der, no. Don't touch things, quit it! Oh. You know, they have them now: women's varsity cheerleaders. Girls cheering for girls. I think that's so . . . perverted.—Yeah, we're the last of the Boomers, babe. Let's go down and catch It's A Wonderful Life. See if your dad will be kind and rewind.

The vanity with the dust-covered Maybelline eye shadow kit. The old 8-track player on the dresser, with the tapes in their little plastic carry-case. Unicorn and rainbow stickers on the pink plastic. Inside, the groovy tunes. Melanie, for real. The Carpenters. Joni Mitchel. Cat Stevens. Amy Grant, The Second Chapter of Acts—the gentle music of an evangelical girlhood. Keith Green. Linda frowned. Who the hell was Keith Green?

The little valanced bookcase. Middle shelf, high interest: teen romances. Bought at the Christian bookstore, like cookies from the health food shop. Born-again girl meets nasty boy, leads him to the Lord. Upper shelf, out of reach but not out of mind: inspirational guidance for young Christian women. Glossy blue covers with white birds. *The Lord Is My Shepherd, He Knows I'm Bulimic.*

Bottom shelf, children's classics.

Easter . . . '92. Window open, yellow-green outside. Sitting on the bed, Linda in her peasant dress. The honest child in her eyes, a moment when a lover was a friend. *Der, really? You read* Little Women? *I never met a boy who did. When Beth died, did you cry?*

Richard Gere poster, over the foot of the bed. Derrick never got around to teasing her about it. He'd only been up here a few times.

Linda walked over to the little space between wall and bed. She stood relaxed, fingers interlaced below her tummy.

She softly said, "My *body* remembers. My *heart* understands. Oh, yeah: I *liked* this poster."

She looked; she laxly swayed her hips. She might have been at the Met, viewing a so-so Matisse.

She added, "I don't know. Do I get to choose who I like, at least. *I* think my tastes have matured. The boyish look just doesn't do me. The shag is way too Seventies. Anyway, the . . ."

She poised still, studying the poster.

She ripped the poster off the wall. Calmly methodic, she folded it in half, tore it, put the halves together, tore it again, doubled and tore till the wad resisted her strength. Til she tugged, grimacing fiercely, and couldn't tear it. She turned and softly gasped, dismayed. No wastepaper basket. She walked quickly from the room, met Shelley in the hall.

Shelley looked concerned. "What's all this?"

Linda slightly shook her head. She didn't know.

Shelley answered her own question. "You threw a tizzy in your room and you tore up your poster."

Linda blinked, dreamily; she'd heard this before. The echoes were here, in this hallway.

Mom, my feelings hurt. I lose control. I don't throw tizzies.

—Oh. But you just said you did.

Linda said, "You're afraid of me."

Shelley parted her lips. She studied Linda coolly.

She decided, "No. No, Linda, it's just you."

The word *you* was a leash, yanked to remind her who she was. A whimpering, loose bundle of weakness, need and silly acts. Linda flinched, startled, when Shelley touched her hand. "I mean, to let this go. This paper. Not important. I mean that it's upsetting me."

Linda said, "Wastepaper basket . . ."

"Drop."

She let the pieces fall to the carpet, afraid that Shelley would explode on her for doing as she said.

Shelley didn't detonate; she calmly watched the pieces fall. Saw something else, informed her daughter evenly, "You're wet."

Linda said, "I'm sorry?"—she hadn't heard her mother right.

"You're wet. You've wet."

Linda looked down, then spread the slack of her skirt so she could see. No dark secret of her sex but just a spreading stain, the navy blue turned black. Only now, she felt the warmth.

She said, "I've forgotten how to control it," even as she wondered: *When did I ever learn?*

Shelley was appalled. "Oh Christ, you're *dribbling!*"

The inevitable human response: don't dribble there, stand back and dribble somewhere else. "Lin . . . thanks. Thank you *so* much. I just had the carpet steamed."

Linda stood holding the sides of her skirt. Shelley stared, Your move.

Linda . . .

. . . dipped her hips: a curtsy. Smirked: things happen. Went into her room and slammed the door.

It was something Mindy might have done. Derrick had been told, by another worker at Pinski Place, that Linda often unconsciously mimicked Mindy's mannerisms. Marvelous. Alone in her room, she stood with her back to the closed door, arms crossed under her bosom. Breathing deeply, trying to regain her calm.

Dribbling. She started to undress. The skirt. It seemed like you had to *squat. There's some way ladies do it . . . maybe, sitting—*

She sat on a corner of the bed. Slipped off the wet skirt.

Stood and threw it. She despised it. Girlie-throw, all hand and hip; it weakly slapped the wall.

Calm, her hands went to her cheeks. She closed her eyes. *I'm going insane.*

Why did she *wet?*—that made no sense. Like many people with epilepsy, Linda was incontinent sometimes. But her *petit mals* were indolent spells. Sitting on a sofa, she might slump, limp; her eyelids fluttered briefly. Then, in the strangely sensual post-ictal euphoria, she might spend some moments looking at

112

her hand. Smile, perplexed, at simple questions. In short, her seizures were the exact opposite of tearing up a poster.

She always had a shrill, explosive temper. She only went off on me, because I loved her. Spoiled bitch.

She quickly took off her other things. Stood naked, looking for a hamper. None. No one lived in this room anymore. It was no one's fault, least of all her own. But now that she was a woman, such concerns were her domain—clothes hampers, and waste paper baskets, and knowing where things like toilet paper were kept, and—

She flung open the door to scream for her mother, who was standing right there—her hand still extended to take the vanished knob. The trim, sweet blonde in her black silk turtleneck, no hair out of place and Linda, like some wild brown Polynesian princess—naked as a jay. The most curious thing was that—in their mutual shock—they looked at each other like two calm, intelligent women. They were, after all, mother and daughter.

Shelley gave a gift. Terrycloth robe, towel and panties. Linda took, said "Mom . . ."—she reached out to touch, to forgive. Shelley raised her hands from reach, breathed "No no no, don't touch."

Linda closed the door, stood with her back against it, hugging her things to her naked bosom. She evenly called, "Shelley?"

After a judicious pause: "Hello?"

"Shell, look: this has gone far enough. I'm not your daughter. I don't deserve to be, all right? I honestly don't know how."

From the other side of the door: silence.

"So what I'm proposing is this: that you just let me leave. Now, like I am. Without any clothes, and I'll . . . well, I'll walk down the road. And I'll freeze to death, or get raped to death, and all of this will have a suitably tragic ending. Okay?"

Shelley said, "Oh stop it!" In some strange way, the classic Massachusetts feminine, Eau *staw*-pit, was more imperative than the words themselves.

Linda asked, "Are you guarding me?"

"I'm leaving." No sound attended Shelley's presumed departure; a perfect lady's steps were weightless.

Linda waited, then went out and found the bathroom. Closed the door. Was Shelley really gone? With suicide threats in the air, that seemed doubtful. Possibly the door would open a crack? A reproachful hand reach in, to place a tube of deodorant on the counter? Hadn't she said her adopted daughter tended to smell, because she wasn't white? This was getting really scary, because it came from nowhere. In five years of marriage, Derrick's wholesome, gentle, giggling wife never once said *You know, my mom's a closet fascist.* And yet . . .

Linda herself was a terrorist. One night, in Dorm Two,

Derrick got a message. His wife had called: Emergency: come home right away. Nothing else. He got someone to cover his dorm, then ran to the shift office. Called home, got Lin's girlish voice: *Hi! We can't come to the phone right now and the cat can't lift the receiver! So, if you'd like to leave a mess—*He raced outside to his car. Flew home, running red lights. Home to an empty apartment, no note. Her purse emptied on the bed. Her clown bank broken. They'd just seen *The Vanishing.* The gold egg . . .

It turned out that she'd wanted to buy a top at TJ Maxx, been unable to find their checkbook. Assumed that he'd taken it. His imagined negligence had thrown her into passive-aggressive frenzy, though she came home two hours later—with the top charged on their overdrawn Visa—all tender surprise, pure innocence. They worked it through in their usual way—a brief, fierce fight, then a night of conversation.

Der, I've never told you. But my mother is insane. *She says she never hit me—she hit me* all the time. *She's so strict and irrational, she thinks that feelings now can* heal the past: *make things that happened un-exist. But more than the physical abuse was the mental cruelty. Leaving to go shopping, say, and making it sound like she'd never come back. Or . . .*

Linda turned the water on, found her hand trembling. The temp control was one of those mystical grooved balls—she shivered, then yelped from sudden heat. *Lin would do this, too—threaten to kill herself, then yelp in the bathroom. Like I did just now—not on purpose. Hopefully, her mom will just ignore it.*

She stood under tepid water, washed herself listlessly. The motions brought back memories. Touching, being touched. Making love.

She remembered her man's body. Lithe and heavy. Peace and power, like an iron core. Hard and vibrant, voice deep as his soul.

That body still existed. But it was no longer hers. It was lying in a morgue or something. While she showered in the Bauers' upstairs bathroom—plain and bland and soft, and frightened of her mother.

She closed her eyes, hair slick to her cheeks and neck. She imagined that the water would just wash her all away til she was gone.

She got out of the shower, dried off. Looked for powder, found a bottle of Crabtree and Evelyn lilac talc, paused for an irrational instant: *I can't use this, I'd smell like a girl.*

She wrapped herself in her towel, hoping she did it right. Her boobs were covered, which felt right enough. She went into the hall, and Shelley was right there. Presumably she'd been there all along. "Lin, suicide threats are not a way of expressing yourself. They're a gravely serious—"

"Mom, that camisole is in my suitcase. I don't think I should wear it. I don't want to."

Shelley fluttered her lashes; they were off one important subject, on another.

"I wonder if I can . . . borrow, like, one of Dad's shirts."

Shelley seemed to ponder a reply. She answered gently. "Your father's going to call you, Lin. As soon as he possibly can. You still have your father, dear. We don't wear Daddy's things."

"Then I should have a . . . nightgown. Plain one."

Shelley said, "Wait here." She went into another room (her bedroom?—Linda didn't know). She came out with a folded garment. Cotton, white. No lacy shit, or anything. Linda took it, went into her room.

It *did* have lacy shit. Puffy little sleeves and it was low-cut, or whatever, so it showed her cleavage. With a little satin bow.

She went downstairs. The lights were off in the living room. The sink light was on in the kitchen. How often had it looked this way—to a son-in-law, a guest? How often had they spurned the guest room's single bed, camped out with a mattress and quilt before the dying fire?

Making love, she'd whispered once: *"Der, this feels so naughty. This is where we used to play Boggle."*

Now it was empty, silent and still, and something terrible was about to happen.

She heard Shelley in the kitchen, quietly talking on the phone. Linda stood and listened, waiting tensely through the "Yes"s, the "Mm-hm"s and endless silences.

Yes, I know all about that. I've done bereavement counseling. Near-strangers, older than myself. This is my own daughter. Shelley's voice wasn't hushed. It was composed, like she was doing her pro gig *now*: talking to some devastated lady at her church. *But what do you call the hostility? . . . that* I'm *hostile? Edna, I really don't think . . . I'd tell you in a minute, 'Look, I'm furious at Linda' . . . am I grieving. For my daughter. As in, vicariously?—or like I might lose her. I don't know which you're . . . No. This is way over the cuckoo's nest, even for her. . . . Like: this house is not her home, I'm not her mother. . . . Oh yes, in those exact words: "I am Derrick."*

Frightened, Linda turned away. Hand to her cheek, she silently mouthed the words *It's not my fault.*

She passed through the dark, softly walked the upper level of the room. Darkened bookcases, glass-framed paintings. They seemed like priceless things in a museum, since she couldn't really see them and didn't recall what they were. A false hearth, mahogany, tennis trophies on the mantle. Lars Bauer, the Great. One little statue had lost its racket, like the player had thrown it to the ground—the Golden MacEnroe for being a shitty loser.

She spun away, wringing her hands. Her eyes roamed the

ceiling, lovely in fear, and she thought: *I'd rather be Linda and just plain crazy than me trapped in her body.*

Our Father Who art in heaven how are girls supposed to pray the same? You're still my Daddy? Help me somehow can You please—?

In the kitchen, Shelley gasped—she was sharing compassionate insights with Edna, who was evidently thick as a post. Linda poised in the darkened living room, pulled from her prayer by her mother's voice—another force to be reckoned with. God was high and Shelley was near. *Fine, she's blaming me—why is my 'defensiveness' the issue? Edna, she can blame me for Hurricane Andrew—I just want to* know. . . . *No: she's perfectly adept at sharing her feelings. She needs* intellectual guidance, since she gets things so tangled in her mind . . .

Linda stopped wringing her hands. Bowed her head, closed her eyes, hands upon her thighs—unconsciously an icon, Maiden In Prayer.

Father, I don't know why You did this to me. Why I'm my wife, standing here afraid in her parents' dark living room. I don't hate You, I'm just scared, and I'm asking for Your love if You still love me. If daughters get any favor, or . . .

If it was an hallucination, it was vivid. The amorphous yet ponderous Hand, a cloud of dark by night; it touched her hair. Caressed her cheek. She held back tears and nodded, Yes I'm blessed.

Turned quickly away; she found herself at the sliding glass door. Her hand moved the curtain, the heavy damask, revealing winter night's cold glass.

It was totally dark out there—nothing but a wooded slope, a pasture empty for the night.

One night, two winters past, Derrick asked about the cows. Were they out there now—just standing there in the dark?

Linda peered, delighted by a flake—a look she knew well, since she often received it.

Lars Bauer was six-foot-two, originally from rural Iowa. When his daughter said something daffy, he'd hang his chin and beam her with a grin, pleasantly amazed by the oddest little girl who ever wandered off the farm. Also, when Derrick and Linda came to visit, he'd stand on the porch and shout "Hello!" from thirty yards away. It seemed that out in Iowa, people were a wonderful rarity.

She'd told her husband, "No, you ditz, not in *winter!* You bed cows in the *barn!*"

He'd been amazed in turn, by a random observation: a stray bit of New England farm-sense had filtered into her genteel world, the natural consequence of growing up at an RFD address.

She touched her palms to the frigid glass; she faced her dim

116

reflection, like a captive facing the wall that confined.

Black-haired girl with serious eyes. She saw what she'd always known—that she was pretty. She felt no pride, because the girl in glass was someone else. Beauty was beauty, all by itself. She wondered whose it was, and where it came from.

She stood away from the sliding glass, holding herself to stay calm. Hugging herself to stay warm.

While in the kitchen, Shelley talked on the phone—a voice in another room, soft and benign and not about Linda.

9

Linda went into the kitchen. She found her body taking its accustomed route, a zig-zag path with pauses to peep, test the water of the room she wished to enter. At that moment, oddly, being Lin felt graceful. Made for quiet meetings. She stood by the table, where her mother sat. Shelley didn't look. "I'll have to call you back." Listened, then laughed. "Oh Edna, please—you're telling me?" Linda's presence was never that important. "Okay then. Mm-hm. Goodbye, now." —Shelley signed off warmly. She'd decided Edna the Obtuse was a wonderful friend, and their talk had been a love feast. She hung up the phone, looked at Linda.

"Mom, it's all right. I know you were talking about me."

Shelley said, "Well, so do I." —she wasn't going to be furtive about it. Busted by Linda—big deal.

Linda touched her finger to a chair. "May I sit?"

Shelley said, "You bet." She winked. She liked when Linda was meek.

Linda sat. She folded her bare arms on the cool rosewood table. "Mom, I feel you're scared of me."

Shelley went prettily flabbergasted—she wanted to be there for her daughter, but this opener was an instant riot.

"You feel there's this stranger in your house. Storming through, livid at fate—"

"That's called *transference*, hon."

Linda stared, impassive. She just wanted to learn what had happened to her, even if the answer was a blasé riddle.

"Lin, you're afraid of *me*. You feel that, by losing your husband, you've somehow failed or offended *me*. Instead of dealing with that, you're switching it around: I am now afraid of *you*. Going berserk in your room, earlier, was *sympathetic aggression*. Acting out my imagined anger, so I would feel your fear."

Linda said, "I . . . don't have any track record of going berserk. I have no history of terrorizing people. I heard about rabies on the news, one time, and I was afraid of squirrels for a month. When I came out of our house on Samara Street, I'd lean out the door and check both ways for squirrels. I mean, come on."

Shelley smiled. "You were always in love with chipmunks, though. Each spring break, home from college, first thing: you had to go out back and 'check the chips'."

Linda understood. This kindly old beauty would not be rattled from her sane, snug nest of how-things-were. Linda could jump to her feet, pound her fist on the table, demand to be heard and taken seriously, and she would . . . just be Linda having a fit.

"Dear, these histrionics don't surprise me. That you're unable to cope with your husband's death, or the loss of a man's love in *any* sense . . . your father didn't give you that skill. No ego, independent of his love. Oh Lin, when you were little. Three and four. Your father picking you up. Saying you were candy, caramel. Your black hair was so pretty. In his mind, you'll always be that little girl, giggling in his face. And in your mind, too." Linda shook her head, less denial than sincere incomprehension. "You'll always be like that, with men—wrapped around their finger. Ego-less but really, egocentric. Since you don't see men as *people*, weak and flawed. You see them as Daddy. God. You don't give *them* a separate self. Oh, it's not bad or anything. You're just a Bauer woman." Shelley noted, superfluously, " 'Your mother's placid disposition; your father's common sense'."—obviously, an old family joke. Like Marilyn Monroe's child by Albert Einstein: her brains, his looks. "Lin, I didn't hear the carpet cleaner going, upstairs."

Linda asked, "Where is it?" Shelley closed her eyes, don't start that shit again; Linda hastily amended. "I mean, I forgot." She watched her mother's eyes, decided it was safe to say, "Mom, adult incontinence is an embarrassing occurrence. I would have expected more sensitivity from someone with your background in—"

"Oh Lin, knock it off. You pee'ed yourself. And no, you did not have a seizure. Like that trip to Montreal when you were, what?—fourteen. You were angry at your father. Kept insisting it was an emergency. The carpet cleaner came out of your allowance." Shelley sighed, wistful. She stood, took Linda's hand. Led her to an upstairs closet, where Shelley yanked out the electric carpet cleaner. Linda was instructed, went to work. Using the circular motion her mom—

She froze, a deer, obedient, feeling her mother's hands on her hips. Shelley's question, soft and strangely distant: "Why are you afraid, dear? Afraid to move your hips? You had a hula hoop when you were little. Just do."

Just . . .

She worked up a lather on the soiled section of carpet. Shelley watched til she was satisfied, told Linda to clean the machine and put it away. Remarked she was sure Linda didn't have "amnesia." Linda said, "Why would I lie, and say that I do?"

"Lin, *I* don't know. This crisis is just blowing you into the Far East. And you *drank* too much. Oh, *Lin*da . . ."

"Mom, I had two glasses of wine."

"See?"

Linda said, "No," rather blandly—she'd learned a woman's *no* was negotiable. Her gaze drifted, down the hallway.

I'm viewing a life that is over, through the eyes of she whose life it was.

One of us is dead, and the other isn't here.

Linda, which am I? Lin, which are you?

Linda, where are we? Where are you?

Shelley tilted her head; she looked at Linda curiously. Her eyes twinkled; she enjoyed games. Her blonde hair curled on her shoulder, a perfect little swirl, like she kept it that length just so it would do that.

She softly said, "Let's go back down. I'll make some tea."

They sat together on the sofa, sipping tea before the fire.

Making the fire was actual work. Something like an ash shovel—an ornamental knick-knack with a brass handle—was something made by men for men to use. And a paper bag full of ashes was something big and massive. Shelley didn't know all this. She scrubbed and scraped on her hands and knees and got mad at Linda for just standing there. Building the fire itself wasn't bad. Lighting it was easy. Now they sat and sipped their tea, ladies after all.

Shelley had changed into her beige flannel nightie. Her hair looked really nice, like she hadn't yanked an iron grate in fury, and been a surly bitch. Softly layered, framing her cheeks and neck—a tress or two mussed, but that was the look. Linda guessed, it must be a *permanent.* . . . since it stayed in place, or . . . ?

They gazed at the fire. Presently, Shelley told Linda to put another small log on; she indicated which one she meant. Linda did as she was told; mother speaks, daughter obeys. But an undertow of resentment—*Has she ever felt a qualm? That she might seem the white mistress, and I'm her little slave?*

—quickly countered by the imagined response: *Lin stop it's too absurd I'm your mother. I love you so much it hurts, Lin why can't you ever know that?*—led to the frightening realization: *I'm internalizing her voice. Becoming my mother. I've got to speak now, before it's too late*—

Linda asked, "Have I seemed masculine?"

Shelley turned her head, regarded her daughter impassively. In firelight, the older woman's expression was handsome and proud.

She said, "We need to talk. Lin, we really do."

Linda knew the moment she had waited for had come. But it wasn't what she wanted, after all.

"Don't be frightened of your *mother*. Linda Bloom!"

Linda, frightened, said, "I'm not."

Shelley said, "Now:—"

Feet up on her cushion, she held her cup in her lap. She carefully dabbed her pinky at the corner of her eye. A speck of soot or something; there, it was out. *Now* did not, of course, mean *now*. *Now* meant *Please stand by, we'll proceed at my discretion.*

"Now: have you 'seemed masculine'. Linda, *God*. Or rather, *when?*"

Linda swallowed; she knew she looked plainly fearful. "Today."

"So . . . *why?* Did you *feel* masculine?" Shelley's voice roamed some airy height of wonder. *Masculine* was too amazing, not a good report. Spotting Bigfoot in the backyard would have been a whole lot better.

Linda lost her nerve. She could only say, or rather weep: "*I'm worried about myself.*"

Tears meant, automatic stop. Shelley sighed regret, and handed Lin a Kleenex. Then remembered the bag of ashes. They had to go out on the porch, by the garden wall. Linda rose and walked, a swift, unconscious errand. Got her bathrobe from upstairs, found sandals in a closet. Interlude, cold mist, a windy February night. *She doesn't have to refute me. I'm doing it myself. Linda, Queen of Sissies.* Back inside, back to warmth and sofa and the half-made thought, *She's* making *me like this*—?!

Shelley savored in retrospect, a connoisseur of her daughter's nonsense. " 'Masculine'. You. It's like, have you 'seemed like an artichoke'—there's no impact. Sometimes you go *boing* and it's just priceless; sometimes, not." Shelley smiled, amused, perhaps reminded of some better *boing*. "But anyway. 'Masculine' *today*. When really, you've been you in spades: timid, anxious, dependent. Clinging to my skirt. So far as manly deeds, I haven't seen them. Not *today*."

"Mom, men get scared too."

"So they do. We're off the subject?"

"No. My . . . mannerisms have been masculine."

"Your mannerisms have been masculine!"—Shelley was delighted.

Linda tried to steel herself. She knew it could be done. She'd seen herself be brave; only her mother was convinced it wasn't possible. "Shelley, come on. You *know*."

"When you used to suck your thumb, I put tobasco sauce on it. I think, from now on, whenever you call me 'Shelley', I'm going to call . . . you . . .—*Hortense!*"

121

"My voice. My speech. The way I talk."

"Well, you're a little hoarse. A little *tense*." Shelley pointed—Gotcha! "*Hortense!*"

Linda remembered their talk in the hospital. "I said that when I was young. That I wanted to be a boy."

"No, you said you *were* a boy. Trapped in a girl's body."

"Like Louisa May Alcott." Linda stared moodily at the fire.

Shelley was complacent—matter settled. "I don't think you need to worry. Not that there's a recommended daily allowance. We fill our worry-quota just by living. Like the salt in food already; we don't need to shake more on. I mean, we have that freedom. To be individuals, in a way men never can. We're not standardized, like measuring cups. Like vacuum cleaner bags should be. A million men in the army have one Uncle Sam, but a woman has only her mother."

Linda said, "It's not that we're 'free'. It just doesn't matter what we do . . ." She fell silent, realizing how she sounded: like a woman, complaining about being one. She knew the tea would get cold, the fire would die, she'd never say she was Derrick again.

"Mom. Do you believe that, within a relationship . . . within a husband/wife relationship . . . something very strange can occur."

Shelley didn't answer at once. Yet she nodded, as if to herself—notions of what this could mean. The den was dark, but for the dwindling fire's amber, ochre light. Outside, boughs creaked in the winter wind. Do you believe in eternal recurrence? Future games, romancing the past? Do you think, so long as there are virgin girls, somewhere there's a unicorn? Maybe not, yet even so, Shelley would have nodded: Yes, she knew what these things were.

"Lin, that question's as broad as the sky. Joint checking accounts can be Kafkaesque, I mean: whatever's your question?"

"Mother." Shelley didn't look, but she was listening. "Mom. When Derrick died. He was holding me. We were both unconscious. Mom, something passed from . . . him. Passed into me."

Watching the fire, Shelley smirked; a spark of interest, quenched. "That's marriage, Lin. Where babies come from."

Linda held steady, patient and calm. "No, we weren't making love. I don't mean my husband's semen—"

"Nor do I, necessarily. A husband gives his wife children. Colds. Opinions. Do you plan to tell me what?"

"Mom . . . I'll just tell you, plainly as I can. Before we passed out on the bed—all my life, until that point: I was Derrick. Derrick Bloom. I was never Linda Bauer. Never Linda, til today."

"That's awful, when that happens." Shelley gazed, serene and

122

precious, at her tea, like she was minding it.

Linda stared, dark girl with a passion; she knew she couldn't simply be ignored.

When Shelley simply ignored her, she calmly asked, "Do you think we'll get more snow this year?"

"I shouldn't guess. Your father's our meteorologist. Why, Lin? Have you overcome your fear of downhill skiing?"

Shelley sipped her tea and Linda waited, watching closely.

Shelley noted, "You were saying something off the wall. I guess you just lost interest. Is it safe for me to rejoin our conversation?"

Linda frowned thoughtfully, circling her fingertip along the glazed mug's rim. It had a squeaky resonance, like dogs somewhere could hear it. "So you think I'm playing verbal hide-and-seek."

"Lin's Secret Attitude. I hate it worse than Twenty Questions—at least I know when you're cheating." Linda was speechless, since Derrick knew that, too—his wife cheated, playing Twenty Questions. Thinking of King Arthur, she'd say "no" he wasn't myth. Insist he was historical. And tomatoes are a fruit.

They watched the fire, burning low.

Shelley gave in; she even sighed. "Oh, all right: I'm intrigued. You're twenty-nine, you've a Bachelor's degree and you feel you can persuade me you're a man. Okay, I'm hooked: persuade away."

Eyes alight, Linda shrugged—so obvious, so plain. "I have Derrick's memories. I do not have 'mine'."

"You said 'mine' meaning 'Linda's'."

Linda froze; the door to truth had not been truly opened. Given two and two, Shelley wouldn't find them four; she'd ignore square roots and quibble on semantics.

"Remember when you were young, and you used to write short stories?" Shelley, then "reminded," touched her head. "Oh—no, that's right, you wouldn't remember . . ."

Linda said, "*The House Across The Glade* was my favorite—mine, not hers. She thought it was naive. I felt that, for a seventeen-year-old author, the piece held deceptive simplicity. Rather like Shirley Jackson, whom she said she was reading at the time. The ending—the mother's note on the bed—was really somewhat haunting."

"Oh, *The House Across The Glade* was self-satisfied kitsch. I liked that autobiographical novel you started. The one you gave up on, since you decided you had nothing to write about."

Linda defended herself—or at least, her other half: "She felt the things that typically happen to girls were not of interest."

"Well, they're not."

"Her husband thought they were."

Shelley was touched by her daughter's naiveté. "You think men are fascinated by women's lives? Like the wonder we feel when we're in love? Envisioning someone's life in all the colors of our childhood? Lin, only girls do that. Men don't fall in love with women, in that sense."

"Sure they do."

"Unfair but simply how men are. Anyway. You found *your* life overwhelming. That was why you wrote fantasy. Such imagination. Yet you could never be bothered with anything so bothersome as consistency. You should have read Mark Twain's critique of James Fenimore Cooper—we have it here, I think, in our *Yale Review Of American Lit.* One of the funniest things Twain ever wrote; no one's taken Cooper seriously ever since. Twain found all these hilarious mistakes—I guess Cooper's editor missed them; putting one character's speech in the wrong person's mouth, or having someone turn into somebody else—"

Linda broke in, furious—a passionate, nubile actress, giving an Oscar-quality performance as a man trapped in her body. "*Shelley, look*: I said 'mine' meaning 'Linda's' for *your benefit, all right?* I'm sure you understood me in that sense."

"Don't assume you're understood. That's why we have language. That same volume, in fact, has Vonnegut's essay on clarity if you—"

"Shelley, *look at me!*"

"Oh. Okay!" Shelley looked and widened her eyes, like a mean big sister. "Oh *Lin*. Oh, shit! I'm sorry, I don't mean to laugh . . . your hair is down for muskrat love. You didn't comb it out after your shower. And you have a ghost of makeup, like you blew off Pond's and just used soap. *Yech.*"

"*No!* Shelley, *I am Derrick.* I—"

She was quiet. She sat calmly. Feet up on the cushion, tucked under her tush, just like her mom was sitting. Tea cup in her lap.

She looked to her left, the room's raised level. A Van Gogh reproduction, psychedelic cornfield, hung over a minimalized, chrome/white velvet slipper chair. Next to a chrome-and-glass demilune with a phone. What did it all mean—you picked up in the den and it was raining auras in Provence?

Shelley said, "Too bad your dad took his camcorder. I'd love to be taping this." She glanced back over her shoulder: Did that connect? Linda was a timid fawn—her mother glanced, she froze. "Like those giddy little skits you made with Pris. Which your dad was never keen on. Said his Toshiba was not a toy but I think it was more that staid Missouri Synod: suspicion of the thesbian. Since it rhymes with something else or . . . I don't know. But you've never had the knack for what you're trying to achieve. Like your stories: dear attempts at 'male perspective'. Lin, you look and sound like an almost-thirtysomething woman,

124

acting like a pre-menstrual teen."

"Shell, my body still exists. It's mine. I want it back."

"Lin, you're whining."

She was, and she verged on bratty tears: "I won't go to its funeral. Cry at my own grave: I won't."

"Lin, your husband's body . . . well, we won't go into that. But yes: it 'still exists'. You say you 'want it back'. Linda, I'm just curious: how exactly is that done?"

Linda stared, a hapless pause. "I'm not sure. Maybe . . . surgery, electro-shock, however they—"

Shelley's voice was like chiffon, in love with all things magic: "Do you think Blue Cross/Blue Shield will cover that?"

"Mom, listen. I wouldn't say I'm Derrick if I couldn't" *you can't Lin you're so unable* "prove it. I can prove it."

Shelley's eyes glowed, feral glee—she only wanted pigtails and a sword. "Oh, cool—*Derrick's memories!* The really spooky part. Should I dim the lights, you think, or—?"—no lights; fire. Oh well.

"Mom, what I'm about to tell you will upset you."

"I'm up for a thrill, Lin. Kick it."

"The time you and Derrick went shopping at Bloomingdale's. For 'my'—Linda's—Christmas gifts. Gold charm bracelet, *Indigo Girls* on CD, Gardenia by Dana—"

"But this is hysterical. You *got* all those things, why wouldn't—"

"I got the potpourri and candle but you said I shouldn't get the fragrance. And I—myself, Derrick—said 'What, is your daughter just this bottomless pit of avarice?' And you said, 'Yes, and I'm the constant yellow ribbon staked around her.' We had lunch at The Nines, across from the Hancock Building, and I saw the black half-slip you'd picked up in lingerie, you moved it and said, 'You're not supposed to look inside a lady's shopping bags.' We talked on the phone that night, your husband was away on a seminar, you were in bed with a glass of dry sack, watching *Melrose Place*, I asked if you were wearing the slip. You didn't answer, so I'd feel embarrassed, then you said 'If you liked it that much, buy Lin one.' Then you said, 'Oh no, she'd spoil the fun—she'd say "Yes! Yes! I'm wearing it right now!" ' and you laughed. Then—"

Shelley turned, an alluring pose, voice casually soft. "I honestly think that's quite enough."

Behind them, in the flickering shadows, the grandfather clock lightly toned the half hour—a vibrant note yet dulcet, Halfway There in D minor. Linda frowned softly, looking down into her tea. The dark round pool of warm cinnamon scent, the cup within her lap.

Shelley gently explained, "You're getting too upset."

Later, she resumed. "Telling you those things was simply

125

wrong of him. It was hurtful to you. And this anger you're feeling is a part of grief. Remembering how the loved one was sometimes . . . well, not just less than perfect. Actually nasty, really mean—as all of us, only human, are. Anger is a *pause* from grief—it's the heart's analgesic . . .

"Lin, my father always told me I would grieve when he was gone. He believed it; so did I. Lin, hate is *so* much worse than grief. And it wasn't just the obvious—the stereotypical, you know, German father/dictator thing. Not the hitting and yelling and insults, though of course we got those too . . . it was, well: drive-in movies. Were 'rutting fields'. Convertibles were 'seduction wagons'. Christ, the Beatles were '*Negro jazz*'! It was *that*, the obstinate stupidity, the trudging through life like a blindered horse, determined not to see or know what . . .

"You try to remember the good. You make yourself. Remember Christmas mornings, the millions of presents. Oh Lin, how we believed in Christmas! Treasures poured like water, all we asked and more. I mean, we weren't that rich so you just knew . . . I mean, I wondered . . . felt that he was buying my love for another year . . ."

Shelley, in profile, gazed into space. Her lips slightly parted. Her eye wet and pretty. A tragic beauty, lost in the past.

Linda watched her mother, tense. She'd just proven, past any doubt, that she was Derrick. Shelley was stunned, but essentially convinced. As soon as she got over her shock, the conversation could finally begin.

Instead, Lin finally realized that her mother wasn't stunned. She wasn't even thumped. She was thinking about something else. Her mind had wandered off the topic.

Alas for Linda, it wandered back. "You've described your problem. I said I would help you with it, and I will. I said that if you fell apart, I'd be there to gather up the pieces. Now here you are, sniffling and pouting and saying you're a man. So."

"Mother . . ."

"You asked for this. Now: . . .

" . . . Hon, are you cold? Move over here." Shelley patted the cushion on her right—her firelit side, warm and golden. Closer to warmth, and to love. Or if any doubt remained: "If you want to lie down, Lin. Your head in my lap. You know Mommy makes a nice pillow. This doesn't have to be a fight. It never does, with me. Here, babe—lie down." She patted her hand on her thigh.

Linda was cold, and apprehensive. Arms crossed, she rubbed her shoulders. "I'm all right." Her smile, brief—Thanks anyway.

"Dear, if it wasn't so morbid, this hyper-empathy with your husband would be sweet. Like Catherine in *Wuthering Heights*."

" 'I don't love Derrick. I *am* Derrick.' " Linda couldn't believe this. "Shelley, I am not Catherine. I am not Jo Marsh. I'm not like any woman. *I am not a—"*

"Oh, did I mention? There's a Tom Cruise flick on Pay-Per-View. Your heart throb and mine. There's microwave popcorn, we can have . . . well, not fun. But this doesn't have to hurt so much."

"Pay-Per-View. Popcorn. Have you any idea what you're saying?"

"Oh Lin, I do. I honestly do. Offering alternatives: I'm so sure it's right. Because I'm able to address this, Linda. Linda, really: I am."

Linda said, "I'm not delusional."

"Fine. This feeling you're having is real. The *feeling* is real. The rest of it's crap and I need you to meet me halfway. Okay? I need you to agree that it's something which needs to be fixed."

Linda said, "*I* have to be fixed. Like a cat. Neutered."

Shelley looked at Linda's lap: nothing there but a tea cup. Linda shrugged: she might be spayed but that was quite beside her point.

"Lin, you know . . . there's only one thing more pathetic than a man trying to be a woman. That is, a woman trying to be a man. A wolf in sheep's clothing is contemptible. But a sheep in wolf's clothing is fatally presumptuous as well. Lin, why don't you want to be a woman?"

Linda answered calmly. "I don't feel bad or strange. I'm not ashamed or angry. I'm just not who I'm supposed to be."

Shelley touched her fingers to her lips, deciding what to say.

"Um . . . here goes: you're mad at God. He took your man so you're saying, 'Take me too. Take the part of me that hurts'—your womanhood. Which would be . . . something I've never heard of. But I guess it's within the spectrum of human feeling. Anyway, it's not an option. So far: do we agree?"

"I'd like to choose my own words."

"I get tired of repeating myself real quick." Shelley waited two seconds, got tired of waiting too. "Lin: okay. Tell me who you are. I'll give you a clue: not Derrick."

Linda couldn't get her voice above a murmur. She licked her lip, like that might help. "I can't admit that. It's not true."

"Then your problem requires professional care."

Not advice. Not assistance.

Care, for which you pack a suitcase.

Shelley stared at the fire. Head lowered, gaze stern. All right, rushing the quarterback didn't work so she'd . . . shoot him. "Lin, tell me who you are. Oh, it's easy. You did it in fifth grade, in front of a hundred people. The Coleman Spelling Bee, and you up on a stage—so happy, so proud. In your pinafore and Mary Jane's. 'My name is'—you say it, dear. 'My name is'—now you. Oh: and you have to believe it. Like I told you that night, when you were so nervous: believe in your*self*. Really and truly.

127

If you don't, then people will know. *I* will know. And this conversation will have been meaningless."

Shelley turned her head. She looked into her daughter's eyes. Her own, though ever serene, were shockingly lovely—cold and clear. As though gazing into the fire had transformed her. Astral transfiguration, lycanthropy in reverse—from mortal woman to angel of light. "You've never been able to lie to me, Linda."

Linda watched her mother's eyes. Nothing else seemed real. The room around them was a theater set, vague and minimal props. The wind outside was some cheap effect, and beyond the wind . . . there was nothing. The winter forests of Merrill, Massachusetts, black and grey and if a tree fell, no one heard it.

"Lin, tell me who you are. It's a snap. There's nothing for you to stop doing, or do. It's already done. You're already you. Choose love and acceptance, Linda. Tell me now."

Linda had been crying all day; she cried again, fresh tears. "But it's too hard. I'm not Linda. If I'm not Derrick either . . . *I'm not here.*"

She didn't know who said that. The room itself had vanished. There were only her mother's eyes, amber truth in firelight and shadow.

Shelley gently said, "You can always just . . . believe me, right? I told you to eat your asparagus. And not to leave your stockings over the shower curtain. I haven't steered you wrong yet, have I?"

Linda stared. Her lips formed *No.* Shelley never steered her wrong. She wasn't Derrick. Wasn't Linda. Wasn't there at all.

"If I tell you the truth . . . and it plainly is true, and it makes clear sense . . . will you believe your mother? Lin?"

Linda's hands went to her cheeks. She stopped; she looked. She *knew* these hands. Her hair, black on her white cotton gown . . . *Hers not mine I'm not—*

"Linda, listen closely. Closely as you can. If you're someone who is dead, and you're not someone who's alive, then . . ."

who ate all the frozen yogurt who gave you the cannoli when did these things happen Linda where was I where are we—

" . . . you're a ghost."

"Mom, I don't want that. Shelley. Mother. Mommy. *Mommy!*"

Shelley flinched, unnerved. "Baby, *shh.* I'm here."

"Mommy, I don't want it! *Mommy, take it away!*"

"What *do* you want? Baby, tell me."

Linda was aware—but only as from a distance—that she clutched at her mother's hands and arms. That Shelley—though herself afraid—gently disengaged, removed her daughter's hands, tried to place them in her lap. And Linda saw the truth at last: *She's the only one who knows me. I'm special, different, epileptic, I'm adopted and bulimic and she loves me, only her.*

"Tell me, Lin. What do you want?"

She scanned her mother's eyes, as though in desperate fever she would find the answer there. Her mouth formed words, half-thoughts; she blinked, and searched some more until . . .

She remembered. She *did*! It all came back—in a twinkling, in a flood. Coleman School, she saw it: grey stucco walls, ivy grown. Lunch table under an oak, a lake of cool-dark shade in sun-bright lawn. Strewn with yellow oak leaves on an autumn afternoon. She saw the stone sign, the planted mums around it. She remembered riding in the chartered school bus every day. Driving through snow, too warm inside the bus. She remembered what she brought for lunch—peanut butter and honey on sprouted wheat bread, an apple sauce, a granola bar. She remembered her lunch box—Charlie's Angels, and being teased about it, *Oh how totally juvenile*. She remembered what she wore: blue and violet dresses, white stockings, patent leather shoes. Because her mother wouldn't let her wear jeans or pants. Her hair back, with a barrette. Friends who said *You'd be so pretty if* . . . She remembered people, everyone. The teacher she adored, the boys she liked who never talked to her. Priscilla—duh?—and everyone else. How did she ever forget?

"Lin, tell me: what do you—"

"—want to marry a man just like Dad. To be a mommy, just like you. To have a baby, a d-daughter, I want to name her Shelley. Sheila. Lynn. I want to live in a nice house in the suburbs no cows country and bake pies all day I want my daughter to make pies with me make a snowman help Daddy pick up pine cones want to work in human services help people *help me people help me—*"

"Are we ready for more tea?"

Linda couldn't see. Because her eyes were crossed; she stopped crossing them. Her wrists were held, as though she were a child. As if Shelley were some calm and gentle judo expert. Shelley was delighted/amazed, like she'd never seen her daughter so lovely or so scary. Linda was out of breath, still gasping softly, "*heh* . . . *peh* . . . *mm* . . . w-wha— . . . ?"

"I asked: are we ready for more tea?"

Shelley slightly nodded; Linda mimicked, confused.

"More . . . tea. Yes."

"Hon, I'm sure that wasn't a complete sentence."

"Yes, more . . . tea. Make. Me."

She stood, her expression stern and alert—a dark, pretty bird, aware of her surroundings, and without a clue what anything meant.

Shelley gave Linda her empty cup. "My honey's in the cupboard."

Linda turned. Her own cup was on the sofa, spilled. Dark stain on white damask. She faced her mother, calm. "Messy girl.

Bad."

Shelley gazed at her, thoughtful. With her master's from Harvard Divinity, she was able to at length say, softly, "Terribly."

"I'll clean it up. I know where things like paper towels are kept."

Linda stood and stared and didn't know where things were kept.

Shelley crinkled her nose. "I'll take care of it, sweets."

Linda took both cups. She went into the kitchen. She eventually found things—tea bags, honey, kettle. Spoon. She spilled. Paper towels. She turned and turned, saw blue and blue. The Bauers' "Chinese" kitchen, hand-painted sketches onto blue marble, walls and counters, an azure-lacquered fantasy and also just a kitchen with a Norman Rockwell calendar, a Brillo box, a James Beard book. She'd seen it all before. A dozen times at least. She hadn't sat here as a child, a thousand mornings of Fruit Loops and sliced bananas. She didn't know what other rooms were in this house, if any. She didn't know if there was a second floor, or if the house was a ranch with only one floor, or if it was a high-rise with twenty. Nothing was real, nothing had meaning, except for the woman who wanted more tea. Linda opened the refrigerator. Milk. Behind a crystal decanter, full of salad dressing. Separated—clear oil on top, the spicy crud on the bottom. She put the decanter on the counter—she thought. Let go before it touched, and it fell onto its side. The glass stopper fell out, the stuff spilled all over. *Oh Christ you're* dribbling. She miserably cried "*Oh shit!*" She got more paper towels. She wiped the counter. It still was greasy, smelled of aged cheese, winey vinegar. She looked down. Night gown. A normal, comfy thing to wear and she knew she hadn't wandered through this kitchen on a thousand sleepy mornings in a night gown. She knew she'd never worn a night gown before, at all. *Camisole. Blue. Are we drunk? —No and if we were that wouldn't explain what just . . .* Her brown feet, toenails still flecked with old polish. A puddle of viscous scuz, specked with dill and oregano. Like a fevered person roaming from their bed, she had a random thought: *Good thing I spilled this; someone might have eaten it.* Like a girl who's made a boo-boo in the kitchen, she got down on her hands and knees. Wiped with the paper towel. Hair in her face, tangled black before her eyes. Wiped and wiped but the floor was still greasy. She got dishwashing liquid, a sponge. Cleaned the floor, then the counter. Washed out the sponge, then scrubbed out the soap from the tile floor and the counter.

Weeping quietly, she made her mother's tea. She also made more for herself. Her mother told her to, or something—she didn't exactly remember. She just knew she was supposed to come back with two cups of tea. She did, her last steps swift—her chore was complete, she could talk again. Shelley took her tea. Said "Thank you, dear"—broken-hearted tenderness. She'd understood, all along, what an ordeal it had been, to simply make the tea. It was all part of the discipline, the cure. Linda sat next to her mother, took her hand. Shelley was calm but not relaxed; her daughter was still in the stratosphere. "Linda. Dear, what—?"

"I was always a girl? I was never a man? I im-m-magined it?"

"Oh! Well then yes; I suppose. If you thought you were a man, that was something you imagined."

"I'm a woman who dreamed she was a man? Dreamed a whole life, but it's over? Ghost?"

"Ditz."

"Mom, it was so beautiful." Linda smiled through her tears, curls damp on her warm cheek; her fevered eyes hopeful, what was lost could be remembered. "To have been a man, and lived a man's life. To have grown up like my father, learned all those deep, hard lessons. To have loved a woman, been strong and brave. Mom, *it was so beautiful.*"

Shelley shook her head in gentle wonder. Beautiful, an awesome dream—she doubted no word of her daughter's report.

"Dear, Mommy's . . . me; I'm just like you. Whatever it is, that makes us Loenat woman. Bauer women. To believe our Father in Heaven's like our daddy here on earth. To think we can have anything, believe and make things true. So long as we are daughters, and accept—we will receive. Be it ever so silly or even strange . . . anything we want, Lin. Anything at all."

Shelley looked at her lap. Linda obeyed, she lay on her side, her head in her mother's lap. She looked at the fire, while her mother stroked her hair.

Shelley began quietly. "Dear, often in pastoral counseling, or in any kind of counseling, you find instances where people have fabricated memories. It's something so common that it's hardly even abnormal. Older people, especially—they do it all the time. They take something they've heard or been told, another person's experience, and they dwell on it. Their imagination works and they envision—they see the whole scene in their mind. Later, they honestly can't remember whether they imagined this event or they actually experienced it.

"Lin, for you . . . this day has been long. Like a whole life, and it's been life without your husband. And you think, in anguish, this day is your whole future. Like when you thought they wouldn't let you out of the hospital. You don't believe in the future, hon, you never trust in what will be. You fix on the moment, like when you have your *petit mal*s. You see an instant neverending, a second hand which doesn't turn. This once, you wouldn't *let* the second pass. You wouldn't let your husband go.

131

He wasn't gone—you 'were' him . . ."

Shelley couldn't keep the laughter from her voice. "Oh Lin. Nice try, at least . . ."

Linda gazed at the fire. Her expression was prettily vacant. She knew where she was—26 Longmeadow Road, her home. She couldn't remember much about it. She felt like a visitor or guest; like she'd only been here seldom, and never stayed here long. She knew Shelley's voice; they were friends. Shelley could talk to her, on an on; her words solved Linda's problems. Her words did all the work, all by themselves. Just like a dryer. Linda's thoughts, like tumbling clothes. Warm. She watched the fire, gently nibbled at the knuckle of her thumb.

In the upstairs hallway, Shelley said, "Don't open your window, if you're hot. Please, dear: use the thermostat."

Linda said, "Like how I drove you crazy. Those summers home from college. When I opened the window with the A/C going."

"Well hon, *I* did the Wild Thing. Your father just turned off the A/C. He skirted your whole realm, like some tender spring garden. Since I was the Punishment Lady. He was strictly the Goodies Guy."

Linda said, "My eating habits made you crazy too. That first summer home." *quick math* "'85. I kept bringing graham crackers and Fluff up to my room. Because I did that at school. I was afraid to eat with five hundred kids in the dining hall."

Shelley rolled her eyes. "I wanted graham crackers and Fluff banned by Federal *law*. You and that old Rainbow got acquainted."

Rainbow what in the world does she "Vacuum cleaner."

"You go, girl. The first time I made you bring it upstairs, you had a complete fit. Called me a 'bitch'. Oh dear, that time you 'fell'? When you and the Rainbow 'slipped' down the steps and you shrieked, like you'd been killed?"

Linda smiled politely, confused. "I was . . . difficult."

Shelley didn't care; she was long over the Rainbow. "It was sort of my fault."

Linda slightly shook her head. She didn't understand why her life seemed dim and hazy, like a story someone told her long ago. But she knew you didn't call your mom a 'bitch', no matter what.

Shelley said, "When you were one year old. So tiny and thin, but you already had your little head of black hair. When you got into things, when you messed, I . . . punished you by making you walk."

Linda stared, vacant as a dreamer. She was a woman, had views about childcare. *Punish by making you walk*—it was either good or bad. Linda didn't know which it was and couldn't even guess.

Shelley said, "On my knees. I held your hands." She posed, hands out, wrists bent—a spritely mime. "Walked backwards on my knees and drew you along. You hated it. You cried. I honestly thought it was harmless, Lin. I thought I was mixing discipline with movement training, and . . . well, you're not supposed to do that. I was young, Lin. I was little more than a child myself. But it made you see movement as punishment. It made you prefer to sit. All day with your storybooks; I praised you for being docile. Linda's sitting, reading; everything's all right. Paper *au pair*. Then the ballet class, because I wanted to make up for . . . Lin, *I* had to take gymnastics when I was young. I thought, ballet: tutus, slippers, piano music. I didn't believe your stories about Mona. Ms. Malchinski. Dance Nazi—please. I thought it was just you."

"Can I ask a silly question?"

Shelley said, "Runway's clear."

"Are you sure it's me? I'm me?"

Both women had to laugh at that, however weakly, fearfully.

Shelley said, "Well let me see." She held Linda's cheeks, gazed into her daughter's eyes. For a moment, Linda thought *She's really looking.*

Mother's eyes widened, mirroring her daughter's fear—not afraid herself, just showing Linda how she looked. "Stop? I'm looking. There: I see. I see *Lin*da," she teased. There was music somewhere far-off in her voice; Linda listened for more. Like the Romper Room teacher, with her magic looking glass. *I see Bobby, and Cindy, and Pete . . . will she see me too?* "Yes, I do see *Lin*da. I don't see anyone else."

Shelley stepped back, gave her daughter's body a critical look, down and up. *She thinks my thighs are big, too. It isn't bad, or . . . she's just wondering* "What will you wear, tomorrow?"

Linda blinked, *Please don't ask me*, since that was too hard. Shelley took her cue, her daughter was unable; stepped towards her bedroom, then glanced back. "Come along?" Again, that music through her voice, that unheard, magic brook. Linda followed through her parents' bedroom. Pearly satin, things so white. The queen-size bed with cream brocade spread. The white shag carpet, chrome/glass vanity. White oak dressers. White Asian lilies in Vogel crystal. Linda now was sure. *I can't be a man. I can be* with *a man. That's what I want.* That was a sane and grown-up thought.

Shelley opened her closet. "Here, choose anything you like." She cleared her throat meaningfully. "From the left-hand side."

Linda glanced at the right-hand side, wondering why it was wrong. Evening dresses, formal suits. Black fur under plastic. Unenlightened, she looked left. Casual daywear. A white, black polka-dot dress. Elvis lives. She was supposed to choose. "This." Her mind made some connection; she didn't wait for her

133

mother's okay. She took the dress. "This was mine."

"Well, obviously. It's a black-haired girl's dress."

"I stopped wearing it . . . before I met Derrick."

"Right, you left it here when you went to look for work in Boston. I wore it for cleaning. What bra size do you take?"

Linda smiled, vacant. "Bra."

"Your size. Perhaps you recall."

Linda fought back panic. The white room was too pretty, pure—a court of heavenly judgment. An angelic being asked her bra size, and she didn't even know what sizes they came in. *Why not why not why don't I know?* Linda held steady, calm. *You don't believe in the future. You never trust in what will be but I do I do know God will tell me why* her mother disapproved of *going braless.* Linda did a lot around the house and went out with a coat when it was cold, No bra so what. Her smile held—uncertain, polite. "My size."

"I'm sure you know."

"If I" *reach back reach deep with all my might I'll remember* "don't breathe I can squeeze into your 34 C."

Shelley was enraptured. "Here we are, borrowing clothes. This morning you were unconscious and I thought you would die. Lin, our God is wonderful. Don't you think so too? I want to tuck you in. Is that all right? Or it's too silly?"

Linda smiled, her adult smile. Her grim Here,—you-get-one-of-these. "You wanna tuck me in, Mom? Sure."

Shelley tucked her daughter into bed. Smiled down, benign. "Baa baa black sheep." She brushed Linda's bangs from her forehead. "Have you any wool."

Linda asked, "Are you going to sing to me?"

"Oh, I suppose. What should I sing?"

There was, of course, one answer.

Linda stared calmly up into her mother's eyes.

tell me please God tell me please God tell me

"*Come to the church in the wildwood . . .*"

"*Oh come to the church in the vale/No spot is as dear to my childhood/As the little brown church in the vale.*"

That was it, token sing; they were two grown women. Shelley kissed her forehead. "Lin, goodnight."

Linda breathed back, "Goodnight."

Her mother turned off the light, left and gently shut the door.

Linda gazed up at the wall, at the faint square of light from her window. She thought *I lay like this a thousand nights. I'll just think thoughts like I did then.* She lay and had no thoughts at all and next she was asleep.

10

Linda sat up and looked out the window. It was snowing, very hard, and everything outside was white. She sat cross-legged in bed, motionless for a very long time. She watched it snow.

She imagined it wasn't cold nor wet. Warm and dry, like cotton. She could go outside and lie on her back and the snow would cover her up. First her body, then her face. But her eyes would still see, flakes falling from above like a box of magic spilled in Heaven.

Later, she got up. She saw her wet clothes from the night before, just dropped on the floor. Some scary lady had a tizzy. But that lady wasn't here, today. Linda took the clothes out to the bathroom. In the hamper. There.

She went back to her room and undressed. It surprised her, a bit, to find she had breasts, and hair under her tummy. *Like Mommy. But I'm too little.* But no, she was all grown up.

She folded her night gown. She put it in her empty drawer, pausing to sniff the vanilla almond of the scented paper liner.

She found her white black polka-dot dress. It was really a big girl's dress. She kept the panties she had on, didn't touch the hose and bra. They were for the scary lady who threw her skirt at the wall. Linda dressed and went downstairs.

Shelley was sitting at the kitchen table in her beige flannel nightie. Linda felt a warm glow of excitement in her tummy, which grew even warmer as her mother looked up. Her mother was so beautiful. And Linda had dressed all by herself.

Shelley said, "Hello, precious."

Linda walked into the kitchen. "See?" She pulled at her skirt, let herself turn in a circle—light as a feather, she knew how from ballet. The skirt swirled lightly about her hips. "All by myself."

"Lin, are you all right?"

Mommy wasn't mad. She wasn't worried. Mommy, herself, was all right. Linda said, "I'm fine." *Talk like a big girl.* "Why do you ask?"

"Oh, nothing. Don't mind me. I just had a sudden vision that you'd regressed to infancy, or something. A mother's nightmare."

"Mom, I'm hungry." Linda looked, to see if something was made. Nothing was. "Mommy, will you make . . . ?"

135

Shelley glowed; it seemed she might laugh. Instead she said tenderly, "No." A funny little tune: "No, no *no*, no." Mother was so pretty, she really *did* glow—amber lights around her, like an aurora. "Daughters are not waited on. A daughter is a servant." On a drier note, she said, "That's good, not bad, by the way. God Himself was a servant." She placidly concluded; the fact was plain. "He washed His disciples' feet."

Linda looked at her own brown feet, wondering if that was some kind of hint. Her feet felt clean enough. "What about boys?"

Shelley said, "My. What an unheard-of topic."

"I mean, sons. Are they servants too?"

Shelley considered. "Mmm . . . so far as we're concerned, no. A son is really an heir. He may pass through phases of discipleship, but his role is to assume his father's preeminence. A daughter is servant to all in the house, all of her life; that is her place."

Linda stared, passively mystified—a child, hearing a story she'd liked once and asked to hear again. "You're not a feminist."

"Um . . . you mean I'm not a *modern* feminist. There's a *Weltansicht* which goes with that, a social agenda and it's not what I subscribe to. Since I don't agree about basic values—like, servanthood, self-denial, are those things good or bad—then I'm not conversant with secular feminists, no. I'd tend to see myself a neo-traditionalist, though with certain idiosyncrasies." She put it plainly. "Quirks." She blinked.

She gazed at Linda, placid: were there any other questions?

Linda said, "I don't know what I am, yet. I listen to Jane's Addiction and embroider pillow cases."

"Tell me in a word, then. From the bottom of your heart. Off the top of your head, you're a . . . ?"

Linda put her hands on her tummy and head, like her mother said; collapsed in giggles. Then said, "I'll make *your* breakfast. I'll make . . ." Linda's favorite. She almost jumped—she *knew*! "Whole wheat pancakes with *straw*berry syrup. Strawberry."

Shelley said, "Why, be my guest." Again that magic in her voice, that lost chord of remembrance. All the wonder of the world was up her ruffled sleeve; it danced, angel lights about her hair.

Linda found an apron. Tied it on. Paused, wandered; didn't know where things were kept . . .

Remembered her mother's question: "Girl." Corrected herself: "Woman." Watched her mother's eyes, to see if that was right.

Shelley blinked, intrigued.

Linda looked around. She'd been *away at school no* living in

Salem, but she finally got out skillet, shortening, flour (whole wheat and all-purpose), baking powder, crushed walnuts, salt, sugar, an egg, condensed milk, vanilla, a tupperware mixing bowl and wooden spoon. And measuring cups, she knew where—cupboard over the sink.

She turned to her mother. "Derrick always made me breakfast."

Her mother was calm and gentle, like when she'd asked if Linda was all right. "Dear, do you remember . . . ?"

"Derrick is dead."

Linda's stare was fixed. It was the look she had when she'd bounced a check, or when she cheated at Scrabble—a thoughtful young woman at bay, clinging to the correctness of her answer.

Shelley softly instructed, "Make the batter . . ."

Linda did. She made an awesome breakfast. As always, the meal was more about behavior than it was about food. Shelley chided, remarked, hinted, demured, frankly told Linda she had way too much syrup, raised the dreaded specter of sugar diabetes. Linda pouted, smirked, smiled, sat nicely, had an attitude, giggled, and deliberately spilled some tea. Whoever said meals were about eating?

Afterwards, Linda cleaned up. Shelley came back down in a maroon sweat suit, tennis shoes. Pearl earrings and her gold heart necklace. "Mom, aren't you going somewhere today?"

"Lin, look out the window. That white stuff, hon. That's snow. They're saying eight inches to a foot by late afternoon."

Linda stood on her toes, peeped over the lace valance. "Neat!"

She turned to her mother, excited. "Can we please go for a walk?"

"Oh, in a blizzard—of course. I should call the group home and tell them to keep you." Linda put her hands to her mouth, "shocked" that her mom was mean; both women laughed. "Lin, get your things."

Linda had no things of her own. Just her light black coat. She couldn't imagine what tough, chic lady would walk in the snow with that coat. Not her. Her mom let her borrow a pink ski coat, gloves, a scarf and knit hat. Stockings and a pair of boots—heeled and pointed, stylish. "Let's hope you don't meet the man of your dreams."

Linda stared. "Ever?" She blinked, confused. "Why not?"

"You got dressed at the dollar store; nothing matches."

Linda said, "Oh." She still couldn't figure "man of her dreams" with "dollar store," but was afraid to ask.

They walked about two miles up the country road, up to a T and back. Along the way, Shelley spoke of different things they passed. She talked about neighbors, their properties and possessions—her peculiar New England reticence; you discussed what people had and did, their outward appearances only. She talked about activities Linda had been involved in. Linda learned that she'd picked strawberries, made preserves, helped with "March Thaw" yard sales. Sat and sewn curtains with older women. She asked and learned that she'd not chopped wood, nor climbed apple trees. The snow-topped cords of split maple, the snow-covered trees in their groves, were a pleasant bit of scenery not otherwise for her. A blue Ford tractor, dormant before a gambrel-roofed barn, prompted a question received as weak wit—she'd definitely driven no tractors, no.

Linda sensed that her mother had been very strict about not letting her do boy-things. She knew she was learning much about herself. She knew she was supposed to already know these things—that not knowing them was bad. She'd forgotten why that was. Whenever her mother asked if she remembered something, she firmly said "Mm—*hm*."

They passed a small house up a slope. The house was painted bright fuschia. The slope was all lawn around big stumps, like someone felt the whole ridge should eventually be treeless. Shelley said, "That was Ed Donnegal's place. That rather dour old essayist, wrote mostly for trade magazines; he lost his wife in '86, cancer, very tragic. You may recall him or not; your father, rather charitably, had him down to dinner once or twice. One of your decent, controlled alcoholics; he was never drunk per se, just never sober. Name any subject under the sun, he'd tell you a little-known fact. He killed himself last August."

"Why—because his house was painted that color?"

Shelley stopped. She looked, then breathed in awe: "*Oh God, you're right! It's the Candyland board!*" She turned and slapped her daughter's arm, soft glove against down-padded nylon. "That's awful. You roll dice to get to his door—Lin, that's atrocious."

A little further on, a car stopped. It was an old Chevy Malibu. A man about Linda's age, red-haired and bearded, stuck his head out the window. "You ladies broke down somewhere?"

Shelley laughed. "No, just walking. Mad dogs, Englishmen and Bauers, I suppose."

"Oh howdy, Ms. Bauer—didn't recognize you with the hat on!"

"Steve Laska?"

"Yes ma'am!" He smiled at Linda. "Hey Lin! How y'doin'?"

Linda found herself standing partially behind her mother. She smiled, but it wouldn't stay. She said, sub-audibly, "Hi."

"Long time, no see! You and your husband visiting or something?"

She murmured "Something like that," which the man didn't hear. He nodded with the far-off look you give old folks who murmur.

138

"Me, I'm laid-off for the season. On my way to plow some snow." He solemnly winked. "Fourteen bucks an hour, under the table."

Linda said "Table" like a frightened child's plea, Leave me alone. Anyway, he didn't hear her.

"'Kay, Lin. Real nice seein' you again." His face, for a moment, showed hang-dog regret; a man who'd met an old friend, only to have her play stranger. He recouped bravely for Shelley: "Don't advise you stay out long—nor'easter like this ain't for playin' in."

Shelley answered laughingly. "We're on our way home. Thanks for stopping, Steve. Good luck."

He widened his eyes. "Good bucks!" He rolled up his window and drove, the sound of his engine soon muffled by falling snow.

The two women walked in silence for a while. Linda, at last, said, "He scared me."

Shelley was surprised, concerned. "Lin, Steve is a friend. You and he played together as children."

After a while, Linda said, "You *made* me play with him. I didn't like it." She pictured it. Loud talk about fighting other boys, and hideous things done to a frog. Fixing a bike with actual tools, while she just watched. Climbing over fences, which she had to go all the way around. Walking through cattails, mud sucking at her shoes. She'd felt like a docile, inept captive. She was suddenly afraid. "Does he live around here?"

"No, he still lives in town. And a boy with patched jeans is a person with feelings. You needed to learn that, Lin."

Shelley reflected. "God, all of you were, what?—twelve years old. Almost teens. Playing *Star Wars* out in back. I thought, They can't be serious. But no, you came inside in tears. 'They won't give me a Lifesaver', I thought you meant candy til Jared explained. 'Princess Leia doesn't *get* a light sabre!' I mean, Lin—" Shelley laughed. "—in a couple years you'd be old enough to *date* each other, there you were, all wounded pride and sniffles—"

"—*because* we were older. Since my idea of how girls could behave was more mature, and he wouldn't—"

They walked, snow falling wet and dense. Linda quickened her pace, fairly raced, then turned. "I don't remember. Mom, I don't—"

Shelley stood and faced her. Linda lowered her eyes. She tried to cover her mouth with her scarf. Shelley gently took her hand away. "Stop trying to hide."

"I'm not. Cold."

Shelley touched her daughter's lip. Showed her gloved finger, so Linda could see what wasn't there. Former snowflake. "Hey, you wanna take the short-cut? Really? Let's."

They left the road, went up a tractor path. The snow was hardened drift. Linda stayed back, fearful; Shelley caught her act. "Oh stop. Come on." The path went through a stand of larch, then opened onto a field. The snow was sculpted in waves by the wind, drifting like desert sand. They walked along the border, partly sheltered by the larch; the snow wasn't as deep. The path went down through a barberry patch, now only crazy-shapes of white. A trickle of black through mounds of snow—a brook. Linda sighed in wonder and her mother turned to see. Snow had fallen from the maples, revealing ice that stormed before the snow. Crystal chandeliers, half-buried under snow. A blue heron stood on one leg—the only thing not made of snow, the only thing not white. It flapped its wings and flew, slowly and low up the path of the brook.

They crossed a little bridge of split maple. Shelley remarked, "Old Ned Huff's cows—rather than keep his fences up, he just made sure they wouldn't get stuck in the muck." She said, "Now, with heels, I don't . . ."—mincing ahead of Linda, her hands poised lightly for balance.

"Mom, don't fall."

"I didn't say I might." Shelley took her daughter's hand and, there—both over the bridge. Now there was a steep little bank. Linda went up. Shelley said "Oh, *hon*. Oh please, be very—"

Linda stood at the top. She blinked. She said, "I'm okay."

"Well, I don't know if *I* can . . . Here, give me your hand. Make believe I'm a Rainbow." Linda was confused—thought her mom meant an actual rainbow. Uncertain, she raised her mother's hand to make an arch. "Lin, what are you—*oh!*" Shelley slipped, lay prone in the snow. Linda thought *What should I do?* and lost her balance also. She shrieked as she fell on her tush.

Shelley got up, laughing. "A fair refrain of 'Ashes, ashes'."

Linda lay on her back. Blinked as snowflakes touched her lashes. She said, "I'm dead."

"Then you should be an angel."

"I am, I think. I didn't get my wings yet."

Shelley laughed some more. Took a both-handsful of snow, tossed it at her daughter's face. "There, you're baptized into heaven."

Linda squealed and swept her arms—made an angel, after all.

Her mother helped her up, and they walked on through the woods.

They came into a garden—level paths of snow. A sugar-loaf of magnolia. Underneath the snow, water dripped from broad green leaves like they were still of summer. Rows of yews like Christmas treats with too much sugar frosting. "In winter, it's a different world . . . oh, okay: there's Jared's house."

"Jared?" Linda looked down the path. A bank of cattails, rustling bare and frozen in the blizzard wind. A field of white—a lawn. A Victorian house, sky blue, with gables and a trellised porch. An oak, a great old bough stretched over buried lawn. A swing, seat heaped with snow.

Summertime, everything green. A black-haired girl on a swing. A boy behind her, catching her, letting her go. Bare feet in the warm wind, summer evening lasts forever. Laughing, look—jump off the swing. Race you over to your place, go—

"Jared doesn't live here anymore."

Shelley didn't reply to that—of course he didn't, anymore.

She said, "Oh, there . . . that way, Lin. If the Binettes don't think we're both too old to be cutting through their apple orchard.

"Lin, come on—I'm freezing!"

They walked down the path, deep in snow. Linda turned once, looking back, feeling there was something she'd forgotten, or had lost.

Back home, Linda found the vacuum cleaner. It wasn't a Rainbow. It was an Electrolux, like the carpet cleaner.

It was frightening, how everything was so strange. It felt like something worse than the end of the world was about to happen at any second. She was the only one who knew, and the only one it would happen to. After it happened, only to her, no one else would care.

She didn't know what it was.

Maybe it was just her feelings. Because she'd lost her husband. Maybe losing your husband was so bad—so cosmically, unspeakably terrible—that you couldn't even talk about it. So no one knew how bad it was until it happened, just to them.

Then they went insane, or . . . ?

Maybe things were strange because she'd been away from home so long. Friends grew up and moved away, vacuum cleaners were replaced. Things seemed strange because they really were.

That made sense . . . didn't it?

She vacuumed the upstairs hall, then the living room downstairs. Dragged the vacuum cleaner back upstairs. It was hard. It wasn't horrible punishment. *I'm strong, from doing laundry at the group home. And they make these things lighter, now. Since women have more power . . . user friendly . . . Fluff is banned by Federal law, or . . . something. I forget . . .*

She put the vacuum cleaner away. Looked at other things in the closet. Neat piles of laundered, mismatched linens and towels. A rose hip wreath. Bottles of shoe polish, silver cleaner, mink oil—they had that dusty, venerable look of having done service then been long forgotten. The smell, perhaps unique to the home of a conscientious, not-quite-elderly couple: the dry, vacuous ghost of must; things diligently cleaned, even when they weren't

141

dirty, yet grown stale through disuse.

Maybe she's lonely . . . ? Linda knocked on her mother's bedroom door. No one answered. She remembered her parents were very liberal in some ways—anything she really wanted to do was all right. So she opened the door.

Shelley stood at the picture window, watching winter wonderland. She turned, prettily startled—she just hadn't heard the knock. "Yes, sweets, what is it?"

"Mom, what will I wear tomorrow?"

"Why don't you come see?" Mother's bo-peep smile: *Why don't you?*

They went to her closet. Linda immediately pointed to a laced pink romper. "That." Shelley almost laughed. Linda smiled, timid. Was it funny? Should Linda laugh, too?—she didn't know.

"Hon, your father bought that for me, years ago. Almost as a joke, I thought. In Avignon, I said '*Oh God it's lingerie!* Who's the designer—Nabokov? Does a lollipop come with it?' " Linda lost her smile. "Oh dear, no. On someone dark, it's sweet. For me, it's just too . . ." Shelley made a face and sound, twittering delight gone sour, jaded—just too fem.

Linda liked the sound. She mimicked "*Eeeew-wugh*," giggled.

"Always such a mimic. 'Daddy's little monkey'. Do you remember Daddy calling you that?"

"Um . . ." Linda shrugged, a happy sort-of-yes. She saw it in her mind—Daddy making fun. That meant she remembered it.

She saw the Pfaff sewing machine in the corner, by the window. Sighed, excited. Pointed. "Sew. Like you. I do. At home."

"Sew you do." Shelley looked lovely. Persian princess fascination. "Linda, do you know this word: *regressed?*"

"I . . ." Linda blinked. Calm; her mother wasn't mad. " . . . haven't been getting my REM sleep. That wine last night did a number on me."

"Quote-unquote. You *are* regressed."

Linda stood, impassive. Her soft eyes roamed the room. The Pfaff. She took her mother's hand, led her to the sewing table.

Shelley seemed to like this game. "I ought to *teach* you. You who taught me all I know. I gather that you want to sew. Sew what?"

There was a white wicker basket. On top of folded fabrics were some patterns—some loose, folded; some still in packages. Linda's finger drifted, like an aimless bee. The package on top showed two designs. A suit dress with shaped skirt, to be worn with a belt. Or a simple house dress. "This. Is what I want to make." Not quite certain what she meant, she told her mother, "Simple."

"It's not a Simplicity, it's a McCall's." Shelley's voice drifted through stratospheric wonder. "**Dear,** *why did you choose it?*"

"For . . . quality time. Mother . . . daughter. Bonding."

"Do you feel you need to focus in order to relax?" Shelley was intelligent and calm. She was saying . . . something about psychology. Some understanding mother had with daughter, from years back. Linda only understood the feeling. Just the two of them here, nothing but a world of snow outside. Daughters turning back into babies was something that happened sometimes. "Lin, do you feel tense?"

"Y— . . . Slightly. Just a little."

"Well then, here." Shelley had Linda stand still, and took her measurements. At first, Linda was skittish. Shelley was enchanted. "I'm not measuring how tense you are. Honestly, I'm not."

Linda stood passively, then. She liked the way her mother turned and touched her, held the tape, like Linda was a light and pretty, gentle thing. Nothing bad would happen, while Mother took her measurements.

"The verdict: 34-22-34."

Linda tried to remember what that meant. Something to do with men whistling at her. She remembered lots of talk, that men liked girls so much and how silly/funny/exciting that was. She'd not been part of these conversations. She'd overheard them, without interest. Maybe it wasn't something she liked, then. *Afraid of men*—that was it. "34-22-34" was a *verdict*: wanted by men, without parole. Or maybe only certain numbers were bad. Maybe hers weren't the losing ticket. "My thighs are fat."

Shelley said "Stiletto." Linda didn't comprehend. Shelley's fingers traced the form; clever and intriguing, whatever it meant. "Derrick cooked for you, see? He wanted to nourish you. Also, he liked that shape." Shelley shrugged; men liked what they liked. "A few *more* pounds, we'd be looking at a young Liz Taylor."

Linda curled her lip. "That's Linette. My boss at work."

The image came at once to mind. A short, somewhat plump girl with ringleted black hair, not unlike her own. The girl was pretty enough, though she didn't really resemble Elizabeth Taylor. There were no strong feelings about this person, one way or another. Linda remembered seeing her . . . once. Cut-off jeans, halter top, tanned thighs, sandaled feet. Because it was summer—a beautiful summer day. Bright green lawn, cool dark shade beneath a tree. The lawn sloped down to a lake. Blue sky, blue water, green grass and trees. Lots of people, many of them retarded folks. Frisbees, volleyball, hamburgers on a grill. A loudly-dressed, well-groomed fat kid with Down's Syndrome, strutting around with a cassette player on his shoulder. It boomed Presley's *Jailhouse Rock* perpetually, like it was the kid's theme song and he was running for Congress, or something. His passage

drowned out the more subdued and agreeable sounds of Jewel
and Blues Traveler. There was a big, boyish guy, rather
handsome in a Polish way—high cheekbones, upturned
nose—named Steve Jurassic, or something like that. He couldn't
go anywhere or do anything without a cute, snaggle-toothed,
teenaged girl showing up, making any kind of scene to get his
attention. Linda knew this entire event—the lake, the people, the
summer day—was something she'd been part of, not once but
several times. She'd only seen Liz Taylor (Linette) once because
Linette was *new*. It was an *agency picnic*. It was the only time
Linda had ever seen or met most of these—

"I said you've got a few more pounds to go, Lin; you needn't
fall into a trance, or . . . ?" Shelley showed Linda how to
transfer, using a marker wheel. How to baste, then make a seam.
How to gather waist and sleeves, til it was early afternoon.

Shelley asked, "Are we hungry for lunch? Hint: the answer's
yes."

Linda said, "Yes," placid—that was easy, since she had a
hint.

Shelley said, "It's awful, though. We pigged on
pancakes . . ."

Linda watched her mother, ready to be unhungry, then.

Shelley said, "Well, it's not life-or-death. Dear, you're so
accusing."—meaning how she looked, not how she was.

Linda tried to smile. *La Giaconda*—for the magnifying glass.

Shelley teased, "Aw, that's not a smile. Your eyes are still
frowning at me."

Linda didn't know how to fix that, so she closed her eyes.

"Where's the button to make Linda smile? Maybe it's . . .
here." Shelley poked Linda's nose with her finger. "*Bink*."

Linda opened her eyes, touched her mother's hand. She
softly said "Stop."

"My turn to cook, Lin. Tell me what you'd like."

"Oh. I want anything." *fem* "With cheese in it. Cheese and
milk. Or milk. And eggs."

"I could make you a little quiche."

Men don't eat it. "Um . . . mm-hm. Yes please."

"What kind of quiche would you like to be?"

Linda laughed; that was silly. She could be silly, too. "One
that's too pretty to eat."

She helped her mom in the kitchen. Beat the eggs, cut the
veggies, poured the mix in the pie crust. Shelley said how long,
and Linda set the timer. Shelley did a quick clean-up while
Linda set the table. "Iced tea's in the fridge." Linda got the
pitcher, went towards the table. "Oh, and mayonnaise!" Linda
turned. A fluid pirouette, her skirt swirled round her thighs.
Black curls bounced softly, cheek and neck. The pitcher in her
hand—she was able to help, ready to serve. Her eyes flashed

144

warm amazement. *I'm a woman.*

Her mother's eyes flashed softly back. *I see.*

Linda got the mayonnaise, took it and the pitcher to the table. The radio was playing a song by Whitney Houston. Shelley said a grace. Being born-again and all, she threw in thanks for her daughter's safety, asked for comfort in this time of grief. Since something in the news had troubled her, she also asked divine guidance for President Clinton. Linda, by then, had opened her eyes—the quiche was getting cold.

Part of Linda's mind knew who Whitney Houston was. Had someone asked, she would have known Bill Clinton was the President. But her universe was really just this house, in a glass snow-globe. A home, where a woman's voice told her she would always be loved. Whether it came from the radio, or from her mother's lips, didn't matter much. Had anyone asked, she might not have known, that the radio wasn't talking just to her.

Linda ate quickly. Done, she put her hands in her lap. She looked longingly at the two remaining pieces. She wanted to ask but didn't dare. Her mother read her mind. "That remark about Liz Taylor was a very qualified compliment, hon." Linda murmured, moved her head—Don't know what that means. "You're fine-boned. The difference between thin and overweight, for you, is only a few pounds."

Linda said "Please." This wasn't about food, so Shelley didn't answer. "Mom, I'm empty." Hand over her bosom. "Empty."

"Lin, that's not your stomach."

Linda lowered her hand, She lowered her head, serious—Alice at tea with the crazy haberdasher, sleepy mouse and funny turtle. Not dubious of anything, just lost without a clue—her cavewoman utterance, if nothing else, sincere. "Mommy, I'm empty *inside.*"

"Lin, you don't mean food. What is it you've lost?"

"Myself. No. My . . . marriage."

"What was it, Lin? What was your marriage?"

"Marriage is . . . becoming the other person."

Shelley was patient, gentle. "No."

Linda was quick to agree: "No. Marriage is . . . I know what it is. Making love. Me, with a boy. Man. Husband. Lying on top, making a baby in my tummy. Me. I would have the baby."

Shelley said "Most likely." She looked like she might cry.

"Mom, was that a reality check?"

Shelley, near tears, nodded—Sure was.

Linda said "I'm done." She stood and took her things. She paused near the sink, wondered when the Awful Thing would happen.

Towards late afternoon, the snow had fallen deep. Shelley

145

said, "I shouldn't go out. But we desperately need coffee and laundry detergent and milk." That was true. She also needed to make a couple of phone calls, which she didn't want Linda to overhear. She said she'd be gone about an hour. Linda watched through the window as her mother—now the only focus of her existence—excavated her Sunbird. Holding the long-handled scraper with both hands, shoving off all that snow. She looked like a tough little fox, out there. She got in her car and eventually left.

Linda wandered from the kitchen into the living room.

This was a little scary. What was she supposed to do? *What do I like to do, when I'm alone?*

I like to sit reading a book, pretending I haven't been doing something else.

Why don't I remember something else?

She'd wanted to ask her mother: *What should I do while you're gone?* She'd envisioned two possible responses:

"*I'm glad you asked. You can always ask. Whenever you're unsure, you should. And yes, there's so much you can do:*"—this, that and the other thing. Or:

"*What should you do? Lin, good grief, you're twenty-nine years old! I'm not doing daycare—you can figure something out!*"

She understood, Shelley was like that—a fountain of love and assurance, then suddenly a bitch out of the blue. That was what frightened Linda: she knew so little about her life, yet understood so much. Walking through the house, she recognized the things she saw. But nothing brought back memories. Nothing was hers, in any special way; nothing was an old friend. In that sense, she knew a lot and understood so little.

As Linda stood in the den, she felt turmoil within her. Not thoughts or feelings, this time—probably the veggies in the quiche. *I need to . . . use the little girls' room. I've done that before, of course. But not since I was two, with my mother. WHAT is WRONG with me?*

She thought, *It's just my metabolism—the way my body works. Quick like a bunny, always. I've often excused myself suddenly, from conversations or whatever, to go use the bathroom. I've sometimes told Derrick, on car trips together, to find me a ladies' room somewhere, and stop. I always thought it was some female thing. I was . . .*

Wrong?

She went to the downstairs bathroom. It was the guest bathroom, minimal; she paused at the sink. Oval mirror, silver frame. Dried wildflowers in blue crêpe bows on either side. On the wall behind, a Matisse poster: *Goldfish*. The mirror's effect: you were in the Matisse. What were they trying to do to their guests?

She thought, *I'm drifting through this day like a bewildered*

146

child. I'm home, and yet feel as if I'm in someone else's house. I know whose, and I know the house pretty well—it just isn't mine. *And I'm seeing things and places, like the inside of drawers and Mom's bedroom, that I've never seen before and if I lived in this house all my life til I went to college this shouldn't be happening—*

She used the bathroom, holding her skirt bunched up at her waist. It felt like something you do, but also like something she'd never done before—like she wasn't really used to wearing dresses. *I'm just hopeless, then.* She took some paper, folded it, then paused.

She'd thought, *Remember to wipe from behind. Wiping from the front makes you smell, and can lead to vaginal infections.* Fine.

She washed her hands. Went idle, then stopped, her limp hands bathed in lukewarm water. *I know how to use the bathroom. But only from being told things, naughtily. Things I wasn't supposed to hear because they're private to women. Something seems totally wrong.*

I think I've been insane all day . . . ?—right up til this moment. Maybe widows are supposed to . . . ? Or isn't there such a thing? To go honorably insane? Holding tight to love and devotion, til only your grip on them remains—a Cheshire Cat of fingers, rather than a smile? Yet Linda's face, familiar, was in the *Goldfish* bowl—wet hands at her cheeks, eyes shimmering with fear, picture-perfect *Oh-poor-me.*

Linda stood at the kitchen window. Her snowy solitude had been invaded, in fact the Bauer home now seemed like the center of all kinds of activity. First guys had come with a green Dodge pickup and a snowblower, to plow and blow the snow. College-type boys in orange overalls, like snow removal was a winter sport. It seemed fantastic that people could be young men—could laugh at the snow, play with loud machines then drive away to do it somewhere else, all just for money.

Now an aquamarine Sentra parked in the driveway, and a young woman walked towards the door. That might be all right—Linda could talk to another woman. Unless she was selling something. The woman kind of toddled up the walk with her hands clasped, like a Catholic who'd just taken communion. Like someone selling something no one wanted. Linda felt scared, but fear of her mother ruled. *Linda, you didn't answer the door? That's the living end. I was expecting her all week, about a really important—*

When the doorbell rang, Linda hesitated. *But she's a girl, like me. Maybe she's scared of everything, too?*—Linda opened the door.

The woman looked pale and slight, in her slate-blue wool

147

coat. She had a rather narrow, angular face; an artist who liked drawing noses and chins would have liked to do her cameo. Thick, frizzy auburn hair, parted in the middle and gathered in a tail.

She was anything but a stranger. Her eyes glowed girl-wit, wonder; her presence here, at Linda's door, was wonderful somehow.

She would only answer to a magic name. Linda picked the only one she knew. "Priscilla?"

"*Linda*?"

Oh, *now* she could see—Priscilla was *beautiful*. Lips slightly parted, eyes softly aglow, calm on the verge of joy-burst. She wouldn't jump or shriek, her joy was gentle. Her hands spread in a winsome *Ecce femina*. "Lin, I'm here." She almost wept with joy. Instead she giggled like, Oh right I'm that important.

Linda already shivered from the cold air, blowing in. She had no thoughts but her heart's response. Cold wasn't supposed to come in; Priscilla was. In fact she just came in and closed the door, like the Bauers had adopted her too. Faced Linda with snowflakes on her shoulders, flushed with joy and cold. Linda motioned her hands—Oh forget these, I never wring them. "Is it . . . cold? Out there?"

Priscilla shrugged: Freezing. Bless the mistress of this house.

Linda spoke softly. "Don't mind if I'm . . . overwhelmed. Unsure, if we should . . . hug, or . . . ?"

"Lin, why have *I* been sure? That I could walk in through this door, and it would still be the same?"

Linda guessed, "Because it's true?" But apparently, it was. A lost language only known to women from Longmeadow Road: *Anything you wish for and believe in will come true.*

"Linda, do you love me?"

Her joy is like a bubble—it could easily pop, and be gone. Because she's exactly like me. Lonesome and anxious and odd—that's why she's come. She had melting snow on her hair. Linda touched, smoothed her hand down: snowflakes off, hair nice. Priscilla's hazel eyes shimmered, hope: This means yes? Of course you do?

"Can I trust you enough to be who you want me to be? Or . . . Oh." Linda shyly stepped back. *I can't believe I asked her that.*

Priscilla bit her lip. She said "Mm-hm" like Linda asked her if she wiped her shoes on the mat, outside.

"Pris, I . . . love you. Always. Yes."

Pris embraced her, soft and snug. A slender pear-shaped form, somewhat like Linda's own. Eau de Charlotte perfume; she smelled like Linda's mom. Linda was overwhelmed, no kidding. Afraid to hug and that was Lin, all right. But of course they would hug. They were *best friends*. They kissed, then stood

148

apart, still holding hands. Priscilla's soul was in her eyes. There'd been happy years, a childhood shared. There'd been grown-up years apart, not so happy. Now Pris saw something wonderful, something Linda couldn't see: she'd walked in through this door, and it was 1985 again. They were both nineteen—right where they'd left off. "Lin, listen: this is what happened, okay? I had to move real suddenly, 'cause of the thing with Paul. You remember how that was."

Linda said "Oh, it was awful."—better than an even chance, the thing with Paul wasn't good.

"And I lost my little thingie, my phone-number book. And I couldn't remember them either. And your parents', here, is unlisted? And mine are in Arizona—you know they finally sold their house? I kept asking them for your parents' number. And they always said Oh sure, they'd get it from so-and-so, but they—"

Linda stared at Priscilla's hands, fascinated. She was wringing them, just like Linda did herself. Linda knew just how that felt. She knew the magic touch—Dear, nothing's wrong, don't wring your hands. Pris held Linda's hand instead. "Pris, don't even bother. Whatever the reason why we didn't stay in touch . . . I'm sure it was my fault. Not yours. I'm only glad you're here. Pris, take your coat off." *Help a lady with her coat no no that's wrong* "Go hang it up right now."

Pris did, presented herself with a flourish: *voila*, try not to faint. Old-fashioned dress; deep purple, plaited bodice, mid-length sleeves. Laced white collar and manchettes; she wore a broach. Dark stockings, clogs. Linda was entranced. "What, are you an extra in the new Jane Austen flick?"

"Oh, no shit—I curl my hair now, so it's just like yours." An auburn curl-that-was: "I left the iron plugged in and it burned out, or whatever."

"Is that us? Our look? Pris, what are we supposed to be?"

Pris blinked. "We're BARBs. Born-Again Rural Bohemians." —what could be more obvious? "But anyway, I did get your number in Salem. A man answered. Derrick's father. Lin, I cried for you all night."

They'd settled into a passive groove. Watching one another's eyes, waiting for the other to lead.

"Pris, I've been hospitalized. And I've been having the oddest symptoms, I'm . . . not who I'm supposed to be."

Pris said "That's odd," like she'd lately heard things odder.

"And Pris, I've . . . got amnesia."

"Oh no. Again?"

"I seem like a stranger who needs a friend . . ."

"But Lin that's how you always seem."

"Coleman. Camping out in my backyard. Candy-apple lip glops and *God I'm so sorry I don't really remember*—" Linda turned despair into a joke—poked her cheek, gaped prettily. "Duh?"

"Lin, it's you."—her "amnesia" wasn't even that convincing.

They went into the den, sat together on the sofa. Close together, hands in their laps. Not like two men, splayed out in chairs, shouting distance apart. Why did Linda remark on something so obvious? "I've often wondered what life is like, for men."

"Lin, you're still so *dizzy*."

"Would you like anything? Hot. To drink. Or cold. I'll make it."

"Lin, I'm fine." On to more important things: "Except I'm divorced."

Linda said, "I'm sorry," and was. Pris seemed too nice to have done anything deserving abandonment. "Paul was always so . . . no: I don't really remember him. Oh Pris, just *fill me in* . . ."

"We last spoke on the phone. Like, almost five years ago. You'd just gotten back from your honeymoon."

Linda gasped, relieved. "Nantucket. Off-season, but barely. We rented a cabin in 'Sconset. Bicycle tour which I *hated*."

"My first anniversary was coming up . . . you were maid-of-honor at my wedding. Lin, you remember *that*."

Linda closed her eyes. Pris and Paul, getting married. In a church. Sure. Spring, and all the maids wore yellow. And of course she remembered Paul. Paul was . . . small. Dark and balding. Beaming pride and joy; who dreamed he would turn out a schmuck? Linda opened her eyes. She smiled warmly, assuring her friend, Yes I remember well.

"Everything was going beautifully still. With Paul and I. We were living in Rochester, New York. I'd never met Derrick. We were both so happy for each other. But I said something about living in Salem. Being less than affluent, and we . . . ended on a cool note. But Lin, if you think that had anything to do with why we lost touch—"

"I'm sure I was twice as mean. To you. Pris, all that matters is that you're here." Linda laid her hand on her bosom, a woman's pledge and quite sincere: Cross my heart and hope to . . . remember.

"I couldn't stop thinking about you, Lin. Always, a lot. I was really sad. Like I had a crush on you, or . . . ?"

Linda squeaked and shivered, like a little animal had scampered across her knee. Not a big black rat, but maybe a hamster: mild-to-medium *ick*. Of course, she really understood: Pris described the feeling's depth, not exactly its nature. Both women giggled.

"No, but what I mean is:—stop. What I mean is, there's been so much stress. In my life, I've been unhappy, and I think about

150

when we were young. And I felt, somehow" . . . Priscilla's eyes flashed, altar candles and her heart's own glow. " . . . I could just *come back*, and it would be the same. So finally I went to the library."

"Where I live is in the library?"

Pris tapped on Linda's head: knock on wood. As forceful and belligerent as a baby rabbit sniffing for its mother. "The phone book for *Salem*. I could have called Information, but I wasn't *sure* it was Salem. I was scared of saying, Then try Malden. No, try Danvers. The operator would have yelled at me."

Linda made a sympathetic sound—the fear of operators, understood. "Pris, our childhood—I know. I miss it just as much. In fact, I told Derrick, the night before . . ."

Linda stared, absent. *You ate the funny flower.*

Pris stood, took Linda's hand.

They went upstairs to Linda's room. Pris sat in the chair. Linda went and lay on her bed, like she'd come home sick from school. Like, naturally she'd do this. *The chair is hers; the bed is mine. Just another chapter in a very long book. There's been juvenile silliness and teenage ennui. Winter, spring, summer, fall. Why can't I remember?*

She did remember Samara Street. Lying in the parlor's navy blue sofa. Derrick in the arm chair. Strangely, she remembered how *she* looked, not Derrick. But anyway she realized, *I trained him to this pattern. The chair was his; the sofa, mine. From all those years here in this room, me and my friend Pris.*

Pris smiled. "I'm your psychiatrist again, after all these years."

"What else should there be, now?—to be just like old times."

Pris said "Jared. Lin, can you believe?—I've lost him too. Lost touch with him *completely*. Don't let me forget, I need his number."

Linda lay on her bed, playing with a pillow's tassle. "Pris, I might not have it. Is that possible, or . . . ?"

Pris sighed, disappointed. "Well yeah, I guess. I mean, it would have been your choice—whether or not to maintain the relationship. I can't see Jared popping back into your life. Telling Derrick 'Hi, I'm your wife's—' "

Linda froze. A feline pose. Playing with her pillow, then someone let the dog in. "Pris, what? He was my *what*?"

"Lin, *chill*! My God! Jared is our *friend*. Okay, no: your *lover*. Lin, you wish."

Linda relaxed. She dimly wondered why she'd felt alarmed.

Pris asked, "You miss him, don't you? Jared."

Linda, lying still, softly said, "Boy. Friend. Boy, who was my . . . friend."

She realized she was sort of hugging her tassled pillow. She put it aside with a gentle *tsk*. Pris noted, "You're a ditz.

Now . . . what else should there be. To be just like old times."

Linda moved her lace curtain. Looked out at falling snow. Dreamily, said "Tell me."

"Chessman cookies. Boy magazines." Pris pointed to the 8-track player. "Funkadelic tunes, Lin. All our smoking hip-hop rap . . ."

Linda stood, went over to the 8-track player as though she'd dreamed of it, then woken. "Which tape, though?"

"You tell me when, and I'll tell you what."

"Our . . . senior year."

"Oh, you were in love with Keith Green—that's too easy."

Linda said, "Our . . . sophomore year. This time of year. Winter."

"Joni Mitchel. *Ladies Of The Canyon.*"

Linda opened the carry-case. There was the tape, label grimed and peeling. *Music our parents listened to. Music we grew up with. What else do I have in here—show tunes?* She looked. She did. *Promises, Promises. Hello, Dolly.* So far as that went she had *Alvin and the Chipmunks.* Oh well. She took out Joni Mitchel. *8-track, God.* She wondered aloud. "Will this still play?"

"Well put it in and see, you goose."

"Put it in and *hear*, I think." Linda plugged the player in, put in the tape. The sound engaged, warbled at first then played, however poorly, through abrasive static. *Blue Boy.* She set the volume low.

Pris remarked on one of Linda's toys—Minnie Mouse, in a pink jumper. Linda was told that she'd had this toy since ninth grade. She learned that she'd gotten it at Disneyland itself, Disney Stores being then a thing of the future. She learned that she'd also worn a Minnie Mouse tee shirt, often enough that Priscilla's younger sister and her friends called Linda, "Disney."

It was wonderful and sad, somehow: husbands came and went, but Minnie Mouse endured.

Their talk went on, softly and with tranquil lulls. Pris asked and Linda answered, somewhat like a bedtime story.

"Remember when we made cupcakes for the open house?"

"Remember when Scott Merkle called you? Your mom yelled from downstairs, and you rolled over and screamed?"

"Remember the hay ride?"

"Remember when we took the train to Stamford to see *Hello, Dolly?*"

"Remember when we smoked pot?"

"Remember when you borrowed your mom's necklace? You said it was all right, and it wasn't?"

"Remember the Easter ducklings? How they drowned?"

"Remember when you talked me into that '*Christian seance*'? Your dad said you needed to have 'a good, long talk' and I stayed away for two weeks so you could?"

"Remember the Halloween party our senior year? You were Wonder Woman, and all the boys wished they'd known you better? That was an important event in your life. Linda Bauer was finally revealed—she was Queen of the Amazons. Don't you remember?"

"The day we walked to the mall and got lost? We walked through the hay field, trying to find the road? The grasshoppers scared us? You thought it was exciting, Lin—you said you felt like Laura Ingalls Wilder in *The Long Winter*. I just felt scared and thirsty."

Linda sat up. "My mother should have been home by now."

Pris said, "I have to go. Meet clients in Pittsfield. In weather like this, if that makes any sense." Her tone had changed, subtly. A working woman of the Nineties. It meant, transition—each of them, back to her life.

Linda asked, "What do you?"

Pris said "Sell houses" like it was some funny albatross around her neck. Linda wondered if she dressed up like Jane Eyre to sell just any house, even a modern condo.

Down in the front hall, Pris got her coat. She turned to Linda, softly spoke like she'd barely found the courage. "Shall we stay in touch, or . . . ?"

Linda said "Oh please. Just wait" and went into the kitchen. Wrote her number on a note pad—she copied it off the phone. She really had amnesia then, she guessed. Pris took the note and said, "If I'm just being silly . . . I mean, if this really is an intrusion . . ."

"*That's* being silly. Where's mine?—I mean, yours. Your number."

Both women lightly thumped themselves in the head—Linda because she was flaky, Pris because she forgot. "Oh right, I need to . . . is a business card all right?"

Linda said "No. I'll tear it up."

Pris fished in her purse, long enough that Linda knew her purse was a mess and her life was impossible. Linda gently told her "Take your time," knowing what the stress was like.

Pris finally found her business card. "This seems so impersonal . . ."

She kissed the card, gave it to Linda.

"Just pray I make it up the drive, Lin. How many BARBs does it take to get a car out of a snowbank?"

Offhand, Linda guessed "Just two: one to get hysterical, the other to call her dad at work, *I* don't know . . ."

They shyly embraced, kissed cheeks.

Linda said, "If I ever seem cold, I'm really just shy."

"You've said so a million times, I don't know why I always . . ." Pris almost cried. She laughed instead. What the hell—she went out into the snow.

Linda said "I love you," softly into the blizzard wind.

Linda closed the door and was alone again.

Venerable and dusty, a patriarch, part of the house—the grandfather clock chimed vespars.

She'd never heard it do that before.

She screamed *"What's wrong with me?!"*

She walked quickly through the house. She looked. She touched. A vase. A lamp. A book she'd never opened. All of it was strange. None of it was hers. Nothing here was ever part of her life.

At the doorway of her mother's bedroom. Memories—yes. The Pfaff. The dress. Mommy's little girl. It happened today. There was nothing from before. There was *nothing*.

She turned. She looked. Doors. *She didn't know what was behind them.* She went into her room. Was safe. How often does a girl go into her room, to be quiet and safe? How often had Linda?

Never before?

She stood at the window, looked at the falling snow. Where was Mom? Would she explain? Did *she* know where Linda's life was?

Did the snow know? Was the answer there?

What about—?

What—?

She slowly turned, and looked at the 8-track player.

Joni Mitchel thought it went round and round, like vinyl records used to. The painted pony went up and down, which pretty much explained it.

Linda took the tape out of the player. She absently remembered, *Take care of your things*—put it back in the pink plastic case.

She lay on her bed and wept. Sometimes she sobbed loudly, same sound of grief again and again—a young woman striving, soul against despair. She sobbed and wept til she was through. Til she lay on her side, gazed calmly at snowflakes on glass—truly herself at last, and truly a child once more.

11

"Linda?"

Shelley came cautiously into the room.

Linda sat up, her eyes wet with tears. She came to her mother and, as she spoke, kept trying to take her hands. Shelley, as she answered, kept taking her daughter's hands off her own. "Shelley, I'm not Linda. Shell, I'm not. I'm really not."

"Okay. Calm down, baby. Mommy's here."

"Shell, I love you but I'm not your daughter. I'm your son-in-law. I'm Derrick. Derrick Bloom."

"All right, so this is really.... I did the right thing."

"You don't know what this is, to become your spouse, *alone*, to—"

"Lin, we're getting your things."

"—no."

"Lin, it's not what you expect. You'll have your own room. Wear your own clothes. You can rest, or read, or listen to music. You can walk outside, there are lovely lawns and woods. No bars or needles or scary nurses. Sympathetic friends who will treat you as an adult. Lin, I've made certain."

"I'm not going to a hospital."

"Darling, yes. The decision's already been made."

Linda said, "I'm not ill. I'm not 'darling', I'm *not a girl*. No hospital can cure that."

"Lin, if you are rational: tell me what to do. You're saying you want to be a man. That's something I'm just hopeless with. I have no magic wand, for turning women into men. And Lin, just by the way—you'd make an awful boy. A boy who should have been a girl. If I were you, and I were a boy, I'd be upset with my mother."

"Shelley, I don't *know* what you can do. I'm sure there's nothing. I just want you to know the real me, who I am—"

"Dear, you've always wanted that. So few people reach you."

"—that I look like a girl, I feel like one, I'm starting to think and act like one but it's this body, it's not me. I'm trapped inside, I can't come out. She said it was a statue. Her body. Metal statue."

Shelley was at peace. This was the final trick-or-treat, but she was out of candy; Halloween was over anyway. "Lin, I'm

talking to an adult: you need medical attention. Dear, please.
Now—"

Linda said, "Please don't." Her mother held her shoulders;
Linda flinched, or tried to. "Shelley, do you love me?"

"Hortense, yes—this is. Now, no fair being difficult. You're
stronger than me."

"No I'm not."

"That shouldn't matter. I'm too old to fight with you."

"I don't fight. I never hit. We both know I'm a cream puff."

Shelley took courage, and her daughter's arm, in both hands.
Grimly determined, she pulled with all her might. Linda crossed
her arms under her bosom, immovable. Being bottom-heavy had
its advantage; a daughter is built to be stubborn. "Lin, I'll get
mad."

"I won't go with you. I refuse." She almost laughed, at the
childishness of her own words. That was the funniest, scariest
part: they were two grown women, both calm and in control.
Linda kept her arms crossed.

Shelley gave up with a heavy sigh: force didn't work, but
she'd dramatized her point. "All right. Then I'm willing to
compromise. While I'm driving, you can talk; I'll listen. If you—"
Shelley rolled her eyes; this was absurd—"*persuade* me then yes,
we'll come back. There, I've been reasonable."

"No. And you can't force me. I haven't been seen by a
doctor, and I haven't broken any law. You have no authority
over me."

"How dare you say that. I'm your mother."

"Mom. Please. Don't abandon me to strangers."

"Lin, I was the stranger you were abandoned to. I would
never . . .—Let's go, please."

"No."

"Then I'm calling 911."

Linda said, "Go ahead. When they get here, I'll be calm. I'll
be calmer than you."

She swiveled her hips, arms crossed. Brows arched airily:
Make your move.

Shelley said "You think? Like I wouldn't know which
buttons to push?"—press *F* now, for *fear*. Kind heart, cruel
hand, innocent cat eyes—Shelley hadn't come this far to back
down from her daughter.

"Mom, give me one more chance. I'll never say I'm Derrick.
Never, ever again. I'm Linda, and that's who I'll always be." She
felt serene, at peace; a single tear fell from her eye. She really
had no choice.

Shelley lowered her eyes. She placidly gazed at something.

She said, "You've wet again."

Linda spread her hands, so she could look down and see.
Daintily stepped back, to view the damage. "I pee'ed again. Oh

my."

She told her mom, "I'm purging, like the doctor said I would. My bladder fills real suddenly. I honestly can't help it."

Shelley looked fragile, saddened.

"Mom, I need to tell you something. To explain. It's not bad or wrong, just really personal."

Shelley met her daughter's gaze, woman-to-woman candor. After all she'd been through, the concessions she'd made, this better not be bad. It better not be wrong.

Linda looked at her bed. Unthinking, she wished to sit. Her dress was wet, the seat more than the front. The "Impressionist" bedspread was clean and neat. No, sitting was out.

She looked around the room. Ice marigold print. Dust ruffles, Waverly lace. Pillows of teal damask. No, she wasn't supposed to wet.

Downstairs, the grandfather chimed three times—vespars were concluded. Eventide fell for a thoughtful, learned Christian and his moral, elegant wife. The rooms were now empty and still. Aubusson rugs and Strass chandelier. The dining room, oak leaves and candlelight, with Vogel glassware and Oneida silverplate. The leather-bound Henredon chairs (contoured to match the velvets in the den) with their gold-tooled rosette. The bookshelves, one of which contained a Gutenburg Bible with annotations by Erasmus. This house, these rooms, held Linda in; she couldn't wander through them. She didn't understand them. She wasn't presently fit to appear in them. Shelley stood with her back to the door, to this manor of which she was mistress. Linda was stuck in her bedroom, with Monet and Minnie and Maybelline.

Linda started to explain. "I try to hold it in. But I forget, I do it wrong. I . . ." Her adult smile, brief: Sorry, I know this is gross. " . . . tighten, like, the bottom of my tummy. I think it's my, um . . . see—el—eye—tee." She swallowed.

Shelley asked, "What is a see-el-eye-tee?" Her voice was like white chocolate, was soft at its most intimate. She was willing to give "personal" a great span of leeway, but this already sailed into "silly."

Linda couldn't find her voice; she had so little news to tell. "Nothing. Something. You know. It's small." Real tiny, they could just forget she'd mentioned it. "But that's wrong, because that doesn't hold the water. It's inside. A little muscle. Further back." That was it unless she pointed at her crotch.

"Lin, this dissertation is mystifying! Whatever can you mean? Some Masters and Johnson report? Different kinds of orgasm . . . ?"

"No, it's just about going to the bathroom. It's really very simple." She ended in sorry despair: "I'm really pretty dumb."

"Well, you've pee'ed yourself. It's not a moment of a

woman's life when she shines forth as brilliant. Linda, get undressed."

Linda said, "All right." Calmly, she lifted the waistband over her breasts. Shelley put her open hand lightly over her mouth and nose. No bra. Unshaved armpits. How *au naturel*, how very European. How altogether Woodstock. Linda lowered her eyes; maidenly shame, she'd not declaim the body beautiful. She stood holding the dress, not knowing what to do with it. She gave it to gravity—Here, I'm helpless.

Shelley distantly said, "And my panties, too."

Linda, for the barest moment, hesitated. This was like shower-room shakedown in lock-up. Tony Biondo, amused by his dark secrets: *The skivvies too, tough guy. Why so slow, got a blade up your cheeks?* Mothers did it too, as something pure and soft like baby powder. "You probably won't want to wear these again . . ."

"Well, I . . . probably won't. Hon, we're family. Just . . ."

Linda stood before her mother, naked. She shrugged, which—being a woman—she found she did with her hip. She knew none of this was her fault. She knew she wasn't a bad-looking kid. She knew what she was in her mother's sight: a very wayward calf.

Shelley sighed regret. Even cowgirls get the blues.

She took Linda's arm, placed her own palm on the bottom of Linda's tummy. Linda felt a thrill of indignation, but it left her, like milk poured from a cup. Nothing there to violate, just her tummy. She was innocent—just a girl. Shelley said "Pressure." She pressed her palm: pressure. "When you feel pressure. Here."

Abruptly, she gripped Linda's forearm and walked, pulling her daughter along. Linda tottered after her, no protest in her mouth; her mother's assault left her breathless. "Now, this is a toilet. Sit."

"I'm not a dog. I won't."

Shelley begged to differ. There were simple, effective ways to make girls obey. She grabbed Linda's hair at the nape of her neck, grabbed and turned her chin. Linda had to turn her head and the rest of her went along; she found it was indeed more convenient to sit. Hand to her cheek, she looked at her mother.

Shelley was a cheerful sprite. "Stand, please." Linda stood. Right response; Shelley stayed cordial. "Pressure, here. Means *sit*." Linda tried to speak but only stared. Shelley languidly blinked; what part was unclear? This house of honey-colored stone, all cream and white within, was made by men for a man to own. The particulars did not concern young ladies—a gentleman provided all. He ordered such affairs, such pleasant homes and gracious lives and always preferred ladies who knew how to use the bathroom.

Shelley's outburst didn't spend its force. It went on and on

158

like some crazy, purposeful drill. Pressure, sit, stand; pressure, sit, stand. Shelley jammed her hand, all bone and resolve, into Linda's bland, soft tummy. "Pressure here." Linda sat. "Up." She sat. She crossed her arms.

There was a grace period—nearly two seconds—then Shelley gripped her daughter's hair. It hurt. Linda rose, as fast—not very—as her mother let her. She whispered "*Okay—all right,*" her voice thin and high on the brink of hysteria. The formula was repeated, again and again and again. Linda sat and stood and sometimes whimpered questions or complaints. These, Shelley simply ignored. She only spoke her three commands. She still seemed bright and cheerful, like this was some vicious rule for being mean to Linda—the basis of love remained intact. Pressure. Sit. Linda finally realized that no self-respecting woman would accept this. She felt she couldn't physically resist, but she didn't have to acquiesce. She calmly told Shelley, "I hate you." Shelley answered only with a wistful sigh. Pressure, sit, stand. Then Shelley took Linda's hand. No force, a pretty smile: Won't you come with me? Back in Linda's room, Shelley placed her hand. "Now, when you feel pressure *here*—"

Linda was afraid to fight. She went back to the bathroom, sat.

Her mother called "Come back, please!" An alpine melody; a lovely view, come see. Linda came back and confronted her mother. Shelley placed her hand and Linda wheeled around to storm into the bathroom. Shelley held her wrist: You're not dismissed. "And hon, try not to flounce. When you leave the room: just walk. Okay?"

"I had an embarrassing accident. I don't think you're teaching me anything. I don't think you're normal." Linda didn't flounce, but didn't float out either. She glanced back, said "Oh screw you."

Shelley was mildly startled. "*Oh!*"

While she was sitting on the toilet, Linda needed to pee, and did. Her mother summoned her back. "I'm using the bathroom, if you don't mind." Like an anxious child, she nearly forgot to wipe, then caught herself spinning the roll. That was something else mothers yelled at their daughters about. Linda came back to the room and, for the sake of sin, told her mom, "I think I did it right this time."

"Dear, good for you. Now we'll get the brush and bucket."

Linda said "Machine."

"Now, we'll get the—"

"*All right all right I* heard *you!*" Linda started for the door then turned, beside herself with passion. "*You expect me to know where it is?*"

Shelley said, "Yes. As a matter of fact, I even—" She came to Linda, swift. Lupine, golden-eyed. "am sick of being screamed at. Abused, your filthy language and—" She raised her hand, to slap. Linda cringed, doe-eyed with fear. "—*if you don't stop, I'll . . .*"

Shelley blinked. She was thoughtful, calm. " . . . do something really mean." She blinked again. "Under the sink, downstairs."

Linda nodded, almost eagerly—Under the sink, downstairs was very useful and important information, since the alternative was a slap. She backed away, like Shelley was an empress. Couldn't curtsy, since she had no clothes; Linda went downstairs. Tits and ass through spacious *alpes chateau* decor, quite sure this wasn't normal family custom. She returned upstairs with the brush and bucket, was sent down the hall for carpet cleaning fluid.

Linda spent fifteen minutes on her hands and knees, scrubbing. Shelley sat on the bed, legs crossed, sedately observing. She might have been a fairy on a rock, enamored of her reflection.

Linda got tired; she started to hurt. Her slender arms trembled, then shook. She whimpered and whined. "Mom, it hurts."

Shelley's rejoinders were langorous; she couldn't feel a thing. "Linda, you sound like a child," she said. And once, as though mildly curious: "Feeling pity for ourself?"

Linda softly sobbed, "Bitch." She smoothed the damp curls back from her face; her cheeks were wet with sweat, though she held back tears. Her nose ran, tasting of salt to her lips. She scrubbed.

Her elbows buckled; her shoulder hit the floor. She knelt weeping, her cheek to the carpet.

Shelley went to her daughter's vanity. She unfastened the mirror—it was held on with wing nuts—and set it on the floor, in front of her daughter. Shelley stepped back. She offered no comment. What Linda saw was supposed to be self-explanatory.

Linda sniffled back her tears. She got up on her hands and grimly looked at her reflection. A girl on all fours, naked. Eyes sultry and wet under tangled black curls. Her narrow shoulders framed by the pale moon of her butt. She was supposed to feel shame.

She stood—not very dramatically. She almost lost her balance.

She said, "I think we've proved your point. Anyone who lets you treat her like this is insane."

Shelley blew a wisp of blonde hair from her eye. A crooked smile. "That one sucked, huh?"

Linda was amazed—Grendel could speak. "Mom, what have you been thinking? How do you *feel*?"

"Emotionally exhausted. Lin, you've no idea. You think you're helpless, just a victim. But you're not—you're very willful.

160

You scare me, Lin. So pretty, so much passion. Your eyes, the way they flash. Like if I crossed that certain line, you would truly and forever hate me."

"Mom, you were rough. You hurt. My hair. You pulled . . ."

"I . . . was too into it; I'm sorry. Sometimes I'm not aware. Lin, remember: Mommy had to fight. Had to actually, physically fight. In Cambridge, where I grew up—there were gangs of tough girls. And we were spoiled and belittled, always told that we were helpless. I had a hard time learning English. Stuck on the disclaimer, couldn't even lose the syntax: 'English I speak not.' We gentle Christian folk, surrounded by these *Englisch* like a clump of cows all huddled, facing outward. Their endearment *hon* except they meant it like, Attila. Disciplined in how we acted, not in how we felt; brought up to be selfish. 'I want, I feel, I demand' until my father said, Shut up. Pig-dog means, unfeminine. Not a girl; not human. I was flighty and shy and my mother dressed me silly. Pigtails and pinafores. That and *braces*." Her cover-girl smile, now gentle perfection. "I had no social skills. No confidence. Linda, you never believe but it's true: I was exactly like you."

"I'd never treat my daughter the way you just treated me."

"I know. That's how I made you. Also, you're of different blood. A different type from us. Dark and slender, nervous. An Indian girl raised by Nordic parents."

Linda parted her lips but in her wonder, made no sound.

Shelley, now, was guileless. She was happy to discuss the whole monstrous episode like it was a badminton match; girlish, her eyes alight as she revealed her fears and doubts. "I've heard of people, you know, losing their toilet training under such stress. So I thought, what's the psychological first aid for that? You were very patient with me. You really were quite kind. Lin, you've always been so delicate. I mean, maybe next you'll have migraines, again. That's why I thought, a doctor. I'm more upset than you are." She made a wry face at her daughter's naked bosom. "You are kinda *ick* though, huh? My icky, pissy little girl." Shelley left the room.

Linda took a shower. The hot water soothed her; she closed her eyes, caressed by the jets. Yet her thoughts ran a repetitious cycle, fevered feelings she couldn't work through. Her body was familiar. Linda's body, yes. Like a drawing for the doctor: pretty, incomplete. *Here's a house, a girl inside . . . where's the man in the picture? Shouldn't there be a man?*

Where is Derrick? Where'd he go?

Why can't I be me?

In her room, she got her nightgown. The dress that Barbie came in. No, that was her camisole. This was her baptismal gown. *Baptized into Heaven.*

Linda went downstairs. Shelley was on the sofa, looking at

TV. Linda went to a bookshelf. She asked her mom, "Can I take a book?"

Shelley cautioned, "Mm."—into what she was watching.

"Did I tell you Priscilla was here? Just now, while you were out?"

"No, just that you were Derrick. It figures, though. Whenever you two are together, there's always something . . ."

Linda looked at the books. Lars had an awesome library of ancient history, anthropology. Secrets of the pyramids, spectacles of Rome—Derrick would have flipped. Linda wouldn't take one of those books, like she thought she was her husband. Her mother's light fiction was on the bottom two shelves. Linda chose *Daughter of Desire*, pretty much at random. At least she could say Well no, I haven't just cried and pee'ed—I read a novel, by Victoria Holt.

Linda went upstairs, went to bed and read three chapters. She'd never read romance before, so she didn't know if this one was good. It was strangely soothing, though, to read a novel by a woman. Okay to be a girl and talk talk talk. Mommy's at her WP, all's well with the world. Linda finally closed the book, turned off her light and slept.

She rose at first light, roamed quietly. The house was cold, this morning. It hardened her nipples, made her move in nervous little spurts, like she was scared. She wondered if she really was and if so, of what. She put on the terrycloth robe her mom gave her.

She went into the bathroom, got the hamper. It was plastic, pretty light, had only her things in it, and was plainly the source of these musky urine whiffs throughout the upstairs. She took it down to the front hall and spaced, having no idea where the Bauers had their washer and dryer. The downstairs was quiet but for the loud ticking of the grandfather clock. Outside, it was snowing again, pastel-blue twilight. Basement. Small hallway past the kitchen, indoor patio on the left, her father's study and an unknown door. Steps down into darkness, a ledge stacked with returnable bottles. She turned on the light, went down. Found the machine, threw in her stuff. Threw in soap and started the cycle. She stood and looked around. Old lawn furniture. Boxes of gizmos that were mostly steel tubes. A blue plastic wading pool. A Toro push-mower. Lars was out there mowing his three-acre lawn with it. Doubtful.

Lots of Lin's old stuff. A girl's English racer—three speed, with a basket in front. A doll in the basket; a brown, black-haired Barbie. Still dressed for her last adventure; polyester midriff, low-slung spandex tights. Suspended in time, like Olivia Newton-John in *Xanadu*. Behind the bike, a stack of games in their disintegrating boxes. Candyland. Awesome. Barbie board game. Barbie's doll house. Somehow, Linda wasn't surprised—that she'd been, like, so into Barbie. She still had her antique dolls, in the den at Samara Street. She still rearranged them and ironed their little dresses, which was—she insisted—not playing with them.

She went back upstairs. She sat on the bed.

After a while, she looked up, her eyes tracking only her thoughts. Her lips moved, silent—

lost you more completely. Than anyone ever lost someone before. Every moment I live, every beat of my heart . . . thought that says I or me denies you life . . . my very existence denies your own.

She wept aloud, "*Oh God, this is so wrong for us.*"

She lay curled on her side. Hid her face in her pillow, and wept.

Shelley had been right. The laced pink romper would have looked ridiculous on her mother, but . . . well, she'd been right. Linda sounded solemn, looked grim, as she explained. "I just want jeans and a shirt. I don't care if they fit. I don't care how they look."

Shelley said, "All right, fine!"—she'd never gotten used to her daughter's desperate whims. She gave Linda Levi's, ladies' cut, size 6, and a tee shirt. An Elizabeth Arden, mauve, with a little floral squiggle. "Now *go . . . away.*"

Linda dressed and went downstairs. Shelley was having her breakfast, microwaved crêpes suzette. A Woman of Weight Watchers, dressed to go out. White ruffled blouse, brown chambray skirt, heeled boots. Pearl-on-a-gold-ring necklace. She was gorgeous.

Linda stood in the doorway, reluctantly presenting herself to her mother, to the day. She said, "I guess I look okay," quite like a sulky tomboy.

Shelley touched her lip: chewing. She sat nicely, one hand in her lap, yet was sort of perched on her seat; the crêpes had her undivided attention. Fueling up for her weekday aerobics. She swallowed, dabbed her lip. "Hon, you *slept* last night. You were snoring." Linda wondered why she wouldn't have slept, then remembered: her husband was dead. That was the event which presently defined her existence. That was good, because it meant she didn't have to be happy. In normal times, Shelley was known for her evangelical joy, making all those who were miserable, more so. She pecked at her daughter with chirped exhortations to happiness, *tsk*ed notations of "someone" who was a "miffy miss" or "petulant young adult." Cajoling reminders that "beauty is in the heart." Linda was happy, yes. She was happy that her husband was dead.

She sat at the table across from Shelley, resting her chin in her hands. "It was weird, waking up this morning." She could say why, but why?—she shrugged. "Guess I'm not used to waking up alone."

"Lin, of course not. The marriage bond's not lightly broken. A part of you is gone—like an amputation. So easy to imagine that what's gone is still there." Shelley lightly cleared her throat.

Linda blinked—she was on. Time to test the limits, the strength of prison bars. "I think passing myself off as Linda is possible. If I really have no choice. Then what I don't know, I can guess about. If I guess wrong, so what—everyone knows I'm a ditz."

"You still think you're your husband."

"No."

"Yeah, you do." Shelley winked. "I *know* you do."

A peculiar staring match. Linda tried on three shades of nonchalance; Shelley found them all appealing, none of them convincing. "Mom, I'm self-realized. I'm Wonder Woman. Okay?"

"That was such a bad idea. That Halloween party. At Coleman. You as Wonder Woman. You and Pris." Linda spaced; it sounded like a comic book scenario. A duplicate spawned from a teleportation glitch, the true Maid of Might confronting her evil impostor. Shelley helpfully clarified. "Pris was Minnie Mouse—it was her turn, that year. You took turns being Minnie Mouse. I wished you'd stuck to Disney. Pluto *might* be a girl, I've never really been sure . . . 'Queen of the Amazons', Lin, *good grief*—you were five-foot-nine and nearly Rubenesque, back then. Tiara and a lasso—I mean, why not jack boots and a whip? At a Christian school. But for your father's prestige, I'm sure something would have been said. The phone rang off the hook for months. You and your hot pants and Gloria Stevens barbell, that summer. Lin, you were insufferable."

She shook her head, But it wasn't me. "I'm sorry."

Shelley waved it off; silly then and silly now. Linda made herself some coffee. Shelley got ready to leave. There'd been no discussion of her agenda, which Linda readily fathomed. Tony Biondo had described the procedure most cogently. *It's called* funeral arrangements. *Here's my ticket, gimme my stiff. It's called* chartering a meat wagon. *You start by looking in the Yellow Pages under F. Get your facts of life straight—the angels don't come and haul your rigor-mortis'ed carcass into the clouds.* Shelley stopped on her way out, held Linda's wrist and kissed her forehead. Linda closed her eyes, felt beautiful in bliss. Affection was like water, when you hadn't known you were thirsty. "Be good. If you feel you should be busy, I've a ton of laundry upstairs."

Linda noted, curiously, this seemed to have been her assigned task, even before she worked at Pinski Place.

Shelley said "Bye-bye now" like her daughter was a doll. Went out the door, crying out against the snow and cold, "*Oh! God, it's . . .*

Alone in the house, Linda thought *Now how will I spend the rest of my life? Is there anything to read?* She found some Cosmopolitans, took them to the den. She remembered that the men hadn't come yesterday, to do the patio. If she heard a truck or something, she would go upstairs—softly; maybe they could hear from outside—and lock herself in her room. They could ring and ring, but she'd stay in bed, under the covers.

She knew she would probably do all this, for real. Derrick's wife was known to hide. It usually involved people out in the street. Derrick grew up in a neighborhood, where streets were a sort of common living space. You met your neighbors there, and talked.

He'd only been full of boyish exuberance. *Lin, come on out—Mitch Yensko's got a '69 Mustang. Babe, you gotta see this!"*

It had seemed okay. Hell, Mitch's girlfriend was out there. She and Linda could stand around and talk about girl-stuff, if they didn't want to look at an American classic. It was a beautiful summer evening. Mitch had a six-pack. BCN was playing a block of The Who.

It had been almost uncanny. The apartment, empty. The bedroom window open, the curtains stirred by the evening breeze. It was like she'd been Raptured.

Oh, he knew that she was hiding. It was one of their unspoken rules, she could. Knowing that her husband swayed her, could seduce her to a hated scene of quadrophonic, turbo-charged, beer-fueled bluster. Hence, no scene, no conflict—Jesus simply took her. Come away with Me, My daughter. You won't get fooled again.

He'd find her, at last, in almost incredible places. In a corner of the wall next to a bookcase, which he'd walked past several times. Just behind the shower booth, a cameo through its frosted translucency. She only needed a little space—eight by twelve inches, times her height. It was an extraordinary talent.

Caught, she'd simply blink. Eyes loud, voice soft, she'd murmur her excuse. *I dropped a hair pin.*

I saw a bad bug.

If she'd hide from her own husband, then later for recaulkers—she'd vanish *sans* regret. She got cozy on the sofa and read Cosmo, which she'd never read or even looked at before.

An article on loneliness—being single, not by choice. I'm beautiful and kind and I haven't had a date in two years. Men could rakishly take the initiative, while women had to languish by the phone. It was ultimately men's fault, since there weren't enough decent ones to go around. A piece on body-image. Hormonal changes of the menstrual cycle had the proven effect of distorting someone's perception of her body. Specialized optical equipment directly linked to computer graphics, showing how someone saw herself in the mirror. The author probably submitted it to Omni, first. *Your science is okay but this is strictly women's interest . . .* fluff it up for Cosmo. She skipped an ad and came to this month's exercise piece. Clever arrangement. Here's your problem, Jenny Craig (your other option), now here's our do-at-home solution. Time-efficient aerobics—skipping the burn and getting the effect. Chatty intro, Who has time anymore. Those time slots we plan get edged out, especially when we schedule close to transitions like evening meals. And of course our kids just come to us with everything. But don't despair, here's—

Linda heard a car pull into the driveway. She took her place at the window. A grey van. *Meyer's Stonework, Interiors.* Two guys in dusted overalls got out, unloaded tools from the back of the van. *Young* guys. One big, with curly blond hair. His little side-kick, lank black hair below his shoulders.

Head-bangers.

Linda's hand drifted to her throat; her heart raced.

Stop seeing them through Linda's eyes. See them with your mind. *That big guy is obviously a* bird-brain. *That's why you don't want them here—they don't know how to recaulk flagstone.*

The doorbell rang. Linda opened the door. The blond-headed guy went from bored to amazed; he saw a pretty girl. *You don't know how to recaulk.* Linda didn't say that. She just said, "Yes?"

The blond-headed guy tipped his hat. *Save it, Bird-Brain.* "Meyer's Stonework." He grinned: You're no "lady of the house," you're a *chick*, come on. "You wanted an indoor patio fixed?"

Linda wanted to mimic him. She recalled that girls could do that, though it wasn't very nice. She just said "I guess." Stepped back as they lugged their tools and boxes into the front hall. She looked at their shoes, not expecting their response—they sheepishly stomped on the inside mat. *Just because I looked?* She said, "Come with me," and turned, curt as a sullen child. Led them out to the patio, where she thought to look at the flagstones. The mortar was crumbly in spots. You hired guys to come fix that . . . ?

The two guys spent some time just standing, smiling at the floor. EEG flat-line. Wonderful. Linda said, "Okay?", since she was only a girl and would just run along if they didn't need her for anything. Bird-Brain started mumbling. Questions. Did she realize they'd have to lift the stones? Could they stack them right outside, here? She'd asked for the slate-dust finish, right? Linda looked seriously into his eyes: happy-go-lucky lemons of brain death. She said, "I guess. It's for my parents, so, you know . . ." *I'm brain-dead, too; ask me what's on sale at TJ Maxx this week.*

166

Bird-Brain cleared his throat. "Can we play our radio?"

Linda felt devastated. She'd been positively mean for no reason. "Oh, sure. Oh, by all means, of course, I was just . . ." *Stop. Now I'm over-friendly. They think I'm coming on. They're going to rape me.* She limply waved, Forget it. "I've got a migraine."

Sidekick said "Bummer."

Linda regarded him calmly. *Some balls for a bird-brain's side-kick.* Bird-Brain himself shook his head, What a stooge. Turned his smile on Linda—she'd a gentleman under her roof. "This won't take us long."

She found her hips swaying, passive-impatient; she stopped. "How, um . . . how long." *Oh no he thinks that's a tease* "—will it take. Does it usually take, or . . . ?"

"Not too. Another job after this, then him and me got tickets to The Keg." *'Him and me'—stereotype Neanderthal blue-collar tradesman.* "Physical Graffiti's playing; SCN's doing live broadcast. Fifty cent drafts—can't miss that." This exchange involved a prolonged eye contact. Linda was a doe in headlights, nodding agreement with whatever he said. She felt (*helpless worthless either he likes me and I'm okay or he doesn't and I'm not*) vulnerable. It was just her nature, even talking about recaulking. A tribute band and watered drafts were a scary subject too, since he mentioned things he liked to do like he wanted to ask her out. (She'd call the cops.) She kept realizing that her eyes were too wide; the realization alarmed her, which made her eyes even wider. Derrick's wife did that a lot—they'd referred to it as her *focusing.* Bird-Brain winked. *Oh stick it up your ass.* "Ladies' Night, too. Drafts on the house before and after the gig. They do a mean *Black Dog*, I'm told."

Linda was confused—thought that was some kind of drink. Almost inaudibly, she said, "I've never had one."

Bird-Brain smiled. "That's a song. They do Led Zeppelin."

Linda felt little, inconsequential. "I'm more into Alternative."

Bird-Brain didn't answer. He'd slouched into action. He wasn't going to rape her; he wouldn't even do much to the patio.

Linda went out to the den. She stood fearful, then decided: she would *exercise.* Shelley's Lifecycle—there. She went upstairs to her mother's dresser, lucked onto Shelley's taupe Danskin. That wasn't enough, with men in the house; she found a denim skirt, and tied it on. Pink leg-warmers, tennis shoes; she checked a top drawer for a head band. *What's this?*—behind the jewelry box, envelopes of different types and colors. *Maybe they're about me . . . ?*

Knowing it was wrong, she nonetheless plucked one, to look. A blush-pink envelope with a light floral scent. It was addressed to Shelley. The handwriting was very quaint. It was actually black letter print, degraded into a cursive scrawl. Someone who'd learned to write very fancily, then virtually forgotten how to write at all. Someone blessed with the name Erminegard. It sounded like a moth repellent you sprayed on a fur coat. Erminegard *Loenat*—Shelley's maiden name. That was nice, huh? —being adopted into a family that named people Erminegard? The return address was some apartment, Minerva Street in New Rochelle, New York. The letter itself was on blush-pink, scented stationery. With tulips at the top.

Shelley look I am gay as tulips!!

Still having more the Big Applish escapades. I seldom write to home as they are mostly now living in post-Wall style, as far from our darling farm as can be. Those whom stay I cannot call since the operators are simply stupid. They say "Bad Neussenschein: this is still in Poland?" I say No I am FROM this place and never even dreamed it was in Poland. I am talking to a tree.

The rest was hard to decipher. The writer slipped back into her native tongue to relate her deeper, or possibly more ludicrous, thoughts. Shopping for a certain brand of ham, asking the deli man to cut the Foch & Schidtt. Work in a garden center, where she admittedly did nothing all day but traipse around with baskets of edelweiss, like Julie Andrews. Spending the night with her friend Carl, who bored her with Womenpolitik. Throwing up in a campus parking lot, then sleeping behind the wheel of her '74 Thunderbird. It had eight cylinders, *Normalündersendung und 380 cc. Kapazität.* She had fun fun fun; she was quite the little surfer girl. Setting the alarm on her wrist watch so when it went bzzzzzzz she turned the key in her ignition, went to work. Getting yelled at by her boss for putting *Pretty Petrol* (2-cycle mix?) in a space heater, cutting Dandy Liars with (her English failed) *das Weidwäcker.* Lastly, giddy nonsense about "Hostess Funnybones" (*Or having the goose with chef hat, this is Gander's?*) She understood at last, why everything in America had peanut butter. Even at the pastry shop on Uhlandstrasse (?), nothing was nearly so luscious. *Darling, I love Skippy most.* —*Your Admiring Baby Cousin, Erminegard.*

Linda put the letter back, behind the jewelry box. She didn't much like this person. She seemed like some sardonic goblin.

Linda went downstairs. The Lifecycle faced the wall-recessed, wide-screen TV. She turned it on. *Days Of Our Lives.* She thought *Oh wow! I'll watch this,* since she was scared of the men on the patio. She thought, *They won't want to come in and watch it with me.* She stood poised, listening, til she heard sounds of work. Muttered curses, the clink of a crowbar set on the floor.

A mumbled conversation. They sounded, somehow, like two seals, tossing a beach ball back and forth. *You know how many stones we broke?—Yeah . . .' Do I know how many bones we smoked'—that what you asked me, a minute ago?*—not about her. Linda was safe. She untied her skirt, tossed it onto the sofa. She got on the 'Cycle, started pedaling. Almost set Derrick's level, eight. That would have come to a full stop. She set level one—typically Linda, assuming she was weakest of all. Level one was nothing, she tried three. It felt okay. From the patio came booming noise, shouts of approbation. Def Leppard, *Yeah! Pour some sugar on . . .* ME!

She paused the 'Cycle, walked to the patio. Bird-Brain turned the radio down, to hear what she would say. She softly asked, "Could you turn that shit down, please?"

They stood chagrined—two bad boys, caught with their pants down. Bird-Brain gulped and said, "Oh . . . sure. Sorry."

Linda said "Thank you." She went back on her vicious 'Cycle. Pedaled, brooding. Took the remote, surfed channels. The Bauers had MTV. *Why?* She shook the sweat from her bangs. Passed into aerobic trance, thoughts drifting. MTV soundbites: sex and cars, cars and sex. Perfect hair, V-6 engine, perfect smile, anti-lock brakes. Nothing for a girl who read Jane Austen, and seldom bothered with makeup; she guessed she wasn't in the race. She got off the machine, felt boneless and breathless. She tied her skirt back on. She wasn't going to shower or change. She didn't trust the guys, in there. She was afraid they might steal something. She briefly met—and dismissed—her true feelings: *Boys are noisy and rude. I don't want them here. I wish they'd finish and leave.*

The phone rang.

Linda went into the kitchen. Her hand froze over the receiver. It couldn't be anything good. Anyone calling her would insist she was someone else, and she'd have to agree. What if it was Shelley, though? Linda could say she'd gone out. Grief-stricken, delusional, traumatized out of her toilet training—she'd run out for Ben and Jerry's and left Bird-Brain in charge. No. She picked up. "Hello?"

"Operator. Long distance call, collect from overseas, Lars Bauer. Will you accept?"

This wasn't the operator, talking to Linda. It was Life, talking to Woman. Things are said and done to you, circumstances imposed. Linda gazed sternly at the ceiling, like a soprano powering up for an aria. "I'll accept."

The distant crackle and click of connections. A second, between two blinks, for thought; her mother's words mingled with her own ideas. *Of course he'll be nice to you he loves you Lin he's your father you can be yourself say anything he knows you if he shouts "Hello!" to get his voice across the Atlantic I'll*

169

hang up I really—

"Linda?"

She calmly said, "I'm here."

"Lin, it's your father."

She was caught off-guard, amazed—it was. She felt undone, her heart revealed; she wanted to be held.

Softly, she said, "Hi, Dad."

"Hi. I flew back to Jerusalem . . . needed to come back anyway. Still staying with my friends Doctors Abe and Rachel Adelstein. Sweet folks, I just love 'em. It's cold and dirty here. The beauty's in the stones themselves—the stones of the Old City. They glow like burnished gold, just like the Talmud says."

Yes, that was Lars. Very German-Lutheran, very Midwest. Talk should always start off small; nothing in Life's all that important. "Short while ago, I was sitting out on the porch. We can just see part of the Via Delorosa, through an old arched gate. I was . . . you know. Coming to Him for guidance. Before I talked with you. Read Romans 8:15. 'For you did not receive a spirit of slavery to fall back into fear, but a spirit of adoption. When we cry "Abba! Father!" '—then I heard it. 'Abba, Abba!', down in the street—a little Arab boy, running after his dad."

Linda smiled. She softly said, "Neat."

"Hon, in Jericho I got some dates.—yeah, right; your old Dad's feeling his oats. I mean, local dates—right from the palms which Joshua's spies saw from the Jordan. I told the Arab postmaster, 'These are for my daughter in America.' I told him how pretty you are, and showed him your picture. The one I carry in my wallet, all around the world. He smiled at your picture. He said, '*Inshallah*, she shall receive her gift.' Arab postal service—We'll deliver your mail, if it's God's will. I guess that means He's watching out for your teeth. Dates are 90% sugar."

Linda said, "I guess He is . . . I haven't gotten any dates."

Silence. He was expecting her to open up, waiting for her to gush. "Dad, I'm home and I was looking at my old things. In my room. That I left here, because I outgrew . . . I was looking at my old 8-tracks. Dad, didn't you take me to see *Promises, Promises?*"

"On Broadway. You were fourteen. We had dinner at Sardi's, first; yes." He chuckled. "Yes, that was one of our father-daughter 'dates'. You needed that, sort of, practice with training wheels. Since the only boy you'd known all your life was that friend from next door, that . . ."

Linda was almost excited, that she knew. "Jared."

"Yep. And you thought all boys were Jared. You thought you could simply share your heart, and there'd be a bond. You thought a boy was a *friend*—someone you could always trust. Who'd never leave you."

170

Linda fumbled the receiver. She rolled her eyes, annoyed with herself. *Yes, that was my cue. And it's no good claiming I don't know the script. I saw them together a million times—it's enough to make Barney blush. It went back to the start of her life—him picking her up, making her laugh, giving her things. Bows for her hair and caramel apples and now I have to play the part. Just do it.*

"Daddy, I miss Derrick." It was like lifting a box from some high shelf, expecting it to be empty, instead being crushed by a weight of things she'd feared to find. The optimistic, honest boy who'd given up everything he loved—the great outdoors, male friendship—to be a teacher, a success, a man in his wife's sight. The idealistic straight-arrow in a world of burned coffee and cigarette smoke. Talking love and truth in that pirate's cove of 11 pm, that members-only dive disguised as a corrections office. Linda wept, and it wasn't an act. "*I miss him so. It hurts.*"

"Okay . . . Baby, I know. They got the news to me this morning. It's evening here now. It was as short by plane to Jerusalem as by jeep to anywhere else . . . I made all possible speed."

Linda then realized that this phone call was supposed to be the climactic event of her crisis. The marriage—so long suspect—had failed, even if it wasn't Derrick's fault. Now here, at last, was her constant beacon, her eternal and unchanging savior. Of course he really loved her. And yes, she'd been helpless and afraid, bewildered and undone, because he'd *made* her this way. He'd *kept* her like this. And now she had blessed relief. Now she could scream at her father about Linda Bauer's problems. She could scream—blame *some*one—for all her hurt.

Derrick's wife had been docile and sweet by temperament, but a spoiled bitch to the manor bred. She knew she could scream at this man, accuse him of things—both of which she did—and he would speak to her all the more soothingly. And it made her all the more passionate and shrill. She strolled around the kitchen as far as the cord would reach—crying, shrieking, waving her hand, going through wads of Kleenex. Why did men leave? Why was Life so unstable? Why had he nurtured her to this illusion of security? (An authentic quote, from years back, when her old Tercel was repo'ed. She'd screamed the question—shrill as it was eloquently senseless—into the phone, as if Lars himself had driven the tow truck.) Why in heaven's name had she married a man just like him? (Another authentic quote, from a Fourth of July there in Merrill, when Lars had taken Derrick's side in a squabble over a forgotten bowl of potato salad.) She said things which would have left Derrick, had he spoken them to *his* father, spitting teeth. "And to top it all off, look at *me*! *Look* at me! You made me a spoiled *bitch*! A miserable, wretched, heartless, spineless *bitch*! Who can't even grieve her own husband! Who needs to talk with Daddy first! Is that normal? *Huh? No! No, it isn't normal!* And you made me this way! You! *You're* the one responsible! You gave me—" *Well, fudge it. Lin's stuff. You know what she's got.* "—a car, and books, and clothes and tapes but you didn't give me *character!* You gave me CDs and no soul! Oh, no—you made me clutching and needy and helpless! So I'd always need you! Now you're in goddamn . . . overseas, now *where does that leave me*?!"

"You're still my little honey-boo . . ."

"*Since when is any almost-thirty-year-old woman still* HER DADDY'S LITTLE HONEY-BOO?!"

She stopped. Bosom heaving, she closed her eyes. There was silence on the other end of the line. From the patio came whistles, and an enthusiastic round of applause.

Then her father gently cleared his throat.

"Lin . . . okay. Since you're taking a breather. Let me say this. That I hear your pain, your anger and grief and more, some very legitimate concerns that have caused you to build up anger. All that you're describing—what your mother terms, the coddling—was my weakness, my human sin. Not letting you grow up, not trusting in your separate personhood. Not letting you be *you*. And now, your freedom to pour out your heart like this is a daughter's birthright. Knowing that your feelings are precious to me, these honest words from my daughter's heart are rubies and gold in my hand. You—"

Linda glanced right and left; she was trapped. She couldn't hang up—he'd call back. She wasn't up to a command performance. She was out of passion, real or faked; she collapsed in genuine tears. He really was so nice to her. "Dad, I'm really sorry . . ."

She said it again. And again, and again. He didn't know what she was sorry for. It made her even sorrier. So sorry, she just cried. He just listened to her cry. It was primal communication. She was still his little honey-boo.

When she was quite finished, he started talking again. He crooned and soothed, on and on; Linda paced and listened. In time, his words lulled her. She sighed, stood laxly; her wet eyes wandered the ceiling, as her father talked and talked.

She'd never been a man's daughter before. It was something like the relationship Derrick had with his mother. Only *she* was the mother . . . ?—she didn't understand it, yet. A soft, intimate bond, purely about love; discipline, obedience were trifles, motions gone through to mollify Shelley. His words affected her physically. It was like having her tummy rubbed—she couldn't help but like it. She blushed, rolled her eyes, asked him more than once to stop. If this had been a church service, Lars Bauer would have been talking, beaming, at empty pews. It would never end.

172

Linda saw it: neverending. The corner of the kitchen counter, milky-blue in winter light through curtains. The angular shadow of the cupboard: that was it. That angle was perfect, unchanging. That angle was forever. Her legs were liquid; trembling, she sat.

"Hon, are you still there?"

"Yes. Daddy, I . . . just verged on a *petit mal.*"

"Yes, dear. Make sure you're seated. You're taking your Dilantin?"

"I think I m-might have skipped, yesterday . . ."

"That's an absolute no-no, presh."

"Dad, I'm *sorry.* The shadow, the . . . not turning."

There was silence at the other end; if she needed to say something else that didn't make sense, he'd listen. At length he said, "Well, you know it's not serious. As long as you're sitting. I don't want you to fall."

"I'm sitting, like you said."

"Good girl." *Sit. It's not just Shelley, then.* "If I lose you, then I'll understand. I'll wait on the line til you're better."

Linda was tough. "Just a *petit mal.* I used to have them always."

Then with no further ado—on and on he droned. Love and acceptance, acceptance and love. She told him very frankly that she was tired of hearing it; she said—as Derrick's wife once did—that "it's too boring," like it was something on her plate she didn't want. It didn't work—the sermon rolled along. Derrick's wife had the option of switching roles—becoming the parent, the firm but gentle mother, setting limits. "Dad, I don't mean to be rude. I can't listen anymore, and I'm hanging up. I love you. Goodbye."

"No kiss?"

Just do whatever he says get it over with "Put the receiver to your cheek." She wanted to just hang up, but thought he might cheat and keep the receiver to his ear. She kissed the speaker, heard a kiss in return. "Dad, you just kissed my ear."

"Well, my aim is off. Like when I used to kiss you good-night, after I turned the light off. Remember when I read you the—?"

She hung up.

She went into the patio. "Hey, you guys want a beer or something?"

Sidekick brightly said, "Yeah, sure!"

Bird-Brain said, "But thanks anyway."

She went back into the kitchen. She felt warm. Glanced distrustfully at the hallway, then untied the denim skirt. If these guys were going to cream their pants at the sight of her bare legs, that was their stupid problem. So silly that pulling a denim slip-knot should be a momentous act, like throwing a Bible onto the floor or drawing a loaded gun. She opened the fridge, found a quart of milk. She stood and drank from the carton, felt powerful and proud as the Queen of all Heaven.

12

Linda decided to get busy on laundry. She got her mom's basket from upstairs. Struggled in the narrow hallway, trying to hold the basket while she opened the basement door. Bird-Brain was right on the case. "Hey, you want me to carry that down for you?"

El Suavo. Linda forced a smile, said "I've got it, thanks." Then it was only a matter of getting it. Finally got the stuff downstairs, got the dryer going and the cycle started. Easy.

Back upstairs, she got Windex and rags, started cleaning windows. Thought about how she'd eventually have to return to work. Caring for retarded kids was fine—if some woman didn't mind doing it. The thought of herself playing mother to a brood of drooling imbeciles was appalling. She also felt she might be scared of Mindy.

She went back down to the basement. Washing clothes was *not* a snap—she'd done it wrong. The whites were stained with leaked dyes, flecked with colored lints. Nylon stockings were stretched into the fifth dimension; wire-framed bras had mangled delicate blouses. Everything was clotted with small cakes of soap. *Stop and think: what would Linda do?*

Call her mother.

That wasn't an option; she had to puzzle it through. At last she got it under control. The whites soaked in bleach, the colors sorted. You put the soap in the water, first. You don't machine-wash wool at all. *I was never Mommy's little girl. I was never taught this, never praised for learning.* Washer on, take two. She went back upstairs, feeling heavy, hot and limp. *Men don't get like this. Take away a woman's strength, there's nothing left but cottage cheese.* The nylon Danskin held in her body heat, especially at her bosom. She pulled the low-cut neck, to let off steam. It seemed the natural thing to do, though she couldn't recall seeing women do it. With a sullen eye towards the patio, she closed the basement door, softly so as not to stir the goblins. It sounded like they were doing something stupid—banging and swearing, to no surmisable purpose. She went into the kitchen, stood aimless.

Dinner. She'd make a nice dinner and have it ready for Shelley, when she came home. Linda was guiltily aware that the

175

woman was doing her a world of favors. Making funeral arrangements. Tying up loose ends—doing more for Linda in a day than she'd done for herself in a month. Calling Linda's boss, arranging an extended leave of absence. (Derrick had performed similar service after their apartment was burglarized, once—a four-day period when Linda did nothing but sleep, cry and have seizures. The manager of Pinski Place was then a bright-eyed, sharp-nosed, exultant brunette with the silken, sinister name of Janice Shapiro. She'd said *Well of course, I wouldn't detract from these concerns. Linda finds things stressful—don't we know. I'm distressed by more global issues: the whole, you know, history of performance-related instabilities*, as if Linda taking to her bed with a bag of Mister Chips posed some slight but ominous threat to world peace.) Lastly, Shelley was—God only knew how—moving a ton of Linda's stuff up to Merrill. Linda found a cookbook, looked for something suitably elaborate. A vegetable soufflé looked good.

Searching for a colander, she learned what everyone else in this house had known for years: you could see the TV from the fridge-side counter. She fetched the remote, to surf while she made the soufflé. Soaps. Derrick's wife had been strung out on *The Guiding Light*, even to the point of setting the VCR to tape it in her absence—an extremity which seemed to indicate a twelve-step solution. This, now, was—*TGL*. Derrick's mother used to watch it. The theme music brought back memories. Home sick from school. Women doing gentle, patient work, while you rested with a fever. Clothes tumbling in a dryer. The music was updated for the Nineties, breezy and up-beat. Like women's daytime TV told her, *Look how far we came while you were gone.* The show itself was probably little changed since churchy organ flourishes underscored the action.

Linda brought up laundry. She ironed and folded while the veggies simmered. She hated being a woman; it made her mad at God. While draining asparagus, she smelled singed lycra. She'd tried to iron a bra.

As she brought up the last load, Bird-Brain squeezed past her in the small hallway; he'd taken the liberty of washing his hands in the kitchen sink. Linda had to stand flat against the wall. She held the basket waist-high, as if that made more room. She avoided his eyes—frowned at indigo sweat pants, unhappy. It wasn't right that she had to be shy and afraid in her own house.

He said, "They're really making you work, huh?" Maybe he thought she was the maid.

She managed one of her brief, solemn smiles. It was somewhat a request: *Please don't ask me anything that requires a verbal answer.*

He made a sympathetic sound in his throat. Boys fixed patios, girls did laundry, everybody worked; Life sucked, but hey. He trudged back into the patio, purposeful and graceful as a stunned ox.

Linda ventured, "Don't work too hard."

He smiled back over his shoulder. " 'Work'—what's that?"

She thoughtfully stared at his back.

Sure, we'll hire you again.

Bird-Brain.

She took the clothes into the den. Iron and fold. Watch TV. Spray starch. Is your maxi giving you full protection? Were you supposed to iron sheets? How the hell was it done?

Just fold them, then?

How?

The two guys trudged out of the kitchen, lugging all their tools. "Okay, we're outta here!" No *Thanks for your business.* Not even *You're all set.* A girl of color, folding sheets, was the maid; what did she care?

Linda, serene, unfurled a slip cover. "Don't drink too much."

" 'Drink'—what's—? . . . Oh."

They left.

Linda put all the clothes away, just as it was getting dark. No lights were on, except in the kitchen and in Shelley's bedroom, upstairs. Outside, the world was monochrome, the glistening blue-grey of winter twilight. Linda paused at her mother's bedroom window. Through the snow-laden boughs of spruce out front, she saw more woods, then the silver river of fairway. Across the golf course, another wooded slope. A house, half-hidden by pines; a single pink square, a light on in an upstairs room. It felt like no one lived out here, and everyone who did was hibernating.

She heard a car pull in. Got her pink ski coat, went out. Shelley stood by her Sunbird. Organizing, fussing. Interior light on, chimes, *Your door is a jar.* Shelley was cheerful, a brisk winter sergeant—Take this, do that, hurry in from the cold. There was something sadly heroic about being women without men.

Once inside, Linda glowingly itemized all that she'd done. Maybe she seemed manic; Shelley was reserved. "And Mom, I borrowed this? Your Danskin? And a letter fell out from behind the jewelry box? From my cousin Erminegard . . . ?"

"She's *my* cousin. I don't think you've met. Believe me, Lin, you're not missing anything."

"What does she do?"

"Not much. She's going to grad school. She gets an allowance from her father—my uncle—in eastern Germany. So she's one of very few people in the US to receive foreign aid from a former Communist country. You want to meet her?—you're *afraid* of meeting her. Well, guess what: she spoke with my sister in

177

Manhattan. She'd already planned to gallivant through New England on a ski tour. Was thrilled to ask if she should drive on the left side of the road.—New *England*, get it? She really does not. Utterly brainless. I can't tell her 'No, you can't come to the funeral'. I think she wants to meet *you*, simply because she's your age. If you do get entangled, just steer her towards men. Or better, towards the buffet. She's a cross-country cyclist/skier, so she's always starving. 'Decarbohy*drated*'." Shelley gestured, fretful—for God's sake, enough about Erminegard. "Lin, I know you're only curious. But no more snooping."

Linda blinked. "I'm sorry. I won't."

Shelley helped Linda put her things away in her room. This was somehow done as if her daughter actually needed help—as if, left to herself, she might "squinch straps into the nook, if they're too wide." Shelley held the dress to light of lamp, a perfect sample of silliness. "Just how it'll look, next time you wear it."

"Mom, how are his parents taking it?"

Shelley didn't answer at once. She ran Derrick's funeral, so of course she'd talked to the Blooms. She possessed all knowledge; her daughter had to ask. Linda couldn't lose her husband independently. "Oh. Well, Ray is . . . you know. Very tight and reserved. Your father-in-law is not the most demonstrative of men. Charlene, poor thing—whom naturally, you're closer to—sounded like she'd been crying for days."

"I want to call her." Having said it, Linda watched her mother's eyes. A calm, dark, intelligent girl who'd thought the matter through, reached the logical conclusion. Live long and prosper, call Charlene.

Shelley handed her daughter a blouse. A nosegay of peach tulle and pearled buttons, worn on casual dates and unwanted-job interviews; Linda could hang it wrong, it didn't matter. "Lin, no. You're too hyper. You'll make each other hysterical."

"But I won't."

"Lin, yes. No. Later." Shelley took blouse and hanger from her daughter's hands. "It helps to *unfold* the shoulder pads. See? You're too willy-nilly to even hang a blouse; why should you be calling anyone?"

Linda blinked wetly at her bedroom window, the all-but-dark indigo of February night. She would have to let it go.

They finished unpacking the suitcases. Linda politely said, "My, you brought everything . . ."

Linda realized. In horror, she turned to her mother, trapped.

Shelley stared back, meek and pretty; she didn't trap, she helped. "Lin, *I* don't see you going back there. To live in Salem by yourself, I mean . . ."

She decided not to finish. Just closed the suitcase, closed the door on Samara Street, South Boston, Derrick's life. Remarked "The Blooms will want to stay in touch. But such things quickly

178

fade and Lin, that's simply human nature."

Shelley smirked, apologetic: No one here but us Bauer women.

"So: you're back on square one. Home. So far as rules, there are only two." Linda gazed sadly out the window. The long, high slope of the neighbor's pasture, blue under moonlit overcast. Derrick's wife had started their marriage with "only two rules"; they'd quickly expanded into a Talmudic codex. Shelley said, "Rule number one: no continental drift of books up to your bedroom. They should be taken one at a time, read and then returned." Linda nodded, absent; reasonable rule. Same as a librarian's. "Rule number two: no science experiments in the refrigerator." That referred to Linda's habit of concocting odd things she wanted to eat—like celery bits in pineapple yogurt; deciding maybe nothing sane would eat it, then secreting it deep inside the fridge like age might improve it. "Oh Lin, I know you've outgrown that. I just want you to hear what you expect. To know you're home. And the way you were today—so helpful and busy—I know that's the real you. That's what *I* can expect."

Back downstairs, it broke Lin's heart to find that her soufflé hadn't risen, and had burned. Her mother was phlegmatic. Everyone knew Linda couldn't cook.

Linda had a suspicion. She fetched the clear jar marked *Baking Soda*. "Mom, is this baking *powder* or *soda*?"

"Well, you can read. What does it say?"

Linda read the label, curled her lip. "Shit."

"No, it does not. And since you're grown up, I trust that getting you into the kitchen won't be like pulling teeth. No more instant 'migraines' when you hear sauce pans rattle." New England gentry, old English terms: *saw*-spins. "You lucked out once but truly, men who can cook are the exception, not the rule." Linda cleaned up her aborted mess. Shelley saw fit to remark, "I'd some notion that my Danskin was a casual fashion statement. You've shown me, I guess, that it's really an exercise garment." Linda went upstairs and showered. Put on her own flannel gown. Something sensible and chaste, perfect for sitting on the apse's window ledge in the morning sun with her paperback, her cat curled warm and heavy in her lap and the terror, sudden horror *I'm haunting this life this gown I'm a ghost* sent her down the stairs, through the rooms, seeking her mother and Shelley—so used to seeing her daughter frightened—simply looked her up and down: sensible and chaste.

"Mom, I'm not . . . Mom, I can't—"

"Baby, hush. Lin, calm yourself. *Shh.*"

Shelley had changed. Into black stirrup pants, an aquamarine pullover. She touched Lin's hand, Come follow me. Time to relax, and watch TV. So Linda was walking swiftly through rooms, bright and beautiful with fear, so what. If she panicked, went wild, had a nervous collapse—it had happened before. It was normally dealt with, here in the home.

They sat on the sofa. After a moment's doubt, Linda put her feet up on the cushion. The gown came down to her shins. Was she still supposed to wear panties? Or was that silly, like wearing boxer shorts under pajamas? She laid her knees down, like her mom.

Shelley turned on the TV. "Oh wow, *The Doors*. More my generation, I suppose." She told Linda to go make them both a rum toddy. Derrick had been surprised, the first time his in-laws gave him a cocktail. He'd thought they were nip-and-tuck Lutherans; evidently they nipped, and tucked the stuff away somewhere. Linda, now, didn't know where. She thought about asking—the sweet Christian girl, *Mom I don't know where your liquor's kept*. But Shelley might say *Oh knock it off, you know perfectly*. Next to the chrome/glass demilune, a Harden rosewood sideboard, lacquered to go with the adjacent kitchen's "Chinese" motif. Inside . . . Linda, stooping, widened her eyes. Her body didn't crave alcohol. But the prettiness, the splendor . . . Cointreau, Glenlivet, Dominican brandy. Bottles all nearly full. The arched cabinet smelled only of rosewood, dust on glass. *They must collect this stuff. It must last them years*. Stuff invented by European monks, with nothing to do with years of time but make a perfect brandy. Stuff made by men for men to have. Tradition. Polished oak, old leather. Relaxing in three piece suits. Talking smoothly of interest rates and shareholdings. British Sterling on a smooth-shaved chin. *Daddy/Pretty*. So many new feelings she didn't have words for. She made the hot toddies, brought them down to the sofa.

They watched the movie, volume low. When little was said on the screen, they softly conversed. Linda thanked her mother for being so nice to her. "Yesterday, especially."—careful sip.

"Oh, right—when you were five years old."—like it had been sort of fun, but Shelley wasn't sad that it was over. Though she added, "The high point, I guess, was when you welcomed me home by screaming in my face that you were Derrick. It was something I could answer, at least. I liked it better than the sewing. Your McCall mind-blank. Sitting next to me, watching me baste, like they'd flown you in from Papua New Guinea."

They watched Val Kilmer rhapsodize about pain.

Linda mentioned that her father called. She assured her mom the call had brought pure bliss. Shelley smiled—she'd been a man's daughter herself. "Laughter and hugs and gifts from afar. It won't be long. Next month, we hope."

Linda said "*Inshallah*."

"You mean, the Jewish calendar?—Oh. Don't mind me, I'm just . . ."

180

Shelley sipped her toddy.

Linda watched her mother—her grim and precious stare. Tenniel's Alice, dubious of what the cat with the hat poured in her cup.

She said, "Dad made me laugh."—it was what Derrick's wife would have said. Her father was funny; Derrick was so funny. All the men in her life were just hysterical. "I needed it. Mom, I miss Derrick so much. I miss being . . . his wife."

Shelley, watching a movie, said, "Well he misses us too. Remember where he is, dear. We're the ones in danger and darkness; Derrick pities *us*."

It was wisdom—that of good and godly women. Gleaned from Christian scriptures, handed down through maternal generations. Yet Shelley's peculiar tone added something. *All right already, give Derrick a rest*—she might as well have said that.

Linda wondered, really didn't know: "Mom, can the Bible explain things? When something happens, really strange . . . ?"

"Good question, Lin. Yours to answer. How much did you learn? Your father used to joke that you only went to church for Friendly's after. Like you needed to feel more ashamed of eating . . . anyway. It was our family tradition. Didn't you love it, Lin? I know I *still* love Friendly's. Everything's so clean, and there's every kind of treat. Though my favorite is vanilla."

Shelley glanced back over her shoulder. Kneeling on the cushion, her slender hand on her thigh. Feral shag of golden hair, amber she-wolf eyes—she loved vanilla most.

She softly asked, "You like Val Kilmer?"

Shelley watched the movie. Linda had no answer to the question, right offhand. She looked at Kilmer, opened her eyes and heart. Sadly at peace, she said, "No, I hate him."

Mother's guidance, soft and automatic: "You *don't like* him."

"He looks cruel."

"Well, he's acting. He's playing Jim Morrison."

Linda said, "I realize that. He still looks like an Indian."

"Interesting, that you say that. Since we've never met your biological parents. But your bloodlines are always fun to guess about. We suppose you're part African-American, but the rest seems so exotic. Indian and something fierce and noble. Really Spanish. A mulatto/mestiza."

"Oh mother, how apt. I'm a fancy breed of cat."

"But not at all. Even in the antebellum South, such women were considered most beautiful. They had lavish balls, where the planters' sons would come and court the lovely girls of color."

"And if they liked her, what—they bought her?" Linda sneered at the TV. "I wish I could have lived back then. Waltzing with my suitor in my low-cut classic gown. So proud as I stand on the auction block, and catch my hero's eye: Go ahead and beat his bid, I'm worth it." Shelley simply watched the screen and Linda knew what she was thinking. Linda had romantic masochistic fantasies; her mom now wondered, was this facetious or an honest lulu. "More enchanting still, the word has a feminine case.—stiza. Like *Negress*."

"Oh, quit. You cranky thing. You're Daddy's Little Indian Princess. Pocahantas."

"Politically correct heroine for the Nineties."

"Lin, scarcely; you know you're a mouse. I can't see you loping to anyone's rescue. Or even, for that matter, paddling a canoe."

"A *weak* little Indian princess."

"Lin, this is cinnamon *powder*. There are fresh sticks in a jar."

"Derrick fell in love with Winona Ryder in *Little Women*. She's not voluptuous or anything. She looks like she reads lots of books, and got good grades in school. He liked that kind of girl. Liked me."

"Oh, an actress is a little tart or she wouldn't be in the movies."

On TV, there was violent domestic trauma over a duck. There was a knife, and blood, and brain-dead jocularity of the Wow-man-your-hand-just-trailed-like-a-rainbow variety.

"Mom, were you, like, part of the Sixties?"

"Um . . . absolutely not, I was in a convent. Really, a Lutheran youth group. We were evangelical, but—by today's Newtonian standards—pretty left of center. Back in the days when Jesus wasn't a registered Republican. Christians protested war, believe it or not."

"Do any drugs?"

Shelley sipped her toddy, watched the screen. "There was a time, briefly, when LSD wasn't immoral. It was used in controlled experiments. I mean, now it sounds absurd. Trippy colors, bell bottoms, Yeah we're probing the human psyche. But, like: when an American psychologist went to India. With a milk bottle full of White Lightning, to see how the Hindu gurus would react to this incredible catalyst. And this guru ate a million hits of acid and said he wasn't impressed. He just felt a tingle at the base of his spine. Then he and this American psychologist at once sat down and started talking about God. We were just naive enough to think, you know: magic, pretty colors. Overwhelming emotion, God—obviously a connection. Because we weren't focused on the visuals and it *was* very emotional. And sure, it tingles your spine just something so delicious. But I mean, there were reputable people involved. Doctors, churchmen, a *Harvard psychologist* . . . we were real naive."

"You knew Timothy Leary."

"When I did my undergraduate, there was some—really, quite

earnest—study into whether it had some theological meaning. Scientific theories and tests, only wanting to learn the truth: Are these people really *seeing God*, as they claim. Lin, honest: we were *straight as pins*. We went to church, we didn't drink or smoke. We wondered, 'cause we didn't know: 'Is this how He's speaking to us, in our age?' "

Linda flatly summarized, "You tripped."

Shelley said, "Sure as hell did," no longer idealistic or naive.

"Well? Did you see Him? How did He look?"

Shelley was quiet, then answered softly. "A gorgeous spring day . . . a lovely old campus. Ivied bannisters, marble fountains. Just the *feel of the day*. You think, LSD, you're floating through this psychedelic ether. But really, you're very here-and-now and we . . . were surrounded by books and professors, by knowledge and wisdom and light. No underworld stigma, it wasn't even illegal yet; we used the Sandoz solution. Tiny vials, translucent; they shone like gems when you held them to the light. Just beautiful. 'Pearly Gates', it actually said that on the carton labels, from Sweden. It referred to the color, of course. An eye-dropper, so many cc's diluted, onto a sugar cube. Like the polio vaccines we got in grade school. Three hundred micrograms: yes, that was it."

"Mom, that's enough to launch a repressed elephant."

Lost in remembrance, Shelley dismissed that: "Oh, it was pharmaceutical. Like something that happened all in your heart, or your soul. You went to sleep at first. They had a cot right there, a pillow. I had my Jocko. Toy monkey."

"Only you . . ."

" . . . got Jocko; yes. 'Where's Shelley's doll'. For my nap. It wasn't like mescaline. Fluid trails, not particulate sparkles. No drunkenness or carnal rhapsodies. Entirely pure. You slept, sometimes you dreamed. Then opened your eyes. There was a window, onto an atrium. Moss on a statue of Psyche, pachysandra. Dust motes, yellow sunbeams. It wasn't really His face. Just His shadow, passing by."

There was a commercial break; an ad for Mercury Sable.

"Mom, were you at Woodstock?"

"Um . . . no, but I was at Tanglewood that year."

They watched the movie. The plot was thinning. Jim Morrison, bearded and sotted, staggered from one drunken debacle to the next, having artistically degenerated into a pile of shit.

Linda woke up and the spacious den was dark. The grandfather ticked and tocked, patient til the morning.

Linda sat up, looked. It was two thirty-five.

She'd been covered with a blanket from upstairs. A sofa pillow put under her head. *It's nice to be a person people care for.* The thought was like a puzzle, then a mantra; it put her back to sleep.

It was snowing hard. A fine, cold sleet, whispering through frozen branches.

The backyard was cold and grey, deep snow. No one was out there. It was late, too late—it was frightening, how late it was. A million o'clock in the morning. God Himself was asleep.

Derrick stood naked in the snow. He had no place to go. No rest, for rest is part of Life. Death is waiting forever.

He saw the back of Linda's house. No lights were on. The roof was covered with snow. The Cotswold stone looked simply grey. He saw her bedroom window. Saw her face, faint Mona Lisa glow. She was sitting in her bed, looking his way. Looking through him, at the snow.

She drew a grey curtain, and Derrick was alone. There was night, and snow, grey Cotswold stone and that was all, forevermore.

It was getting light outside. Linda took the blanket up to her bedroom.

She looked in her vanity's mirror. Whatever women do to stay pretty, she hadn't been doing it. Saggy lines of character. Whose? *Some unknown woman who gave me birth. That's who I'm going to look like.*

She turned from her vanity, hugging herself. shivering a little; the room was cold. She went to her bedroom window. Touched the "Monét" curtains, which looked so much like a white sheet spread under a messy watercolor project. The designer, frustrated at having her work rejected, might have gone to throw the sheet away, only to be stopped by her boss: Wait, what are you doing? I love this, it's great. Linda found the store tag. An evil fortune from a cookie: You, young miss, were adopted.

Even though light shone bright through the linen, she half-expected to see the sepulchral gloom of her dream. To see herself, her true male self, standing out in the snow.

She parted the curtains, stood squinting at daylight. The neighbor's steep pasture, blazing white. Bare trees, deep blue sky. It looked windy, and cold as a witch's hat.

She went downstairs. Smelled gourmet coffee. Hazelnut, she thought. Shelley sat at the table, having hers. She was reading the Berkshire Living section of the Sunday paper. Some kid had delivered the Sunday paper to 26 Longmeadow Road, not knowing it was a magic house where a man had been turned into his wife. Shelley looked sweet and soft in her lilac gown. Anyone's dream of a lovely blonde. She said, "Good morning, presh."

Linda murmured, "Morning," got herself some coffee.

"There's some of that gourmet cream, you know. Hazelnut. It's very nice."

"Just caffeine for me, thanks."

"Someone drank milk right from the carton. Not like the brazen sin of old—no lipstick on the spout—but my specially trained eyes discerned a rim of, perhaps, brown sugar. It might also be a clue to the disappearance of a box of granola bars."

Linda said, "Your forensics are . . ." She flapped her hand, too drained to be a wordsmith. " . . . impeccable." She stood and sipped black coffee.

"Do you know what you'll wear to church today, Lin?"

Linda set her cup down on the counter. Cold, she slightly trembled; calm, she watched her mother's eyes. "To church. You're asking if I want to go to church." Her hand held her gown, drew the hem from her bare feet. Her body's new language, and what could it mean?—that a woman might leave the room, or pull away from her mother's touch.

Shelley said, "Well really, I assumed." She gazed as calmly back, the dominion of one shy woman over another.

"God took my . . . husband. Life. Myself, Mom God took *me*." Linda squinted, perplexed. "So now I'll *turn* to Him?"

"Linda, don't be hateful."

"I'm not. I'm sorry. I just wasn't ready for this. I mean, you want me to dress up. Look nice. For *Him*."

"I'd wear something dark, and a veil. *I* would."

"I should hide my face. *I* should hide *my* face."

"*That's* what I don't miss. These early morning explosions . . ."

Shelley set down Berkshire Living, neatly folded.

"Lin, God didn't take your life. You gave it to Him. You were twelve. You came into your father's study. Said, 'I want to know the Lord'. We prayed, and your father anointed your forehead. Linda, spiritually, you are my sister. If you feel yourself more within the modern tradition, that's fine with me. Go to your Father just as you are. In jeans. Whatever. To offer your heart in sorrow and praise. Lin, you're mature in your faith. Do as you feel best."

Shelley gazed, a tranquil sphinx.

"I gave my heart to the Lord. Maybe it was a bad investment."

Shelley said, "Be careful." Her tone was purely Lutheran. Come kick the football, Charlie Brown—I promise I'll pull it away. "Lin, you don't have to be perfect. You know what our church is about—you've been part of it for so many years. You know this Pollyanna piety, or to use our term 'exterior innocence', has never been our fashion. We're real people, searching for true spirituality and you're being so unfair."

"I'm so unfair." Linda savored the words and the thought. A tin of bon-bons, with the tiny lemon-verbena sachet on a ribbon, too pretty to open. A melody lost on a vernal breeze: "Linda's being so unfair."

Shelley gently said, "Then be a bitch." She collected her things and went to the den.

Linda thought of making herself a nice breakfast, now that she had the kitchen all to herself. Then again, she didn't want to feed her body. No more nurture. *I know you, now. You're a greedy brat, a scaredy-cat. You only want to hide and eat granola bars. Greedy cat, scaredy-brat, passive saintly Linda. With your spinster face, dumb boobs and child's voice. I hate you.* There, she was being spiritual—pommeling her flesh into submission. She drank coffee and read old magazines, while her mother got ready for church. Hot hazelnut bitterness, covers splashed with selfish slogans. *Women First, Me First, Making Time For Yourself. Learning To Put Yourself First—8 Inspiring Women Share Their Struggle.* Inside, instead, it was all about men. *How to read Him. When to watch for His signals. What all those little facial expressions* really *mean* like a crazy religion, with men as catatonic gods.

Shelley left, with no goodbye. Linda paced through the downstairs. Hugging herself—it was *cold*. Her *feet* were cold—the waxed wood floor was like stone. In the dining room, she turned on a wall heater, minced quickly over to a chair and sat, *Brrr*, it was freezing. These people had a *real* Monét sketch above their Steinway baby grand, and they didn't heat their home. *Well, that's why they're rich. They're frugal.*

" 'Like a gold ring in a pig's snout . . .' "

She sat at her vanity, wearing just her underthings. She leaned towards her reflection—poised for a moment, critically intrigued by her own critical expression—then carefully drew the pigment tube along her lower lip. Pursed her lips, then viewed the result. She guessed it was okay.

" ' . . . is a beautiful woman without discretion.' "

Who said you had to be taught all this stuff? There was rose-tinged foundation, dark rouge. There were powders and stuff and you just painted a pretty face over your real one. If it didn't turn out like you wanted, you used the cold cream to take it off and start over.

Confidence was the thing. Woman's Day had expanded her mind.

Smooth on foundation . . . all those lines and shit were gone. Then rouge. *I want to soften this expression of my eyes. And the problem seems to be my nose and cheekbones. So I want to buff them out, bring the focus outward with this stuff. Since I'm Latina, I think I'm supposed to . . . look florid. Flower-like.*

'Livid with pride, you now blush with false shame' . . . *My brows are dark—'Dare to make them darker'* . . . *just a touch of this applicator: add a sharp edge. There, that's . . .' interesting', I think. Eyelids. Line them . . . oh shit. Now I'm kohled like an Egyptian . . . princess. Actually, that's kind of neat. Shadow softly, out and away . . .*

I look so fragile. Guess I'm supposed to. Beauty isn't durable.

Mascara. Do I really want to look like Mary Pickford? I supposedly have 'dramatic' eyes, but is that good or . . . ?

She looked at her reflection, vaguely amazed. A cool, proud lady who had Life by the reins, the world by the balls: *Now, who the hell are* you?

She took the Eau de Charlotte spray she'd swiped from her mom's dresser. A puff on either side of her neck, tingle of alcohol mist. Flowers, fresh; a puff on her bosom. Fanned her hand, you didn't want it as a film over perspiration. Shook out her hair. *That easy?*

Shelley was at the kitchen table, writing in her weekly organizer. Linda came into the kitchen to look in the fridge. She wore a black leotard top with deep vee-neck, a black velveteen skirt with silk-screened florals, wooden sandals. Silver-set turquoise earrings, matching silver necklace. She'd made her face beautifully, done her nails. Shelley said, "Linda, you're lovely," with a mother's melting condescension.

Linda shrugged. "Thanks." Her mother wouldn't understand the torment, inspiration, of a male soul locked within a female body. Like any true artist, she was misunderstood. "I can be real pretty when I want. I used to think so, at least." She took the quart of milk and drank straight from the carton.

Shelley said, "Ew, germs."

"Sorry. Anyway, it's empty." Linda threw the carton in the trash. "Look, I'm sorry about this morning. I know I was an absolute . . . *c*-word." She paused, wondering if her mother would take umbrage at the expletive, even deleted.

Shelley just said, "I'm aware of that, as well."

"I woke up feeling awful. I think I'm premenstrual or something."

Shelley said, "Well, deal with it. I expected a real apology."

Linda looked at her hands. Yes, she was wringing them; she clasped them instead. "Mom, I'm sorry. I was wrong."

"Lin, I wish you'd come to church. I miss our long talks, after. Beauty and virtue and truth. We're made for that, you know. We women are in our purest glory, talking about these things."

"Some women would be furious to hear you say that."

"Someone will always be mad when you talk about virtue; yes."

187

Linda said, "I'm running out." She stared blankly: There, I dared. She was flying out the door for the most unvirtuous thing that came to mind. "For Ben and Jerry's."

Silence like a firecracker, fizzled. *No you can't. You're mentally incompetent.* "Lin, what a wholesome brunch. Oh—could you pick up an item or two?"

Linda said, "I suppose." She stood with her hand on her hip while her mother wrote on a pad, watching the list lengthen with diminishing favor.

Shelley ripped and handed. "You're a dear."

"Doe."

"Hm?"

"A deer."

"Yes. I have to go back this evening and run the nursery, and I want to make gingerbread cookies." Shelley motioned at the window, the blue-and-white outside. Her eyes twinkled—a sweet old lady hidden in that vixen bod. "Something warming. You can help."

Linda got her coat, her own black leather with embroidered velvet. Slipped on her high-heeled boots. Looking good with no one in the world she wanted to impress—in misery, she'd chanced upon a state some women strive for. *Maybe I should write a book.* Zen And The Art Of Doing Laundry, *or whatever. Maybe God has a plan for my life, other than death by despair. Maybe I'm called to be some sort of New Age Erma Bombeck.* She took her hand bag, off a hook. Fringed black leather, it matched her coat. She'd held that bag a hundred times before. *Lin, I need the ATM card. Where's it at, what pocket?* It felt no different, now; she just didn't have to treat it with respect/aversion, anymore. Didn't have to hold her breath while she made a tunnel-visioned search for that one thing she needed, careful not to look at anything she didn't need to see. It was just her bag, full of her stuff, none of which was really that mysterious or exciting. She checked her purse. Wow, cash. There since before The Event. She'd been holding out on hubby. Crafty little bitch. She went back to the kitchen. "Keys? Please?"

Shelley gave her the Sunbird keys. "Please be very cautious."

"Where's the nearest store?"

"Lin, quit. It's still the Talcott Meadows Market." In fact, Linda remembered now. The yuppie delicatessen *cum faux* country store. It had been a natural stage of their many trips to and from Merrill. *Lin, can't it wait? For what they charge for Perriére, you could buy French wine.*

The owner, however—or perhaps, not surprisingly—was an authentic Yankee. His wary "Yer not from around here, ah ya" with its silent suffix, *I hope.* He'd always been nice to Linda, though.

"I'll be right back." She remembered that little gesture.

Pinky and ring finger, toodle-loo. You wanna see *me* again?
Throw another party and I'll cater. "Bye." She went out into the
cold.

Linda leaned her tush against the counter, spooning the last
from a Rainforest Crunch while she watched her mom knead
dough. "That's what I should have gotten—Cookie Dough. I
almost did. I thought it would be like licking the batter spoon."
Shelley said, "Oh, yes—*that's* what daughters are good for."
She asked, "Did you see Mister Barnett?"—the owner of the
store.

Linda smiled fondly. "Oh, yeah. He was too funny. He made
me giggle and *blush*—so fresh. Said I was 'prettier than ever' "
and charged me $3.49 for a pint of ice cream.

Shelley was kindly ambivalent; said, "He's getting old."

Besides making cookies, they'd been folding sheets and more
were in the dryer. It felt like they were busting their butts,
especially since it was Sunday. Maybe Shelley wasn't really that
religious. She said, "There. I've kneaded the dough, you can roll
it."

"The dough."

She handed Linda the roller. "You're a dear."

"A female deer."

Shelley untied her apron and gave it to her daughter. "I need
to check the quilts."

Linda rolled the dough. Her forehead soon was warm with
sweat, her bangs in ringlets, damp. The slight muscles of her
forearm stood out; she pressed the dough. She smiled, unendingly
patient.

Shelley came up from the basement, muttering something
about a lint screen. She turned on the oven, to pre-heat.

Linda smiled, rolling the dough. "Mom, when someone . . .
you know, like an older man, Mister Barnett, tells you you're
pretty, and all . . . and there's really nothing you can say back
that's intelligent or even grown-up, you sort of *have* to blush and
giggle . . . can't it make you resentful?"

"Lin, stop."—automatic; not what I want to hear, therefore
invalid. On second thought, a reason: "He's sold you so many
magazines and freeze-pops, since you were old enough to hand
money over the counter . . . he can tell you you're pretty. I give
him permission."

Linda shrugged, a slow and soulful resignation. She said,
"Well, he's old," drawing out the final sound like there were
millions of things to love about the elderly, she just couldn't
think of one offhand.

"And I'm sure you were . . . you. Made a point of seeming
all grown-up and . . . *likeable*. Which is fine. Though knowing
Mister Barnett, I'd advise you to be a little more reserved. Since

189

he's liable to be *really* fresh and then we'd *all* be resentful."

Linda rolled the dough, lightly said, "Oh, mother! Barf-o-rama!"

"Well Lin, it's not unnatural per se. Women your age do go with men his. I just think you can do a lot better than Mister Barnett."

Linda smiled. She rolled the dough so nice and *flat*. "You know, I'm stretching my mind to its broadest limits . . . say someone his age had money. And they were handsome—well, Mister Barnett's *okay*; sort of distinguished with that white hair, I guess . . . say he was *rich*. Say he was *kind*, which matters even more . . . I'd only get it twice a month, or . . . ?"

Shelley was looking at a recipe book. "What is 'it', dear?"

Linda said, "You know," coy and sweet; girl talk was such fun.

Shelley closed the book, she *tsk*ed; perhaps she needed something they didn't have. "Lin, you're thinking of an older man with an older woman. A buttercup like you would make a man your father's age the Eighth Wonder of the World." She came over to the sunlit counter, a vigilant instructress. "I think the dough's rolled. Now you get to do the fun part." She gave Linda a gingerbread-man cookie-cutter. Linda made a face—eyes wide, jaw dropped, sheer joy. As soon as Shelley turned from her, Linda frowned broodingly. The tin cutter was faintly frosted with ancient flour. She touched the tin mold's crotch. No, it was not anatomically correct. Gingerbread *person* then, really. Maybe that was right for Shelley's church, since they used the New RSV Bible. The one that changed *men* and *sons* to *mortals* and *offspring*, though it prudently left God Himself alone. Anyway, time to make gingerbread folks.

Shelley wistfully murmured, "We need confectioner's sugar . . ."

Linda stood at the counter, one hand on her hip. Not sugar-and-spice but a woman with body hair and sweat glands, she . . . *pressed* the cookie-cutter. *One* cookie-wookie . . .

Shelley was on tiptoes, looking through a cabinet. It was a regular square cabinet, not one with a revolving lazy Susan. No lazy Susans in this house. Shelley turned and noted Lin's demeanor. Couldn't have been meaner. "Dear, come on. You're making cookies for kiddies—be sweet. Don't be a miffy-maid. No one wants a miffy-made cookie."

"Mom, you're so right. I'm just . . ." Linda smiled, shaking her head. Mother was a constant fount of wisdom. Daughter was her foil, the paradigm of error. Lips pursed with mounting tension, she jabbed the cutter into the dough. One, two, three, *four*, this-is how-we make-a *cookie*—

She squashed the cutter into the dough, ground it into the linoleum with vengeance. She stepped back and crossed her arms

190

under her breasts. Daddy's little Indian princess wasn't grinding any more maize.

Shelley was right there, of course. "What in heaven's name—?"

Linda turned on her mother with swift, soft-spoken vehemence. "This. Me. *This.*" She yanked at her apron. *"This."* She fiercely squeezed the flesh of her breasts. Her mother, face askew, winced in sympathetic pain. *"This."* Linda put her hand to her cheek: undeniably pretty, soft, an angel's face—her eyes were cold. "And this." She pointed to the dough. "This is stupid, Shelley. It's stupid, stupid, *stupid*. The cookies are stupid. The dough is stupid. The recipe is so fucking *stupid. I'm* so stupid, cutting dough in silly shapes and I'm doing it wrong 'cause I'm not *happy!* I shouldn't be a '*miffy maid*'! *Happy* maid! *Honey* maid! Graham cracker! Everything's babies and sugar and dough, everything's simple and puffy and dumb, I'm a big dumb chick and I'm supposed to lay an egg? And leave it on the floor or do I go—" She struck a winsome pose, in frenzy doing a fair young Shari Lewis. "*Oh, my!*" she twittered musically, "*I* just laid an egg! Now I'll get the broom and—"

Shelley slapped her daughter's face.

Linda touched her numbed cheek. She was thoughtful, no more sensitive to mere physical pain than any other woman. The slap was just really *hard*.

Shelley tilted her head, gently curious, like Linda was some pretty thing but Heaven knew just what.

She said, "I'd like you to go to your room, please." She sounded very tender, like a child. She even dropped her *r*, your woom.

Linda untied her apron. "All right."

"I realize you're an adult. This is awkward for me too." Shelley was having an awful time with her *r*'s; really, letting her English slip.

Linda gave her the apron. "Did you find confectioner's sugar?"

Shelley took the apron. "No. After I had you get sugar dots, even. Silver, and I shouldn't think what's in them. I forgot confectioner's sugar. Filled the bath, forgot the baby . . . scary when I act my age."

"Is this normal?"

"Sent to your room. Well, it's normal for us. I'm not aware you've expressly outgrown it. You're very young, when you're with Dad and I. As for me, my mother sent me til the very week she died."

"Did you go?"

Shelley tied the apron on, girding her loins with strength. The apron of responsible adulthood of which her daughter was relieved. "Certainly not."

Simply puzzled, Linda told her mom, "I'm twenty-*nine*."

"You don't want to be like me. Darling, you're so docile. You'll go to your room now, as I asked."

"Is docile good?"

"Docile's dear. I made you so. I think it's too adorable."

"You're taking advantage of my docile nature?"

"Sure. Since you *are* so very docile, you won't mind. I'll come up and see you in . . . well, I'll come up *later*."

Shelley made no move, but Linda flinched. She told her mom, "I have every intention of going. But I'm scared you won't respect me."

Shelley viewed her dismally. Linda made a sound she couldn't help: a whine of fear. Miserable, she shrugged: I couldn't help it.

"If you went calmly, gently shut your door, I'd see that as ladylike. Honestly, I would admire you. If you stay down here and we fight, I . . . probably won't." Shelley blinked, unsure if this digression was to any good purpose. Linda went to her room.

She lay on her bed and stared at the ceiling. Detached, she tried to analyze her feelings. They seemed those of a girl who's been disciplined by her mother. She needed . . . a stuffed toy donkey. She held it to her shoulder. They both felt so much better.

Shelley came in about fifteen minutes later. Her eyes glittered magically at sight of the donkey, but she kept a straight face. She sat on the chair, curled into a winsome pose: Cuter than you, and I don't need stuffed animals.

She softly asked, "What do you feel, right now?"

Linda twitched her hip.

"Mom, my living at home . . . I think it might not work."

Shelley agreed: "You're still regressed. Only now, it's adolescence. Though Eeyor seems to think we're not quite out of the Three Acre Wood."

"I knew I was venting in your face. I'm sure it wasn't pretty. But you didn't have to *hit* me."

Shelley said, "Oh, you needed it," like it was a kiss.

Linda held the donkey on her tummy, peered sadly at its long, narrow face. "I think she's a *girl* donkey. I think her name is Stubborn Linda." She hugged it to her shoulder again. "Don't cry, Stubborn Linda."

Her mom was really tickled. "Oh God, your husband trained you. Act three years old and ride the pretty pony."

Linda corrected her, absently: "No. I was always on the bottom." She studied her donkey's button-eyes, said "You were very bad. You got smacked, and you deserved it, and that's only sad but true."

"Linda Bloom, Sad But True,

"I think that's a good name for you."

She murmured, "I don't like that. Someone else can be that."

"But dear, it's not unlovely. Sad but ever faithful and sincere. Another man will love you, Linda. Just for who you are."

"Is that what this is all about? Is that who I'm going to be?"

Shelley didn't answer. After a certain point, her daughter needed to find her own way.

"Mom, when did Daddy spank me, last?"

"Hon, you were twelve. Your dad made sure your religious conversion went to your head: 'Princess of Israel', *really*. You used some phrase you'd picked up at school. Oh, right—you told him to *shove it*." Shelley laughed, a little minx herself.

Linda said, "I didn't like it? Or . . . ?"

"You were shocked, is how I'd put it. Like a young lady, you told him, 'I'll thank you to know I'm not spanked'. Then, like a twelve-year-old, fled to your room."

"He didn't want to do it."

"He did not. And he told you, it was on my orders. Then gave you an accelerated series of love-pats. Oh, shit—I said 'Give her to *me*!' *I'd* fix you, my pretty."

Linda touched her stockinged heels, ready to go home.

Shelley went to the door, then turned. "An entire pint of ice cream? Lin, it's not even two o'clock."

Linda softly told her mom, "I'll miss you, when I go. Being your daughter has been a total trip."

Shelley stuck her tongue, and went downstairs.

Linda lay on her bed. She stared at the ceiling. It didn't seem like there was anything else she should be doing. It seemed like Derrick's wife spent half her life just staring into space.

It didn't look like she'd be going out again, and the velveteen skirt was too warm. She got up and undressed, put on her nightgown. It also seemed like Derrick's wife spent two-thirds of life in her nightie.

She looked through her bookshelves, selected *The Secret Garden*. One of Linda's favorites, though her husband never read it. She lay in bed and read two chapters, realized she was reading a children's book and put it back.

What an odd person's life I'm assuming. Yet everything feels sensible. So normal. Like man comes out of woman, returns to her later in life, and I've just closed that circle in a way that's too complete. Like I'm female after all, and it's only sad but true.

She idly stirred the window's curtain. She looked at her hand. Slender and soft like a child's, though imbued with adult cleverness. Gentle and brown, in sunlight filtered through linen.

She looked out at the neighbor's pasture. White snow with patches of chocolate mud, like some melting dessert. A clump of dun Herefords milled at a corner of the split-rail fence, where pasture ended and woods began. That whole corner was trampled mud—the place to be, for whatever reason. She saw the farmhouse, flanked by ancient willows, at the summit of the slope. Gambrel roof, narrow windows, painted somber slate. It was a New England house—dull, functional, built to last. It seemed, somehow, like a Puritan house—home to many generations. Under grey winter skies, rolling black summer clouds—they lived without displaying great emotion, worked hard and died in peace.

I wonder if they spanked their daughters . . .

I wonder how I really feel, because my daddy spanked me.

She knew she had all Linda's heart; the answer was inside her. She wouldn't have to wonder long, if she really wanted to know.

Well, I . . . didn't like it. *Then. I was disciplined by my father. Humbled. I felt I was becoming a woman and he took me over his knee. Took my adulthood away, like it was his to give or take. And I felt he had no right. I felt I was more the adult, because I drew it from my own heart. In that moment, I didn't need him.*

Guess he should have spanked me more often.

Later, though . . . years later. Looked back in my heart and found myself held and handled. Warmth and love. Pearl around a grain of sand; it turned to sweetness, deep inside. My body, not my own. My pride laid down across his knee.

She gazed out the window, her dark eyes softly vacant.

Her fantasy was like an early Technicolor romance: simple and vivid, elegant and naive. Deep in body images, drenched in tropic moonlight, dappled waves and languid palms.

Soft thighs squeezed together, she already felt the little squish of wet between her legs. She hugged her hair-sweet pillow.

Her special someone was someone she knew. He looked like Derrick, sort of. But way handsomer. Handsome as only she could imagine, but she liked him just for who he was. The big brother she'd never had. Someone who could fix cars and do layup shots. He'd always look out for his little sister . . .

They'd come through this together. They'd both suffered, long and deeply. But while she'd been eating quiche and peeing on Shelley's carpet, he'd been on a dreadful mysterious mission. He'd returned from Death itself. He'd come back just for her, to take her home.

He met her on the beach. He was wearing a black body suit of thin elastic, with wrist and belt ballasts and a waterproof chronometer. There was no special reason why Death had to have been underwater. She just felt that a black scuba suit was the sexiest thing a man could wear.

She wore a strapless gown, white silk. Her black curls were

stirred by the tropic evening wind. She looked really good—she was beautiful. She sort of needed to be. She'd never been a woman with a man before. She really wasn't sure about her part of the script.

He saw that she was scared; he held her. Safe in his strong embrace, she laid her head on his shoulder. Watched the surf cascade and flow, moonlight melt across the silver sand.

He lifted her chin, Be here with me now. *Share with me. What's wrong.*

So afraid I'll wet myself.

Linda glanced moodily at her bedroom door. Her damn mom better not burst in.

After a while, she lifted her hips and pulled up her gown. Touched herself. She already knew how.

am I wet?

Not . . . really. She licked her fingertip.

Aren't you going to talk to me, first? Or . . . ?

He smiled. Careless, like a boy. He'd be with her, then go play basketball. *What should I say?*

I don't know. That's up to you.—she liked that. Something easy.

He picked her up. Feet out of the water, *Wheee.*

He said he'd keep her, care for her. He'd never let her go.

She said *Let me go,* just to see if he was lying. He laughed at that, No way. His arms were like two cypress roots. She was just a tidal nymph—trapped in tree, for good.

He set her down. Feet in water, gritty sand. He smoothed her skirt, wet silk around her hip. She looked at him, thoughtful. *Who said you could touch me there?*

As though in answer, he held her. His arms up her back, holding her shoulders. He kissed her and she closed her eyes. Took his tongue and shivered in the crystal-cool sea breeze. He held her hips, she moved them. *There, is that what you want?* He took her gown, her sacred hem, held it wet against her waist. She laughed, *Hm.* Liked him, kissed his lips.

He touched her. He knew how.

Her arms around his neck, she wanted to take him. Driving her crazy. *Feels so . . . oh.*

Suddenly, she felt afraid, that people might be looking. Turned her head, her hand to her lips. He didn't mind her looking. He thought it was cute, how she looked. Tropic beaches in old movies were like Eden—all alone.

His finger probed, it found the nub. Touched the button, turned her on, inside. Electric water in the bottom of her tummy. Spread warmth into her heavy thighs. God, she felt like a beast. Like she was turning into a man herself. Held his neck like she would take him down, licked his lips and tongue.

195

Too much—he picked her up again. Nice for her, to know who was boss. She gazed down at the sand, wondering how she could be so high, feel so safe, just being held.

She looked at him, calm. They kissed again.

They left the beach, went away in a convertible, which everyone in early Technicolor seemed to drive. They went to his bungalow, out on the beach. A patio, trellised hibiscus. He said she could come and go like a cat or simply stay. Be quietly frantic, read her books, make potpourris, he'd never question or be jealous. He'd tell her want to do, but he'd never criticize her. Never show her anything but love.

They made love on the moon-bathed sheets . . .

She wanted something to do with her legs. Something to hold. Her pillow, which she put there hoping it wouldn't get raunchy somehow. She held on with her legs, *Oh yes* . . .

They lay entwined, limbs gently astir, quiet but for her soft sighs, the light smack of their kissing lips. They lay in tropic evening's light blue gloom, so much like the monochrome "night scene" tint of vintage Technicolor.

How can I win your heart?

He really wanted to know. She could hurt him, if she wanted to.

She smiled. *I don't know. How did you?*

She held his neck like she needed kindness, always needed more. So he'd know, he owned her heart. He worked his will, a rhythmic pacifier. On the outside. On the lips. *Baby needs it most right here.*—in. He came inside.

She wanted something to hold in her arms. Something to love. She wanted . . .

My donkey. Oh for chrissake. Well I guess you're not a girl donkey after all.

As one in warm, dark stillness. *I'll never let you go.*
Lie beneath you, always . . .

After a while, she got up on her knees. She took the pillow, looking to make sure she hadn't pee'ed. It sort of felt like she had, though of course she hadn't. She lay on her side, feeling that she'd lost something. She drew up her knees, wanting to hold in whatever she had left. She felt empty and alone, in a way past all understanding.

Abruptly up on her knees again, she clutched the donkey, studied its face. Pretty silly excuse for a man. She threw it but—since she was spent, and didn't quite know how to throw—it only tumbled on the carpet.

Linda cried out with all her heart—the only words that came to mind:

"*I want my popsicle back!*"

She dove into the mattress, bounced on the bed. Flopped onto her side, lay fetal, wept. And wept and wept.

She'd forgotten about that part.

13

Two days passed quietly. The Bauers' house became familiar. Monday, Linda felt some cozy vibe on the indoor patio. She sat in the wicker love seat under the potted ficus tree, and finished *The Secret Garden*. Then she went to the Bauers' outdoor greenhouse, vaguely hoping for some miracle. Instead, Shelley put her to work. Potting seedlings. The soil was sticky-black as could be and they mixed it with liquid fertilizer that stank like fish. Linda didn't realize she'd been averse to it, or complaining, til Shelley put an azalea blossom in her daughter's hair. "There, still sugar-and-spice."

That afternoon, they did the other McCall's pattern—the suit dress—in paisley which was all they had enough of. Shelley asked if Linda wanted to go to "the Shops"—at Talcott Notch—for a belt. After Abigail's Fabrics they could browse the Country Craft Shoppe, have a croissant at the Halfway Café. (The Shops were across from the fairway's ninth hole.) Linda shyly smiled, shook her head—she'd pass.

That evening, they discussed the funeral. Linda wanted the casket closed. She had to scream and cry to get her mother's agreement. Her angst was partly sheer frustration—she missed the sufficiency of speech. That was one of many reasons why she hated being female—you got so mad you cried, and nobody backed off. In fact they got closer, to pat and coo and tell you to stop.

Tuesday morning, Linda got up at first light. She put on her robe, her own quilted cotton with iris-and-tulip. Went down, soft and swift, to the den. She stood at the sliding glass door.

It was warm outside—an ephemeral fog, losing the neighbor's slope in pastel haze. The snow on the lawn was mostly melted—just isolated, hard-edged bergs, stranded on the sodden lawn. She went out onto the porch. It was cool and wet, but not cold. Stray breezes brought chilled scents of water, bark and somehow fern. The forest's abiding musks, hidden through the winter, now released.

She looked at the woods, beyond the lawn. The snow, melted and refrozen, bright and smooth like glass, like ocean waves through pilings of pine and sugar maple.

Action to her right, a frantic flutter. The bird feeder was

doing business. Two chickadees, black-masked, swooped in and out like nervous commandos, taking turns with a matronly, more leisurely titmouse.

From somewhere deep in the empty woods came the monotonous/complacent ticking of a chipmunk.

Linda turned, saw Shelley. Excited, she asked, "Do you hear it?"

Shelley smiled, nodded; she seemed sad.

Linda said, "The *chipmunks!* I love them. They're mine."

"Yes, dear. You're in charge of the chips."

The vacant woods broke Linda's heart. "They think it's spring. When it gets cold again, they'll die."

Shelley was phlegmatic. "Well, many of them do. They're quick breeders, and not all that bright. It's Nature's way of keeping them within reason." They went inside and closed the door, Linda stealing a last, worried look at the warm-too-early woods.

Later, they baked a vanilla layer cake for a neighbor child's birthday. They drank coffee all morning, heightening Linda's perception of the Bauers' kitchen as this blue, adrenalized stage of the absurd. The first batch of layers fell when Linda closed the oven door too hard.

She stood, then decided to cry. While she was at it, she sobbed.

Shelley consoled her, trying not to laugh, since *MacArthur Park* was playing on the radio. For Shelley, having the radio on meant LYT-FM or nothing; vintage folk and themes from Sixties movies. They'd earlier played *A Summer Place*, perhaps to hit a nostalgic note on this foggy February morn. Shelley couldn't have known, nor could Linda have explained, that *MacArthur Park* was why she cried—it was dear to her real mother, Charlene Bloom.

Shelley asked if Linda wished to take the finished cake up to the Baldriges'—just up the road, at the T. They were old friends, they'd be thrilled to see her—variation on a mother's perpetual theme, *I promise the people there will be nice.* Linda shyly smiled. Slightly shook her head—You know me, I'm just too shy.

That night, she went to bed with one last, wild flight of hope. Her body still existed. If she prayed with all her fervent heart, maybe by some miracle . . .

She woke at seven, a girl in her bed. Sat as sullen, and as sad, as wilted violets. *It's your funeral.* And she had to go.

Shelley supplied the black dress, hat and veil. Linda said, "I've never wondered about these before—I mean, where they come from. I don't recall seeing, like, a funeral boutique with mourning mannequins in the window—"

Shelley was in no mood to reflect. "I don't know where they come from, either. Probably, from wherever matching socks disappear to. That's one of Newton's laws, dear: the Conservation of Rayon."

The long ride to Boston. A pretty winter's day, snow-patched fields before evergreen hills. "Mom, let's stop and get something to drink."

Shelley watched the road. Linda looked at horses.

"Maybe just a . . . pack of wine coolers. Pink. Passion fruit, I think . . . I just remember how it tastes. We could crank up . . . well, Carly Simon is all right."

Shelley had no comment, just slipped a tape into the deck. She hadn't the time for the pain.

The funeral home was on a quiet residential street across from Columbus Park. It was in a nice neighborhood, though—in that way unique to Boston—only blocks away from the horrors of Dorchester. The home itself was a modest Greek Revival, purplish brick, white-plastered columns on the porch. It was on a corner, yard dense with oaks and doubtless more acorns than grass in the summer. Inside, the walls were papered a brooding magenta without manifest excuse, except the brick outside was sort of purple. The floors were polished oak with runways of burgundy carpet. The house had that indefinable aura of a venerable past, which buildings sometimes possess just by virtue of being old and well-built. It felt like it had once been an important place, the office of some prominent law firm. A place of strict rules and officious memos. It had probably just been someone's house.

Reverend Gershing, from Derrick and Linda's church, gave the eulogy. Linda spoke to him after the service. He'd often talked with the Blooms after church, and had visited their apartment. Now it seemed like he'd had some heavy raps with Derrick, while his wife served tea and carrot cake. No manly exhortation, no rugged road ahead—he spoke to Lin about her feelings. Her relationship with God, her acceptance of His will. He covered all of this without resorting to big words.

The reception was *à la* South Boston: beer. No wine coolers, though.

Charlene was as Linda had feared—emotional, dramatic. Yet Linda went to her directly, at the reception. Charlene said, "You're still family, Lin. You'll always be a part of us."

Linda said, "But that's too kind. I feel I don't deserve it."

Charlene lifted her own veil. Then *please Mom don't* she lifted Linda's.

Linda blinked, impassive. *See? Just me. Just Linda.*

Wasn't that unforgivable, or something? To lift a widow's veil? Or was she thinking of Saudi Arabia? Charlene kissed her daughter-in-law. Linda closed her eyes in anguish. *Mom, I'm right here. I'm not gone. I'm miserable, unhappy, in this dress I wasn't born to wear but I still love you. Mom, I do.*

200

Ray Bloom didn't want to talk. Linda didn't want to hear his pained and careful choice of words, like women were these weird little senile grandmothers and he needed to speak some special language to them. Linda knew he was just mad at the world and doing what he knew was wrong, being cold to his son's widow. *How he talks to Mom, sometimes. I don't see how she stands it.* Linda stared sullenly at the floor behind Ray's back, as he tiredly reeled off the list of stock phrases he felt all women expected to hear. "You know, that father/son thing . . . we talked and talked but never really opened up . . . there was always that guy-thing, you know, that competitive tension between us . . . it was how we both wanted it, though." She felt the emotional distance as she never had before. Partly because she was much more sensitive to it, meeting him with a daughter's heart but also because the distance was much greater. She was just the dark, dim, pretty little skirt his son had—for unfathomed reasons—married. She recalled a vicious statement—*so feminine for a colored girl*—heard in passing then absorbed in family silence, something he would never say and that she hadn't heard. Ray finished with a clumsy, reluctant hug. He knew she didn't want it but he thought it was the right thing to do and so, she endured it. *Dad,* "stop you're squishing my" *boobs.* She stepped back, someone's daughter but not his. Someone people loved; she blinked languidly, *Goodbye.*

There were people from the Bauer side whom Linda didn't know. There seemed to be lots of old women, and an inordinate number of old men. The men were almost cheerful, and a lot of their conversations seemed to be about business and financial matters. She even caught the tail end ("—*walking across the water hazard, said 'That guy just teed off with a nine iron!' So the priest tells the rabbi*—") of a golfing joke. Shelley touched Linda's arm, startling her slightly. There was someone for her to meet.

Erminegard looked very young; in fact, Linda knew, they were both twenty-nine. She was, no surprise, a ravishing blonde, though with gothic, green, malevolent eyes. Suzanne Somers, demon-possessed. "In light of all things, just Erma's fine"—she was cosmically important. She wore a long-sleeved calico dress with pleated bodice, in a pattern that looked (at first) like autumn leaves. That might have been okay, but it was actually olive-gold magnolia. The whole thing looked like camouflage, suggesting that she either had outlandish notions or had given it no thought and now looked festive, surrounded by black. She said she was on extended leave from Fordham, where she was *pursuing her master's new, clear physique.* Her scent was an almost intolerable honeysuckle/sandalwood; it seemed inconceivable that she wouldn't be pestered by bees in warm weather. She was apparently treating the funeral as a cocktail

201

party to which—like the cynical parvenu in a British comedy—she'd been invited by mistake. Linda realized, with alarm, that Shelley had left them alone.

Erminegard asked, "Lin, do you smoke?"—they clearly weren't a love match, but Fate had made them companions.

Linda, uncomfortable, said, "Sometimes. I'd like a cigarette . . . yes." She'd wanted one for some time. She just hadn't recognized the craving, since Derrick had never smoked.

They went out onto a little balcony like two kids home from college, bored by a family gathering.

The balcony was balustraded, raised just over a tiny garden, hidden from the street by mature rhododendron. There was a bird bath, now holding a wheel of melting snow like an over-sized dish of sherbet. An amorini, encrusted with lichen and all but swallowed up in yellow-fronded hasta; perhaps an appropriate symbolism, Life's trifles come to nought. Linda realized that this balcony was so designed and intended, as a time-out room from grief. She also saw that you wouldn't be conscious of this ambiance unless you didn't need it—unless you were just stepping out for a smoke. Linda took her hat off, set it on the beveled banister. Erminegard said, "Oh! That thing with the hair; I like it."

Linda was wary of her new acquaintance. "It's a French braid." Her mom did it for her; she knew it was right.

It was warm, in the forties at least. It felt like spring though Linda had a nostalgic feel of autumn. Perhaps from the smell of wet leaves. Erminegard offered a pack of Virginia Slims. Linda took one, accepted a light. Drew smoke and stood gazing out through the broadleaf hedge; a narrow vista of receding lawns, bare trees, a distant playground. Distant growls of urban traffic. She didn't stop to think that she was smoking like a pro, having never in all Derrick's life even held a cigarette.

Erminegard chattered away. She was so animate and enthused that Linda thought she was on diet pills. She talked about her recent adventures, touring Massachusetts. Shopping at Neiman Marcus in downtown Boston. Compared Faneuil Hall with an Oktoberfest. She discussed women's fashion, like she had any business raising the topic—an esthetic analysis almost metaphysical in its obscurity. "Post-existential romanticism. Really, dear, that's all that is left." The girl's relation to Shelley came clear, in her face but more in her mannerism. Linda ignored what she said, watched her face. Girlishly expressive, oddly unfocused on her listener; Linda felt like a mirror. " . . . as when I was in Europe, last. Pursued by Carl, my Fordham friend—one of these American students of physique who must look for transcendental meaning." Linda was starting to suspect that this oblique passion for her master's physique had more to do with quarks and neutrinos—that Erminegard studied nuclear

202

physics, but felt that she couldn't just say so. "Everywhere I go, he is always at my heel—*das Wanderer und sein Schatten. Aber Sie bicht ein Deutschespracher, ja?*"

Linda said, "Not really. I understand when it's spoken to me. Sometimes." She tapped her ashes, frowned at the distant playground.

Erminegard said, "Oh I see," like Linda's inability to converse with her in German had drawn some emotional curtain. Went on to question Linda nonetheless. Her views of different philosophies, her ideas about clothes. Linda found herself playing a role which somehow seemed imposed on her—the sullen, self-righteous American girl. " . . . to be so skinny: more the West. At home, the *Ostfrauen* still are big. Like *Marilyn*—okay?" Linda had to know who Marilyn Monroe was; that was non-negotiable. "All buxomy is fine; is how men like and so, our diet—meat and bread. Under Communism, we were told it was most healthy. That tofu and bean sprouts were a capitalist subterfuge to weaken women. I guess, because of 'Lenin's Law'—Vegetables go East. Or because it's true; who knows. We altogether worked on farms—strenuous like *gymnastique*. Like with the weights, with the barbells." This last was so garbled by her accent—*mitsy vades, mitsy baubles*—that Linda pictured couture based on dolls and their accessories. Fashion Mitsy, with her vades; baubles sold separately. "So really we are all too strong. End up in Olympics, getting medals for our masters." She rolled her eyes, blew a blonde wisp from her mouth—a perfect impression of her cousin.

Linda dropped her cigarette. Arms crossed under her bosom, she crushed it out with her shoe. "I used to be a man."

Erminegard said "Oh!", as if simply agreeing—yes, then that would be one-up on female gymnasts.

Linda said, "I'm male.—I'm *supposed* to be male. I'm female, but it's wrong for me." She added, "I like men, but that's just my body's feelings."

Erminegard remarked on this as though from mere politeness—Oh, so you enjoy racquetball. "Oh, so you're female gay."

Linda answered coolly; she was in fact cold, and ready to go back in. "The English word is, lesbian. No, I am not; I just said."

"No, not that; I mean, *female gay*. A man who loves men, trapped in a woman's body. The opposite of *male lesbian*."

Linda, rather absently, pondered a reply. To explain that her identity was separate from her sexual feelings would have been absurdly tedious. She decided to leave it alone.

"Linda, don't pout. I wasn't being cruel. I honestly don't care."

Linda felt the girl was too close, too bright and malicious. A pretty white cat, excited by a bird. Linda looked away, shy and proud; the sound of passing cars was more interesting than this conversation. She said, "You might not understand. If it seemed like I was approaching you somehow, that's—"

"—not it at all. Darling, this shyness of yours is so dear. I'm used to so much worse." To emphasize, Erminegard gestured: thrust her two fingers, made a sound like a little boy shouting a toy gun. Charmingly childish; a five-year-old girl who'd seen a ten-year-old boy do something cute.

Linda said, "What's that. I don't know what it means."

Erminegard said, "Oh, you know:"—repeated the gesture. "Like the lightning bolts. Two lightning bolts. Why we are sick, as a people."

Linda calmly watched her eyes. Slightly shook her head, Scared of you, yes. What do you want?

"Linda, do you know this term: *matriarchal*?"

"That's . . . myth. Anthropologically, that's . . . not true. Feminist . . . reconstruction of anthropology."

Erminegard clicked her tongue. "Oh dear, it's worse than that. There's one exception. In all of history. Those were ancient Germans."

"I . . . don't really know, but I don't think that's true."

"Yes. Primitive people. Barbarians from Asia. Fair-skinned, blonde; the oldest, those westernmost, angels. *Angles*—to fish. Same Sanskrit as *to watch*, to be an angel. They wandered cold forests of Europe."

Linda leaned to look at the street, like someone was coming to pick her up.

"The Romans feared them. They drove Emperors mad. '*Varus, give me back my legions.*' They were fiercer than the Slavs, crueler than the Celts. Hellenes thought their speech was all *bar, bar*—original barbarians. Linda, do I frighten you or something?"

"No. You don't fwighten me. Frighten me. No. I'm just . . ."

"When a village was attacked. The men drew steel to defend the village; the women drew steel and stayed inside. When the Romans came with horses, they were strong; crashed through walls. Crashed through into the longhouse, and there she was. The Blonde Beast of legend. Sword in hand, her children at her back. As tall as the Roman man, and little weaker. They were obsessed with her, you know—the Romans. All their women bleached their hair. If you study the classical sculpture, Lin, you see the evolution: Roman goddesses, into German women. High cheekbones, braided hair. At last, the heavy bosoms."—Eye contact, suspicious; Mine are smaller than yours, so what—Erminegard shrugged. "The icons were originally painted, so we know: Juno and Minerva 'had more fun'. Like the commercials for the dye. Much later, the Germans absorbed the Roman infrastructure. I say the English right?" —she did, but barely; "absorbed" was *ah-soir*-bed, like some fancy continental dessert. "Became Christian, with the Pope like the Emperor was before. With the Church like the old Roman government. Same laws, same roads. Same language, for the Mass. Same temples, though now churches. Because every temple had, what? —a statue of a woman with her baby, right? Isis and Horus? Damuzi and Tammuz? —they just called it something different. Madonna Mary and her Kid. But really, same religion. Of dark; of Yin; of Earth. Death and fertility. Recognizing Woman is the Beast inside of Man. And loving this, making it spiritual. Knights and ladies, cultic love. Romance, a new invention." Erminegard smiled, which—in that manner so German and sadly unfeminine—she did with only half her mouth. "So unlike the calm, clear *Weltänshauung* of the Arabs and Chinese. We never stopped being barbarians. Never peace with Nature. Never friends with God. We never even liked ourselves—Darkness was our only friend."

"Cold. Did they say it would snow, or . . . ?"

"You know this myth, right?—that Woman destroys all things? She even damns the gods? Wagner was obsessed, he personally held the auditions. He said, Okay if she's not blonde—that is a problem for hairdressers. Didn't care for her soprano virtuosity, whether she could sing the lovely arias from Mozart. Only that she make 'the floorboards creak. The chandeliers rattle, the audience quail'. Lin, he wanted a blonde-haired girl to get up on a stage and scream at the top of her lungs, her man was dead and she would kill God to get even. German men watch this, and it's sexual. Religious. *Both*. Lin, don't you think Wagner is decadent?"

Linda said, "I wouldn't know. I'm more into books." She just wanted to escape from all this gaseous German nonsense. The thought so strongly took her mind she almost spoke aloud: *I'm going to tell Mommy you won't let me come inside.*

"Lin, what a world of dark ideas! Votan—God Himself—was ruled by his wife Freida. Like the father of a German family—he bangs the table, screams and roars, the impotent rage of a child. Because he is ruled by his wife. The ancients didn't bother God. They only prayed to His daughters."

Linda said, "I've read lots of books. I've never heard any of this. I think you're making it up."

"Well, so . . ."—a tilt of golden head; being brainless didn't hurt, cost nothing and was scads of fun. "Runes are still obscure. They weren't an alphabet. Ideographs, like Chinese. But fewer. Denser. There are two runes for the noun *walküre*. The transliteration, symbols *choice* and *death* and then, *epiphany*. Bolts of lightning, two. Goddess comes to Earth, which can't endure Her; She must leave at once. The lightning flashes twice, like Iron Maiden."

Linda looked back through the glass-paned door, into the

reception room. Carpet, quiet, family, warmth. She wanted to go back in and be a widow. She wanted to hear gentle words about loss and love and hope after all. She had a vague but present wish that some older man be nice to her. She yearned for big and heavy hands, a dark grey suit, British Sterling cologne.

Erminegard said, "God hurt her so." It seemed some tender echo, as of something Linda had said.

Or maybe she meant something else. Dreamily, Linda slipped into her mother's tongue, the one she claimed she couldn't speak. *"Wos ist Eisenmaedel . . . ?"*

"Dear, you know. The cruelest thing, the worst. The Counter Reformation. The Jesuits, in the south. So sick. They copied the old knights—the chivalric love. Devotion to the Lady, and they made a metal girl. For the man who spurned the Mother. The lightning was her eyes. The statue's eyes. Were tiny lenses. Made of tin, made perfect. Like musical instruments. Toys. Like we've always been so wonderful with children. Glockenspiel and fairy tales, kindergarten, cuckoo clocks. Dresden dolls and torture-things in Nuremburg. Like the Babylonian bull, that roared when men were thrown inside—their voices from the bronze machine came out. The iron girl was lead inside. Lined with lead, you hear nothing. Only his screams make her eyes flash. Lenses vibrate. *Oscillation.*"

"They hurt . . ."

" . . . the man inside the Maiden. The nails are short and the worm does not die. Lin, I've been inside of her! Me! At the museum in Nuremburg! You pay, you know, ten marks and they put you inside. They let go the chain, though of course they cannot do this all the way. But you feel what it was like. The nails are to hurt a man. To carve him, push him into shape. Woman's shape. Me, I feel . . ."—Erminegard shuddered. Deliciously; she'd tasted lemon sherbet. "I'm such a chicken! Screaming 'Let me out! Carl, make them let me out this *instant!*' Of course they do, at once; the rules are very strict."

Linda said, "I wish *I* could get out."

She smiled bravely. Tried to laugh.

She cried.

"Oh Linda, I've been stupid. Telling you silly things when it's your husband's . . . Shall I hold you?"

Linda wept, *"No."*

"But I must. For me, or I'll be too ashamed." Linda weakly raised her arms, like a child allowing herself to be dressed. Erminegard held her. She was strong, like Shelley. If it was possible to die from honeysuckle/sandalwood inhalation, that was something Lin needed to worry about.

Erminegard took her hand, led her back into the reception room.

They talked a little longer, on more normal topics.

206

Erminegard stood within reach of the buffet table, eating paté and crackers one after another like it was an uncontrollable nervous habit. She said, "It's so nice veda quacker, you know?", licking the tip of her finger like a satanic elf.

Linda, who hadn't tasted it, said "I know" and left her. Glanced back and saw her gobbling, oblivious to a smiling man who'd quickly filled Linda's place. Linda bumped into Shelley. Still weepy, she said, "*I did what you told me*"—steered Erminegard towards food.

Shelley spoke softly, gravely concerned. "Lin, you must attend your own husband's service. You've barely spoken to your Aunt Martha and Uncle Eric. People want to be nice to you—you have to be available. And you've been crying again."—for which she was out of sympathy. It was just another one of her daughter's messy habits.

So Linda laughed, instead. "I know, at the drop of a hat . . ."

"Your hat!"

Linda turned to go back out and get it, faced Tony Biondo.

This was more than strange—it was slightly too intense. And she couldn't play dumb or shy—Biondo and Lin had been friends.

She said, "How's it going, Tony."

He gaped, appalled. "Terrific. Got a new kid in Dorm Two. Name *Monarro* ring a bell?" Linda sniffed back the last of her tears, shook her head. She felt mildly entranced, like Derrick's boss was now a funny puppet. He made her want to giggle. "How about the initials M-A-F-I-A? That spell anything out for you?" Linda crinkled her nose, Oh stop. "Got a new dude working nights, says he was in the Green Berets. That means, a sign lights up in my head: *Basket Case.* Hire him anyway; life's too dull. Dorm Three got feisty, he orders them 'Sit on the floor, place your hands on your head.' I was so embarrassed I was gonna sit down *with* 'em. No other business known to God attracts so many crazies." This was on good authority, coming from the man who'd assured the commissioner he could staff the facility during all-staff training. Staff it he did—with his former bro's, Hell's Angels. "And Joe Castellano, got him as my new Assistant . . ."

Linda willed her expression blank; the name meant nothing to Derrick's wife. *Ton, that lazy sleaze-bag. He took my place? Why?*

Biondo swallowed, looked away. Humble, like a knife was to his throat and he'd spilled his guts. "Lin, I don't know what to say."

She swallowed sympathetically. "I don't either."

"Nothin's the same no more. The dorms, the meetings . . ." He said it working-class Boston: *me-ins*, like a Seventies seminar in self-involvement. " . . . even this here, this wake: it isn't the same without Derrick."

Linda said, "I know. There's" *no don't say it* DON'T "one less drunk."

The room fell silent.

Everyone turned to look.

Linda looked around, as in a dream: *I said it . . .*

She held Tony's wrist. "*Ton, why'd he do this to me?*" She was taking Linda's license to the limit—Mediterranean passion, unbridled. She'd been that way before—but only with Biondo. It was somehow unique to their chemistry. To loose her passion over slights to her burned roast, her Yorkshire pudding like pancakes with meat drippings instead of syrup. *I don't know how to cook, Ton—okay? Is it all right?!*

Tony put his free hand over Linda's, clutching his wrist. It was an eclectic gesture, peculiar to DYS; a soothing pat or a wrist lock, it could go right with the flow. "Lin, slow down. Doll, it's me. I'm here."

Their eyes met. For a moment, frozen in disbelief . . .

They surely were a picture. The juvenile corrections boss with his ponytail, mustache and sentimental-pirate eyes. The shy, dark girl, shapely as sin in her mourning dress, clutching his hand, electrified with passion. In his eyes, she saw his thoughts: She mimicked people, all the time. Unconsciously, a lot. She was doing Derrick, now—so perfectly, Tony just spaced.

She all but yelled in his face, even bounced up on her tip-toes; he blinked, relieved, and she read *No, that's Lin.* "Why did he leave me, Tony? I needed him! I *need* him!"

"I'm hip, babe. Get a grip, then you can tell me all about it."

Linda blanked on that for a second. *What's he going to do—walk me down to his office?*—then she clutched his wrist with renewed force. Men had changed, they were all big and hard as rock and nothing she did could possibly hurt them. "Why do men leave, Tony?"

"We're all for the birds, hon, I know; the writing's been on the wall all along. Let's go sit; c'mon."

She wouldn't go, and of course he wouldn't force her; she was Derrick's wife, not a delinquent. She looked around the room, at the wall of silent faces, and she knew she'd made no splash. Everyone knew she was flaky.

Shelley came and took her shoulders. (Biondo tenderly whispered, "*You got her?*") Mother and daughter departed the room. Linda found herself mincing, afraid of what Shelley might say once they were alone. They began their soft and gentle consultation. *I'll go sit in the car.—You may not.—Then I'll sit in the ladies' room.—No, that's absurd.* While Erminegard followed with Linda's hat. After all her twaddle she was just their fair-haired cousin, wanting to be good.

Shelley later said that at the burial uptown, Linda had an "attitude." She only remembered thinking, *This business of being my own widow*, and it plumbed some fiery pit of woman's bitterness.

Derrick's two brothers faced her in turn, both oddly grave and distinguished in their black suits. They, like all men, had changed. They'd become huge, loud, granitic slabs, impossibly dynamic and handsome. They'd become wiser and stronger than Linda, fields of competence more able. She wondered when this had happened—when these two jerks had transformed into lifeguard/executives.

Derrick's wife had been cool to them both. She'd chosen one man and the rest were dismissed. When Dan or Jenson came to the Samara Street apartment, Linda's worst fear—repeatedly voiced—was that her husband and brothers-in-law would drink beer and watch football. That was her absolute worst-case scenario, the moral equivalent of getting burglarized again. Now, Linda thought (not too clearly) they might tease her.

Dan lifted her veil to kiss her cheek. She softly spoke in his ear: "You're not supposed to do that."

Jenson took her hand, muttered some stock condolence and moved on. He knew she didn't like him. *But I do*. She turned to him but he was gone, and someone else was in front of her. Charlene. Linda gestured, lost. *That boy, I like him, or . . . ?*

Charlene said, "I'll call you. I won't leave you alone." Miserable, she *tsk*ed and took a Kleenex from her purse. "Oh, look at us. Your face is a mess, dear, let me . . ." She lifted Linda's veil, dabbed at streaked mascara. Linda closed her eyes. *I want to be your child, this last once.*

Murmured words, and Charlene gestured, hectic; her own grief, too much. Someone took her aside, and Biondo took her place.

He hung his head, like this was all his fault.

"I'd like to stay in touch. Tony, if I . . . gave you my phone number, maybe . . . coffee, I'm meet you someplace, or . . ."

"Ah . . . nah, babe. Human nature being what it is, I don't . . ."

She parted her lips, thoughtful. *Who do you think you are?*

She remembered *He honestly sees himself, still, as a 27-year-old stud. He thinks no daughter of Eve can resist his charm.*

If I hung around with him, I might believe it too.

That would be disgusting. "It was sweet of you to come."

He said, " 'Sweet' got nothin' to do with it. If I'd had my way, the kids would have been here also."

"Would they have done the Three Him's?"

Biondo frowned at his shoes.

Linda explained, "While they lowered the casket."

"Hon, that's like a DYS tradition. What all the kids do when a counselor quits or gets fired. Whatever Derrick told you the Three Him's meant, it ain't something nice."

Lin lowered her eyes. Tried to smile. Tony moved on.

The casket was lowered. Pastor Gershing said the rites.

Shelley said softly, "You may throw a flower, Linda. Onto your husband's . . ."

"I'd rather not. His mom can."

" . . . if you ever expect me to speak to you again . . ."

Linda went, took a blossom from a wreath. She went and stood at the foot of the open pit. *Throwing a flower onto a box . . .*

. . . surrounded by steep walls of dirt. Hard, packed earth. That will be on top of me. How will I breathe?

She dropped the flower, fled back to her mother's side.

Jenson took a shovel, took a shovelful of earth . . .

Shelley said, "A spouse is closest. 'A man shall leave his mother and cleave unto his wife.' You're the woman, here. Derrick was your husband. Yours and yours alone."

Linda was cold. She trembled with cold. She held her shoulders, shivering.

Jenson handed the shovel to Dan.

"Baby, are you really . . . ?"

"Cold. Mom. Mommy, I'm *so cold* . . ."

Shelley held her daughter. Linda didn't weep. She trembled in her mother's arms. She was just so cold.

Towards evening, they went up to the Samara Street apartment. The darkening sky was clear, but a chill, sea-scented mist was blowing in from the harbor. As the Sunbird parked, Linda looked up at the building. The eroded tar walk up to the scuff-marked door meant, home.

She'd had a strange belief: that the apartment, with all it contained of his and her married life, had simply phased out of existence. She'd envisioned boarded windows, the seared lawn strewn with garbage. Neighbors who, like Rip van Winkle's townsfolk, couldn't for the life of them recall any couple named Bloom.

In fact, their last month's rent was good to the end of March. Nothing had been turned off, locked up or removed. It was still Linda Bloom's apartment.

Linda Bloom, Ms. or Mrs. at her preference, wife of Derrick Bloom, deceased. Hispanic, US citizen, over twenty-one. Registered Democrat, taxpayer too. But it didn't seem real, somehow. It seemed like she'd be all this, but only when she grew up someday. It seemed like she wasn't really allowed to drive a car. Like she couldn't really leave the house unless she asked her mom.

Just her feelings. *Lin, it's just you.* And yet . . .

She'd somehow lost her majority. She was only a ditzy girl and when push came to shove, others would make her decisions for her. Confined to a house in the kindest words—*darlings* and *dears* of internment. She'd needed to wait until she was asked, listen until she was spoken to. If she walked around she was "anxious"; if she gestured, she was "upset." If she wished to visit the ladies' room or simply get some air outdoors, she asked to be excused and it felt like an actual request.

Of course, no one ever said "No! You can't go to the bathroom!" Or snapped, "Who needs air?"

But rather, "Oh my! Are you purging still, do you think?"

Or "No, stay; sit. Here, I'll open the window a little."

(Shelley was the worst one, for treating her like a dog. On one of their walks in Merrill, an irritable "Come along" seemed but a step removed from *heel.*)

Or maybe—as she'd been so reliably assured—it was *just her.* Maybe a gentle, thoughtful woman was willing to confer with those who cared for her—to put her desire to pee as a proposal, up for discussion. That seemed rather doubtful—yet Linda wasn't free to voice her doubts. "Treating you like a *dog*! Linda, that's ludicrous! Babe, all I said was—"

Her perceptions were invalid. "Oh Lin, stop. That's just you"—wanting what she didn't need, afraid of things not harmful. "Although, if the doctor thinks best—"; "All right, but if Ray prefers—"; "Yes, assuming your father approves—": assumed, she was subject to men. Their sober judgments outweighed her childish thoughts. Nor was she merely "so precious"—she was actually, intrinsically less important. She'd just attended Ray's son's funeral. She'd been coached on things to say and do, also subtly cautioned against trying to steal attention. (There'd already been some biting words about her scene with Tony.) At the reception, Ray said he might have a cup of coffee. Shelley gave Linda a look: *Well, what are you waiting for? Go fix it.* Sweet-and-sour, Linda asked Ray how he liked his coffee. Ray declined, like Shelley was nuts; you don't put the widow to work serving coffee in any sane universe *he* knew.

And now, here she was—back *home.* Back to the crumbling walk which Derrick carelessly trod each day—responsible for his own, answerable only to his conscience. Linda, standing on the sidewalk, drew her collar against the twilight chill. The retaining wall still needed stones remortared; the small, sparse lawn still had to be thatched and reseeded, come spring. Her breath, still warm, condensed in the cold. Nothing had changed. She was home. Her signature was on the lease.

Here were their cars: Derrick's all-but-wholly rebuilt Rabbit.

211

Linda's all-but-holy '93 Tercel. This being Salem (tarnished jewel of Greater Boston), they'd no doubt been ticketed and booted for situational infractions, til Ray seized hold of his Irish chums and Shelley of her Brahmin peers—Tell City Hall, Lay off.

Nor had the cars been vandalized. It was a Crime Watch neighborhood and more—it was Polish. Staid, outspoken, civic-minded Poles. The Blooms weren't of their own, but they were still part of the neighborhood. The Polka People loved their clean and happy little block. Cops and punks get lost, we have no king but Bobby Vinton.

Shelley insisted on getting the doors—her key was somehow better than her daughter's. The apartment was cold and, til they turned a light on, dark. Charlene had been there, to do what needed to be done—the cat fed, the plants watered. Ray had appeared, without clear purpose—a sentinel, a witness. He'd done his duty—been there—and gone.

The parlor was unaltered—a still life, verging on death. The coffee table with Anchini linen and Pfaltzgraff china. The candles melted down to the stick, like the Wicked Witch's hourglass. The white carnations, long dead, and the remnants of the meal had been decently disposed of. The glasses were gone. Linda supposed there had been a police investigation. She asked "Did they ever find Pazia?", not expecting an answer. She hung up their coats.

Linda's dress was the only other black one Shelley owned—not really right for mourning. The hemline was short and the collar had white lace appliqué. "I'd like to get this off. I feel like a French maid."

Shelley said "Good heavens."—what an ungodly remark.

Linda's tabby lay curled on the sofa. Linda crooned, "*Aaaw.*" Then, idly curious, asked "Is it dead?" Shelley didn't respond—she knew Linda's love for her pets needed the brake, not the gas. Linda sat next to the cat. She poised her finger, like a typist contemplating a word, then—*boink.* Tip of her ring finger, on catty-watty's nose. (The animal's name was Skittles; Derrick never used it.) It woke up, narrowed its eyes at her. "Mommy's home!" She fussed and teased, then lifted it over her head, swinging its heavy bottom. The cat—ten years old, and as many pound overweight—meow'ed a feeble protest. "Poor witto thingie-wingie. Poor witto *itty-bitty* thingie-wingie, aw, there, there."

Shelley returned from a tour of the apartment. "I know you'd never swing a child like that, Linda. Harmful to the spine."

Linda went to the kitchen. The cat followed, tail erect, knowing that this gliding lady gave her milk. Linda sniffed the Light and Lively jug to make sure it was still okay. Women nurtured, they sniffed before giving. Derrick always wanted to give the cat strychnine. Cats were good if you had mice; you suffered one big varmint to be free of many little ones and otherwise the ideal cat was roadkill. But a girl who thought ant farms were cruel (no privacy) would lavish love on Skittles. She set the saucer on the floor. Stood, asked "Mom, do you—" Her eyes flared dramatically as she tottered backwards, half a step. *These damn heels.*

Shelley said "Be careful."

"—want anything? Coffee? Perrieré?"

"Oh. No, I'm fine, thanks. You had your chance to play hostess at the reception."

"Mom, I was upset."

"You were not valorous in your grief. Is how I'd put it."

"Of course you're so right." Linda went to the cupboard, got a can of Nine Lives. Served the cat which, duly grateful, twitched its whiskers at the food and went back to its milk. Shelley said "Nine Lives is so expensive."

Linda threw the can in the recyclable bin. "Oh. It was supposed to be for me. After Derrick bought his Sega."

"Dear, I hardly find that amusing. Anyway, just go find what you need. It's freezing in here."

"Mom, I'm staying."

"Lin, no. I've got someone's space, out front."

They both knew what Linda meant, though.

"I've lived here five years, Mom."

"Not alone. There's no man. There's no one to care for you."

"Does NOW do house-calls, like the Jehovah's Witnesses? I'm giving them your address." Shelley was mortified—this was no joking matter. "Mom, look: this is the Nineties. And I can take care of myself." Shelley was appalled—these jokes weren't even funny. Linda conceded, toned down her boast: "I can scream and call 911." She sighed, her hand on her hip. "I'll be fine. Just like him."—the quietly lapping tabby.

The case had been heard, the verdict reached; Shelley answered calmly. "Lin, I'm hardly impressed. You're not a cat, you're not one of these self-sufficient modern girls. You're simply not."

"Mother, please don't be upset. I'll get you a chair."

"Making me 'upset' will not work either. No: you need love, and people caring about you, every single day. You need comfort and warmth and beautiful surroundings, you need books to read—"

"I have them here."

"—and clothes and no, I won't bring them. You need quiet and peace. You need constant assurance."

Linda laid her hand on her bosom. She said, "I have them here." Her mother didn't answer. "You gave me those things. Now I have them. Here."

Outside, some blocks to the north, a police car wailed its siren around the Commons. Shelley lifted her hand to the sound—there, that said it all.

Linda said, "I still have those relaxation tapes you gave me when I was young. The ones you made me listen to when I had problems relaxing at home. The rainy forest and the surf. I play them every night. It drowns out the noise, outside."

Shelley tried sweet reason. "All right . . . what does this say, in itself? A girl living in a safe and pleasant home, with no real stress in her life, needing to lie down and listen to these tapes."

"That was then. This is now. And I was being somewhat facetious."

"You went to a psychologist each week all through high school."

"I'm quite capable of opening a phone book, if I feel that is something I need."

"I can't believe this is happening."

"Mother, I'm not asking. I have decided to stay."

Shelley motioned, Shoo fly shoo; her daughter's dictates, dandelion puffs.

"Mom, if you insist—if you absolutely insist—then I won't go against your will. I will choose to submit; you're my mother. But this is what you asked of me. That I assert myself. Like when you tortured me in my bedroom—"

"Excuse me?—dear, I'm sorry. My hearing, you know. The traffic here's so deafening, and at my age I—"

" 'Pressure. Here.' "

"Lin, if you're imagining things, that doesn't persuade me to leave you alone."

"I imagined 'pressure, here'."

"You imagine that it was torture."

Only the kitchen and hallway were lit. The apartment was otherwise as it had been, winter days and nights on end—abandoned, dark and silent. The sole survivor of a life shared, ended now stood and talked with her mother, as gentle women do—not loudly. The cat lapped its milk.

"You said I asked for that. That you only answered my cry for a mother. Now *you've* been crying, 'Be a woman. Stand up.' And now I'm—"

"No. Let me speak: no. My helping you, that night, was steadfast kindness. Just one of those awful things that go on behind closed doors. Within our family, Linda. I alone saw you beside yourself, peeing all over the house—"

"Oh *stop* it! *Quit* it!"

"—*and this is the same sort of hysterical act, and you're*—"

Both women paused, having both shouted.

Linda crossed the finish line, winded and with joy. "Mom, I'm staying."

214

Shelley said, "Then I'll just cry," like that would never happen.

Warm and serene, as though she were the parent, Linda had her mother sit. Shelley wanted to anyway, waved off her daughter's unwanted attention. She wept in stoic misery, rheumy-eyed and simply sad. Linda went and got Kleenex, which Shelley accepted as though it materialized from thin air. Linda, kind tomato, smiled as she stroked her mother's angel-blonde hair. Oh, the roots were white as snow. *But she's beautiful, she really is. It's how she sees herself that counts.* She went and made tea, told Shelley, "It's mine; there's no caffeine. Watch the cup, though—this one's pewter. It'll burn your lips."

Not afraid of pewter, Shelley resolutely took a sip.

Linda heard all her mother had to say, the overflow of her wounded heart. In lecture form, of course—even Shelley's sorrow was didactic. Yet Linda was in control. Her mother's words were funny and sad and they couldn't hurt a fly.

"You *should* stop being smug, Lin."

Soft melodies of compassion. "Oh stop. You know I'm not."

"No smiling at my tears, unless you shed some of your own. Stop being so steady. You always think you're my son."

Linda smiled at that, too. Shelley and her blithe self-contradictions. So mild and harmless, compared to someone like Derrick's grandmother. Shelley's chastisements were whispering whips, not lyrical scorpions. She asked for Kleenex to dry her eyes, not gin to fuel her madness. Nor was there a grandfather in the subdivided loft next door, alone with his Camels and memories of war, inclining his ear to the plywood wall like a priest in confessional, hearing.

Linda sat on the floor, before her mother. Radiant with love, almost mischievous, she smiled. Docile as a plant receiving water, ever faithful, a *mensch* beneath her lycra slip. She heard her mother's pain then went and made some more herb tea.

Shelley finally rose from her chair. Sniffling—God, scarce able to breathe—she noted her little mess of tea-things and used Kleenex, There it serves you right. It was time for her to leave unless, of course, she wished to spend the night. Linda stood waiting, lovely and light on her feet, ready to go change linens and unfold a nice, warm quilt. Shelley gasped the notion aside. Were there still cockroaches in the apartment?—Uh, no; they were silverfish, and completely gone. —Oh. Well, they'd been *horrible* silverfish then, Shelley thought. But anyway, she would relent and—at her convenience, and against her better judgment—bring Linda her things. "Mom, no. I'll come get them. I'm not disabled."

"Darling, yes. You are." She'd been brought up helpless, lost her husband, she was who she was and it was too late now to blame her mom.

Linda almost laughed. "Of course. But you're so right."

She walked her mother out to the landing. Linda motioned, tenderly uncertain; she wanted a hug, a kiss. Shelley said "No. You need to . . . no." She went down the stairs.

"Mom, be careful. Those steps are simply awful."

Shelley gestured, fretful—everything was awful.

Linda went back into her apartment.

Derrick always locked the door, to make his wife feel safe. Now this was a whole new deal—*Perils Of Pauline*, and she wasn't the guy on the horse. The neighborhood outside was like a video game: a blue-grey maze of hedges and driveways, through which any phantom could steal. Linda didn't want to play—she locked the door.

She went to the bedroom. His, her bedroom. Still his, still hers; everything was the same. Everything she needed, right where Derrick's wife had left it. Her Secret, her jojoba soap. Her Clairol Herbal Essence. She suddenly felt anxious, thought that she should soon go round up all of Derrick's things, all traces of Irish Spring and Mennon Speed-Stick and give them to the Salvation Army, or whoever. They didn't belong in a single woman's apartment. She was scared of them.

Most of her clothes were gone, but not all. She went and opened the storage space across the hall, pulled out dust-covered boxes. Caught her stocking on a nail-head in the wooden floor. The dust made her sneeze; she'd forgotten she was allergic to the world. Also afraid of all medicines, which she considered instantly fatal poison. The boxes held things she couldn't believe she'd ever worn. A turquoise slip dress was a fold of fabric in the palm of her hand, something for some slip of a girl. She knew she was much too fat. It seemed incredible, now, that Derrick looked at these cavewoman thighs and saw . . . she couldn't even remember. Swimsuit model, or something. *Starvation is the key to guilt-free binges* . . . Derrick's wife said that. Worth a try, at least. She set aside neatly folded jeans and blouses, which only a child could wear and which—if she had tried them on—would have fit her fine.

She found things Derrick's wife just hadn't wanted; they were out of style, or whatever. From a girl who still had her pet rock and lava lamp, that was pretty final. A peasant dress which Derrick's wife had felt was "too organic"—too Seventies, too Earth Mother. Though Linda felt it must have been a favorite. Bauer, after all, means *Peasant*. The dress gave her a sane and simple feeling; it looked like something to wear. Loose and sturdy, it wouldn't tear; the cotton would feel soft. The *Impeach Nixon* statement didn't matter; she didn't plan to go out. She unfolded it, sniffed. Apple-cidery mothball tang, dead flowers of old Halston's. Under the puffed sleeves, a must of her own scent; she'd lived in this dress for years. She looked for a label to see if

216

it was her present size, 7. It was a liberated dress, it just said *Large, 100% Cotton* and to wash it in warm water. She spaced on *Large*. Maybe Derrick's wife was right all along—she was truly, officially fat. *Five-nine; I'm tall, for a girl. That's all they mean by "large."* She went into the bedroom, took off her mourning dress. She was done feeling sorry for herself.

She looked under her side of the bed. Derrick's wife had the habit of putting things there, if they'd been worn but weren't yet dirty; consigning them to this limbo of things she intended to wear again soon. There was a scrunched-up cotton nightie, some clean-enough panties, two white elastic rings which she didn't know were stockings til she unrolled them. Linda tried the peasant dress. It fit like her own skin.

She took a paperback romance off the shelf. *I might start reading all her books—there sure are enough of them. A whole undiscovered world of . . . whatever she got out of reading them.* She made herself some herb tea. It tasted like the raw juice of some virulent weed. *I won't drink all her herb tea, then.* She went into the apse, took her place on the window ledge. She drew the curtains just so, just so she could see and not be seen.

The cat came and nestled in her cross-legged lap. Linda tickled its chin. She touched her finger to its nose. Curious, it sniffed.

She said, "It's just the same, hm? Mommy's lap, still soft and warm . . . you can't tell I'm any different."

Linda didn't like that. She wanted the cat to realize she was Derrick, bound off her lap and run for its life.

But it just went to sleep, purring softly, vibrant, in her lap.

She read and, as the hours passed, the story drew her in. It never crossed her mind that she was waiting, like she used to wait, for someone to come home.

14

Linda woke up in the morning and her ear lobes were all sore. She got up and looked in the mirror. Forgetting she wore earrings now, she'd gone to bed with them still on. She was wearing a cotton nightie and gold earrings. She looked cute and dumb, like Mindy. She'd never wanted that.

She dressed and went downstairs to check her mailbox. It felt like something scary. Derrick's wife was postal-phobic. She'd been hassled by people—a video store in Weston, Vermont; a clothing boutique in Pittsfield—to whom, so far as Derrick could judge, she didn't owe a speck of lint. The video store wanted $392.98 for two tapes which Linda mislaid and forgot and returned a few weeks late. The bill listed "legal fees" and "compounded penalties"; it was obviously meant to express how someone felt, not to be read as an actual bill. Linda had paid sixty dollars late fees when she returned the tapes; Derrick called the store in Vermont, told them to get a life. Linda then got a letter from a lawyer, which made her almost hysterical. She feared that she might go to jail. Now, Derrick's widow faced her mailbox—throat dry, pulse racing. The mailbox was as ominous as the episodic still-frame at the end of *Twilight Zone*. The clock that broke and ended time. The cornfield where awful things were kept. The little magnesium door marked *Bloom* which someone opened one day, and—

There was a paycheck for her from Cape Anne Community Residences, Inc. A sympathy card in a separate letter, from Pinski Place. It was signed by a bunch of retarded folks. It might have been quite touching, had Linda known who they were. Exuberant scribbles, laborious prints; a firmer hand tucked underneath, *We miss you Lin Love Steve*. It gave her a strange, warm feeling. She wasn't sure who Steve was, but it was nice to know he loved her.

There was a paycheck for Derrick from the Massachusetts Department of Youth Services. *All personnel must report in person to get paid* but the State has a human face—if you're really dead, we'll make an exception.

There was a payment, to her, of five thousand dollars life insurance on the policy of Derrick Bloom, deceased. He'd been dying to get it. Actually, she hadn't even thought of it. Shelley had spoken with Tony Biondo—that strange, resourceful man who played golf with the Commissioner, had lunch with the Mayor, yet hitch-hiked to work each day because he didn't own a car. Tony told Shelley to relax—"maybe someone" would pull a few strings, cut through the insurance company's red tape. In view of Tony's reputation for faithfulness, it wasn't hard to guess who "someone" might have been. Money meant nothing to Linda, but it seemed like people were doing so much to help her. She decided to go to the bank.

First, though, she was curious . . . she sat at the bedroom desk. Found old papers signed by Derrick and by Linda. The two hands were completely different. His was a compacted, angular scrawl. Hers was rounded, close to perfect. She'd retained a childhood habit, in modified form: the *i*'s dot was a squiggle, suggestive of a heart. Linda closed her eyes, wrote *This is how I sign my name*, signed her name then looked.

Linda's handwriting, but pinched, with sharper angles.

She looked out the bedroom window. The sanded-tar roof of the porch down below, the lawn, the cars, the vacant street, the angle, always there.

Diatomaceous shapes, translucent, drifting through grey water.

No, the water was the sanded-tar roof of the porch, outside. The diatomaceous shapes were bacteria, on the mucal surface of her eye.

She looked at her hand instead. She saw it for the first time. It was a lovely, ingenious thing. It did whatever she wanted it to.

She eventually realized she was slouched in her chair, as if she'd been asleep. The bank . . . she stood, felt suddenly dizzy. Her body felt boneless and heavy, all useless curves and soft, round bulges. She'd been slightly incontinent. It hadn't seeped to the seat of her dress. She went to the bathroom, took her Dilantin. Went back into the bedroom, changed her panties. She used some FDS spray, though she didn't think it was for that and wasn't sure it would help. The unmade bed looked heavenly. But she remembered something Derrick's wife used to say, that she couldn't go to bed every time she had a little seizure.

She endorsed her two checks. She didn't think about how she did it. It looked like Linda's sloppy, post-ictal signature. Groovy.

She wouldn't "forge" Derrick's check—her own check; no. She envisioned a phone call from some pompous, powerful banker—a man in a grey suit with heavy jowls, voice quavering in righteous wrath. *Your husband died on the fifteenth, miss.*—she'd be a kid again. *This check was issued on the twenty-first. Do you know the PENALTIES FOR FORGERY IN THIS STATE?!*

She didn't need the money, really, anyway. She'd ask about

it, at the bank. If they wouldn't accept it or whatever, that would be okay. She got her bank book, purse and coat. Her keys. Off into the wild wintry yonder.

Out in front of her apartment, she hesitated. She felt pulled to the Rabbit, but then quietly retired to her Tercel. She thought, *I don't know how to drive a standard. I don't even know what "standard" is, exactly.* That wasn't true and yet, it had to be.

The Tercel was a mess. Papers, books, soda cans. Bushels of lipstick-stained Kleenex. Linda tensed with sudden fury. *I didn't do this.* She went quickly back inside to get—in dramatic overstatement—a garbage bag. Cleaned out her car, then got in. Turned the key and BOOM—Melissa Etheridge. Blasted at two hundred decibels, like she was Deep Purple. Linda yanked the tape. Turned down the volume, put in Guns N' Roses. Started on her way.

As she rolled past the bare trees and yellow houses, Guns N' Roses bothered her too. The snarling menace seemed directed at her personally. The singer wanted to make skull n' bones of all weak, timid women named Linda. He needed some time on his own from scared, clutching females and, if he didn't get it, would drench them in a driving sleet of anguished guitar chords. At the corner of Samara and Lafayette, Linda switched the player off. *Sound the air raid siren, clear the streets—Massachusetts lady drive on the loose.* She pulled out onto Lafayette.

She kept feeling like she was forgetting something, kept remembering that the Tercel was an automatic.

There were pedestrians on the sidewalks. A couple times, men looked at her abruptly, as though she'd honked. Pretty face, pure reflex. She didn't know how to react. She felt absolutely certain she was not supposed to acknowledge them, though. Just yesterday, she'd had the scare of her life. On their way to South Boston, Shelley stopped for gas near Fenway Park. Linda went into the little Patco mart to buy a Snapple. As she came to the door, a really rough-looking Spanish dude came out. He smiled at her and said *"Hi, Linda."* She looked away and her heart skipped a beat. *Oh God help me this animal* knows *me.*

But he'd only spoken to her in Spanish, which—if Fate had taken a different turn—she would have grown up speaking herself. He hadn't said anything awful, like "I want to get you in bed." He'd only said, "Hi, Pretty," like that was her name, which unfortunately it was.

And the funeral wasn't much better. When talking to people, she lowered her eyes; if she made eye contact, she tended to stare and raise her voice. The most embarrassing thing happened when she talked to men: she swayed forward slightly, as if light-headed. Not wanting to be held so much as assuming they wanted to hold her. *I give up, you win—hold me.* No one seemed to notice, though.

Now her mind was occupied by the familiar problems and aggravations of Massachusetts urban driving. Good thing she knew where the bank was. Street signs were absent; if you weren't from around there, you'd no business being so nosey. Lights were red for all-way stop, green for all-way go. She drove past a man in a Buick LeSabre who decided to play chicken pulling out of a parking space. He blew past her at the next yellow light, honked and gave her the finger. Derrick's father taught him that the proper response was to smile and wave cordially. Linda felt too vulnerable; she gave him the finger back. She didn't dare honk, but she yelled "*Coward!*"

It was a Spanish girl's expression—Derrick's wife had picked it up. (She could "act Spanish" whenever she liked, since she really was.) It meant that you, a man, were unchivalrous, a bully, to insult a lady like that. Linda felt a little better, imagining that the guy in the LeSabre heard her.

She got to the bank, cruised through a full lot, then parked on the street. The meter was buried in a hardened snow bank. This situation made Linda tense and upset. She gasped in dismay, first at her skirt and high-heeled boots, then at the meter. How was this supposed to be possible?

She angrily decided she couldn't follow their stupid rules, because they'd left a big mountain of snow on the sidewalk. If she got ticketed, she would (*start a petition. No: this isn't college*) appeal. Not in person. She knew the terror of mean letters; she'd write one herself.

She went into the bank. Stood near the door, scanned the lobby. Looked at all the women, found her fear confirmed. *My thighs are twice as big as anyone else's.* She took courage from her mother's words: *Just stop.* She took her place in line.

But men were really staring. At her body.

She glanced, to make sure. They were.

Other women, whom she assumed were more attractive than herself, weren't being treated this way. She wondered what it was about her, that made it okay to stare. She wondered what to do to make them stop. It should not have been so upsetting and unpleasant to wait in line inside a bank. Yet her thoughts were out of focus; she felt it was her fault. She didn't *know* what she could do. *I can say that men are staring at me, but that somehow doesn't seem right. I can't remember anyone saying that. Who would I say it to, anyway?*

While she had these thoughts and feelings, her affect was completely normal. A tall, slender woman with an alert, rather stern expression—she didn't look the way she felt, as people normally don't. The woman in front of her turned and softly entreated, she needed a deposit slip and would Linda hold her place? Linda answered as softly, "Oh!—yes; mm-hm. Of course."

For a moment, she was not alone. Women were an underground, united in senseless acts of kindness. But the other went to get her deposit slip, leaving Linda alone and alarmed: *Why didn't I tell her?*

An older man in a three-piece suit was scariest of all. His bad-dog eyes roved up and down her body, seemed especially fixed on her thighs. Her coat, so stylishly form-fitting, now betrayed. Her peasant dress had to cling, show off her thighs like the robe of a Byzantine angel. She wanted to fight back, except she didn't want to fight. She couldn't think of a role model. *Shrill, accusing bitch* just wasn't a cultural icon. She thought of simply freaking out and screaming, *Why are you staring at me?!* But she knew she wouldn't do that. Her timid body would hold her in, make her behave. Anyway, if she screamed she'd have to leave the bank right away, and never come back. She thought she might get one of those slate-blue, carbon-paper letters you have to rip open on three sides before you can even glimpse a hint of what it says. She envisioned a terse description of her behavior, followed by a statement: her account was thereby closed. She ended up minding her place in line, trying to avoid the man's eyes. Hating herself, feeling that only she would passively submit to such an insult—in short, the response of almost any civilized person.

Then she saw the impossible. She saw, but could not believe. The man's trousers bulged at the crotch. This grey-haired pillar of the community was standing in a bank lobby, in broad daylight, blatantly staring at another customer, with a big hard-on. She stared herself, fixed on the impossible threat, like a frozen chipmunk watching a snake. In terror and, dimly, female wonder: *Daddy's Thing I* see *it and he wants to put it* in *me . . .*

He was old, and had a bank account, and no right whatsoever. She met his eyes and briefly was an adult—a woman with pride, offended, demanding of him why he stared. He looked away, unconcerned. She was beneath his notice, and that was his only shame. Perhaps, even, that was his thrill—he lowered himself to flatter some ethnic slut in a tawdry dress, black leather coat, who'd come to cash her welfare check. So she could go buy pot and baby food. Linda looked at the security guard. She looked at the other customers. She realized nothing would be done, no matter what she said. This was Salem, where they used to pillory lechers, and now it was perfectly okay to publicly, visually rape total strangers.

There was a female voice, irritable and jaded, which Linda gradually realized was irritable and jaded at *her.* "Next. *Next,* please. Ma'am, over here. Ma'am, you are *next.*"

She twirled toward the counter, unleashed her dismay on an unrelated topic. "There was someone ahead of me. Deposit slip, she—"

222

"Ma'am, there are people behind you *waiting*."

The teller was in her early twenties. Prissy, thin, high cheekbones. Vacant sloe eyes, potentially soulful; thin, indifferent lips. She was quite pretty. And she, too, was a Latin girl—black-haired, dark and volatile. It somehow made them sisters, somehow didn't make them friends.

The girl—slightly, briefly—altered her expression. Linda saw, though she couldn't believe, it was intended to mimic her own. The teller *mimicked* her, like they were two kids in third grade.

Yet surely, the girl had seen. Surely she and Linda were somehow together on this. A customer, another woman, was being attacked by a man. Surely the teller would . . .

. . . not. She didn't care about Linda, didn't like her, wouldn't help. *Of course* she saw what the man was doing; she felt that Linda deserved it. That was why she hated Linda: she saw, and it was shameful, and it happened to Linda, not her. Linda was the victim. The dishrag. The chump. And this check to Derrick Bloom was not endorsed.

Linda strove for confidence, poise. *I am Mrs. Bloom, a customer of this bank.* She took the insurance payment's stub from her bank book's organizer. She kept her bank book in her purse, like any other normal, respectable woman. She spoke in a low voice, yet wanted her June Cleaver diction heard by others in the bank. She explained that Derrick Bloom was her husband, he was recently deceased and this was a payment on his life insurance policy.

The girl examined the stub: a dubious ploy to get money.

Linda said, "And anyway, the account's in both our names, still." Yet she hated her own voice—the hesitant, soft stammer of a woman who can't assert herself, who knows it's not her place. "Look, we're known here. Look, maybe you're new, or . . . Are you? New?"

The girl made no attempt to mask her sarcasm: "There's no need to be *unpleasant, ma'am.*"

Linda's throat went dry. No, there wasn't. "I just . . . I'm sorry. Please, we've done business with this bank for five years. If there's a problem, maybe . . . you could ask someone? Or—?"

The girl surveyed her calmly. Linda felt her unspoken response. "*My husband, my husband*"—where? *All I see is you. A greedy little crotch, like me.*

The girl went to another worker, an older woman. Linda read faces and lips. *Yes, of course it's all right. What the hell's wrong with you? This woman is a widow. Give her whatever she asks. Go do it!* The girl trudged back, sullen and bored. She enacted the deposit and gave Linda cash. She made her voice silk, unassuming: "And we'll assume the account is now in your name, only?"

223

Unassuming, she blinked: *Your husband's really dead, or . . .?*

Linda verged on tears. She smiled warmly. "Have a nice day."

The teller slightly shook her head.

Linda shrugged: All right, don't. People glanced—the light heel clicks of a lady's calm departure.

She kept forgetting who she was, now.

Linda had a trauma response to any kind of confrontation with men. It was to flee, to hide somewhere and recover strength, often for many days. Derrick's wife, a maturely developed woman, had learned to do all this while functioning—while going to work, doing all of her stuff. Telling Derrick, *Nothing happened. Der, I'm fine. I need my space. No, I didn't say, kiss. Now you're bugging. Go away.*

Now Derrick was gone. His widow imagined. That the man in the grey suit followed her to her car. That he grabbed her arm, demanded *How much*, insisted that she was a prostitute. That he revealed himself as someone powerful and important—a police commissioner, a politician—and that he threatened her. With all righteous Anglo-Saxon might, saying her car was illegal somehow. He'd call a cop and have it booted. He'd have her investigated. Then, he would turn—be gentle and kind, like the old man at Domina's. But she'd know that he could turn at any second—that his wrath could explode without warning. If she tried to pull away, if she refused his kindness. He would stay calm and mild, but only if she stayed under his hand. She'd try to explain that she had a life, she belonged somewhere and couldn't just be taken. But he'd step on her words like a cigarette butt. *Yeah babe, I know. I know everything about you.* He'd say he just wanted to buy her a drink. He'd gently take her shoulders, turn her. *There's the bar, babe. Nice; nice place.* A red brick front, a small dark window. *Michelob* in neon blue. Ruin her life or buy her a drink—easy, simple choice. But he wouldn't even wait for her to choose. His big, strong, diamond cuff-linked hand would pull her plain and skinny arm. And she would have to go, have to enter his world, become part of his life. She knew that once she stepped from the curb, she'd never return to her own.

She decided to stay in the apartment. She'd be mean (*to the cat?*) and not bathe. She wouldn't wash her hair, til it got all stringy and oily. No one would stare at her, then.

She thought, *Linda wasn't perfect. Do I really need to copy her mistakes?*

Well, *She practiced those mistakes for many years. By now, they should be perfect. Someday I'll be an old lady, so I won't postpone the inevitable—I'll start being one now. This apartment is now a one-woman convent. I am* en réclusion, *and I'll never come out for the rest of my life. I'll have food stamps mailed to me, and I'll go to the grocery store once a month, at two o'clock a.m.*

Before Linda knew what she was doing, she'd gotten out two Hefty Cinch-Sacks, and the biggest cardboard box she could find.

CDs first. All the hillbilly shit. Guns, malt liquor and pickup trucks, women-ain't-nothin'-but-trouble-blues: into the silver Sack.

Metal, next. *Blue Oyster Cult, oh right. I* am *afraid of the reaper, okay? Metallica, as if.*

Books. Books, books, books—all into the Sack. Anything about war, guns, cars, karate, computers, science *all morally depraved and I* abhor *it.* Video games. *Mortal Kombat, I don't even want to touch this.* Into the bag.

There—all the icons. She went to work on the matériel. Packed all of Derricks' clothes, neatly in his travel bags. She packed his suitcase, all his things. Electric razor, aftershave, soap dish, sweat band. "Here's your toothbrush, Der." She sat on the bed, next to the open suitcase. "Remember to brush . . . brush at least . . ."

She went to her knees, her face to the bedspread. Linen soft as marriage, warm as all-my-life embrace. She wept.

She tried again. " . . . at least twice a day . . . after each meal . . . your wife loves you, Derrick. I care about . . ."

She wept, til she was through.

She put on her coat and boots. Took the plastic bag, a suitcase and two travel bags outside to the curb. It wasn't Garbage Day. It wasn't even Garbage Eve. Collection was on Monday. She found a piece of cardboard, and wrote with magic marker:

FREE STUFF FOR WHOEVER WANTS IT

She put the sign on top of the pile, then went inside quick, since she was cold.

She fixed herself a nice, big mug of herb tea. Now that she was learning to like it, she had a favorite: Chamomile Sleepy-Bye. Derrick's wife didn't drink it before supper, insisting it really did put her to sleep. Derrick's sadder, wiser widow didn't think something was true, just because it said so on a box of herbal tea.

She sat and sipped and soon she was calm. She looked out the kitchen window, at the bird feeder hung from the eave. Charlene had kept it filled. There were chickadees, same as in Merrill—two. No crested titmouse. But a long-beaked, badger-headed, upside-down nuthatch, the messiest bird in the world.

225

Throwing away all the millet, taking only sunflower seeds. Linda sat and watched the birds til it started getting dark outside.

She went and looked through her bookshelves, thinking an authentically childish thought: *I wonder if there's a book here about a girl who was afraid of everything.*

She chose *Alice in Wonderland*, which was sort of the same; anyone but Alice would have been scared insane of this place. Linda took her book into the apse. The cat followed, hip to the scene. She sat and read on the window ledge, the cat asleep in her lap. Read the fall down the rabbit hole with an English major's eye. No harping sisters, no one saying she was stupid or lazy—the fall is lackadaisical, euphoric. Poetic puns, droll musings. Linda liked it.

She felt her life had *some* prospects. There were things she'd just discovered—sewing, indoor gardening—which she'd sort of enjoyed and could learn more about. Life was an unopened gift, but only from a distant aunt—what's inside might well be nice, but nothing to get too excited about.

Because I want, more than all the world . . .

To walk outside without a shirt on warm-wind summer evenings. Get into my Rabbit and go anywhere I choose. Country, city, parts unknown—just seeing where the road goes. Through green wet meadows, open fields, and anywhere along the way I'd stop. Just walk over, see what's going on. And no one would say Oh what's wrong, miss? Why'd you have to leave your car? *No: they'd say* What's up, man you want this? *toss me a Dew. Because a big boy's presence speaks for itself—he does whatever he wants.*

If my car broke down, I'd care less—stuff breaks and you fix it, that's why you've got tools. I'd buy a six-pack, get the Red Sox on the radio. Unscrew my speakers, put them on the pavement. Any place I broke down, I'd make that my little camp. Tie my black bandana to my car's antenna: international signal for Guy Working On His Car, Don't Stop Unless You're A Pretty Girl. Broke down, son?—Nah, just chillin'. Hey, hand me a 9/16th?

The world would be my personal backyard—full of friends waiting to be met, toys waiting to be found. The sunny sky would be my roof over my head. When it got dark, no problem—boy scouts come prepared, dude. I'd have my Sears Roebuck ground lamp—plug that baby right into the cig lighter. If it rained, so what? I'd be under my V-6 hood, warm and dry as a termite. Drinking my beer, rolling on my tunes. Want a hand there, bro?—You got your own beer? *When I finished playing with my car, I'd go walking through the warm, wet night—looking for a party, for stuff going on. I'd sleep in my back seat; when it got light again, I'd get out and go look for breakfast.* Then what? Work on my car some more? *Not when I see the morning sun on water, over there. Pop the trunk—tackle on board. Fishin' time!*

Fishing . . .

She sat, cross-legged on the window ledge. The book lay open in her lap, forgotten. She gazed out through the curtain, winter's urban grey in fading twilight.

Maybe we're all female, all along. Maybe this is really Life, when you take away the magic and the colors.

She looked out the window, looked only somewhat bothered, bored.

Father, I'm sorry. I want to be a boy, and that's . . . wrong for me, not what You planned. You made me Your daughter, not Your son. Anymore. Because I didn't deserve it, somehow. Or maybe because I was happy, too beautiful and happy, You were jealous, it was . . .

A tear fell, ran down her nose. She touched her finger, caught it.

I guess this is a woman's tear.

Only a woman. Merely a tear.

And I only had a lovely dream.

I know what every woman knows, that dreams weren't meant to last.

She sniffled, read her book. Alice shrank and swam in her own tears.

The cat tried to leave. Linda made it stay. She was still boss over the cat. Still made in God's image—mistress over the beasts.

She stayed up til eleven, finished *Alice.* Closed it with a smile. Derrick read it once, when he was eight. It scared the living shit out of him.

I'm braver now, I guess.

It's funny, too—how I was in the story, like I wasn't when I was eight. I was that little girl, listening to a stoned caterpillar. I felt no little resentment, that the Queen of Hearts was such a bitch. And I felt salvation's bliss of leaves, falling on my sleeping face.

The thought occurred to her, only then: *Why don't I go to a doctor, or someone. Tell them what's happened to me.*

Well . . . interesting notion. How would it go?

Okay, I . . . don't understand what that means, Mrs. Bloom.

—Oh. Well, it means that I died, and my wife was still alive but her soul had left her body, and I transmigrated into my wife's body. Or maybe I'm just not good at explaining things, or . . . ?

How would she prove it?

What would she know that Derrick never could have told his wife?

Linda fell asleep that night with Shelley's voice, imagined: *Lin if you wanted attention so much, why didn't you just ask?*

By late afternoon, Day Two of reclusion, Linda was bored to tears. She'd already called Shelley, who had a guest and was not a happy hostess. Erminegard was eating her out of house and home. "At least when her mouth is full, she can't talk. And at least I'm spared S-and-S."

Linda was confused, awash in fear. "Two lightning bolts . . . ?"—the fearful query trailed off in a whimper.

Shelley waited til it was quite extinguished. "Um . . . no. *Spudenschnitzel und Schneisenschnorkel*—thank God, they're in a pound in New Rochelle." She answered her daughter's bewildered silence: "Her *Dobermans*, Lin. The two most disreputable dogs on Earth."

They talked for over an hour, covering a range of topics—clothes, nutrition, health and well-being in general. Shelley seemed to impress the fact that Linda was still capable of giving her grandkids someday. She imparted this through subtle hints, like "When you have your first."—such a done deal that Linda glanced at her belly, to see if it was getting big.

It was worse than talking with her dad—not gently refusing a surfeit of love, but running from a pushy witch who tried to run her life. Linda didn't really want to hang out with her mom. That left . . .

She found herself pacing the apartment. *I don't know why I'm making myself so tense over this. Sure I do. Because Linda did. She wanted a girlfriend more than anything. She'd focus on someone she'd met, almost like she had a crush. Yet it never came about—she was no less shy of other women than she was of men.*

Am I going to call Priscilla, or not?

Well . . . yes, she was. Right now. She sat on the bed, by the phone. She reached to pick it up, then pulled her hand away and bit her thumb. Derrick's wife did that, sometimes—I'm cornered and I'll bite (myself). Shelley once alluded to some vague origin of this quirk, a male teacher in first grade or something. What was her problem with calling Priscilla? *Is this done? Do adult women really call each other, just to ask if they want to hang out? I'll bet it is not done. I'll bet this business of exchanging phone numbers is an empty courtesy, and the last thing you're supposed to do is actually call the person.* She stared at the indifferent phone and her fear came into clear focus. *She'll think I'm some lonely, passionate eccentric with my cat and peasant dress and unshaved armpits.* Clearer still. *That I'm a lesbian. But I'm not, I'm purely seeking companionship and that's . . . somehow more embarrassing.*

She remembered male protocols, like that would help. The chums of Derrick's youth: guys with earrings and tattoos who called everyone *pisan*, but a friend was just a dude you hung with. Then there were your Nordic types, Lars Bauer and his ilk. Men who valued friendship and did not bestow it lightly. When you shook a man's hand, it meant hello or goodbye; when you *gripped* a man's hand, that meant a great deal more. Lars always shook Derrick's hand—he never gripped. He'd only known his son-in-law five years; in his Germanic perspective, that made them barely acquainted.

Shelley's words came back as well. *That's them we're different we're tuned to feelings others' and our own we're individuals in ways they'll never know oh anyway you're just two girls who cares.*

Linda decided: *I'll call. I'll ask, Would you like to do lunch. Or whatever. If she says she's unclear on what this is about, I'll say You're my friend and I care about you. Which is honestly true.*

She remembered Don Burgess, in lock-up. Short, round and black as a chocolate Easter egg. Straddling the fence between the program and the gang, set up for a fall. Shouting accusations, til all the king's horses and men came into the dorm. Derrick and Biondo rushing him to the office, like Spock and Kirk getting Nomad off the ship before he exploded. *You're a homosexual, Tony! Tony, you're a homosexual! You touched me—that was a mistake! Error/imperfection:* Faulty! *Must . . . sterrr . . . illl . . . izzze . . .*

Oh for chrissake. She dialed Priscilla's number.

Three rings, then a voice Linda didn't quite recognize: jaded, rather langorous. "Hello?"

"Hi, Pris."

A pause; Linda's heart raced. She wanted to hang up, and then: "I thought you'd never call me, Lin."

Linda spoke softly. "Well, um . . . you didn't call *me*? Or . . . ?"

Another pause, which was now a reminder: *She's as shy as I am.* "Well, I didn't want to intrude? On you losing your husband, or . . . ?"

"What, like it's a party or something?"

Another long pause, then Pris almost shrieked: "*Oh God you're just too weird!*"

Alone in her apartment, Linda blinked. In a cool blue world of godlike men, she'd finally found a sister spirit tangled up in pink.

"Linda, my life sucks. I mean it. Meet clients, come home, watch TV. Call clients on the phone. I'm not a people person. I'm not a money person. Everything is sucking up for money, money, money. Lin, I wish we were still—"

"If we don't get together, Pris, I'll die."

"Yeah, huh?" Pris giggled. Dying was assumed—the natural consequence of their not getting together.

"Pris, how about . . . um . . . well actually, tonight is even good for me. The rest of my week is just—"

"Lin, tonight is fine."

Linda showed Pris through her apartment. "I hope you feel

229

like you belong. Because you do. I mean, I feel so honored that you're here." The Singer sewing machine. The Black-eyed Susan throw on the rocker.

Humbled, Pris whispered "Okay"—she'd strive to be worthy of this grandeur.

They sat in the parlor and talked. "Lin, are you allowed to drive?"

"Not really."

"How's your epilepsy? Has it been a problem?"

"No. I go blank, then wake up in a chair—it's real easy."

"Lin, you're strange. Unidentified Flighty Object."

Shy, dumb giggles.

Linda kept steering their talk away from the past. "That's old, Pris. Oh God . . . that's so old."

Pris, watching her carefully, began to recount a shopping trip in the summer of '87. A breathless tale of Girls Unleashed: after Mai Tai's with their lunch they traipsed through Caldor's, tried on things they'd never buy. "Spandex pants—wow, Pris, that's so old. The last time I wore them, I got clubbed over the head and dragged into a cave. Honest, I burned my mammoth roast. Wow, spandex pants are *old*."

Pris shook her head—not spandex, then. She started on a weekend camping trip in '82. Linda gasped, Why don't you get it. Pris trailed off, uncertain about "bug spray . . . ?"

"Pris, look: . . . I'm not sure how to say this. I want a rela . . . I want a *friend*ship that's more here-and-now. More who we are, today."

"Oh, okay. Who *are* we, now?"

Linda was startled; she'd expected some kind of resistance. No, I'd rather wallow in the past. Now the ball was in her court and she didn't have a clue. "Well . . . who we were, back then. Just a little more mature."

"You wanna go see male strippers?"

Linda calmly studied. Pris wore a white turtleneck, a small gold cross necklace. A somewhat shapeless skirt, low heels. Her wavy, frizzy auburn hair was gathered loosely in a tail, like all she could do with it was bunch it into the neatest mass she could around her face. Her pale, lightly freckled complexion was almost childish; like Linda, she didn't routinely bother with makeup. Her greenish eyes were matronly, warm and unassuming.

"Male strippers" needed no response, because it was a joke.

They talked about jobs, home and family. Linda had grievances against Shelley, issues she'd developed over the past eight days. Pris gently redirected, Don't bitch about your mom, like she'd been hearing these tirades for twenty years. Pris mentioned that they were both single again. Eventually, they could double-date and (Pris smiled) go dancing in clubs. Derrick danced with his wife but once, in a cocktail lounge in Montreal. Linda's idea of dancing was to sway in place to Christopher Cross' *Sailing*. Slow-dancing worked about as well; she was mortified, feeling her husband's embrace was too intimate to demonstrate in public. She cuddled like some frightened little mouse, losing herself in his arms. "Dancing," too, was a joke. "Dating again" was—?

"Pris I can't date 'cause I'm scared of men." Linda stared, in awe of herself—*I said it, and it's true.* "More than I was before."

"Oh, shit—is that even possible?"

"I want nothing to do with them, Pris. I had a horrible experience yesterday and I'm not a lesbian."

Priscilla stared at her, vulnerable, transfixed—a rabbit caught in headlights.

Sterilize.

Linda twitched her shoulder, staring rather spookily herself: *Well, what? I'm not.*

Pris said "Sure you are."

They'd spent their teens discussing men, a soulful competition: Lonelier than thou, and ever faithful.

Linda tried a breathy recoup: "So, would you like to do something?" Pris gaped in shock, delighted. Lin explained, "Go out"; Pris dropped her jaw. "I mean to get, like, a tape to watch. Or, to eat."

"Mm-hm. Let's go get a tape to eat." They got their coats, took Linda's Tercel. To Blockbusters, close to the Cabot Street bridge. The night air smelled of tar and fish. The parking lot went right down to the wharf pilings: except near the store, it wasn't brightly lit. Three young men were standing near an old Dodge. Loud talk of college dorm life and a guy who was a wuss. Slacker uniforms: grunge coats, baseball caps on backwards over close-cropped scalps. All three turned to look, as the two women walked to the store. One of the men said "Oh my, my." Another whistled, softly but long. One said, "Yes, there is a God"; another made a sibilant sound. Whether he was adding—*ess* to God to make it Goddess or just hissing through his teeth to be a jerk was not too clear. Linda didn't look at her friend. It seemed understood, you just keep walking. Linda had a thought, like a mother's protective, ungenerous notion: *Pris has nothing to worry about; I don't think they meant her.*

They got into the store: light and safety and The Little Mermaid. Walked around together. Linda remembered that: *Girls stay together. We're taught that early: hold Mommy's hand.* Pris went happily from one tape to another, making little comments—she'd never seen it, she thought it might suck, she'd already seen it and *knew* that it sucked, and so on. Linda said, "I'm worried about those guys outside. I'm afraid they might still be there when we leave."

Pris said "pffth," somewhat like a tiny horse. Then noticed they had *Sleepless In Seattle*. Men said things, you kept walking; it was part of Life, so deal. Linda felt like a child caught breaking an unknown rule—it was now her place to politely dwell in shame and fear. She said "No really, I'm uncomfortable." It seemed like something women had a right to feel and say, though Lin imagined Shelley's voice *Oh knock it off you're fine*.

Pris said "They won't bother us. You look like some Puerto Rican chick, who would pull a knife."

A woman about Shelley's age stood frowning at the New Releases. She was black-haired, trim. Black dress, tan coat open like an Iverness; Linda sort of liked the look. The woman's face tightened into an almost cruel expression, then she turned and spoke calmly to Pris. "Pardon me, miss—there is something that you have against Puerto Rico?"

Linda realized that, ridiculously, Pris had stepped behind her—not hiding exactly, just taking cover. Linda spoke on her friend's behalf: "She was talking to me. I *am* Puerto Rican."

The woman answered caustically in Spanish. Some motherly remonstrance, like Linda was her daughter. Unknown words to a familiar tune, Your generation makes me sick.

Linda said, "We're in America. Why don't you speak English?"

"Because I teach it all day, and I feel that's enough. Why don't you wear makeup?"

Linda, wide-eyed, said "Oh well."

The woman went to another section.

Pris was thrilled. "You were always the protector." She lived in Ashland, a hinterland hamlet much like Merrill; race issues were an exotic adventure. "What do you want to get—have we decided?" Her energy level seemed daintily frenetic. Linda could envision her cleaning house, like a squirrel getting geared up for spring. "A foreign film, Lin? How about a romance?"

"I'm just not into that . . ."

"I'm talking about a movie."

Linda said, "So am I. This is a video store, right?"

"If you're so smart, why don't you wear makeup? Look, let's . . ." Pris walked; let's stroll around and see.

They passed through the adventure section. Films Derrick would have loved. *Death-Meat 4: The Ultimate Carnage*. Linda looked in wonder, trying to remember why she used to love these films. Pris stopped and looked at her, perplexed—why on earth was Linda looking *here*? Linda didn't know either; she *tsk*ed, and they moved along.

They browsed through Comedy. Linda was disturbed when Pris presented *Home Alone*: "No, not boys. Too . . . energetic, or . . ." Pris somehow understood exactly, put the box back on the shelf.

232

She said, "Oh Linda, here: goofy guys trying to get laid."

Linda looked at *Steel Magnolias*. An "inspiring portrayal" of older women, bonding left and right. An army of Shelleys gloating over their triumphs. Pris came over with a box. "Did you ever see this? It's with Ellen Barkin. About a man who wakes up in a woman's body. Someone said it's funny, though I—"

"His . . . wife's?"

"I'm sorry?"

"Pris, put that back where you found it, please."

"Lin?"

"Just take it away. *Put it back!*"

The clerk behind the counter glanced up from his book. Another customer turned to see. Linda hadn't raised her voice but she'd been really shrill. Not in anger—she'd just keened her voice, like Pris said "Hey look at this" and had a big black spider.

The clerk went back to his book. The customer decided there was no live entertainment, went back to reading boxes.

Linda put her fingers to the side of her nose; closed her eyes, remorseful, like her shriek had been a cataclysmic sneeze.

Pris gently said, "Just tell me. You don't need to scream."

Obligingly mild, Linda said "Please put it back."

They finally agreed on *Groundhog Day*. Took Cabot Street back to Lafayette—a narrow, winding drive past dark, gabled houses which looks unchanged from Puritan days, except for cars and streetlights. Pris said "This is route 1-A! Doesn't it go to Boston?"

Moody, Linda shook her head. No one from the Boston area asks that question. It leads into a number of jokes.

"Lin, why'd you get upset about the tape I showed you?"

She didn't answer for a while. She focused on her driving, which—in Salem—is always a good idea. She was, of course, allowed to drive. She had *petit mal* fugues, not grand-slam tonic-clonic seizures. Her diagnosis was *Mild Epilepsy, Controlled*. They circled the Commons, entered Lafayette's shop-bright, four-lane stop-and-go.

Linda said "That gender-bending stuff upsets me. Boys should be boys and girls should be girls. Life's already confusing enough."

"I remember when we were young. You worrying that you had too much hair on your arms. Then in your Bible phase—telling me all female believers are really men, inside. That we'd stand before God as men." Linda shook her head, mystified. "You got that from First Peter. The King James Version, the woman's 'hidden man of the heart'. I remember your dad telling you, that was just Elizabethan English. How it was poetic, not precise; they called boys 'girls' if they were pretty. And stuff. Yet you always wore skirts. Long black skirts. And you got upset when you saw two guys on the football team hug. You thought you might have witnessed a crime."

They stopped at 7 Eleven, got wine coolers and TV dinners. Linda hadn't eaten a real meal all week. They got a little buzzed and watched the movie. It was sort of like an old Beaumont/Matheson *Twilight Zone*, played for nervous laughs; both women got absorbed and they broke down in nervous laughter. "Oh shit. He's trying to kill himself by letting the groundhog drive the van. Oh I think I pee'ed myself. Oh my ribs hurt OhmyGod."

After the movie, it was late. Pris said she'd head on home. Linda said, "You should stay. Spend the night. I want you to."

"Oh, right—like in the old days. Walking each other across the golf course at night—afraid of our shadows. You'd make me promise to stay and watch, then run back so fast, your flashlight looked like a ghost. A green glow on the lawn. Then you'd make it to the other side and shine the light at me. So I'd know you hadn't been killed. We used to tell our mothers anything, so they'd let us sleep over instead. We hated crossing that golf course." Now it was the world outside—a bigger, darker golf course where the goblins were quite real.

Linda said, "You have to stay. 'Friends don't let friends . . .'"

"Lin, all that laughing woke me up. I'm October as a drudge, gonest to odd." To cinch the discussion: "I had a neat time with you tonight."

Linda said, "I'm glad. So did I."

"You're so narcissistic."

It took Lin a moment to get it. She knew that, once, these silly jokes had been a world of giggles. Once, slipping out to the golf course on a moonlit summer night, with an 8-track player and a bottle of wine, was the height of pagan debauchery. Tibbling on the gazebo; puffed-sleeve blouses moonlight blue, murmurs hushed under the breeze. Playing at impassioned musings, movie actress poses—a world of allure all squandered and kept secret since Prince Charming never came out on the golf course. It was Longmeadow Girlhood stuff; you had to have been there. Linda couldn't laugh; she only smiled.

Pris said "Next one's on me. At my place. Tomorrow night . . . though you mentioned, the rest of your week . . ."

"I lied. I don't know why. I do. I was trying to sound . . ."

"Which failed. I'm having two other friends over."

"Then I'm surely sure it's a date."

Pris, fascinated, echoed *surely sure*. A catchword of their childhood, not just something Derrick's wife used to say. "These friends of mine: they're old and dear, just friends. But they're two guys. Is that okay?"

Linda withdrew into her thoughts. All of a sudden, Pris was

a threat. The estimable nose, decided chin and hopeless hair made her look like Emily Bronte. Perhaps she wrote secret poetry, got bitten by a dog and cauterized her calf with a hot poker. Linda said "Um . . . with men. I can't."—her Broken English of the Heart, like Pris was now her mother.

"Lin, if you're scared of *me*, then forget it. You're pure yin. Nothing but solidified estrogen. Turn into a bubble and float away, like Tinkerbell."

"Pris, these friends . . . you say they're 'old and dear, just friends', they wouldn't happen to be gay? Or . . . ?"

"No. You're not heterophobic, are you?"

The question multiplied into so many possible interpretations—to one of which, the answer was *yes*—that Linda just said "No."

"Linda, I won't pressure you. Just tell me how you feel."

Linda thought, *Same as with Shelley. Everyone wants to be nice to me, I can have whatever I want—and I manage to screw it up.*

"Lin, I know you; I know exactly what you're feeling. I know that you're going through grief. These are friends, they go to my church. They're open, sensitive guys. We don't have to be separate, like nuns. They can be your friends, too."

Linda wanted her friend's approval, said the boldest thing that came to mind. "How are they on looks?"

Pris narrowed her eyes: Come on. And Linda, all at once, saw the amazing, hidden truth. Pris was the Sensual Jewess to Linda's ethereal Vicar's Daughter. Pris was, in plain English, hot. She was lusted after, obsessed with, feverishly sought by men. The aquiline cast of her nose and chin weren't homely, they were *wanton*. Her heavy breasts and ample thighs were Ishtar's call. She could get in any man's face and command his attention. The shapeless, schoolgirl clothes were the water poured on Elisha's altar—they could only damp, not quench, the flames. Her narrowed eyes meant: *You know us. We only choose the best.* The rule obtained from the first day they were allowed to wear sheer stockings: Average Joes need not apply. "Lin, they're sweet. Regular masculine guys who are nice. Okay?"

"Are they, like, 'Alan Alda types'?"

"Lin, what would you want with an 'Alan Alda type'?"

"I simply don't know. I don't know what I want with *men*—even just this, just socially." Pris rolled her eyes, expressive as some silent-movie starlet: same old sissy Linda. "Pris, it's who I am. Who I've become and you don't understand, I'm not strong enough to be this weak. If men challenge me in any way, if they play any games . . . well, they'll win."

"Lin, you're a wuss."

"All right, I'll come. Where do you live?"

"Are you sure?"

"No, I'm not. I'll need directions."

Pris wrote them out on a scrap from her purse. Linda held the paper without taking it. "This is strictly a 'friends' thing, right?"

"No. They'll pull the walls away and you'll be on *Love Connection*. You'll have to choose between Rush Limbaugh and David Koresh." Linda curled her lip; she took the paper, reluctant. "Lin, it'll be a *she-thang*." Lascivious, Pris winked. "The guys will just be there for us to, you know: play with."

"I understand. Little attitudes and mind games. Could you do that part for me, though? I . . ."

Pris viewed Linda dismally, walked out to the landing. Linda followed, and Pris turned and took her hands. "Lin, this wasn't an accident. The way our lives have crossed like this."

Linda wasn't touched to hear of Someone's machinations. Every time He came to her desk, she would bite her thumb. She preferred to believe in accidents. She had a smile for her friend, however sad. "It's late. I'll walk you to your car."

"Oh, *right*. Then I'll have to stand outside and wait, til you run back upstairs and wave to me from the window. 'Chile, we're too old and it's too cold' "—another classic line from their teens.

Pris began her descent of the building's notorious stairs. A sequence of dainty poses; a Lorelei stepping down stones of a brook. *She can't weigh more than one-twenty, and half of it's lady-fat. Yet she's afraid of falling. I understand, now, what a big, hard, noisy world she lives in. And how a Bartles and James seems like a big bottle of booze.* At the bottom of the stairs, Pris turned. Her upturned face was girlish, bright with mischief. "My. What creaky, creepy steps you have, Granma."

"The better to watch you from the top of, my dear."

They wiggled fingers, Bye-bye.

Linda went back into her apartment. She drank half of the last wine cooler, walking slowly through her rooms, then poured the rest down the sink.

15

Linda woke next day with an obscene and furious shout, spinning onto her side. The cat—done clawing her behind—lept from the bed, galloped guiltily out of the bedroom.

She gasped, outraged, then collapsed onto her back. It pissed her off to be woken like this—in a woman's body, to a woman's day, painfully informed that her wholesome peach of a derriére was just the thing to claw.

She abruptly sat up, fished through clarifying lotion, an old apple, wadded Kleenex for her little Cosmotime. 10:12 and now she knew, why Derrick's wife hid her clock. Obligations were lead blankets, keeping her in bed.

She went into the bathroom, showered. A daughter's toilette, unlike a son's. No hearty romp beneath the jets, nor swaggering forth to rule with just a towel around one's hips. No, you just go in and wash. The less you smell—or talk, or eat—the better. Cold cream, foundation—make yourself disappear. Nothing matters, but that you come out—since others are waiting to use the bathroom. Linda was alone in her apartment; nothing mattered. She combed out her wet hair.

She caught her reflection in the door's full-length mirror. *A naked woman combing her hair is really not an impressive sight.*

Yet this is what I'll see, each time. Year in and out. Broadening, sagging, softer, more, til I'm nothing but cleavage and rolls. And thighs. Hating my body more and more. I should start developing character, or something.

So boring. So hard. She combed out her hair.

She stopped, and saw her reflection again.

If this was a stranger I saw—in a health club, or whatever—I'd think nothing of her, good or bad. Yet I find no comfort in being an Average Jane. Nothing there I like.

But I know that's all I am. Not an angel, nor a beast, only arms that work and feet that ache. Thighs and hips large, to bear children "we" decided not to have. That my husband wouldn't give me, so: an embarrassment of softness. Breasts to nourish lips that never were. Now they're just heavy, they chaffe underneath.

But it's not my fault. I . . . sort of want to be a mommy still. To have a baby girl, my little . . . Lynn, and she'd never be lonely or scared. She'd never wonder why she had to be a baby girl in such a loud, hard world, 'cause I'd be there. I'd explain everything. As a mother does, like God should—I would always smile, always love. Because I'd know just how she feels. When she was hungry, I'd feed her, right from my own body, all she wanted. She could just suck, like my nipple was candy; I would have time for that. Or if she was really starving, if she wanted all she could get—Mommy has plenty; I'd hold her til she was full. I'd sing until she went to sleep and then I'd hold her still.

Thoughtful, Linda held her breasts. Touched her little fingertip, the hardened nipple, magic thrill, warmth deep inside, a secret in her tummy. *My breasts are okay, then? Beautiful, or . . . ? They're burdens of hope, and . . . ?*

Sad. For now I'm unused, alone—a world of love that might have been. Born to dry tears and wipe noses; to stand before those new, a guiding light. That part of me is angel; that light appears as God. And yet alone, just for myself, my she-beast stomach growls for bread with jam. I'd take it, loaf and jar, and binge, and screw the starving children in Rwanda.

She looked at her reflected sex. The tummy's curve down between her legs. Baby-doll innocence, then little nook of cleft and hair, Oh just forget it, nothing there. Same as you'd see on a mare, a cow or ewe—no mystery. Husband in, baby out—birds, bees and flowers nice, but not intrinsically germaine. A cleft that bleeds and smells but it's okay, No no don't touch. A daughter is a sturdy piece of work, after all. Spank her bottom, make her sit, No bread and jam for you. Sweep the floor, fold the sheets, while precious sons are sung to sleep. *And when you wake, I'll give you some cake . . .* Shelley's wistful reminder: Oh, *that's* what daughters are good for, besides licking batter spoons. Good for folding sheets, and giving pony rides. *Don't be a pouty pony, Lin. Be a pretty pony, and some prince will want to ride you. Some lovely man will love you, Linda. Just for who you are. Sad but faithful, blue but true. What's a mother to do with you?*

She sadly blinked at her reflection, *I forgive you. I accept. At most, a faithful someone for some special someone else. A pony for a gentle groom. A husband. I won't nag.*

So sad to be a woman, such a lovely and sad little tragedy. Men love and pity women as once their mothers loved and pitied baby sons and so, I guess, the two ends of the circle meet. So sad.

Choosing something to wear. She couldn't lift her heart to the day. She wasn't Natalie Wood. She felt neither pretty nor witty. Miss America's crown was secure.

She found her old petticoat dress, under her side of the bed. It surmisably had been worn. But she decided to receive it as a gift from God and pretend it was also miraculously clean. She got a jumper from the storage box. The jumper was a Faith Mountain, with a teddy bear motif. It was mostly brown. The petticoat was white. She'd find a way to mismatch something with white, but it seemed only marginally possible. Her panties were the ones she'd found under the bed, Wednesday night. She added up the hours she'd worn them, and decided to divide that by three. The dividend—actual hours—was reality: doing what Derrick's wife did at home, scads of nothing much. Lying on the sofa, dreaming. The divisor was a working woman's day: a girl with mountains of faith, with calculator and daily planner and teddy bears on her pockets, like nothing was too hard or too absurd or just too cute. That fictitious girl worked a whole nine-hour shift, and her panties were okay. Lin could comb her hair and do her buttons; maybe panty math was okay, too. She dressed and went outside.

It was sunny and warm, in the upper forties. Sparrows perched on the telephone line, across the street. She could hear the distant rev and rumble of trucks down on Canal Street. You didn't hear them when it was really cold. She wondered why that was.

She got into her Tercel, destination Filene's Basement. She chose to go there because it was close. She didn't know if it was good or bad, or how it was different from Filene's. The fact that it was underground, though, seemed kind of a plus.

Once there, she found it was a regular store. It wasn't really a basement. Everything was white, even the low-pile carpet on low-traffic aisles. There were racks of clothing according to type—dresses, blouses, etc.—but otherwise miscellaneous.

The strangest thing were the mannequins. They were silver, faceless, and wore visors and/or hats that weren't part of the outfits they displayed. It seemed like some sort of in-thing, which everyone but Linda understood. If you came and looked at five hundred blouses and found the one you wanted, you'd obviously know why the mannequins had to look like robots. Moreover, she imagined all the women in the store were watching her: *Let's see if she knows how to shop.*

Linda strolled through different sections, looking at different dresses and skirts like she had complex and subtle thoughts about them. In fact, she would have been quite receptive to anyone who stepped up and told her what to buy.

The PA played soft music. Billy Idol's *Eyes Without A Face.* Linda found it soothing, somehow. Idol crooned the phrase like it evoked a romantic and compassionating image, rather than the title of the most disturbing movie ever made.

One of the clerks seemed to have her under discrete surveillance. Why be non-white and wear a leather coat, unless you wish to portray yourself as Substance Abuse personified? This wasn't like being a big, rough man whom people were afraid of; it was worse. No one wanted to play dolls with her, she smelled. Lin looked harder for a dress, disturbed by how she felt. *"Maybe if I'm prettier, they'll like me"*—oh my God.

239

Linda found a dress. Dark green velour, with rayon lining. Elegant daywear, relaxed evening. Draped neck, cinched waist, a gathered mid-length skirt. See, she'd learned a thing or two just from sewing with her mom. The dress looked cut for a fuller figure, but Linda was convinced that she was fat. Nor did she understand that it was a winter dress, reduced for spring clearance. It was on sale, and she vaguely wanted it. The forest green fabric looked velvety, soft. It was on the size 7 rack; she took it, went to the dressing rooms. The clerk glanced sternly in her general direction, like there was a jack-booted crack dealer *some*where in the store but the clerk wasn't quite sure where. Linda wondered if she might confront the clerk in a ladylike fashion—say something light and pleasant that couldn't possibly offend, yet still get her point across. *Oh, I know you're spying on me. I really think you should stop.* Yes, that sounded right. *If you don't, I'll kick your ass.*—then she would laugh, since that was obviously a joke. She ended up just going into one of the dressing rooms. Her tall, gentle, coltish form minced nervously; she felt there wasn't enough room to get undressed. She knew she wouldn't kick anyone's ass. She could hardly get out of her own way.

The dress fit, and she supposed it looked all right. It came with shoulder pads, which she wouldn't wear in the evening. There, she'd gone to Filene's Basement, bought a dress. Almost. She changed back into her own clothes, went to look for the cashier. The PA was now playing Olivia Newton-John's *Magic*. The Eighties aren't over yet, you still have gobs of cash; they probably played the whole *Xanadu* soundtrack on slow sale days. She saw some things near the checkout, put where a woman might say *I need that too*; it worked. An older clerk kindly asked if she'd like any assistance. Linda felt like she'd been caught, looked and sounded like a lady shopper. "Oh!—no, I'm fine. I'm only browsing, thanks."

"Browsing." 34 C, if it's not fluorescent green or something, grab it. Here, pick this up and read the package. Demi-cup underwire décolleté cups with cushioned underwires sold. I need pantyhose, here: "French cut," lacy shit, I can't even read the writing: fine. *Oh hell, they come in sizes. 24-28, is that waist or hips? Anything user-friendly? Okay:* large. *We covered that tune with the peasant dress, it means tall. Though I'm scared it really means* tall-but-we-know-you're-fat-too. *Who cares, just . . .*

A girl behind a counter spoke to Linda, softly said amazing things. It took Linda several moments to realize it was a sales pitch. Germainé Montaile was doing free makeovers. Linda didn't care, but someone was treating her as an educated consumer of beauty products and she somehow couldn't walk away. Uncertain and unwilling, she murmured, "But I'm sure I need, you know, an appointment, and I don't have time to—"

The girl said, "You're in luck, we're doing walk-ins." Now the clincher: she pointed to Linda's stuff. "You can pay for these here."

Linda didn't know how to say she didn't want it. If anyone took charge of her, her will was not her own. She didn't like the fact that even other women took control of her. Like Alice, she kept getting smaller. "Well . . . where would you like me to sit, or . . . ?"

The session took about twenty minutes. Linda sat on the thin, stark chair, two cushions on metal tubes, inside the counter booth. The store was bright, white. Her mind was empty; she saw herself as though outside her body. The mannequins looked knowing, like when the store was closed at night they came to life and worshiped Satan. Linda felt detained, caught in a sliding glass web.

The girl said something startling. "You're very pretty. One of the prettiest women I've ever seen. I guess you're just somebody's mom." The girl felt she could share this, since Linda wasn't really as imposing as she seemed. Linda also realized she was older than this girl. It felt nice to be admired, even by mistake; she smiled, shyly sharing warmth.

"Now, I see you're doing the natural look. Minimal makeup. You've done it so well it looks like you're not wearing any at all."

Linda felt startled again. *She doesn't like me. She doesn't hate me. She's getting some kind of commission for this.* "Well, I . . . saw an article in Elle and thought I'd try it."

"That's West Coast, hon. It's been, like, totally passé for months even there."

Linda swallowed. "It w-was an old issue then, I guess . . ."

"Your eyes are wide. Are they *always* wide? They're *large*. Go like this." A face: surprise. Not unpretty. Linda mimicked. "Yeah—see?" Linda poised still, large eyes looking for a mirror that wasn't there; No, she couldn't see herself. "We'll want clear definition. No rouge, we'll lose your cheekbones." Was this *Le Yeux Sans Visage* for real?

"What are we trying to do?"

"Well, we're *trying* to create a look." Was it hard? "Monotone simplicity: your eyes carry your whole face. Bring your lips out dark for counterpoint. Do you really want all that hair?"

"To c-cut, or . . . ?" *Oh talk like an adult at least.* "I mean, I don't know what that has to do with makeup."

"Well, in terms of getting it layered back—that's just my suggestion. Since you want to show your face. Affirm your . . . plainness. You know what I mean." The girl sort of winked, herself unsure of her meaning.

Wary, Linda looked around. This sounded like a spiritual

journey, and she just wanted to go home. "I'll ask my stylist. What she thinks."

"Hon, *any* stylist—please. We're all in the Nineties. —that's just my suggestion."

Linda ended up buying thirty dollars worth of cosmetics she didn't want or need. She took her bags and quickly left.

Walking through the aisles, she felt trembly and weak. She didn't feel hungry, yet knew she must be starving, having scarcely eaten all week. There was a TWBFY out in the mall. She pictured something fruity, and very, very light. A non-fat, sugar-free raspberry dessert. A really small one. She left Filene's Basement, wandered out into the mall. Looked for a directory, saw none. Sam Goody's, Lane Bryant, Jo-Anne's Fabrics, Toys-R-Us. No yogurt place. Sparro's Pizza, dear God no—the thought of oil and oregano made her stomach contract into a bilious knot. The central plaza was up ahead, she'd walk and find a directory. She stopped, took off her coat, put it in the bag with her new dress. Ambled along with her mind far away, a woman with three bags and a purse. But the mall felt pretty safe. Standard lunchtime crowd, she thought. Lots of young to middle-aged women, mostly in pairs, some with toddlers or babies in strollers. Young men with ties under their windbreakers, walking purposefully—office go-fors. Clumps of men in suits, women in suit dresses. All in grey, like soldiers of some well-heeled army; yuppies doing lunch. No one stared at Linda baldly. Artful glances like a brother's kiss, part of the human family; like a mother making rules, she decided to allow it.

Past Victoria's Secret, Shannon Jeweler's, Au Bon Pain. (The thought of a croissant was almost scary—so much salt.) The central plaza, wow—open space and light. A two-tier arcade around an elevated concourse, with glass elevator, escalator, modern art and climbing gardens. A permanent platform for seasonal attractions, like Santa's North Pole—kids are never too young to start confusing their geography. (Pris had mentioned that for three consecutive Easters, she and Linda worked as "helpers" on an Easter Bunny gig at the Twin Oaks Mall, near Merrill. They brought small children to the Big Guy, who wiggled his nose, made bubbly jokes about hiding eggs where only good children could find them, etc. and gave them Munson's cream-filled eggs. The "helpers" wore pink pinafores and rabbit ears.

(*"Mall Bunny", God—what a thing to have on your resumé.*)

In the center of the plaza was a tree—a real, live elm. The sun roof seemed a lofty, spacious translucency, pearly white and high as heaven. Above the plaza, on all sides, the shoppers walked the upper tier or lounged at the railing, looking down at stores and people. Yet Linda knew there wasn't just one upper level. There were more—many more—there were levels up to the

242

heavens. They *were* the heavens, a progression upwards of Disney Stores and Radio Shacks and Laura Ashleys *ad infinitum*. Hosts above, ringing the ascent to the light, looking down at her like the faces on the Sistine Chapel's ceiling. Only they weren't God and His angels, but a starry host of consumers, all buying home computers and velvet dresses with lace appliqué, and lastly Linda saw that they were real. The tiers were multiplied into the stratosphere, thousands upon thousands of stores, millions and millions of shoppers, and only Linda could see them. Yet even as she learned this awesome secret, she knew she couldn't share it. They were high, very high, and she'd sunk as low as she could go—all the way to the floor.

> *lookit this oh my Gawd the girl had some kinda fit*
> *if someone should call 911 or we should just find a security*
> *guard*
> *out of the way please I know CPR let me through*
> *She's fine.*
> *something I heard about putting a spoon or something in their*
> *mouth so they don't bite their tongue*
> *give her air come on stand back*
> *let me in I know CPR*
> *Lady, look: I have CPR, First Aid and I* know her. *Okay?*
> *She had a grand mal seizure. It's over; she's* asleep. *If people*
> *weren't being so aggressive . . . you have a nice day, too.*
> *Linda, can you hear me? Hon, are you awake? Ground control*
> *to Minnie Mouse, is anyone flying your plane*?

She saw the shape of a man's head, framed by a pearly white halo. Oh . . . no, it wasn't a halo. It was a translucent skylight. She was in the mall. It reminded her of a mall she'd seen—long ago, she thought. But this one only had two levels. The one she'd seen before had more like fifty or a hundred. It was the World Trade Center of shopping malls.

She saw the man, now; he was kneeling, right beside her. Smooth, boyish face, longish brown hair, high cheekbones. Handsome, but for a funny ski-jump nose; cute, then, perhaps. He looked at her very calmly, like he knew everything about her, knew she was all right, but still wondered where she went when she was gone.

"Hi, Lin."

Watching him, she moved her lips: *hello.*

"Do you know where you are?"

"World Trade Center."

"Um . . .—we'll go best two out of three. Do you know what happened?"

"Yes. I had a seizure. A . . . ." She wanted to use the technical term, but wasn't sure she remembered it. She thought it was *tonic-clonic*, but that sounded like something from *I Am The*

Walrus. " . . . big one."

"Correct. Now, the deciding vote: do you know who you are?"

She said, "I'm a retarded girl. I live in a group home. You're my staff person. I'm in love with you, or something."

"I'm deeply flattered, Linda. And really glad the person you're describing isn't here."

Linda recognized the man. She knew that, for some strange reason, she had to act like she knew him well, even though they were barely acquainted. She couldn't remember what the reason was. Maybe because she was trying to overcome being shy. She said his name. "Steve Jurassic."

"That's Mister Park to you, young lady."

He put one hand under her head. It made a perfect pillow. His other hand took her finers, like he would kiss her hand but instead he raised her, sitting up. She felt like Sleeping Beauty; she looked at him, dreamily bemused. *He's had a lot of practice, taking care of helpless girls.*

The world swam back into focus. There was a crowd of people, staring at her and talking, some genuinely concerned, others only curious. A short, plump woman with short, brown hair seemed angry or indignant. Linda realized it was the lady who knew CPR, who hadn't been allowed to save the day. Linda had some nerve, being all right without her help. Anyway, the fun was over; the crowd was breaking up. The man wore a chartreuse Jansport jacket. They were in front of Hit Or Miss. Half-Off On All Sweaters (purchased with an accessory).

"I was over in Hermann's Sporting Goods, and I heard someone bit the dust. I told the guy I was talking to, 'I'll bet it's my partner from work!'—you know, kidding. Who can't believe there's a God?"

"Faith Mountain." She looked at herself. Woman's shape in child's garment. She explained her remark: "I used to be my husband."

"Well, I see you're quite recovered."

Linda missed the irony; she blinked, confused. "It was wrong for me? Before I was sick and now I'm okay?"

" 'Was blind but now I see.' "

"Steve." (His name was *Juraska*, of course. He didn't even remotely resemble any kind of dinosaur. She dimly recalled he was into white-water body surfing, or something similarly crazy.)

He took both her hands and raised her up, like a dance master lifting a little ballerina. Bottom-heavy, slender-armed, she felt herself float upright. He did that for a living, she knew; picked twenty-year-old children off the floor.

He lowered his voice discreetly. "Probably need to use the ladies' room, huh?"

"No. I didn't wet. I don't drink much."

244

"You never do."

"I mean, water. Anything."

"Obviously not. Your new box of Jasmine Joy is still untouched. And Mindy put a goldfish in your mug, so no one else would use it."

"What do you use goldfish for? . . . oh. This is my second seizure."

"*Shh.* You're under a ton of stress. Naturally you drop off like the Dormouse."

"Put me in the teapot . . ."

She leaned forward, swayed; he caught her. She made herself held, thinking that was what he meant; she was half-dazed, and simply needed a hug. She laid her cheek on his shoulder, cuddled, like a woman waking from sexy dreams, content in her husband's embrace. After a moment, he gently placed her half a step back, like she'd semi-swooned and he was helping her get steady.

She stared at him, blinked wetly, amazed. Her body remembered.

She held the hem of her jumper, like she would curtsy, acknowledge that she'd once been his.

She waited, as for him to speak to her, lead her somewhere.

He looked at peace with her and with himself. He was the focus of Mindy's obsession—used to seeing women pull all kinds of freak shit.

She looked around at the floor, spacey, half-asleep. "My stuff. I bought cosmetics." He gathered them off the floor—gave Linda her purse, held onto her bags. She said, "You're awful nice to me."

"That was a cry for help."—she'd never say that in her right mind. "I'm buying you a coffee."

She said, "I'm too embarrassed. My seizures are real personal."

"So I saw you in curlers."

Almost inaudibly, she told him, "Stop."

"Lin, you *petit-mal* even more than you think. If I had a nickel for every time I took something out of your hand and helped you into a chair . . . besides, the guys do it all the time." The "guys" were the clients at Pinski Place.

She said, "I'll just go home and sleep."

"Are you okay to drive?"

"I'm licensed to."

"Ill?"

"Steve, honestly, I'm fine. You're being way too sweet."

He rolled his eyes; she was just another difficult retarded adolescent. One with a college degree and, unfortunately, a driver's license.

Lin saw him through her wet post-ictal haze. Limp and

sleepy-eyed, like she'd just come; in fact she'd come undone.

We take turns doing dishes. Argue over how to raise the kids. What do you call that?—we don't even wonder.

But he's my other husband. We've spent the last three years in a three-to-eleven, celibate marriage. I've been polyandrous all this time; I'm so dumb, I just assumed it was okay.

Since what happened is behind us. We've forgiven each other, forgiven ourselves. I've learned to put up with him, love him, as a brother. Knowing me, I'm sure it wasn't easy.

"Lin, you better come back. They've got me working with Ramona."

"Oh, no. You poor thing." *Who the hell's Ramona?* "In that case, I probably . . . will."

"Have a coffee with me—decent. I knew you'd smell reason; Au Bon's right there. I'm sympathetic up to one cappucino."

"Nn . . . no. Raspberry. Buy me a fat-free yogurt."

"Yogurt place is way the hell down there."

Linda looked, the endless hall of storefronts. Sweet red ice . . . too far to go. "Oh Steve, I see enough of you. I'm going home."

"Ladybug, ladybug."

She gave him her hand—a dizzy girl's dead fish. He held her fingers, Sir Walter Raleigh in blue jeans. Loaded her with bags and turned her, set her on her way. She tottered like a sleepy child, turned and said, "I'll call you. At the group home, or whatever . . ."

He gravely pointed his finger, We know where you live—she'd better call. She saw him enough—he was gone in the crowd.

Outside, at the bus stop, a Spanish woman about Linda's age was waiting with a baby in a stroller. Linda paused, to shyly see. The black-haired baby girl looked up at her, serious and thoughtful. She was precious.

Linda bent slightly. She smiled, then crinkled her nose in delight. She told the mother, "She's beautiful."

Mother smiled, brief; There, don't say I never smile. Said "She one-and-a-half," looking for the bus.

Linda leaned close, bright and tender as the simple mind she'd lately claimed to be. "What's *your* name, huh? What's *your* name?"

Mother, distant—where was that bus?—said "She don' understand no English yet."

Linda, enraptured, touched the child's bib. "*Pullelos, usté? Cant los pullelos, con el pio pio? No?*"

The child looked at Linda's finger, then thoughtfully at Linda herself. I have chicks on my bib: yes.

Linda set her bags down, opened her purse. She timidly asked Mother, "Her nose is runny, can I . . . ?"

The woman glanced at Linda, sadly blinked: If you really must. Linda never would have dreamed that the woman was afraid of her. That she thought Linda might be some boisterous flake who would sit with them on the bus, be chummy and intrusive. Shy people seldom recognize each other.

Linda lovingly wiped the child's nose. Put the used Kleenex in her purse. "I just love her. I want one just like her, someday."

Mother said, "She shy but very playful." She looked at Linda, shrugged—a playful hint, Please go away.

Linda said, "I was like that, too." She smiled at Mother, Thanks, picked up her bags.

Mother shyly smiled back, Thanks for leaving me alone.

Linda went to her car in a dream. So cold and bright, so blue and white—in awe of a winter day.

Back home, around two, she vacuumed and dusted. She turned on both the TV and radio, filled her apartment with daytime stars and Top 100 glitz, as anxious people often do.

Her body wasn't done giving her trouble. The jumper felt too snug, especially around her hips and tush, of which she was self-conscious anyway. The fabric felt constraining, like she was too fat to wear it and should have known. She felt irritable and edgy and she had this awful itch where it couldn't be scratched. Twinges up inside that made her wince and clench her buns and think *Don't ever do this in public.* She shut off the Hoover, looked in the medicine cabinet for hydrocortizone cream, but Derrick's wife had used it all. She felt hot, and opened a window. She felt cold, and closed it again. At last she sat in a chair, wrapped up in anxiety. *Yes: I'm probably pre-menstrual. And I have a yeast infection, and I had a grand mal seizure, and I'm anorexic, starving myself and hallucinating that I'm fat. I'm unwell. I should go to the hospital. When they ask what's wrong, I'll ask if they've got a few minutes—otherwise, I'd just like to be sedated.* But at once she imagined some man's unfeeling voice. *Ah, yes: Mrs. Bloom. The doctor you were mean and rude to said you "seem psychotic." We were just about to, um, call you. Here, please sign this form.*

No hospital.

She went into the bathroom and carefully checked. No blood. How much of an assurance was that? Complete? Conditional? Not a damn bit?

Should she wear a pad or something, just in case?

Women got nervous, edging towards afraid, when they felt they might need pads but didn't have one. *What would happen?*

Derrick only knew that it was frightful. Entry into the apartment, the quick and furtive closing of the door. The swift flight into the bathroom. A long and ominous residence, audible gasps of dismay. Repeated flushing of the toilet. Afterwards, all traces of the rite removed. Sink cleansed, like a chalice. The only tangible signs, sink-washed pantyhose over the shower curtain, and half a roll of toilet paper gone. *Der, it was frightening. I was gushing. Look, I'm shaking. I'm too upset to answer questions. I'm going to call my mother.*

She opened her top dresser drawer, found the box. Four left. That was enough . . . wasn't it?

You walked into a store and purchased them.

Four was enough.

She sat on the bed, momentarily mystified. Strip-off adhesive. *I guess you stick it right on the panty . . . ?*

She finished her vacuuming, watched a little tube. It got dark outside. Time to think about getting ready.

She wasn't the least bit happy about this. She was doing this for Pris, but didn't want Pris to know that.

Are you super lonely, Linda? I mean, is our friendship that important to you? I'm not sure I can cope with that. Maybe we don't really need to stay in touch.

She was doing that, a lot: vividly imagining all kinds of devastating things which people might say to her. The very worst was that Pris might look at her strangely, then say *You know, you're awful close. Do you need a boyfriend, Linda?*—then stand and walk out of her life.

She sat on the sofa in the darkening parlor, absently staring out the window. Sad and afraid, she almost wept. *But* Pris *is lonely and scared. She wants from me what I want from her: kindness and strength. Like a mother, always there. So I'll be what she wants, I'll do what she expects. I'll be there.*

She dressed, then looked in the mirror. Basically the same as in the store's dressing room. Dark olive skin, dark green dress. She looked like a very pretty Martian.

The makeover was surprisingly nice. The Germainé Montaile girl's unfathomable vision—"One of the prettiest women I've ever seen"—transposed onto her self. She blinked at an exotic stranger. Some cool, foreign lady with an English accent, maybe. She added earrings with a string of pearls. Those might have been wrong, too cool and white—they made her cleavage simmer. But Pris would understand; women dress for other women. The men would just be there for them to tease, or something.

Linda posed before the mirror. In dulcet tones of Her Majesty's own, she asked, "Is there a lift to the ground floor? I've got to telly home that I shan't be missed for tea.

"I rather do fancy your shirt—is it a turtleneck or a henway?"

She *tsk*ed and got her things, tired of this already.

Priscilla's place was nice, and should have been—to sell

houses and not have a nice one yourself, seemed unfair. It was off on some paved cow path, pastures sloping up on the right and maple woods sloping down to the left. Past Cold Brook Cider Mill. (Pris had written "Apple Place" and Linda had been watching for a street sign.) The house was set back behind a row of old Weymouth pines. The yard sloped down to a brook; just down the road was an old covered bridge. The house was small, a one-story cottage. Plaster siding, French eaves and persienne windows; mock-Provincial. Three cars in the driveway. *Why am I doing this.*

Linda took her time, walking to the door. The night was warm, felt balmy. Pine-and-water scented breezes stirred the boughs. A midwinter thaw on its way. The moon was full and wreathed in thin, grey clouds. *I wish there were roses. I'd stop and smell them, then go home.*

She rang the doorbell then sighed, looking disappointedly at the porchlight. Like an old-fashioned storm lamp, or whatever. She was uncomfortable with her self-image. With her light wool coat, her Halston's scent, holding her purse in both hands. Not unlovely, but spinsterish. Miss Linda Bloom, unmarried. *I know I'll never get used to this. Being a woman's just tiresome. I hope this doesn't last long.*

Pris answered the door, like she'd bounced to get it—health and joy in a crisp spring dress. Linda knew she would, herself, be hot. The velvety rayon felt nice in the fluorescent chill of Filene's Basement; Pris had a fire going in her small and toasty living room. *Oh lovely—I'm going to sweat like a milkmaid.* Linda took off her coat and, like it was rehearsed, Pris promptly remarked on the new dress. "Oh!—that must have been spring clearance." Linda returned a dark look. Pris dipped her hips, I'm sorry. Old Maid Winter meets Little Miss Spring.

Inside was small and cozy, well-appointed. Victorian comfort, minus the clutter. Everything was green. Linda was a chameleon.

Two men stood up. They beamed with affect and energy. A lady had arrived. The lady was cool, subdued by brute size and masculine zeal. *Standing, giving me all their attention—a real woman would appreciate it. So I guess I'm fake.* This was already a nightmare.

Moments passed in cold terror. A man, who seemed to own the room. Black hair and chiseled, rather Romanesque features, like some tipsy Welsh poet. One whom an accident of birth had placed too far from the soft-flanked Cambrian hills to muse on anything better than betting on the Celtics. He had a cynical smile, which Linda shyly mimicked, as though it were her own as well, small world. He spoke with eloquence of nothing much; his joke, it seemed, that the best of words were a waste. She stared at him like a goose. *Wait til he finds out I don't have a personality.*

Pris made introductions; names flew by, unnoticed. A hand . . . not a shake. He *held her hand.* Hers on top. Honor the weaker sex, or something. *I don't want to be this* yet he held her hand, she was. Asked to sit, she sat, on a sofa whose upholstery magically matched her dress. He asked if she wanted a glass of chablis. Linda felt little, embarrassed. Men weren't supposed to serve her. She parted her lips to speak but only smiled, gasped. He chided her. "Oh come on, we're all doing it. You wanna be accepted?"—then she couldn't be a stuffy lady's daughter. *She taught me how to be a girl, not how to be a woman.*

All these thoughts went through her head and no one else could see them. She softly said, "Oh stop. All right." She didn't seem shy or confused. She seemed like she might have wanted chardonnay instead.

He said, "You wait right here," like a kindly, take-charge uncle; he could do nothing for her unless she was immobilized.

The fire was warm. The sofa felt satiny, green like her dress, like a bed with matching cover sheet and spread. The man came back from the kitchen, gave her a tall, thin glass of white wine. It glistened in the fire's light, amber, clear and cold. She didn't have to stand to receive it; she was a lady. She didn't want to look at him. She smiled at the glass, like a somewhat spoiled girl. Took it in her hands and sipped it. Sweet. She closed her eyes.

Everyone came back into the living room. The men were roaring, laughing giants; Pris, a delighted pixie. Giants in your house, what fun. Linda felt herself fade into the sofa, as though she were snow and the fire melted her. Chablis moment, over. Oh well.

Minutes dragged by. There were incidents, transitions. An evening unfolded.

The two men weren't *bad*, if only they'd stop being so *present*. Like friendly bears, they did as they pleased and always had the right of way. If they invaded her space there was nothing she could do, except be still and soothe them with soft modulations of her voice. She was frightened, introspective, put where she was and fondly kept there, like a delicate bouquet. Shy, quiet women were a normal fixture of social gatherings; she could sit and be petrified, that was all right.

The man who'd held her attention came near, to put a CD into the deck, so naturally she wanted to . . . bite her thumb. No. She wanted him there, but she didn't want him to talk to her. It was confusing. He told her, "Let me guess. You like STAR 104. Superstars of the Eighties and Nineties. Slow sounds for the fast track. Miami . . .—Sound Machine."

She blinked at him, thoughtful. He seemed to think she was his daughter. He *had* a daughter, she could somehow tell. He wanted her to smile and she couldn't, since Miami Sound

Machine was not the key to her soul. In fact she thought they sucked. She said, "That would be nice."

There was music, which was helpful. Words got in the way.

Both the guys were in real estate. Chuck, who she wanted to go away/be with/not talk to, was in some level of middle management, developing. Rich assessed property values. Both were bottom-rung white collar with hands-on backgrounds. Linda picked up bits and pieces, gathered that Chuck still had to occasionally wear a hard hat, even run a back hoe every once in a blue moon. Both were jock-*cum*-health club types; jeans and sweaters, college manners. Small-town heroes, laid back on their modest laurels. They talked shop with Pris; their professional circles overlapped. Coveted accounts, impossible clients, colleagues on the skids. Pris laughed at one of Rich's jokes, excused herself and went into the kitchen.

Chuck said, "So you're in human services, right?"

Linda stared. Her smile was fixed. She blinked.

She said, "Yes. It's very fulfilling."

She asked, "Could you—?" She remembered to include Rich; asked them both, "Could you, um, excuse me? A minute?"

The guys barely said "Mm-hm," like Linda's flight was inevitable.

She went into the kitchen. Pris was there. A kitchen. Counter. Cook books. Pots and pans, utensils. Spice rack. This was like home, like Shelley's house; everything made sense. *Maybe I can stay in here.* "Pris, do I need help?—I mean, do you? Can I—?"

"Not yet. Everything's basically set to heat and serve. What do you think—should we play a game?"

Linda softly said "*Oh*," like some dread and secret new dimension was revealed. *Game?* Was this something really sinister and deep? Put LSD in the guys' glasses, then start a satanic ritual? Drop black widow spiders down their backs, then run away into the moonlit woods? What kind of *game?* "Like Monopoly?"

Pris frowned, worried—that was difficult to respond to. "Well, I meant, like . . . Trivial Pursuit."

Linda opened her mouth, but didn't speak. It *was* some kind of torture, after all—to live in this magic, evil night and be asked random questions.

They went out into the living room. It seemed Linda's chore to announce that they would play Trivial Pursuit. By virtue of being a girl, she was somehow co-hostess. The guys thought it was a cool idea. They were like all of Derrick and Linda's friends, quasi born-again young professionals; board games were major kicks. At the coffee table. Rich pulled up an armchair. Pris and Chuck sat on the sofa. Pris opened a card box, her hair fell over her shoulder. Chuck touched her hair, moved it back like her puff-sleeved shoulder was some lovely, delicate thing, remarked they'd played so many times they'd played with every card and Pris mentioned you could buy new cards or even special sets, like Current Events or Movies. Linda put a cushion on the floor: a place for a grown-up child to sit. Less responsibility, easier to run away. Pris asked "Should we play teams?" and both the guys agreed. "Boys against girls, or . . . ?"

Linda didn't like that; it seemed like two against one. She said "That's dumb."

Chuck backed her up. "It doesn't have to be."

Pris said, "Oh. All right. Then let's have . . . ?" She looked at Linda, neutral: Your idea, your call. There was some distance between them, now; Linda was a traitor. She didn't want to be her best friend's partner.

Linda told Chuck, "I want to be on your side."

She contemplated her empty glass, a lady who hadn't just said anything.

Just for that, Rich told Pris, "I want to be on yours." Pris dropped her jaw, delighted by this unexpected compliment.

Chuck said, "But why?", overwhelmed with wonder.

Linda said "Then maybe you won't tease me." She went into the kitchen, refilled her glass, came back. She said, "I'm good in Arts and Lit." *In Sports and Science also, but I have to keep that secret*. She flashed her eyes at him: *Be nice or I'll just be completely stupid*.

Duly noted; Chuck told Rich, "You're in my partner's chair."

Lin told Rich, "No, stay."

Rich stayed. Chuck could only remark, "Good dog."

Linda looked at Pris, at Chuck and then at Rich, amazed to learn she was a mistress.

She showed Rich her pillow, on the floor. Her hand's clever sweep introduced her little move; she descended like a flower dropped. Crossed her legs, smoothed out her skirt, I took ballet, so there. Like any girl's enchantment, it entranced and was ignored.

Chuck asked for a marker, shy of his voice, like the air had been sexually charged. Linda vaguely wondered who had charged it. Chuck supplied the answer—he gave Linda the die. She rolled to see which team went first, and lost.

Forty-five minutes later, two things had become clear. The first was that Rich and Pris were winning—the vindication of the snubbed.

The second was that, for Chuck and Linda, the game was less about trivia than about their strange rapport. They disagreed, quietly but at length, over every answer. Rich frequently joked about a time limit, but Chuck and Linda ignored him. They were into thoughtful questions, patient waiting for response—a game

252

of dog and cat.

Linda rolled a five. Pay dirt: Sports.

Chuck said, "I've got this," before the question was even read. Linda watched him closely, ready to smile if he stumbled. Their marker had two wedges, to Rich and Priscilla's five. Jake LaMatta lost his title to . . . "Sugar Ray Leonard."

(Even Pris touched her finger to her cheek, Uh-duh?!—Rich *shh*ed her.)

Linda said, "Sugar Ray Robinson."—her voice at its softest and lowest, like a woman telling her husband, Don't send me away. Chuck just shook his head; it was worth being wrong, to say he was right. "Chuck. That was the Forties. Sugar Ray Leonard wasn't even born." If nothing else, babies and births were her domain.

Rich chuckled. "She's right."—and took the die.

Linda frowned in dismay, watching the die being taken away. "But it's our turn again!"

Chuck said "I had the question; we lose."

Rich gravely concurred: "You lose."

Linda spoke to Chuck as though the other two weren't there. "That's not right. We should have agreed first."

"Two cannot agree. That's why we have committees."

A long look between them: Chuck tolerant, too old for this game; Linda, his dubious conscience.

Later, Chuck rolled a three: pay dirt, this time Geography.

The Soviet Union's Baltic seaport. The game was copyright 1994. Linda said, "It's a trick. It specifies 'Soviet Union' so it's Leningrad."

Chuck said, "They're not smart enough to make trick questions. We'll go with the obvious answer, St. Petersburg."

Rich sadly shook his head. "Answer's Leningrad."

Linda gave Rich the die, warmly told him, "You can tell we've both been married."

Rich took the die, winked at her. "I know, I have that indefinable aura of carnal knowledge." Linda softly laughed, like she and Rich just hit it off.

Later, Pris excused herself to get dinner on. They played a turn without her. Then Linda *tsk*ed and stood, and gently said, "Oh you're an asshole. Chuck, it's only a game."

Chuck answered her as gently, even took her hand in passing. "I'm an asshole in this *game*. It's a role, it's part of the *game*."

Linda slipped her hand free, went swiftly to the kitchen. "Pris, can we do cocktails? I'm a nervous wreck."

"You like each other. Go with it." Pris was tossing a salad.

Linda became very serious. "You're . . . I don't believe this. I'm being abused. You're *jealous*."

"I doubt it. I told you, they're just friends." Pris bit a slice of cucumber, walked by Linda. Paused to look and touch: Linda had a perfect French curl on her dark breast, like a Creole duchess on the cover of a romance novel. "Wow, neat. Curling iron?"

Distracted, Linda looked. "Oh. No." *Consider the lilies of the field.* "It just does that, sometimes." She remembered why she'd come into the kitchen. "Can I help? With dinner? Please?"

"I'll call you when it's time. Go entertain the guys—that's how you can help." Priscilla's yoke was easy. Her tone was sweet. "Okay?"

Linda slightly shook her head. Her perpetual response to everything now, to Life itself through a woman's eyes, *this can't be, it isn't me, no no no no no.* Entertaining the guys wasn't a treat. It wasn't something fun, disguised as a way to "help." It was the fire she'd quit for the literal frying pan. She said, "I can't cook?"

"It's not like I don't get it, Lin—Chuck is making you crazy. He charms you to death and then plays with your head. Am I right?" Linda gestured, tense and silent ambiguity; it looked like *of course* but was really *how would I know?* "He's only been impossible the last few months. The divorce was just . . . oh shit, I forgot to tell you."

With her apron over her spring dress, Pris looked buxom and maternal. Her thick and frazzled auburn hair framed a face incapable of guile. She had a stoneware dish of mushroom strudel, a boat of burnaisse sauce off to the side, and it didn't seem like evil people bothered with such things. "Lin, you're widowed. Rich, Chuck and I are the Three Faces of Divorce. I mean, you're not the only one. We're not some bubbly sitcom, twenty-somethings without a care. You're with friends. You can be yourself."

Linda parted her lips, but found she had nothing to say. She went back into the living room.

She immediately came back for a refill of wine. "Pris, don't even start." Linda sipped from her glass, then bared her heart in passion. " *'Like each other'*? Pris, when have you ever seen me this *tense*?"

"Well . . . every time I've seen you with some guy you liked."

Linda gasped in disbelief, and went back out to fight over trivia.

16

Chuck and Lin sat silent, gazing into each other's eyes.
She softly said "A tomato . . . is a *fruit*."
Rich looked at his watch.
Pris called from the kitchen: "Okay, Lin!"
She stood, not taking her eyes off his. "I have to go help Pris."
"I fully understand. Peel apples, or some other vegetable."
Twenty minutes later, dinner was served. Pris and Linda served it. Linda moved quickly, with somber purpose. She knew how to work, how to move with the flow and do things efficiently. Passing Pris in the kitchen doorway, she said under her breath, "I thought this was the Nineties."
"It was. Your submissive nature triggered this dormant domination reflex." Linda stared, thoughtful; Priscilla's eyes went loony, It's a joke.
At last, everything was set. Chuck strolled in, his hands in his pockets. "Anything I can do to help?"
Linda twirled to face him, her lovely eyes aflame. Her black curls fell across her shoulder, lay still as she twitched her hip. "You can stir the burnaisse if you like."
He gazed into her soul, entranced, though not without a faint and taunting smile.
They gathered in the dining room. The guys wrapped up a loud and jocular talk about the baseball strike, while Pris and Linda discussed the table's centerpiece. A flowering herb arrangement. Roses, lavender and lady's mantle, a wreath of rosemary and pastel-shaded marjoram. Hollyhock and thistle, all ringed with mistletoe. The guys just had a stupid game played by pot-bellied men in their thirties, who might not play at all this year.
Pris said, "Seating arrangements. We'll do boy-girl, boy-girl across." Linda thought, *Pris* stop *it. Just*—"We'll keep our Trivial teams together, too. Oh, Linda's blushing—everyone look!"
Linda glanced about, demure; she was dark, how could anyone tell?
Linda sat across from Chuck. He pleasantly nodded, like a subway commuter acknowledging someone he sees every day. Pris said, "Linda, pass the strudel." She slightly shook her head, like

255

she didn't acknowledge a stranger's nod. Pris tactfully prompted, "I'd like to see if the recipe worked; if the dough flaked, like it said. Lin, strudel dough . . ."

Chuck said, "And Strudel-Dee; dear, pass your friend the dish."

Linda did, and looked at the piece on her plate. It had seeds in it. She couldn't tell if they were caraway or fennel. "Lin, Bermuda onions."

"Oh.—none for me, thanks."

"Well, we want some. What big eyes you have, Mother Goose." Linda passed the casserole dish, glanced moodily at Chuck. She didn't trust him even eating strudel, temperate and serene as Saint Augustine in his cell.

There was a salad, which finally got Linda's attention. The cold, crisp slices of cucumber tempted her, like candy. She put some on her plate and mainly looked at it, sipping her wine.

Chuck said, "Have some dinner with your wine there, kid."

Linda froze, petrified. It was absolutely her worst-case scenario, that a man would actually tease her. To be with friends her own age in a casual setting, free to relax like a girl at home with her brothers, was . . . a nightmare, since she didn't know how. Anything she said would be silly if contrived, juvenile if genuine. She opted for genuinely juvenile—stuck her tongue at Chuck.

Chuck resumed eating, angelically unassuming.

Linda looked at Pris. Pris stared back, in awed delight: What will you do next?

Linda giggled uncontrollably. Then told Chuck, "I'm so sorry. That was, like, the rudest. I don't know why I did it."

"Yes, dear. Eat your salad before it gets cold."

The other two had been silent, this far. Rich was the male pair's quiet one—a slight, mustached, balding young man. He watched this interaction—Chuck, in rare form; Priscilla's friend, enchanting and odd—with mild interest. Pris watched brightly, proud of Linda for being so unusual.

At last Pris said, "*I'm* not bashful! Boo!—there, I said boo to a goose!" She gaily laughed at Linda.

Linda told Chuck, "I'm newly widowed."

Chuck said, "I know." He added, "I'm newly divorced. We're sharing the same experience, except my departed other half still phones me twice a week."

Linda said, "Life sucks."

Chuck said, "And then you live. I feel I should explain."

"Oh. No, if you don't want to, don't feel you—"

Chuck said, "She was a Polish lesbian." He took a bite of salad. "She liked men."

Rich made an elaborate effort not to laugh, like he knew the whole story and that summed it up neatly. Pris said, "Chuck, that's cruel," like she was hip and tickled by it also. Linda didn't get it, not even the joke.

Rich got started on gay marriages, carelessly scornful of both sides of the controversy. The conversation got rolling again. Politics, society, Decline of Western Civ, 101.

Pris told Linda, "Both these guys go to my church. Talk about Jekyll and Hyde . . ."

Linda calmly said, "I don't want to go to Heaven."

Chuck said, "Now, now—I promise you'll enjoy it, once we're there."

"No, I mean about God. He's been really, really mean to me." Linda weakly laughed; her eyes flashed wet with tears. "Can we talk about something silly, please?"

The guys then talked about her. "We've heard all about you." (Chuck.) "Pris portrayed this outrageous character; we expected someone with pierced nipples. I mean, I of course would never look below a lady's necklace . . ." (Rich.) They seemed to still expect her to burst forth with flamboyant views; they acted like she already had. Relationships, sex—that was always a favorite, right? Men and women. Us against you, which was simply scary. Linda's inner woman was a frightened child, ten days old. Unarmed with anger or insight. She couldn't bear to hear what she ("you") had done to make men furious. She especially didn't need it from Chuck. She felt that she'd reached out to him, tried to make friends on his terms. Now his bitterness stung like a whip, however it was couched in friendly humor. She bowed her head, sullen under his sarcasm; she looked at him, hurt, when he said she was bad. "—so come on, Lin, you *know*: a woman will bury the hatchet, but she won't forget where. And don't even start with the chauvinist rap. 'Some of my best friends are women'—a ridiculous statement. Why? Because a man bonds with his woman like with no one else on earth. She has power over him, second only to God's. So yes, I can speak more truth, be judged less harshly—maybe. Since you know how you—"

She stared at him, head lowered; she involuntarily cringed, whenever his voice sharpened to underscore some pungent irony. She was hot, she felt sticky. Her crotch felt like a swamp, and the maxi pad felt like a diaper. Her itch was driving her out of her mind. She'd fantasized relief: getting up on a gymnast's sawhorse with a sandpaper strip along the vinyl upholstery. Gripping the soft vinyled padding with her thighs, slowly massaging herself on the sandpaper. It seemed like something heavenly. Langorous slow-motion, jaded pastels, light-filled empty space and she in an aquamarine leotard, like some godlessly seductive commercial. Chuck exclaimed with glee, " . . . which is a *double standard*! Feelings count, sure—they count for everyone! Like an automatic handicap, already in the score!" She felt she was being yelled at, scolded. Bad girl. Weak,

257

whiny, hypocritical, selfish, lazy thing. " . . . *why you bite the hand that caresses your cheek*, then fall at the feet of the first insensitive lout who—"

"*Will you stop?!*"

The table fell silent. Pris and Rich had been conversing in cynical counterpoint, murmurs and giggles, but Linda's yelp had pulled the plug. She didn't look at Pris or Rich; she wasn't concerned with them. She stared at Chuck, wide-eyed with alarm: *What do I get, for yelping?*

After some moments of stunned silence, Chuck said, "I've made you upset. I didn't mean to. You win, I'm completely refuted."

Linda saw what Pris had meant. Tenderness and sarcasm, flowers with thorns.

She said, "But no, you *always* win. That's why we just freak."

"Linda, you're wrong. You hold all the cards."

He shook his head, hand over his eyes, OD'ed on hyperbole.

Rich told Pris, "This was asking for trouble," like a man who knew what his friend was going through—nothing to do with Linda. She wetly glanced at Rich, That's very sweet of you.

Pris, in turn, apologized for Linda. "She's very emotional. Always."—a poodle who'd gone hyper and caught people with her leash.

Linda told Chuck, "I'm sorry I bit."

"That's okay, I've had my shots."—from the school of hard feminine knocks.

"Chuck, don't say *you*, like it's me. I'm not Woman, with a capital *W*."

"Not strong. You're not invincible."

Rich said, "Good point!"—anything for peace.

Chuck was right back on. Like any man struggling with bitterness, he never failed for words. "But that's not *really* true, Linda." He lingered fondly with her name; he liked it. "I know that you're *a* woman. If I get into your head, there are certain things I'll find. You—"

Rich signaled Let it go, jovial and unconcerned. That was his role—Allegro, leading his friend through the Slough of Despond.

Chuck graciously caved. "—don't like Bermuda onions."

Pris said, "What were you guys even talking about?"

Linda said, "Alimony. Legal mumbo-jumbo. Women have too many rights. I don't know." She wanted to leave.

After the meal there was a tawny port, with a fruit cocktail. While no one trailed Linda through the stratosphere, no one was going to leave exactly sober, either.

After dinner, the two men went out to the living room, while Linda and Pris cleaned up. Linda complained, "But this is so blatant."

"Well, they're guests. You are too—go sit down!"

Miserable, Linda decided, "I'm your friend," and scrubbed a pot.

Afterwards, the living room. Pris and Rich shared the sofa, had an endless conversation about people, places, things that meant nothing to Linda. Chuck sat deep in his armchair, still but not at rest—Coleridge, awaiting the return of his muse. Linda sat cross-legged on her pillow—hold on to your mood ring, the Seventies aren't over yet. Alert, seldom speaking, she got quietly, controllably drunk.

She was close to Chuck, enough to have her hair stroked, though of course that didn't happen. When she wanted more tawny, she softly asked and he filled her glass from the bottle on the coffee table.

Early Fleetwood Mac on the stereo. Those future games, go figure. Pris was getting sleepy. "Lin, go open the window."

Linda went, opened into darkness and warm, wet wind. The pines were far grey mountains in moonlight.

As the evening progressed, the wine had a strange effect on her. It erased her self-awareness. She felt herself deeply, passionately involved in conversations when in fact she only listened, watching faces.

Pris brought out munchies—bagel chips and onion dip. Chuck, progressed in lecture, held a chip with dip and didn't eat it. Linda watched his hand, how it lightly tapped out emphasis, like commas, to his speech. Chuck noticed her. She slightly moved her hand, I want it, and he gave her the chip. She ate it from his fingers, two quick and gentle nibbles. Chewing, she listened. Everyone was high.

Chuck said, "Love the feminist, hate the philosophy."

Linda said, "Okay. Really, I'm not selling anything. I told you before, I lost my ego. I have no opinions."

She felt, in her cups, that she'd told him everything—that all was understood. He knew she was her husband and it made him mad, like she'd chosen womanhood and all the values such a choice expressed. In fact she'd only told him three unusual things: that she'd lost her ego, that life could look easy but be really hard, and that God sometimes spoke to her over the radio, to which she hastily added that it wasn't MRQ-FM. MRQ played mostly alternative. It didn't take a holy roller to doubt that God would share the air with Alice In Chains.

Chuck said, "Change will come. We ultimately want what you want."

Linda said, "What's that?"—she honestly didn't know.

He said, "Well . . . whatever it is that you want." He couldn't preach togetherness and be a prick; he lightened up.

"We want for you what you want for yourselves. We want you to be happy."

"It might not be easy. Some Englishwoman said we're the 'soft, unhappy sex'. I know I am, at least."

"Why?" he asked, softly. "Why are you unhappy?"

"It's hard to explain. We're less full of ourselves and we . . . see a more beautiful world. The feel of a day, the mood of a place, and we think you do, also. We think you enjoy life as *we* would, having your power. That's how we think and feel when we're in love. It's different. Maybe you understand, sort of? Or . . . ?"

Rich drawled, "Yep, you're right, Chuck: she's an iron-clad, whip-toting feminist."

Chuck resumed his original train of thought. Reactionary Apologetics, Updated and Revised. "Change will come, but let's face facts. Change will come through the system. Men control the system, men will make the change—that's not a proposition, that's reality. Screw us while we're working on it, fine—just don't ask us to screw our*selves*."

Rich found this alcoholic construction rather amusing. "Screw yourself, Chuck. Go screw yourself."

Chuck said, "And Lin, you're right; we're really not enjoying this."

Linda said, "I used to understand all that. Is it ego? —I'm just guessing. It all sounds weird to me, now."

"Well, sure it's ego. What I advocate? No, Lin, I'm like you—I'm not advocating anything. It's just the nature of the business. You can picket out on the sidewalk, or you can deal with the men inside the building. Real change is never about tearing things down. It's never about turning things loose or 'letting people be free'. That sounds real groovy and all, but . . . well, you end up with shit."

"Do I look really Seventies or something? Is it the bangs?"

Chuck squinted blearily at Rich. "Am I making any sense?"

Rich said, "Not a bit. Don't let me interrupt you."

Linda said, "It's all boring. I'd rather you two talk guy stuff. Football or whatever. I like to listen."

Rich said, "Chuck—look." Pris was asleep, curled up at the end of the sofa. "A Victorian print. In an oval frame of honeysuckle garland. *Beautiful Dreamer.* Huh?"

Chuck saw what his friend meant. "*Wow.*"

Linda looked and only saw Pris sleeping.

Chuck went on. And on and on. It sounded like the preamble to some business prospectus. Linda touched his hand, so he'd let her talk. "Chuck. It's not negotiable. Not on those terms—not to us. The fact that you're angry, you're stepping back, your arms are crossed—that's the issue. More important than some convoluted argument. That's how women see things. That's our truth."

"Why, you sound like a traditionalist."

"I'm one by default, since I don't know anything else. I copy my mother a lot. I already said, I lost my ego. From drinking home-made wine. It was pretty special."

Chuck didn't miss a beat. "I knew all that about you from the start. Lin, do you smoke?" She sighed, desire; a closetful of cravings. "Pris won't let us smoke in here. She doesn't understand that it's sophisticated and glamorous. You wanna go out on the patio?" Linda raised her listless hands, You may pick me up. Chuck stood and took her hand, helping her up from her pillow. He waited, still holding her hand, while she smoothed out the seat of her dress. They went out through the kitchen.

Chuck opened the door and Linda wandered out. The night air felt like balmy spring. It smelled of chill, dark earth and growing grass from far away. The pines seemed to stir, as moon shadows shifted under swift-passing clouds. She heard the secretive trickle of the brook, down below the hedge of azalea.

She turned and smiled at Chuck, Come on out.

By her side, he asked, "Winston okay?"

Linda was in love with the evening, and a man's cigarette didn't bother her. "Yeah."

He lit her cigarette. She whispered thanks, leaned her tush against the wrought-iron banister. She crossed her arms, took absent draws, looking towards the night-dark forest, past the brook.

After some time, she asked, "Why'd you divorce?"

"She was very domineering. I admit. Still respect me?"

She thought it over. "I think it depends. On how we feel about you. We may wish to show you we're not like that. Be kinder than her, even meeker than you."

"Then the woman-thing. Pleading victim status while you're bulling someone into a corner . . . ultimately, it was a justice issue."

"Do I remind you of her, somehow?"

"If you did, we wouldn't be out here."

Linda thought about this.

Softly, amazed, she said, "That gave me a really warm feeling."

He only blinked, But of course.

She said, "That domineering isn't good. Because I wonder. How men really feel, since I'm the total opposite. I'll always do the dishes, wash the sheets. I'll always be a servant to the man. Like when he makes love to me, I'm so honored. That he loved me, came inside me. I don't want to bathe. I want to keep his smell."

He parted his lips, but kept his peace. She twitched her shoulder, eyes alight: I'm not afraid of you.

261

"I like to think a man admires that; it's something good, in me. I like to think he would open doors for me, light my cigarettes. Because he admires the way I am. Reveres it."

She inhaled, softly blew smoke. Noticed the length of her cigarette's ash.

He extended his palm—her ashtray. She giggled, he snorted a laugh.

They finished their smoke. Linda asked, "Is there any rush? It's nice out here."

"Lovely." He put his hands in his pockets.

"Chuck, I drank too much. It's so embarrassing."

"No; you've been quiet. When I get to review the hungover text of tonight's conversations, I'll see who put foot, ankle and calf down into his esophagus."

Linda laughed at that, happily and long.

She touched her finger to her eye, said, "No. I could listen to you all evening."

"You've already accomplished that feat."

"And I liked it. Thank you for a very enjoyable evening."

Chuck took her hands and drew her, boneless ballerina, from the bannister. She held his hands, swayed like she was standing in her sleep.

He asked, "Where's that warm feeling?"

He placed his palm on her tummy. She looked into his eyes, only curious: Where will this go?

He asked, "Is it here?"

"Mm-hm. You gave it to me. I'll keep it inside me, always."

"I just felt it kick."

She tried not to laugh, but it burst from her mouth. She giggled, sighed as he lightly held her hips.

She said, "I'm very regressed. I keep thinking you're older than me. I guess you're about my age."

He said, "We're at opposite extremes. I'm pure bitterness, you're pure grief."

"Somewhere deep inside, though, we're the same."

"Both cold. Let's go deep inside."—the fire was still burning.

"Do you know what it's like? Having no ego? I hear myself talk, then wonder what I sound like? Wonder if that's who I am? If it's someone people like?"

"You really miss your husband."

"Flaky social-worker type? Angels and auras?"

"Do you need a hug?"

"That's what they say?"

She realized it was sort of a joke, since he already held her. She laid her head on his shoulder, gazed at the kitchen window. Softly lit, looked warm inside; she knew it was. She remembered things that happened there—Priscilla's histrionics over hot pads. Their nervous laughter when the noodles were soft and they

262

couldn't find the colander. *How quickly we get used to things. How soon a place is home.*

She said, "I want to ask you something. I'm just curious. It's about Pris." His embrace warmed around her, she was deeper in his arms; she widened her eyes. *I'm her, in the dark.* "It sounds awful. Since she's my friend. But . . . what do you *see* in her?"

Chuck pondered, then shrugged. His sublime truth: "Her breasts."

But you can feel mine and they're bigger than "Hers?"

"It's more than that. It's hard to explain. The way her skirts hang limp from her hip. The way her eyes light up when she's witchy at someone's expense. You'd have to be a man, to understand."

"I guess."

He held her closer, no more talk.

There was music from inside, still Fleetwood Mac. *Brown Eyes*, Chris McVie, voice plaintive and pure as though rock had died, leaving her alone at her piano.

He kissed her forehead. Linda blinked and lowered her head, as though he was too kind and she didn't deserve it.

He gently lifted her chin. She surveyed his eyes, impassive. He lightly kissed her lips. She softly said, "Okay. Can we go inside?" She glanced longingly at the kitchen window. She feared what Pris might say or think and, now that she considered it, she feared where this might lead.

He kissed her neck. She frowned at the night sky, worried. Whispered, "All right. I just wanted this, being held. Nothing more."

He said, "I know."

He kissed her throat. She said, "Don't," though some passive reflex made her lift her chin to receive it. She placed her hand on his chest, to show she would even push if she needed to.

He said, "I have a confession to make. You've been driving me wild from the moment I first saw you. I've wanted you all night."

It wasn't pleading, wasn't even urgent. It was more of an advisory. Like she'd met him at an oasis, with a water jug on her hip, and he'd taken it from her and set it down on the sand. Like he'd brushed her cheek with a clump of dates and said, *You shouldn't eat these. They're 90% sugar.*

She opened her mouth to say he couldn't have her. He kissed her neck and wouldn't stop and finally she just sighed, she sadly endured it.

She distantly said "Lower." He kissed her lightly, just over her collarbone. She stiffened slightly, drew a sharp, small breath.

He said, "Experience. Why married men are best." He eased off, gave her space. She held his hands and dimly thought, *That's it . . . ?*

263

She asked, "Was she your friend? Your wife? I mean, do you have women friends?"

"Sure. Not all men do, though."

"Because I need a friend. A male friend. I'd . . . like you as my friend . . . ?"

He smiled. "I thought that line comes after the second date."

She giggled, swayed her hips. She let herself be held again.

"Lin, you're sad. You're lonely. You see the world you described to me, the one dripping with tragic colors. Not all women see it; only you. And I see one that's the color and texture of coffee grounds. Not all men see it, just those who are recently divorced."

"You're sure you don't want a girl as a friend? We make good ones."

He drew her in, close to him. Hips touching, breath felt on lips. Linda scanned his eyes, lovingly astonished. He wanted sex, she wanted a friend, two wires connected: *We want . . .*

He kissed her lips. A light, chaste kiss, except it didn't stop. A boy who liked his sister just a little bit too much. He'd stop if she just turned her head; he left it up to her. Being liked felt lovely; she relaxed, and held his neck. He held her hips just so, a sculptor finding quite the shape he wanted. If she fainted or something, she wouldn't fall. Her part was so easy. She closed her eyes, turned loose her thoughts.

She found him so exotic. So ominous and thrilling, the way their two worlds touched. Brut on Halston's, wool on velour, the bristled maturity of his hard chin on the soft, plain humanness of her cheek.

He gave her time, let her learn and explore. Let her touch his chin, like a father who would get around to teaching his little girl, what Daddy did with shaving cream and razor in the morning.

They kissed again, stood quietly joined in the whispering, cloud-grey night.

She abruptly decided that was enough; stepped free, and turned toward the door. He caught her hand and brought her back. Not roughly but with certainty, her adult sovereignty was overruled; like a girl with little feet she tottered back. She faced him—for a moment, outraged. He gazed at her calmly—would she be so kind to him, would she be his lady. She blinked languidly, surprise—she was beautiful and kind. Desire tingled deep within, spread heavy through her loins. She'd given herself, surrendered. She knew, at least in some animal sense, she was no longer her own to take back. He pulled her in, his palm to the small of her back; pressed just so, tilting her hips. The magic touch and she gasped, thrilled. *How did he know . . . ?*

She suddenly imagined—tasted, felt—him bare-chested, undoing his belt. Skin soft and thin and tight over bone of hip, ridge of abdominal muscle. Leather strap pulled rudely, loose, a careless prelude to discipline or simply getting clothes off. Dark must of sex, unbuttoned denim, and it drove her wild. She held his face, uncertain what she wanted, where to kiss; breathless, she couldn't decide, just parted her lips, *Just feed me.* His tongue, strong as an animal's. His hands massaged her hips, the pads of flesh she didn't like—he wanted her. She moved her hips, felt the smoothness between her legs like she'd melted, warm and formless underneath. *Oh dear I'm* wet. He smoothed his hand along her tush as if she'd told him that, *I'm ready.* She snuggled in, swayed heart and soul, a worm on his . . .

   . . . hook?

She paused, because it was a little scary—his hardness, pressed against her lower tummy. She looked down, then smiled at him shyly. *I did this to you. I made this—it's for me.* It was something they held in common, between them, like a baby.

She crinkled her nose, playful: *More, please.* They kissed deeply, he pressed in with careless rhythm, lazy power, and she arched her back as she would to receive him. Her body remembered its fever, vixen flesh and angel soul, steel sizzled into placid water, melded against her will.

Their lips parted, and he whispered in her ear. "I think we've come to the point where . . . we should go inside, the recommended option, or . . . to my place. For a drink."

The final, empty courtesy was endearing, even as her thoughts and feelings flowed together, vivid and confused. She gazed over his shoulder, her dark eyes soft with wonder and emotion.

He gently chided, "I asked, Lin. Your turn to answer." She held him, hoping he would answer for her, hoping the question would go away. "You have until the end of this kiss to make up your mind. Okay?"

She closed her eyes, let her answerless lips be filled. *Is this fair? It's like proposing while making love? Or . . . ?*

The kiss ended. She said, "I'll do anything, let you do anything. Be your total slut."

He spoke very softly, like some terrible bet over racing cars on an empty, moonlit highway. "Will you suck my dick?"

"Only if you promise to come in my mouth. I've been thirsty for your cum from the moment I first saw you. I want every drop."

"Will you take it up the ass?"

"Oh God yes."

He let her go, she stepped back. Looked at him thoughtfully, smoothing her skirt over her hips.

"Lin, we're playing. Words, that's all. It doesn't have to be savage, like that. Rough—it doesn't."

"I know. I just get very passionate. I don't want to be hurt.

Physically, or . . ."

"I mean, I've been married half my life, it seems. Same for you, I suppose. Really, it would be more like . . . well, I live a few miles out of town. Back from the road, on Sharon Pond. Queen size bed, down pillows. Wood heat, we'll be warm. My wife left some things. You could find a nightie, or whatever. I'd hump you, then we'd read in bed. Lots of her books. Do you like Danielle Steele?"

"Um . . . if it's one I haven't read yet. I like her. Yes."

"We'd kiss goodnight, turn off the lights. I'd hold you, if you wanted. Tomorrow's Sunday, we'd sleep in. Wake up, make love . . . is that okay?"

"I like it better than 'hump'.—the morning's nice for me; yes."

"Then you could go make breakfast. Fresh blueberries, for pancakes. We could eat in bed. I get the Sunday paper, delivered."

"Chuck, it sounds lovely."

She shyly reached. He took her hand.

They turned, she saw their shadow, grey on moonlit plaster siding. His a mountain, rugged and unmoving. Hers small and clever, independent at his side. She saw herself having her own opinions, taking his with a grain of salt. Receiving dinner guests with pride and warmth.

So far as shadows knew, they made a couple.

What will he think of my throwing up after blueberry pancakes?

She let go of his hand, stepped toward her shadow. *My thighs are that big?*

She turned to him, happy; peace was something wonderful.

"Chuck, you don't know me. I don't know you. It was a super idea, though."

For a moment, his face showed how he felt. Nothing there to pity, nothing there to fear—the accepting smirk of a boy who's hooked, and lost, an eight-pound bass.

"It was just a game, Lin. I wanted for you what you wanted for yourself."

"Yeah, I'll bet."

"I wanted you to win."

"You made me do the hard part. 'Guardian of virtue'."

"Magnificent performance, Lin. I really, truly mean it."

She said, "I'm newly widowed. I suppose I should slap your face," with all the passion and vehemence of a get-well card to a long-lost aunt in Sacramento.

He said, "It's late. I should leave."

"Shall I make you a cup of coffee?"

"No. I'd sit and steam, and someone might drink me."

A gust of cold wind blew. They drew close for warmth,

266

looked annoyed at the grey-blue moonlit sky. They shared a look, like naughty kids—*That was just ridiculous, but didn't we have fun.* He opened the door, and she went back inside.

17

The morning was warm. It was a midwinter thaw.

Linda, hungover, lay on the green-velvet sofa. The window she'd opened the night before was open still; she heard the off-key laughter of distant blue jays. The white wine hangover left her body langorous and heavy, thighs warm with sexual longing. She thought, *It would have been awesome. I would have been wild, impaled on him, while he poked and poked all he wanted. I would have come and come. It would have been transcendent. It transcended me right by.*

Yet I think of it as, it—*like something I had a craving for. Like a chocolate-covered banana. Doesn't that say it all? What does a chocolate-covered banana symbolize? Two flavors that perfectly cancel each other out, so it's just a tiny cloud, frozen on a stick.*

Pris came out of her room. Her lavender gown had a ruffled hem and she seemed to solemnly float, like a Victorian ghost on her appointed rounds. Oddly, her hair looked magnificent—sculpted waves of burnished gold, like she was destined to be ravishing in her fifties. She glanced at Linda sternly, No hangover jokes. She opened all her windows. It was sunny out, a blue-sky day. It felt like you could go out on the porch in just your nightie, smell the green, renascent earth.

Linda went into the kitchen, stood and had coffee with Pris. Pris laughed. " 'I'll treat you like a goddess'—'I'll call you on the phone.'—'No, no! Never!'—'Blueberry pancakes.'—'I'll go with you! Yes!' " Linda smiled, What, are you jealous? "With *Chuck.* Oh, *ouch!* There wouldn't have been a paper bag thick enough. For *me*—for my embarrassment next day! Lin, please—one more time. Show me how big it felt through his jeans." Linda spaced her hands. Pris pointed, gaily laughed at her.

"Pris, I showed terrible judgment. We both knew it was wrong. Pris, bereavement's not what you think. Not spiritual, it's all of you. I didn't want sex. I wanted the biggest, longest hug."

"Lin, *I* can give you that."

"It would have been nicer from him. Thanks just the same."

Pris gasped for breath, wiped her eyes like a tragic heroine who'd wept. "Linda, I don't judge you. I'm made of the same stuff as you. Eve's fallen daughters, or whatever. But I mean, shit—I meet 'em, you snatch 'em away."

"Well, you laughed at me til three in the morning."

"Lin, I'll laugh. I'll scream at you. I'll hang up on you for a week. I'll never say you're not my friend. Never, til we die."

"Pris, go back to bed. I'll bring you breakfast. And clean up."

"Just make breakfast. I'll clean up."

Lin cooked, and they ate at the table. Lin muttered, "Why did I put peppers in my omelet? Putting vegetables in eggs, that's so perverted . . ."

"Lin, I'm going to church."

Linda played with her fork, picking peppers out of her omelet.

Pris said, "There's no pressure."

Linda swiftly stood, her hand over her groin. "Here." She went into the bathroom.

The toilet flushed, and she came back out. She sat and took a bite of her toast. Then: "Yes, I'd love to go."

Pris said, "*Really*?", delighted and amazed, like pigs had finally sprouted wings. "I'm sure you'd like it. It's the same as our church in Merrill—you know, Lutheran, evangelical." —meaning not Evangelical Lutheran, but Lutheran and "Spirit-filled." The distinction spoke for their whole milieu, of liberal/intellectual New England Christianity. More CS Lewis than Jimmy Swaggert; more Narnia than Beulahland. A sweet, simple New Testament creed, of pure white doves to go with girlhood's unicorns. "But it's a little more subdued. You'll like our pastor, though. He's . . . dynamic. He's *young*."

Linda, smiling, shook her head. "I don't know what that means."

"Well, he's . . . great. But compared to Pastor Schmidt, in Merrill—you know, that Gentle Shepherd style . . . I mean, he's simply young. Like, all of a sudden he gets real reactionary. Swings to the right of Darth Vadar for no reason, but it's only happened once or twice. He's *learning*. But he's wonderful. You can tell him anything."

Linda was politely puzzled. "I'm supposed to talk to him? I didn't think you normally . . . oh well."

"Lin, I'm *describing* him. Isn't that okay?"

But of course, that was all-important. Linda saw it clearly: religion through a woman's eyes. God was a diamond glow, back-lighting a wonderful man. She said, "I'm sure I'll be blessed. Do you think my green dress is okay?—it's been partied in."

"Well, now it can be worshiped in."

"Oh Pris, I'm so excited. I can't wait to be in church. To offer myself as a woman before God, with my hands upraised in thanksgiving and praise."

"Why are you so mad?"

269

Linda said, "Just me. You know how cranky I get." She winked. "I'll go get ready."

They took Priscilla's Sentra. (It was every bit as cluttered as Linda's Tercel.) The trip was rather long, through apple orchards and pasture land. The sky was clear, but the wooded slopes were faintly fogged with evaporating snow. It was beautiful; they drove with the windows down. Few other cars were on the road.

Linda said, "I've been thinking about converting to Roman Catholicism."

Pris laughed. "Wheee!"—waved her hand out the window. Like crossover dreams were a well-known symptom of hangovers.

Linda gazed thoughtfully out at the passing stone walls and misted meadows. "I had an experience yesterday. I saw a child. A beautiful baby girl of my own race. I mean, we could have been related. And I spoke to her in Spanish. Pris, I've never spoken it or even understood it. It was like I'd spoken in tongues. Maybe it was a sign, or . . . ?"

Pris said, "All right . . .," respectful of religion just in case.

"Pris, I might learn Spanish. Buy a set of tapes, or whatever. Maybe even someday . . . you know, return to my real mother's homeland. I mean, it's part of the US, right?—you can just move there? With my qualifications in human services, I'm sure I'd find a pretty decent job."

Pris said, "In Puerto Rico," her laughter on hold.

"I could live in a villa on the beach. With palm trees. Can't you see me? All torrid and dramatic, like one of those UNI soap opera ladies?"

Pris watched the road, like she saw a zebra crossing; the problem was with Linda being torrid and dramatic, never mind in what language.

Linda said, "They thought my mother came from some important family. I could be, God only knows: heiress to an avocado empire."

"Avocado empress."

"Seriously, though: I think I should live a very simple life. Outdoors. Doing simple things each day. Feeding chickens. Drawing water from a well. I should only own a dress. A crucifix necklace. That's how I would be myself, be really close to God."

Pris didn't answer right away, as if sensing that Linda was serious. "Sort of like . . . a nun, or . . . ?"

"Oh. No, I should have a husband. I should have kids, be a mom. I mean a way of *living* life, not hiding from it."

"Well, Lin . . . you can do what you want. If that's . . ."

"You know, this rural America, whitebread prosperity—even this Lutheran religion, this tired German God with all His windy whys and wherefores—these things were *imposed* on me. They're

270

not mine."

Pris queerly said "Just stop"—it worked for Linda's mom, sometimes.

The church was across the road from some river, near a long stone bridge. Across the bridge was an historic-looking factory: red-brick arches, *Keene & Sons Foundry* in faded white letters under the eaves. Directly across the river from the church, a rocky slope rose steeply, dense spruce and white fingers of birch, wreathed in mist. Though they were half a mile from downtown Ashland, this particular view might have been somewhere in the White Mountains.

The church itself was physically beautiful. Mock-Gothic, with buttressed spires, all of grey New England granite. It was flanked by a couple acres of wooded park—bare lindens, beige lawn, all but sighing for spring's green.

Inside was a little warm—the sexton, or whoever, had neglected to take the thaw into account, left the thermostat cranked for winter. Linda and Pris hung their coats in the lobby. A pleasant usher seated them in the middle of a pew near the front.

The church was pretty inside, as well. Stone-arched ceiling, buttressed walls. Green carpet, stained-glass windows, lots of yellow crocuses up on the altar. Their scent, like that of some Middle Eastern rice dish, mingled with the forever-new incense of polished rosewood.

Linda softly told Pris, "I like this. This is nice."

There was an invocational hymn. Both women stood and opened their hymnals. Pris whispered, "Lin, *sing*. You sing so beautifully."

Linda touched her throat. "I have a cold."

There were standard Lutheran proceedings—prayers, announcements, responsive reading, another hymn. The Lutheran standard: *A Mighty Fortress Is Our God.* The host of Christian women were like a lovely filter. They strained the Viking dirge and made it vernal melody, like God was love and sweetness and it said so in the hymnal. Just for that, the pastor told them "Please be seated."

Linda turned around. "Are Chuck and Rich here?"

"*Linda!*"

The two women sat. The pastor began his sermon. No nervousness or humor; he muttered and paused like he willfully disdained the art of public speaking. He seemed *terribly* young, no more than twenty-five. Blonde hair, cropped close on the sides, rimless glasses; he looked very German. He talked like he came from Connecticut. He had that frightfully serious air, of a handsome boy who could have had a Mustang convertible and a million girlfriends, but had chosen to serve God instead. Or worse, he hadn't chosen—it had simply been his chore, next on

271

his agenda.

Linda sat still, eyes wide, lips reposed—prettily in awe, a woman before God.

The Old Testament passage was from Job. He burned to speak with God, but was afraid—even if he was right and God was wrong, God would make Job's tongue condemn him.

The New Testament reading was from Luke—the parable of the ungrateful servant. Forgiven of a national debt, he went out and shook down a friend for pocket change, was called back before his ruler and destroyed.

The sermon concerned human anger at God. It began with a word of ellucidation about the book of Job. The book's premise was that Job was furious at God with every fiber of his being but he never sinned against Him with his tongue. The pastor said that Job's words, therefore, are inerrant wisdom from Man's perspective. It seemed a fine distinction, like you needed to have heard preceding lectures in the series. The congregation's mood seemed subdued, almost absent. We'll just sit this one out. Linda knew she was witnessing a prodigy. Like someone who visits the zoo on that one day out of a thousand when the Tibetan leopard comes out of its cave—she'd lucked onto one of those fabled swings to the right. Human anger at God was no occasion for sympathetic homilies—this guy was all on the side of the law. He would stridently announce incoming fire, then hit the deck himself.

The pastor, talking, noticed Linda. He noticed her again. He decided, then, he was talking to her. His congregation of one. The dark, pretty woman in her forest green dress . . . wasn't the Whore of Babylon, no. But some toned-down, domestic equivalent. The Feminist on the Fringe, perhaps. Anyway an archetype. At first, Linda felt self-conscious. Then she met his eyes. She refused to be ashamed.

The sermon itself wasn't Fundamentalist. It was worse: mainstream neo-orthodoxy. Exigetical explanations, hermeneutical hair-splitting, a classic Lutheran two-steps-back from Protestant liberality. There was a discussion of *insane impudence*, like that was some established catchword. Linda looked around, at people who came to hear this guy talk each week. They looked disturbingly normal. Note of the futility of any attempt at self-justification. Digression: a passage from Jeremiah. The people of Jerusalem felt they could cope militarily with the Babylonian army. God said that, though every Babylonian soldier lay bleeding and maimed on the floor of his tent, at His command, if He so wished, every soldier would stand, take his weapon and they all—of one terrible, silent accord—would storm Jerusalem and take it.

("*Oh God, it sounds like* Night Of The Living Dead. *What happened to nice little stories about angels and babies and stuff?*"

272

("*Lin, hush!*")

That, said the pastor, was the extent of man's ability to contend with God: an empty boast, his back to the wall and a blade to his throat. This remark, at least, wasn't addressed to Linda; he spoke, with a quick grin, to someone else in the congregation—probably another man—who could appreciate a good blade-to-throat metaphor.

Linda spoke loudly aside to Pris: "The Gospel According to George Romero, I mean it! Shouldn't we leave?"

Petrified, Pris didn't answer.

The pastor continued, unperturbed. All human suffering was a pittance, a token in return, related to the cosmic debt of individual guilt. A glimpse of the man behind the collar: something not a *pittance* but a *piss-ant* of remorse; it seemed a verbal slip and no one stirred. All suffering, against which people cursed and railed, was only the loving touch of God's guidance; the fist of His wrath, no flesh on Earth had yet felt, nor could the Earth itself withstand it. Speaking to Linda, he arched his brows: Think it over.

Linda told him, "Oh give me a break!"

Pris held her shoulder, soothed her. "Linda, no."

From problem to solution: the spiritual disciplines of humility and self-examination. "This message has been pastoral, rather than evangelistic. Meat for those saved, not milk for the lost." He invited everyone to stay for fellowship after, and urged those who couldn't to return for evening service. Then pleasantly broke from his script—told Linda, "We'll serve our more usual sweetness and light." He even, by way of apology, grinned—like Erminegard, with only half his mouth, though on him it seemed appropriate. A kindly young man who slopped hogs, fixed tractors, and explained why people are going to Hell. "It helps to shock the system, now and again."

Linda stared at him coldly—a mature Christian woman, sure that all Christendom's pralines and tea would never seduce her into this fellowship. Reserving the right to withhold her approval, to think that his meat, milk and system shocks were altogether a load of crap.

The congregation stood for the Doxology, voices raised in joy, Praise Father, Son and Home We Go.

Pris said, "We need to just leave."

Linda said, "I can't. I may need you to wait." She walked up the aisle. Her remarks had been conversational in volume; it appeared that some people had heard her, were now talking in groups about her, while most hadn't heard and were unconcerned with her, except insofar as a beautiful and impassioned woman, walking swiftly, was a natural focus of attention. The question of a tiny child, *Why is Mommy mad?* and the gentle reassurance, *Mommy's here.*

273

The pastor was at the door, speaking with departing members of his congregation. His demeanor was as personable as it had been from the pulpit—solemn acknowledgments, grave benedictions. Linda quietly waited in line, holding her purse in both hands. I'm a little chipmunk, striped and meek. She'd not gotten her coat. When her turn came, the pastor extended his hand. "Good morning. Are you visiting for the first time?"

She didn't dare *ignore* his hand; she looked and twitched her shoulder, like his hand was something scary. "Sir, my name is, um, Linda. Bloom. I feel that we should speak."

He said, "Ms. *Bloom*," as if he'd heard of her. Yet he was unassuming—Clark Kent, asked what Superman was up to, these days. "I'm available, yes. After this; after people have left."

"Now, please." She flared her eyes, like he'd toyed with the wrong lady. In fact she was appalled at herself for giving a minister an order.

He said, "Excuse me one moment."

The pastor walked away, while people milled, impatient and bewildered, behind Linda. There were, of course, no comments. The people were Lutherans; Swedish and German-Americans, comfy middle-class. They preferred not to address someone they'd not been introduced to, especially if she was beautiful and clearly upset. Nor did they have the sense God gave a goat to walk around her.

Another man, perhaps a deacon, took the pastor's place. He graciously received whoever he saw, but didn't see Linda; her cue, You're out of line. The pastor touched her arm; she was startled, since she didn't see him first. He murmured a few words—"This way? The office is available, I just needed to check"—to the effect of, *I won't bite*; strange, since he already had. She walked with him, permitting his hand on her arm. It seemed she was upset and being cared for, not bad and being hauled away. They passed a bulletin board, mostly taken up by an exuberant colored poster. KING'S KIDS SPRING CLEAN-UP!, that coming Saturday. Refreshments served after, in the Fellowship Hall. A pressed-on Xerox enlargement of Charlie Brown and Linus, rakes in hand but vaguely unsure about work. Linda felt like a wicked intruder. *Oh give me a break.*

She stopped at the office door. "You may wish to have another person present." She explained with a listless gesture: she was a woman, he was a man, Life was more trouble than it was worth.

He said, "Um . . . that's not really necessary. I'm not an Hasidic rabbi." Linda gestured again, Silly me. They went in, he closed the door—double nonHasidic. A chair and a desk, he offered the former. Seated himself at his desk.

There was the needful exchange of trivial remarks, by which people show they are sane and civil adults. He said, "It's unseasonably warm. I'll have to check the thermostat."

Linda, tense but poised, said, "It's a March thaw. Early." She managed a brief smile. Then "See, you've got sparrows or something, in that bush outside your window."

The pastor turned in his chair, to look. He said, "I believe that's a junco." He studied it for a moment; it appeared to be singing, though one couldn't tell through the glass. He said "A junco in the . . . hemlock," like he was starting to recite a haiku, but then he turned and faced Linda again. "Do you feed wild birds, Ms. Bloom?"

"My . . . husband used to." Another quick smile. "You can't help but get interested, after a while. You have to be consistent, though. They get dependent. On being fed."

The pastor nodded. Linda blinked. So much for trivial remarks.

Linda knew she was supposed to begin. She hadn't been called into the office; she had called. She already felt like she'd made a scene over silly feelings that were already gone. "I . . . okay: a woman should be silent in church. If she has questions, let her ask afterwards. Let her ask her husband, so the pastor's not bothered with frivolous female concerns. That's in First Corinthians, I think."

The pastor said "Um . . ."—it was a long and brooding *um*. It was nearly *Om*. " . . . someone's amplified version, perhaps."

She said, "I'm sharing how I feel." She couldn't believe she sounded so calm and lucid, like she knew what she was talking about.

He said, "I've previously stepped on feminist sensibilities. While that's certainly something that can be talked about, I don't deserve it *today*. Since my sermon wasn't about that. Unless you're also mad at God, I'm not inclined to serve you."

She remembered Chuck, her glass of chablis—she didn't have to stand for it. "How is that 'serving' me?"

"On the premise that I'm a repository of knowledge." Already self-abased, he wouldn't fall for her.

Linda said, "Well anyway, I wasn't being facetious. Paul addressed the believer herself. Right?—so I've received it."

He acknowledged her with open hands—There you sit, redeemed.

"So obviously, it's not about you. I'm the one at fault. I spoke in church, I honestly did. I want you to forgive me."

He stared, as if waiting for more. The daylight through the window happened to reflect off his glasses, so she couldn't see his eyes.

He shook his head, as if to clear it; she'd made a simple request. "Uh . . . okay, sure: I forgive you. Anything else?"

"Your sermon was, like, directed to me. You spoke to me. I feel."

"Well, you . . . felt that I was speaking to you, personally."

She knew that she'd been speaking very softly. Electrifying this conversation with a submissive, seductive current, but she simply couldn't help it; she was nervous, and her mouth was dry. "Oh spare me the Rogerian psychology."

He spread his hands again: Then it's still your turn.

"You spoke to me publicly. Really, you admonished. As a visitor, I felt singled out. I don't think Jesus would have liked it."

He looked at her, inscrutable, pale in the light through gossamer curtains.

She sat with her purse in her lap, looked around. If he wasn't going to answer, then she needed something to look at. His desk. It was covered with books. Some were right-side-up facing her, like someone had been sitting right where she was now, discussing things more weighty than a lady's feelings with this pastor. She pictured that person as an older man, with a corduroy suit—elbow patches, vest—and a pipe. The books were dense stuff—Bultmann, Barth. *Critical Historicity. Christ In Culture.* A xeroxed manuscript, its face sheet proclaiming *Qumrun's Implications On Masoretic Syntax.* She thought, *Then maybe he's right, about everything. Maybe that's why he wears glasses—he's some kind of rocket scientist of the soul.*

"My dress?" She looked down at its neckline, then at him, curious. "You feel it's immodest? That's all?—I mean, that's it?"

He looked at her, unreadable, surrounded by his unreadable books.

He spoke in a mild, easy tone. It was almost spooky, like he'd never been distant or unreadable at all, she'd just imagined it. "Uh . . . I'm not all that attuned to women's concerns. I mean, they're private to you. If your dress is something you're anxious about, then I'd tell you it's okay. I don't see anything wrong with it."

"Is this something we should both be somewhat embarrassed about?"—she *thought*; she wasn't sure. If in fact he flattered her, she didn't want to lessen him. "I mean, if we can be that specific. I'm not offended. I'm a little mortified. I'm staying with a lady-friend, and this is all I have."

"I can't see what's wrong with it."

She helpfully said "You're young. I'm a few years older. This is a delicate situation; you haven't dealt with it yet. Am I right?" She paused, to learn if she was or not. He waited, to learn what situation she referred to. "Relations with unmarried female parishioners . . . ?" He languidly blinked. She hastened to explain, "I mean, I know how I come across. Dark, passionate and flighty. Unattached. Hair on my arms—don't look. I just mean, people think Oh, she has male hormones and a flaming libido."

"Well, you're . . . concerned that people perceive you this way."

"You fear that I'm eccentric. You . . . suspect that I'm unsaved?—you have doubts about my morality. You're uncertain how to approach me. You're afraid I might storm out the door, and never set foot in a church again."

He lightly cleared his throat. He didn't stir.

He said, "You're obviously an intelligent, sensitive person. You appear to be upset. Those really are the sum of my impressions." He had a bit of a Yankee drawl, which didn't come through from the pulpit. He might have grown up on a farm. He might have been a farm case.

"You think I'm a carnal believer. Like, I'd entice some wealthy widower, here at your church."

"As for your leaving the church . . . it's not my church. It's God's. It's between you and Him. You talk about problems of character, but so far as I'd guess, that's why you're in church."

She started to speak but stopped, puzzled by the odd perspective. "Bad people . . . ?"

" . . . are bad; that's why they're in church."

"I drank, last night. Too much. My breath . . . well no, I won't breathe on you. If it smells like a florist's shop, that's me. Chablis, and too much perfume. It's very fruity. Chablis." He gestured, slightly distracted, like a Halston's-scented butterfly had lighted on his hand. "I'm afraid people noticed. 'Some hungover tramp is in our church.' Last night, there was a man. He wanted me to, like, be his wife. For just one night. I wanted that. To be something normal. Someone loved."

"This is upsetting you."

"Yes." She realized with alarm, she would cry if she talked about it further. "I feel I need guidance. Older Christian women should admonish me. Teach me to be chaste and sober. Bring me into my place within the fold."

"You went wild last night and you're misquoting the second chapter of Titus."

"Uh."

"Ms. Bloom, you obviously come from a Christian background. You appear to be having some crisis of your spirituality, and it seems to be hard for you to share this with me. You suggest you'd be more comfortable talking with another woman. I'd like to arrange this for you . . . here." He reached for a phone, presumably an intercom.

If Linda didn't speak, this scene would change. The pastor would quietly exit the stage. There would be another woman, and a conversation in some other room. That conversation would be about God, and about her soul, and it would have meaning. But, "That's not what I want."

"I felt myself directed to address you."

It took a few moments to sink in. He admitted he was preaching straight to her. He excused himself saying, he was only following orders. Like someone slipped him a memo from the CEO. He looked at her blankly, like he received such directives on a fairly frequent basis.

Linda said "Oh. Well, this is getting good, then. You felt yourself 'directed'. Sir, I'll thank you to know I'm a Lutheran. If I want to be charismatically singled out from the pulpit, I'll go to one of those store-front tabernacles in Roxbury." She was mad, and didn't try to hide it. "Oh, you are *young*."

"You have a quality."

"Excuse me?"

"You feel things deeply, you're very vulnerable, and you're somehow misplaced. You're not who you're supposed to be." The broken smile, apologetic. "That won't stand up to intellectual scrutiny."

Linda started to say he was right, she agreed with him, it didn't make a bit of sense.

Linda wept.

It was just a calm lady's *pauvre-moi*, a self-involved sniffling as she fretted through her purse. The pastor sat with his hands clasped on his desk. Her weeping was her business. It was happening in his office, taking up his time, but there was no nice way to curtail it. He was getting paid to sit and wait.

At length, she mentioned, "I'm already saved. I've known the Lord since . . ." Her eyes widened, wet and lovely at the door of numinous awe. *How will I stand before God? As Derrick or as Linda?* " . . . I was twenty. Or possibly twelve." Her voice choked out on little-girl anguish, *"This really isn't about that."*

Later, she managed a womanly, droll comment: "You know, they say women always have lots of Kleenex, but sometimes it's not enough."

The pastor stood, strolled over to a bookshelf. A paisley-pattern tissue box, wedged between Neibuhr and Neimoeller; a compassionate concession, Sure, this stuff can bore you straight to tears. Linda took an offered tissue, dabbed her eyes. Absently she motioned, Thank you, you may leave. He returned to his desk, steepled his hands. Remarked, "We do get groupies. You don't seem the type, though."

She frowned at her Kleenex, it was sooted with mascara. She tucked it into a corner of her purse, behind her powder blush, along with the Kleenex she'd wiped the baby's nose with. She clasped her purse shut with decision. "God did something unforgivable to me."

"Well . . . God does not sin. To accuse Him of that is injustice."

"Oh. No. If you knew the truth about me, you'd agree. This body is not the vessel for my soul. It's not my birthright. He

278

robbed me of it, He . . ." The pastor sat relaxed in his chair. Flanked by shelves of books. A wall of conviction, not to be turned. A blur of motion, trivial and random. "The junco. I recognize it, now." The pastor slowly turned, to see. She said, "They're always first when you fill the feeder. It's like they're telepathic."

"You commonly hear that barnyard *geese* are telepathic. I hadn't heard this trait ascribed to any songbird." He turned back, said, "I think you're going through a sustained crisis."

"Oh. Do I look really awful, or something?"

"No. Whatever ladies do to look unawful, you do very well. Now . . . are you sleeping at night? Are you . . . well, I hate to say: using any substances?"

For an instant she was utterly confused. "Like n-night cream, or . . . ?"

She closed her eyes, took a breath.

"It seems like all I *do* is sleep. I've been drinking lots of herb tea. It doesn't make you high or anything; no."

"Are you safe?—at home, I mean. When you go home, will you be—?"

She said, "I'm presently living alone. So far as some man beating up on me, no. I couldn't deal with that for even a moment, I'd go instantly crazy for life. No, the person in my life Who's mistreating me: I already said."

"Were you abused by your father?"

"My Father in Heaven."

"Okay . . . a woman's relationship with her male parent may predelict her feelings towards God. That's part of His redemptive work in our lives—a good Father to those whose fathers were bad. Because this happens, we have fathers who are irrational and sadistic—"

"You're telling me *your* problem."

He said, "You're right." It seemed like the throwaway answer of a man too tired to backtrack.

Linda said, "Besides, you're wrong—my father wasn't bad to me at all. My . . . father is Lars Bauer, and we're very close. I'm . . . my daddy's little girl, and everything's all right."

He said, "Then, wrong guess. Just, the mention of something being done to you, which you're leaving me to guess about."

She suddenly felt a great emptiness. She said, "You were rude to me during your sermon. That's what I'm upset about." She glanced down at her watch, her dainty Fabergé, one of daddy's many gifts. She sighed, gazed at the ceiling.

He said, "All right. Then *I'm* asking *you* to indulge my curiosity. My life's work is focused on God; I always thought He was a pretty cool guy. You say you have contrary knowledge. No man is killing you stealthily. Then the gods are sending you pain—"

She said, "You'll think I'm crazy. You'll have me committed."

"My doctorate's in divinity. On a hospitalization form, that would look very strange."

"You'll call someone."

He said, "No I won't," with a tinge of exasperated laughter.

She examined her nails. She needed a new polish. She was down to the last of her bottle, and it was flaking along her cuticle. She wouldn't get the same color, though—not burgundy. She'd read in Cosmopolitan that dark polish and lipstick for dark-complexioned women was out of style. Beige was in. She said, "I was abused."

He waited.

She explained, "It was more subtle. He'd hold my bottom and kiss my ear. I sat in his lap when I was fourteen. That's not right, you know, you shouldn't do that after you've started to . . .—not that it's, like, messy or anything. Just that your father should know. He *does* know, so you feel . . . I can't describe it. To a man. You feel so dirty. I feel so ashamed."

He waited. At last he shrugged. "We can begin to help you with that. There are professional services affiliated with the Lutheran Church."

"I wasn't abused."

"I know, Ms. Bloom."

"You won't tell anyone. If I tell you, you—"

"Won't."

She murmured something to her fingernails.

"I'm sorry, Ms. Bloom."

"Oh, stop *calling* me that. If you insist on being formal, then it's Mrs."

"I didn't hear you."

"I said I want you to . . . swear, or something."

"Bullshit."

She looked at him, drearily, through misting tears. He didn't look like he'd been humorous. He looked removed and austere, in the wan winter light through the gossamer curtains.

She said, "You'd never say that from the pulpit."

"Well . . . if I felt I was *supposed* to, I might. But I'd probably have to hand someone my keys on my way out. Though it's something of a Lutheran tradition. Luther seldom minced words. He called Erasmus *ein shreckkopf*. Anyway, I'm not about to swear an oath. Jesus would have a fit."

She tried to get mad, so she wouldn't cry again. "You know, for someone in the ministry, you're really snide."

He told her, "Be quiet." Not like the priest in *The Exorcist*, telling the demon *Be silent*; more a sibling variant of *Just stop*.

Linda sat docilely, looked at him indifferently, obedient to men without resentment.

She asked, "Has anyone ever come to you, and said they were really a member of the opposite sex?"

He looked at her closely. He even moved his head as if trying to view her from slightly different perspectives. Trying to see her gunning down on a Harley, or ballistic on ice with a hockey stick, or even playing co-ed foozball. At last he pursed his lips; it wasn't there to see.

He said, "Not to me personally, no. I've needed to study the phenomenon of sexual identity disorders, as part of my pastoral counseling curriculum."

"My mother has a master's in it."

He somberly said, "All right," and she realized he'd misunderstood—thought she meant her mother had, metaphorically speaking, an academic degree in warping her daughter's sexual identity.

He said, "Sexual identity's a semantic artifact." He seemed to be starting a lecture. "Like *the totality of human experience*. It references dichotomy between form and self; blame Aristotle." He paused. "Or a woman could say she felt like a man if she was really mad at her mother," like he was bored by Life in general but especially by his own lecture.

Linda piped up brightly, like she was bored by it too. "Has anyone ever come to you, claiming they were dead?"

"Um . . . no, but at least we're not off the subject. Such a claim would have to come from Old Testament Sheol—*ex oblivione*. It would argue the immortal soul against the Resurrection—again confused by Aristotle."

"So you don't think someone's soul can leave their body, or . . . ?"

"Let's pick the pace up slightly: tell me what *you* think."

"If I tell you, it's secret? Like Catholics? In confession?"

"Is that what this is?"

She said, "No, it's not." The room got bright, like God was mad—no confession, indeed. She said, "I don't know what my sin is. I only know how I'm being punished."

She saw that he knew, too—how *he* had once been punished. He was unturning because he was *tired*. A thousand summer days, dark to dark on a tractor. Back and forth across the same old field. Ever since he was very small—work and work, line upon line, over and over, again and again. At best, he could get into another field—the winter corn, up top. Now he rested at his desk, while birds sang in the bush outside his window. Everything was finished. It was all taken care of by someone else. Clothes tumbling in a dryer.

Her hand was really neat. Dark and slender, funny and clever. It could have been anyone's hand. A farm girl's. A waitress'. A duchess'. A boy's. But it was hers. It did whatever

281

she wanted it to.

She felt really nice. Lazy and so relaxed, like a little girl slumped in the back seat of her parents' car. School was out, they were on vacation, driving somewhere far away. She felt heavy, vibrant, all of one piece. She liked her long legs, so heavy and warm, so part of her. She liked her own smell, of warm caramel.

But most of all, she liked her hand.

She felt a little wet. She thought maybe she'd come. Then knew that she'd just leaked. A very little. She was wearing a pad. Worry-free.

She was in a big room in a very big house. A big, important man was there, and he would take care of everything.

It was a beautiful day outside.

The pastor looked quasi-busy. Like he'd been doing a little of this and that at his desk, shuffling papers. Whatever.

He smiled, then stopped. His smile was familiar—it was just like hers. It didn't stay on by itself.

He told her, "I said, 'Mrs. Bloom, Mrs. Bloom'. I tried 'Linda', once. As it happens, I've an aunt who *petit mals*. Awake you're indelibly you, even as my aunt is plainly she. Yet the startled look, the absence then the awakening bliss are interchangeable. It really does appear as if your soul has left your body—curious, since we were discussing that."

She realized she was slumped in her seat. She sat up straight. "I almost never have them, anymore. But I've been under so much stress."

"If God is being mean to you, that surely must be stressful."

Her eyes drifted, dreamily; she gazed around the room. Her mouth opened and closed, opened, then closed, like a fish out of water, gently seeking air.

She looked at him, alarmed. She'd found someone to listen, but it was only another trick—God was in this room, and He wouldn't let her talk. She touched her throat: *Can't talk.* She shook her head: *Help me.* Yet she knew it was hopeless.

He said, "There's no spiritual Heimlich maneuver. I can't come over to you and make you cough up the truth."

Linda blinked. She could talk; of course she could. However, she could not.

"Would you like my help?" He spoke to her, now, as a child. Tenderness tainted with irony, since she wasn't a child. "Would you like me to ask questions?"

She nodded, tight-mouthed and embarrassed. *This must appear so childish.*

"Okay. Linda. Were you raped?"

"Uhn . . . nn . . ."

He asked again. He was gentle and patient; he enjoyed being gentle and patient. He was undoubtedly wonderful with children. "Did someone hurt you, Linda? Did a man? You can tell me; I'm

282

a minister."

"Nn . . . n-no, I wasn't. What you said. Not rr . . . ray . . ."

"You're sure?"

"Um . . . mm-hm."

He liked and cared about her—this was true. He saw her as a challenging puzzle, a test of his skill—this was true as well. He really couldn't help, and this was the truest truth.

He said, "This involves a member of your family."

"Yes." She closed her eyes. They felt like they were moving closer together, gradually, like two people rolling an enormous boulder. She understood she was fighting a barrier which she, herself, had deliberately built.

She opened her eyes. "There's been more. Worse. Than a death. A new . . . a different kind of death."

He frowned with interest. Death was a major part of his job.

"A luh . . . luh . . .—someone I liked a lot, died and now I have to live. Her life. For her."

There was quiet. At length the pastor said, "A form of mourning."

"No. Yes. Yes." *And there was evening and morning, one day.* Her girlhood had lasted only one day. It was hard to remember, hard to reclaim the skills. *Shelley Mommy help me. Choose which don't point use words whole sentences. Oh Mommy I want to come back to that day, I want to come back to my home. I want to sew take a walk in the snow make quiche make wholewheat pancakes. Say you'll always love me Mommy please let me come home.* "A form of mourning."

"To live a person's life for her: your life is not your own. Your mother was ill for a long time. You cared for her."

"No. My mother is living. Shelley Bauer. Twenty-six Longmeadow—"

"Who are you mourning, Mrs. Bloom. Linda."

"Yes."

"Who."

She was startled. It felt like falling asleep, thinking you fell out of bed, but it was only a dream. She woke up in front of the pastor's desk. He said, "A girlfriend. Another woman, whom you were close to. And this person has died."

She looked at her hand. A woman's hand; it had never been anything else. *Man and maiden made He them.* "I think I'm unable to tell you."

The pastor seemed to weigh this, silently concur. "Try to describe other things, then. Feelings. What it is you experience."

"To . . . always see the person, to . . . see her face in the mirror every time. To lie in bed and she's there, to always . . . always . . ."

" 'The dead are in deep anguish.' "

She blinked.

He said, "That's from Job. The spirit is integral to the living body, only. But the dead are not entirely extinct. I . . . don't think you want a hermeneutical discourse."

She slightly shook her head, a little girl before the dentist.

"II Samuel and Isaiah both confirm the possibility of what you're describing. When you say, a face in the mirror. A presence in the bed. When you seem unaware of what you suggest, that this person who is dead is still actually present in your life."

She gripped her purse, her adulthood. "No, I am the ghost."

"Have you been in a lesbian relationship."

"Have you changed the subject."

"No. I haven't time to explain the correlation."

"Goblins. Dykes." She shook her head.

He went soft again, gentle—Mister Rogers with rimless specs, and a military buzz-cut. "It's a sin. But it's only a sin. Mine aren't any better."

She softly said, "Oh you're grossing me out."

"You had a friend. There was love. Love per se is good; that part's all right."

"Oh, it's 'all right', my ass. What kind of minister are you?"

"Okay, I was wrong. Should we start again?"

"I think maybe I should leave." She rose from her chair. She felt directionless, light. She'd just *petit mal*ed.

He said, "Where will you go?" He sounded purely curious. If there was somewhere to go where troubles couldn't find you, cool—he'd go there too.

She turned away, turned back to him, motioned to the door, motioned at him, despairing of both her options. It was the same way she'd gestured at the meter in the snow bank: *How is this supposed to be possible?*

"Mrs. Bloom . . ."

"Stop *calling* me that! *I'm not my mother!*" *Don't scream.*

"Linda. Sit down." His voice held kindness; it was like a physical force, bending her knees and making her sit.

She said, "An inverted haunting. The body is alive, okay? The soul is gone. Departed."

"Where?"

She said, "Into the light," and almost cried again, since she sounded like Shirley MacLaine.

Think: your wife's body. Your wife's character. You're Linda. Try to remember. You can solve problems, you can cope with stress, so long as there are simple rules which everyone understands. So long as pencils aren't chewed, spitballs aren't shot, and the clock on the wall says when it will end. So long as people are nice, and rules make sense. Take any of that away, and you go haywire. Panic, and rage that your guidelines aren't clearly defined.

Words. Make Sense.

"She's gone. I'm haunting her body."

He said with calm finality, "I don't know what that means."

"Then you don't, and I can't help it." She started to cry, for real; the tears she'd only tapped before, now flowed. "I've done something terrible, I can't imagine what, but I've done something very, very awful."

"Well . . . this happens. We do things. We sin."

"I'm a very bad person, and I'm being punished very, very severely, and part of my punishment is that I can't tell anyone."

"Well, then . . . maybe this happens." There was less and less he could say.

Linda wept. She wept, and began to sob.

The sobbing became tremulous, high-pitched. She began to tense, release the sound in soft, piercing wails. The sound transcended emotion; it was animal agony, purest essence.

She spoke to him thinly, from the cold, lonely height of her grief: "*I'm so ashamed to be crying like this.*"

He shrugged. "You're allowed to. You're a woman."

She flashed her eyes at him, gorgeous fury through her tears. "It's not '*freedom*'! You don't know—being a woman is *bottomless*! You cry and it's like falling and falling, you . . ."

She hid her face in her hands. No man could understand.

The pastor came over, stood next to her. He placed his hand on her shoulder. A function of his office, impersonal as a quoted psalm. "You said you've been saved. You know the Lord."

She wept, "But He doesn't know me. He says I'm someone and something I'm not."

He said, "You're a daughter of God."

She put her feet up on the chair, covered her ears with her hands. It was her body's last resort against unbearable stress, a behavior lost in early adolescence. She covered her ears and screamed "*No!*"

"Linda. Yes."

"*I will not be His daughter!*"

"Daughters are . . . loved, I guess. Cherished."

She twisted away from him. "*No! No! Noooo*—aah!"—the scream ended wildly.

She collapsed, hugging her knees; she shook with silent sobs.

The pastor stood by, stirred and fascinated—but only as some type of clinician, intrigued by a new phenomenon. The door opened, and a woman looked in. The pastor absently waved her off; the doctor had his lab under control. The woman closed the door.

Linda wailed again. She wailed and wailed and couldn't stop. The sound from her mouth, from deep within, carried her along, she knew not where, like a swift, ferocious wind.

The pastor said, "Anguish is not godly grief. Pain like this is

285

not from God."

Linda wept, she shook her head—she didn't know where it was from. She hadn't asked for it, she'd refuse it if she could. She wept and wept, and then—

It finally stopped. She was empty.

Empty!

She stood. She took her purse. At the door she turned, and softly told him "Yes. Just so you know: my Father sexually abused me."

She opened the door. Turned and said, "Don't pray for me. It's between Him and me, like you said."

She left the office, walked down the church's outer hall.

The pastor stood in the hall before his office. Without irony, without any feeling as such, he said, "Do come back, some time."

She got her coat, put it on as she walked out the door.

Beautiful out! So warm. It was like spring. Priscilla's Sentra was alone in the lot. Pris herself sat reading a pamphlet. Linda got into the car.

"Well, I saw the pastor take you to his office . . ."

"Oh Pris, yes. God really spoke. I'm so at peace." Linda motioned happily, Drive. Pris started through the parking lot.

She said, "I'm glad it happened, then. You had so much pain. I remember when you would have just gone home and gone to bed. Instead, you were so bold. I think that's really neat."

Linda stretched in her seat, luxurious. Toying with a curl, she looked at a stone house, enclosed in arborvitae hedge. Ivy up the chimney. The parsonage, no doubt. *I wonder what he does there, day and night.* "Well, you know, I played my part: the weak, emotional woman, turning for help. The men in our lives, we just revolve around them, like . . ." She shook her head, wistful: time and again, so true. " . . . but Linda Bloom has changed. The cornered rabbit's going to start fighting back. The little lamb lost will start finding her own way. Let other people cry—I'm going to laugh. I think I'll remarry. Live in a gorgeous mansion and have five beautiful daughters. I'm going to be happy, Pris."

Pris smiled, watching the road. "I know you will be, Lin. The other things, though . . . I seem to recall Linda's Declaration of Ascendence as the anthem of our youth."

Linda twitched her shoulder, gazing at the clouds above the hill. *So I'll still be timid. I'm still going to be happy.*

They passed nice houses, far between along the wooded stretch. A lot of them were family farms, with little orchards and fields nearby. They had signs saying things like, *Pick Your Own Apples*, with stickers slapped on saying, *Closed For The Season.* Though one place had a billboard: *From Our Family To Yours—Have A Happy Winter And Stay Warm.*

286

Linda looked at the houses, going by. Her mind didn't work as it formerly did; she didn't see how foundations were dug, how frames were raised or wiring installed. She only saw the beauty. She thought, *Life there must be pretty.*

Some of the houses were set far back in the woods, surrounded by their shaded lawns, like magic homes in secret glades.

She saw a long lawn, sloping up to a Victorian gingerbread house. It was painted bright yellow, with lavender shutters and bargeboard eaves. It was surrounded by elms, and she saw the house in autumn: bright yellow, framed by dark purple. In spring, bright yellow framed by light green, with samaras snowing down to the dark green lawn. She felt, or her body remembered: this was Life, how things should be.

Matters settled, lawns mowed, cars washed, bills paid—Daddy took care of it all. Life was to be lived, the seasons to be savored: sweaters and apples in leafy fall. Coats and cranberry preserves in snowy winter; windbreakers, strawberries in fragrant spring. Bare feet and peaches in long, yellow summer—all provided, all just there. So long as a girl was a daughter, was faithful and loving and true.

Linda looked at the passing homes. Looked at Life imagined, moved her gentle lips, *I want it.*

18

"Do you like Natalie Merchant?"

Linda said, "Um . . . sure." Pris put in the tape.

Linda said she was starving, she wanted to eat the whole world. Pris said, "Start with South America. The Amazon's loaded with fiber." They agreed it wasn't church without lunch, after. They agreed they should have something bad—Pris knew just the place.

They went to a weathered, Cape Code-style shack just off the main road. The crushed-stone parking lot was crowded with four-wheel drives and motorcycles. Pris said, "Trust me—it isn't *quite* as rough as it looks."

Linda looked, wondering what was "rough."

On their way in, they passed a big young man getting off his hog. Leather jacket with an American flag, the stenciled motto *Helmet Law Sucks*; his head gear matched. Linda said "Nice bike," then quickly turned to follow Pris; she wasn't supposed to say things like that.

The guy said, "Why, thanks. Would you like to ride it?", like he'd seen every movie Jack Nicholson ever made.

Linda said "Oh." She stopped. "No. See, I've got high heels and I'm wearing a dress. See?—pantyhose. I'd freeze."

The guy spread his hands, a sublime gesture; there was only one answer to a pretty woman complaining of cold.

Linda shyly twitched her hip, Sorry; you can't hold me either. Went along with Pris, who was nearly at the door. Linda stopped to look at a slate board mounted next to the door. "Pris, stop!"

"*What?*"

"They've got Bloody Mary's half-price on Sunday. Look, they've got flowers in the window. You were right—it's okay for women to eat here."

Pris gasped, like Ofcourse it's okay for chrissake. The lobby was a warm vestibule—frayed green outdoor carpet, a giant trout mounted over a community bulletin board. Wood for sale and missing dogs and business cards, *We Rent Equipment*. Pris asked, "Are you *nuts?*"

Linda, blameless, said, "I'm hungry. So I talk to strangers. So?"

There were rough-hewn tables; polished cedar with chipped rose-hued edges, too perfectly rough-hewn to be anything but ordered from Maine. Booths whose decor was late Used Auto Parts. The two women went to a corner booth. The place was crowded and noisy. A juke box played The Maverick's *Crying Shame*, so no one smiled. They were blue-collar guys and their girls, doing pitchers. Two guys on one side of the table, the girls on the other. The girls ran towards facial scars and leather jackets. No pierced noses or tattoos, though; they were just New England rednecks. How quickly one forgets that rural New England is like rural anywhere, USA: boozy, Bible-ish, everything centered on piston engine and paycheck. Linda liked this place. "Let's come here some night, just to drink beer—you wanna? Chuck, Rich and us? Would it be a blast?"

Pris dismally said, "Yeah, we'll ride motorcycles." She added, "You might want to visit the ladies' room."

"Why? What's special about it?"

"Nothing. You've still got mascara, that's all."

Linda went into the ladies' room, which was truly unremarkable. A thin blonde in tight jeans and halter top was standing tensely at the sink counter, looking at the mirror. She told Linda's reflection, "Men are such assholes."

Linda said, "Oh, I know," arriving at the mirror to see her mascara: a surprise-burst of flecks around her weep-darkened eyes. "Oh shit, I forgot my cold cream."

The blonde opened her own purse, slapped a tube of rinse cleanser onto the counter, angrily prompt like she'd seen Linda walk in and thought *Oh hell, here's the chick who wants cold cream.* Linda washed her face, said "Thanks." She went into a stall, sat and pee'ed.

The blonde said, "My boyfriend is a *rare bird*. He's a Yellow-Bellied Cocksucker."

Linda said, "Yep! Men are really going to seed." She rocked happily, told the stall door "Get it? Bird? Seed?"

The blonde said, "I get it," like it was angina.

Linda finished up, paused to look at a condom dispenser, faintly surprised to find it there. She felt it should have been a strictly male concern. Besides, it advertised a condom which was studded with tiny latex nubs, like some Teenage Mutant Ninja accessory. "Have people gone insane? Would you want that inside you? I think I'd rather get AIDS."

The blonde said, "Ask my boyfriend. He'll probably give it to you."

"Oh. No thanks." Linda went back out.

The waiter soon came to their table. Linda was pleased to chat with him—she was stronger, since her debacle at Domina's. Also he was just an artsy college kid with a cannibal haircut. He wouldn't plow her under with Neapolitan charm; he could barely

289

get their order straight. She chided, like a mom. "Two Bloody Mary's, one no-salt. One with double lemon. I see you didn't write it down; I hope that you'll remember."

He smiled, simple friendliness. "Sure! Two . . . whatever."

He left, and Linda conferred with Pris. "It's a woman's drink, right? I never had one. Do you get to eat the celery, after? If you eat it before, do they give you another?"

Pris smiled, through her teeth said, "Will you *chill*?"

"But hon, I'm frosted." Linda touched Priscilla's hand, concerned. "People are nice, I'm being civil. Why do you feel threatened?"

Pris, again, spoke through her teeth so it would look like she was smiling, not talking. "I'm only having lunch with you, all right? Go ahead and write your number on your napkin."

Linda curled her lip. "For that Gen-X twerp? If it's not online, I doubt if he could read it."

The meal was an imbalanced affair. Linda ate clams, french fries, onion rings, cole slaw, rolls with butter, drank two Bloody Mary's. Between bites she waxed eloquent, waving her fork around: she still found fault with the Lutheran Church. Catholicism seemed nice, since you could by-pass God and deal with Mary. Pris picked at salad, fed into Linda's monologue as little as she could. Linda finally said, "You don't want that, do you." She took Priscilla's plate, not shy of her friend's germs. She ate and then remarked, "Mm—I'll never order this. The breading's way too thick."

Afterwards, they went back to Priscilla's house. They watched TV, then Pris said she had stomach cramps. Linda was alarmed. "Oh no, it might be botulism."

"Of course. You ate the food, now I get sick."

Linda said, "Well I'm taking care of you," and "helped" Pris into her bedroom. It was nicely decorated—jade greens, lace curtains. Grapevine wallpaper, matching the carved motif on the mahogany bedposts. The bed itself had an opulent, forest-green satin spread. An imitation Tiffany lamp on the night stand. Yet the room was cluttered like Pris was an overgrown teen. Brochures and magazines, a half-eaten candy apple and a huge stuffed Lion King, which Linda deposed onto the floor.

"Lin, I can put my own nightie on . . ."

"Nuh-uh, you're too sick." Linda put her friend to bed. She took Priscilla's temperature, made her an herb tea. Aired the room, fluffed pillows. Rubbed her friend's cold feet and put on socks. Cooled her forehead with a moist cloth. She sang to Pris ("Lin, it's too queer"), made chicken soup, fed it to her with a spoon.

As it grew dark outside, the bedroom lights still off, Linda sat on the edge of the bed. She smiled down at Pris, said,"Mommy's always here. Lin will always take care for you."

"Just . . . don't do that to me anymore."

"What did mean old Linda do?"

"She was too strong. Scary. I want you to be scared, like me."

Linda smiled fondly at the pictures in her mind. "Two scared girlies holding hands, running past the graveyard on an autumn day? Two proud swans, floating past the rude boys on the sidewalk?"

"Of course. That's how we were. Lin, that's who we are."

Linda laughed. "You're right. I promise: no more courage. Though I walk through the aisles of Stop and Shop, I'll fear all kinds of evil."

"We've so much catching up to do . . . Lin, sometimes you seem like someone else. Another person."

Linda said, "I understand."

"Yet other times, you're Linda. More yourself than even you."

"I understand that, also."

"And today you were just wicked. And you thought it was funny. You came out of church 'so at peace', then acted like a biker chick. Who were you guys praying to—the Devil?"

She kissed Priscilla's forehead. "Just a Father/daughter thing."

By the time Linda got home that evening, she felt a little off, herself. She took Pepto Bismol though she knew it wouldn't cure Eve's Curse. She'd used all four of her pads. She'd noticed—or possibly imagined—a faint unpleasant odor, like a tuna can left overnight on the counter. The pads had seemed satiny, fresh and clean from their pink wrappers like some little Easter present—like the proper band-aid to put under the problem. But now she found that she was spotting. She *guessed* that it was spotting. If it wasn't spotting, she had to admit—she didn't really know what spotting was.

She took a long, warm bath, then read in bed for a while.

She fell asleep with the light on, and—it never fails—woke feeling like she hadn't slept. It was early morning, and something wasn't good. There was blood, and it was bad. Little smears on the sheets, like the brushes of color on those damned "Monét" curtains. Her thighs were smeared too, and her gown was stained over her crotch. She also thought she stank—low tide under the sheets. Though Derrick never noticed such a thing. Just morning huggles and her pushing him away, *Quit I feel disgusting.*

She got up and made herself tea, feeling like she wanted to cry. She decided she had nothing to lose and did that—went back to bed and wet her pillow.

She got up to open the window, belatedly thinking *What's wrong with you? You're standing in full view of Samara Street, looking like you've been stabbed.* She bent, so no one across the way could see below her waist. Hands on the sill, she squinted out at the bright, cold winter day. The Orlowskis had their shades drawn. The Karpinskis' black Lab was trotting along the sidewalk, wagging its tail. All quiet on the Polish front.

Linda pulled the curtains over the open window. Took off her soiled gown, put on her quilted bathrobe. Went into the kitchen, gulped her lukewarm tea. It sat in the pit of her stomach, a puddle o' tannic acid. She went to the bathroom, couldn't avoid her reflection. Her eyes and cheekbones, shadowed. Her natural *café au lait* seemed spectral and translucent. With her serious, large eyes and pensive little mouth she looked so wan and spooky, like a vampire—afraid, not of crosses and sunlight, but of just about everything else. She opened the medicine cabinet. Stridex. Midol. Pepto Bismol. No need to dial 911 and yet, in a way, she did.

"Hi, Mom. It's me."

The voice in the receiver was from another world: a jet-stream of abundant life, of flowers, wealth and wisdom. "I was just this minute thinking of you, precious."

"Mom, something's wrong with me."

"Well, of course there is—you're Linda."

Linda nearly dropped the phone. Life was a Halloween ball, and Shelley had just unmasked. Yes, Linda was her husband—everybody knew. Then she realized Shelley just meant, her life was an unending crisis. "Mom, I'm having my period."

"Poor baby."

"And I'm bleeding."

"I'm amazed."

"No, Mom I mean, a lot."

Shelley's voice registered the remotest trace of anxiety—she prepared herself for the unlikely event of an actual problem. "Well . . . specify, for heaven's sake. Think measurements, hon. Ounces."

Ounces? She'd thought menstrual bleeding was a token amount, like the sip of wine at eucharist. "One or two . . . ?"

Shelley sounded annoyed. "Well, that's normal for you. You're a heavy bleeder. Maxi pad and tampon both—God forbid your husband might detect a spot. Like toxic shock's a bugaboo. You're wearing both now, I assume."

"I'm not wearing anything at all." Linda thumped herself on the head, explained, "I'm wearing a bathrobe, I mean I'm not—"

"You're sitting there, bleeding."

"I'm standing."

"Much improved. You're anxiously pacing." (She was; she stopped.) "You're whining, which means you're bouncing on the balls of your feet." (She made an elaborately sour face; she'd gone out of her way to call the one person on Earth who would make her feel like a pre-school toddler.) "Thank God you don't have carpet."

Linda stepped back, like the blue polyester had given her bare feet a static-electric shock. "Mom, that's simply gross."

"Linda, the potential's there. You do things."

"Shell—Mom, please. Don't abuse me. I'm ashamed enough, okay? You trained me to be ashamed, now I'm doing it all by myself."

"So this is why you called?"

"And I'm early. I *think*. I think I'm a week early. And . . . *I don't know*, maybe it'll get worse like a faulty valve, or—?!"

"Linda, you're not early."

She roamed with the phone, stunned by wonder. At the threshold of conspiracy, worldwide. "*How could you possibly know?*"

"Because I'm having mine."

Linda was silent. She thought of something she'd read, once, in Omni. Something so wild that Derrick even told his science-challenged wife. The simultaneous polarity reversal of non-interactive particles, all laws of logic refuted. Yet her mother sounded flatly authoritative. Any further inquiry would be the final straw. Yet mercifully, Shelley explained. "It never fails. When you're home for even a few days, we're back together. On my cycle."—never forget who's boss.

But didn't older women—? "Mom, but you're, like, fifty-three."

"Um . . . yes! Why? Does that have something to do with anything?"

What else could Derrick say? "I thought you were closer to my age."

Linda closed her eyes, stamped her foot and pulled her hair.

Shelley answered warmly. "Sure. I married your father at gunpoint in the Ozarks, drenching my teddy bear in my tears. Lin, did you call to make ridiculous jokes? Did you make a potpourri?"

"A p-p-po—?"

"-po-potpourri. You put nutmeg shavings in your herb tea, after, and get higher than a bat. Don't think I don't know these things."

"Mom, I can't deal with this. Mom, I have blood on my *hands*."

Shelley said, "Oh, Linda," pity mingled with disgust. "You've been a woman sixteen years, and never once coped with your period."

Linda was amazed. "I *always* call you?"

"You have never *not* called me. Though usually, you have a better grip—you pretend it's about something else, at first."

"When are you bringing my clothes?"

"Today. And if I see a pig-sty, I'm leaving your things on the sidewalk."

"Mom, can you . . ." Linda tried to sound nonchalant, like she'd been through thousands, not just four. " . . . bring me a few pads?"

"I cannot. You're three houses down from a corner store. Shower, dress, and walk."

Linda found herself lost. Confused. Her own heart was a stranger.

She wept into the phone. Upset, she said, "*I'm scared*."

There was silence on the other end of the line.

At last Shelley told her, "I'll bring pads. Now calm yourself. Go sit by your window and read. There, that's a nice, quiet girl."

Linda said, "Mom?" and waited, til she heard a dial tone.

The afternoon with mother was a nightmare. Shelley wasn't a drill sergeant—she was worse, a friend. Some older gal who didn't really care how Linda lived, just thought it was a scream. Even so, it was a bust. All of Linda's sins revealed, all her drawers and closets opened. Linda stood by, offering what apologies and explanations she could muster. Shelley said, "Yeah, huh?"—her daughter was *outrageous*! She pulled the spread and blanket from the bed like a coroner uncovering an unlikely corpse. Her eyes flared in delight—it was a shriek-fest! "Oh my God, you didn't strip the *bed*!"

Lin feebly dissembled: "So you could come and see . . ."

"I came. I saw. I vomited. *Eew!*"—a luscious shiver. Shelley dropped the covers, looked for something to wipe her fingers with. She wore a cling skirt, violet blouse with pearls. She looked, not merely gorgeous, but glamorous. She might have been a soap star, or an Avon district manager.

In awe of realization, Linda said, "You're going through this too."

"Going through what?" Shelley glanced curiously, thinking Linda meant a drawer or cabinet.

Linda said, "Oh, you know." Touched her tummy, waved her hand—her body, her life, the world for good measure. "This humiliating sickness. This diarrhea of the body and soul." Linda smirked—good sport.

Shelley said, "Oh. No, dear: *you* are having your period. *I* am mildly indisposed. I've not called anyone about it; no."

Shelley helped Linda unpack her things. Then they sat in the front parlor. Shelley drank her civilized dharjeeling; Linda, her notorious herb tea. Shelley studied Linda's face, at last remarked, "You're grieving."

Linda, listless, said, "I am? . . . Oh. I am, of course . . ."

"You scarcely know it. Yet I see it. So many of Derrick's mannerisms. You're keeping him inside you."—it was marvelous,

294

somehow.

Linda, sick and weary, contemplated Shelley's gaze. "I'm not Derrick. I'm your daughter."

Shelley lowered her eyes. Her finger carelessly, elegantly, swept a speck of lint off the aster-patterned cushion. "I think it hardly matters. Since in marriage you become each other anyway."

Linda felt less lost than simply sad. She could do the impossible—prove the incorporeal soul. Prove that she was Derrick. And the world would pat her hand. Tell her *Well, this happens.*

After Shelley left, Linda went out to the corner store. A totally weird feeling: *The last time I came in here I was Derrick.* She came to the counter with a one-pound bag of M&Ms, half a gallon of Heavenly Hash, a gallon of milk, a jar of peanut butter and a box of maxi pads. The boy behind the counter was myopic and obese. Linda's eyes flashed, Go ahead. Make fun of me. I dare you. The boy demured. Linda Bloom—of outlaw jacket, vixen bod and raven curls—had always been one of the more chic, mysterious people to come into this store. Not your standard housewife with kids in tow, piling kielbasa and bread next to the register. Linda didn't realize that. She fully expected the kid to tease her. Yuck, yuck, yuck, you're going to eat all that at once then make yourself throw up.

On the third day *apres le deluge*, Linda went and joined the YWCA.

The club rep was an ectomorphic young brunette. Linda didn't like her. She seemed mannish or at any rate, more masculine than Linda. She felt that signing someone up could never be complex enough. She picked Linda's brain for her potential *visa vis* complete commitment. What were her needs, exactly? To take charge of her life? Oh, she was *widowed*. A group was getting started for the newly single, and it promised to be real affirming. Linda asked about Nautilus. What?—oh yes, they had it. *All* of their programs were geared towards personal autonomy. Was she reaching out to other women? There were studies in native American life-ways, focus on interpersonal bonding. Linda asked about a StairMaster. Yes, they had one. Did she feel *safe.* Was she presently exposed to any form of harassment. There were assertiveness seminars, self-defense classes taught by and for women, exclusively. The club rep knew how important that was to Linda. Linda asked if there were any, like, light dumbbells. The club rep was laughingly flustered. Yes, for goodness' sake, they had exercise equipment—was Linda some kind of fanatic?

After an exhausting tour of the facility, Linda signed up for a year. She wasn't happy about it. Everything was dark green carpet, milky pastel walls. Except for the yardage of mirrors—potted plants redux into infinity. She hoped they'd just leave her alone, and let her swim in a pool.

Linda got a locker number and combination. She soon felt different and dumb. All the other women had Elizabeth Arden spandex suits and Polos by Ralph Lauren and elaborate toilettes in sleek suede cases. Linda had her canvas carry-all. It contained a long-sleeved Danskin top, a short blue skirt, blue socks and scruffy Reeboks. She'd put no thought into this choice. It was just what Derrick's wife wore when he made her come play Frisbee in the park.

Some of the women looked at her. When she shyly smiled back, they looked away. She had an empty feeling that she didn't have a clue.

The Nautilus instructress was a bored college girl. Cool WASP princess, paid as much attention to her hair as to her quads. "Have you ever exercised before?"

Linda, startled, said "Oh!"—a question only a girl would be asked. "Well, I've done lots of laundry. If that counts, or—?"

Princess smiled: Laundry, how charming. "You've no medical conditions?—though right, you've signed the waiver. I'm certified for CPR, just don't get any major kicks from doing it. I mean, sorry, sis—if I have to put my mouth on yours, I'm calling the paramedics and taking lunch."

Linda smiled happily, like a sweet, forgiving Christian girl who thought the diss was on somebody else.

She fell easily into her role—the ethereal airhead who didn't know push from pull. As it turned out, that was actually a problem: on some of the machines, it wasn't clear which way to go when the girl insisted "Pull. No, *pull*."

At last she languished, warm and breathless. "I did good on the leg press, at least."

Princess twisted her mouth. "Well that's all your birthing muscles," with a glance at Linda's thighs.

Linda spent twenty minutes in the wet sauna. It felt nice, to sit and melt. She felt limp and heavy and for once, exactly who she was: Susie Creamcheese, after lifting a bunch of things that were way too heavy for her.

Driving home, she passed Subway, had a vision. Tuna. Green and yellow, lettuce on fresh bread. Yet she felt sufficient. She didn't have to eat and maybe never would, again.

Next day, Linda resolved to do nothing at all—something that had a high chance of success. But Pris called. She'd exceeded her quarterly quota, and had a couple bonus days off. "Why don't you find a *boy*friend, Pris?"—yet Linda took the forty-five minute drive out to Ashland. Belt unbuckled, tape deck cranked—Axl Rose lamented having to kill the woman he used to love. Linda drove aggressively, she cut people off. A man gave her the finger and she languidly blew him a kiss. She'd heard the horror stories from the heartland: male motorists running women drivers off the road, dragging them out of their cars, beating them. Linda wasn't scared of things like that anymore. If it happened to her—hopefully on an overpass—she'd just return to the spot some moonlit night in her wedding dress, with a bouquet of dead roses. She'd kiss a sixteen wheeler and they'd find a note pinned to her corsage. *Death will not refuse me and He'll never let me go.* What was so hard about that?

At Priscilla's now-familiar cottage, they decided to go for a walk. It was apparently something they often did, when they were young. It was something Derrick's wife used to ask if they could do. Derrick didn't feel that it was normal, and a year or so into their marriage, she stopped asking.

They went to a nature center, with trails around a pond. Another nice day in the Winter That Wasn't; the sun had warmth, the earth had smells.

The nature center was literally overrun with chipmunks. Pris said, "I was reading about it. There's this, like, population explosion this year. Years from now, they'll be saying '1995—oh God, all the chipmunks.' " There seemed to be one on every rock and stump, chipping. As they walked along the trail, chipmunks dashed maniacally for cover, as if fleeing from some crime.

Two small girls were standing uncertainly near the water. Pris murmured, "Where the hell's their mother?" They stopped to talk to the girls. Their mother had gone to her car for a camera. Their Barbie had fallen into the water. They got her out, but she was wet and dirty. They were sad.

Linda knelt, and spoke to them in earnest. "Okay: first of all"—she touched the doll—"this is an evening *dress* and it's not at all appropriate for hiking. You need to get her jeans and a sweater, all right? And this is nylon, so don't put it in the dryer. Swish it with your finger in warm water, with a teeny bit of *liquid* laundry soap. Then pin it up somewhere to dry." The girls stared in awe. This tall, dark, pretty person must be Someone Else's Mommy. Whatever she said about Barbie was the indisputable cosmic truth.

Pris and Linda went their way. Linda said, "It's nice to be a woman." She nodded to herself, like it was something she was in the process of making herself believe. "To be trusted by children, like that. I never—" She halted and squeaked in shock, then both of them laughed. Two chipmunks chased each other, zig-zagging down the trail, over a rock and out of sight.

Pris said, "They are *so* mean and greedy. They're really territorial." She was cynical and worldly—all illusions of Alvin, dashed.

"You don't think they're just playing? or . . . ?" They left the pond for a trail through the woods. Gently rolling ground, with New England's ubiquitous moss-covered boulders. Hemlock and spruce, evergreen and blue; the ground, red-needled carpet. And *tick, tick, tick* from far and near. It seemed true, then—it really was a benign plague. If you took away the trees, you'd see—all Massachusetts was Chipmunk Nation.

Linda went on about babies, which finally had to do with men. Husbands and fathers, real and ideal—feelings and theories she'd recently formed. It was pretty much a peripatetic monologue: Linda talking, sometimes with passion and eloquence, Pris listening. "Lin, one thing hasn't changed: so much power in what we say. We need to bring a tape recorder. You should start a book."

Linda smiled sadly. "Oh, that's silly. It's just girl-talk."

Yet she knew it was kind of a miracle, too—that after years, divorce and death, a black-haired girl and her gentle friend still talked as they walked through the woods.

Shelley called, next day, in the late afternoon. She said, "A surprise is coming your way. Be sure to answer your doorbell."

Linda promptly guessed. "Dad is home. He's coming here." *That's not a surprise, it's an ambush.*

Shelley said, "No. But I think it's every bit as special." That music in her voice, that secret, far-off melody.

"Mom, why wouldn't I answer my doorbell?"

Another magic secret: "Lin, we understand."

They talked of trifles which bored Linda to tears, til at last she said, "I'm in the middle of doing sixteen things at once."

"Sixteen different ways of lounging around in your nightie. Lin, I'll let you go."

She supposed she'd better get dressed. She decided on her black velveteen skirt with silk-screened florals, her black Danskin top. She languished some more on the sofa, looked at some of *All My Children*, then put on gold shell earrings and a matching necklace. She spent some time on her makeup, playing with a couple of different shadows til she got pretty much what she wanted. It was something to pass the time, before she had to deal with God-knew-who. Maybe it would actually be someone nice.

She came across her curling iron, in the lower drawer of her vanity. Funny, how Derrick must have seen it twenty million times and never wondered what it was; just oh-yeah-that. Part of the miasmic void of Lin's Stuff. She still didn't know how to use it. Luckily, it was in its cardboard box, with an instruction sheet that Linda never bothered to throw out. She found the spray bottle and holding solution.

There—two long, tight curls, in front. She sneered at herself; she looked like an afghan. So, some bigger, looser curls in back. A couple on the side, which came out nice; they lay on her shoulders, black, bouncy and soft. She teased her bangs a little, too. Made eyes at her reflection. *There, I'm pretty. I really am, and I . . .*

. . . don't care, I'm so tired of this. There's no reward in this for me, there never was or will be.

She watched some more TV, did her nails. A pretty bird in a cage, serene. How many more days of this could she endure.

The doorbell rang.

She went down the stairs. The damn steep stairs. Like it was built for sailors, who'd be glad it wasn't straight-up vertical. Damn Salem, with its crazy Sweethaven architecture, its wimpy, popeyed people, its olive oil, salted scrod, its bloated Blutos in pickup trucks. This damn long skirt, she lifted her hem, not trusting it not to catch on a nail head. She opened the door.

A young man, tall and built, though he looked hungry; shaggy dark hair framed a pensive child's face. His army coat looked traveled in. His eyes were lowered, like her door mat was of interest. She thought, *Yeah, he's my type. I can believe he was part of my life, at some point.* He looked up, met her eyes. *Oh God he's really my type.* She widened her eyes, spoke a voiceless *Yes?*

"Hi, Lin."

19

She leaned into the door, half holding it open, half hiding behind it. At last she twitched her hip, *Well what?*

He said, "I don't suppose you remember me," grave like he read an improbable script.

She shyly smiled, Sorry, no.

"I heard you were in the hospital, Lin. Shelley mentioned 'memory loss'. She told me you're being very shy with everyone."

Suddenly, it was clear that her friend had no business standing out in the cold. Cold herself, she stood behind the door.

She waited.

She looked. His hands were in his coat pockets. He was standing out in the cold, since he hadn't been invited in.

She said, "Well, you . . . should come in. Please, come in."

He came in, closed the door. She fled from him, up the stairs. Thoughtful, she paused, as if safe enough halfway. "Um, these stairs, you should watch . . ." *Not my tush.* "Your step."

He said, "Your fear of heights." as though reminded of this.

They went into her apartment. He closed the door. She felt like he belonged here, like now she could relax and tell him things. "I'll take your coat. Why don't you sit down."

He looked at the parlor's furniture. He went to the chair. In a sudden dream she thought *He knows the couch is mine.*

She hung his coat, came back, stood. "It's colder today. Your coat. Feels cold." *Act human.* "Brrr."

Cold and comfort were meaningless, except a woman asked; he said, "It's nippy."

"Can I get you . . . ? Make you? Warm, tea, or . . . ?"

"Oh. I'm fine, Lin. Thank you, though."

She said, "You like me. You're someone who is very, very nice to me. I . . . sound like I'm five years old. I mean I'm . . . ?"

He looked at her, benign and calm. He already knew what she was.

She went and sat on the sofa. She watched him, blinking, alert.

"Jared, Lin. Jared Lennox."

"But you're white." She thumped her head, waxed giddy. "Sorry. I say nervous things when I'm silly. I mean, at least I'm

300

not afraid of you, 'cause then I lisp. I mean, people meet me on the phone and think I'm white. Then they meet me for real and think I'm black. Then I tell them I'm not black or white, I'm Spanish but I'm not."

She closed her mouth, put her hands in her lap. Her expression was brightly neutral, like her words were only water spilled on linen.

"Linda, I'm not 'meeting' you. I'm . . ."

She widened her eyes, unconsciously dramatic: OhmyGod, *what*?

"From Merrill. Two doors down. Lin, I'm your best friend."

They looked at each other. He was relaxed, had all the time on earth. She tilted her head, simply curious.

"Well . . . Priscilla's my best friend. She mentioned you. Once."

Jared shrugged, pleased to play Lin Has Amnesia. "Well, I'll mention her twice. I love Pris Daigle, even if she's this jealous."

"Of our . . . friendship. Of us being close. I'm just guessing." His eyes smiled at her; he rolled his hand inward, Guess some more. "—but I don't doubt you. I just can't remember. Who came first. Time-wise, which relationship—you or Pris?"

"Me, by a number of years."

"Then we were babies. Then you're like this really-real important person in my life. I mean, I feel like I should stand up. Serve you. Honor your presence. I mean, I shouldn't worry you'll undress me with your eyes if you've already—?"

"Lin, we went to Baker's Grove Elementary. I held your books as we waited for the bus, in front of your house. I was told, many times, it was officially my job to make sure you got on and off the bus with all your things."

"Was I retarded?"

"You were scared to death of school. We shared our lunches, if you had deviled ham and you wanted my peanut butter and Fluff—"

"Coleman, too? Were you there with me, at Coleman?"

"No. Sissy private school. Yuck. You can have it. Then all of a sudden, everything was 'Pris'." It took her a moment to realize, she hadn't offended her guest. These were things he'd said and felt when he was eight, or seven.

"But we were still neighbors. Friends . . . ? We . . . ?"

" . . . played hide-and-seek. Looked for things in the woods. Though we never could agree what we were looking for—wildflowers or cool-looking bugs. When it snowed, we rode your toboggan down that hill out back of your house. You would only ride in back. I was your back-seat driver's airbag."

"Jared—"

She'd started to say something, but was caught on his name.

Sitting in one of her yoga-like postures, one leg folded over her other thigh, she leaned forward slightly, like she wanted something from him.

He affirmed, "Linda."

"I'm . . . sure you're telling the truth. But it doesn't seem like I would have played with boys. My mom was strict. I had to be real feminine." From her very own recent experience, she told him, "It sucked."

"Tell me about it. It was all I could do, getting you to come out of your house, most days. You'd hide behind the door, like you did a minute ago. Only then, it took half an hour. I guess we've made some progress."

She said, "You trained me. To talk. To come out."

"And you trained me how to ask."

Linda was happy. "Can't I get you something? Coffee?"

" . . . and you trained me to endure your playing hostess."

"Then die of thirst. Whatever." She felt playful. She'd found someone inside her whom she hadn't known was there—a little girl who wanted to fly kites and look for flowers. Or ride a toboggan, safely in back. "Did we do boy-things, then? Or girl-things?"

He looked solemn, like he had a sudden headache; like girl-things once were the bane of his existence. "I recall some arrangement involving turns. 'What I want today, what you want tomorrow.' You'd have us read books in your room, I'd bring my Batman comics. I'd get us out looking for fossils down at the old quarry. Which you'd try to turn into a picnic. You'd bring your parasol and plastic tea set. Made me carry them, since you had your dolls."

"Did you play with my dolls?"

"Yeah, I played with your dolls like you helped me build my go-cart. Wouldn't even hand me a wrench."

She said, "I see. I *feel* that—I'm feminine, with you. You're definitely the man. Jared, try to understand this: my mind is blank. My *body* remembers. Like with . . ." *What was his name? Redbeard/Malibu.* "Scott Laska."

"Oh my. Lin. You were *terrified* of him. Which was hysterical, since he wasn't a bad kid. I mean, he was rough. His dad's still in prison. But I had a beer with him, just last November. But when we were kids you even got *me* thinking he was this villain. Like that time up at the Baldridges'. I told him, if he squirted you with that water gun, he was going to eat it. Remember me pinning his arms with my knees, trying to get the muzzle into his mouth?"

Linda rocked back, clapped her hands. She laughed.

"Jared, so when did this end?—I mean, the relationship. Ours."

She knew his answer even as he gave it—what any man

would tell the girl he played with as a child. "We never stopped being friends, Lin. We just haven't been in touch."

He said, "You went to Franklin, I went to Springfield Community. You were in Vermont, I was still in the area. We saw each other during breaks; we wrote, though that dropped off. Felt kinda sappy. 'Dear Linda, Love Jared'—we were at that age, enough's enough. Once you met Derrick, I was gone from the picture. And Lin, I'm sorry. I'm really, truly sorry."

"That Derrick's dead?"

She touched her fingers to her mouth—she'd made Derrick sound like yesterday's trash.

"Jared, I feel awful. I'm your childhood friend—God, whatever else—sweetheart, or"—she went painfully tender, "your first, and I'm treating you like a total stranger. I feel what all of this means and I just can't connect. I feel horrible."

He gazed at the floor; he wouldn't fake indifference. He'd been there with her through it all—the spats with Pris, the bad grades in math, the haircut that made her look like a boy. The captain of the football team who dated her once and never called again—Jared knew the taste of Linda's tears.

She gestured, helpless; she did the best she could. "So what are you up to, these days?"

"About five-eleven, still.—oh. I live in Ipswich. I'm a mason, and I sculpt. Statuary. Mostly commercial."

"Well . . ." *This* should *be personal.* "Are you married? I mean, I want that for you. Happiness."

He shrugged. "Been in and out of relationships. Mainly caught up in my work. My sculpture's not all commercial; I work for my money all day, work for my heart all night. Drawn to Bohemian types, but urban sophisticates just . . . I don't know. Spiritually tepid."

"Jared, I need to ask you something. Please be nice."

"Lin, just ask. If it's something you need, or want, that I can—"

"Have we been seeing each other." She immediately cleared her throat, like the utterance had just been an amazingly articulate cough.

When she finally looked his way, he was staring at her, curious, like he saw a white rabbit with a vest and pocketwatch.

He said, "I doubted it, at first—you 'have amnesia'; right. Even though Shelley told me, 'There's something really the matter'. Lin, it's me. I. Jared. We haven't been having an adulterous affair. We haven't been in touch, these last six years."

A car alarm went off outside; at the far end of the street, it seemed. Linda only noticed it when it stopped.

She said, "I'm just curious. Have we ever . . . ?" She twitched her shoulder, a reluctant coquette. "You know."

"Hon, I was your first. Yes."

303

She lowered her eyes. "I'm sorry I don't remember."

"Don't remember your first kiss. I feel I've been used."

She brooded on how to respond. Then firmly took a sofa pillow, threw it at him. He didn't bother to catch it; he took it stoically, in the neck.

"I'm sure there was more after that." She looked at him thoughtfully, played with her hair. Calmly instructed, "Tell me."

"What's to tell. One time I recall, we'd just seen *West Side Story*. At the Merrill Cinema. Third and fourth-run movie classics, for a buck. We lived there, Lin. Those two seats in the gallery, just under the projectionist's booth, were Reserved For Lin and Jared." She gently shook her head: Don't remember anything, don't remember that. "I mean, we were *friends*. So far as tumbles in the clover, Pris and I were more—"

"Oh God. Just tell me about the movie."

"We were thirteen, I think. We were *playing*. I was Tony, you were Maria. We sat on the steps of your patio, since your house didn't have a fire escape."

She slyly winked. "Bet you got your finger wet."

"Linda Meredith."

"Did you tell your friends?"

"You *were* my 'friends'."

"Oh." She considered this. Decided it was nice, and crinkled her nose at him. "What about when we were older? Were we ever a couple?"

"We talked about it, once or twice. I mainly made you giggle. You didn't think I could be serious. I guess I doubted it, too."

"So we dated. Other people. And that was quite all right."

"Not totally. I think we were emotionally possessive. 'You can do whatever you want with Pris, so long as it's not a date'—you remember telling me that?" Tired of denying things, she simply rolled her eyes. "Then that time I finally got a date with Laurie Parnell. It was supposed to be the turning point of my life. Up til then, you'd said I was only your friend because you actually knew Laurie Parnell. You gave me your hand, to be kissed: 'This hand *shared a hymnal* with Laurie Parnell.' Then after the historic date, you 'couldn't find time' for me til it fizzled. About a week. Then you were my sister in misery, assuring me I was too good for 'that stuck-up twit'. It was funny, how we were."

Linda had perfect objectivity; what was "funny" to Jared was plain in her sight. "We *were* a couple. Always." Her voice was soft with wonder.

"Well . . . we were kids. We were *close*. You have total amnesia. I wish it would go away."

"So, all these years. All these *years*: you've been living, basically, just up the road. Sculpting. Building walls."

"I got back from the Persian Gulf three years ago."

"Oh my *God*. Jared, why?"

"Back in college, I was one of those 'weekend warriors'. National Guard. Thought I was the cat's ass, at the time. Well, guess what: that made me a reservist. They wanted a lot of us over there. They firmly requested the honor of my company."

"Was it awful?"

He made a wry face, but his eyes clouded; he wouldn't tell her anything. "I was in a rifle battalion. The whole thing was mainly . . ." In female-friendly terms: " . . . planes and missiles and stuff. The Iraqis, the ones we saw, they . . . came to us on their knees. From the bunkers. They were nerve-shocked. Because of what we did with the missiles and stuff. They were weeping, begging . . . the normal human reaction. I mean, *we* came unwrapped, and we were miles to the rear."

"And I didn't send you anything. No basket of fruit, or . . . I just feel unpatriotic."

"Lin, you didn't know I was over there."

"Oh. Well, now that I know, I'm appalled. Don't ever do that again."

"Deal."

She said, "I never told Derrick about you."

"I hope not. I had no part in your lives. You grew up, hon. You became a big girl, with your own husband and your own life, and that made me very happy." Jared glanced at the window, cold urban outside. That was where he belonged. Her life was her own; he'd only stopped by for a visit.

Linda shook her head; that didn't seem right.

She said, "You want to tell me something."

"I do?"

"Oh, cut the crap. Don't tease me. Linda's house, Linda's rules." She guessed: "Same as always."

"You were always so curious, Linda. That was my last resort, to get you out of the house. I'd tell you I had a secret. And you'd come right out the door."

"What was the secret?"

" 'Fooled you.' "

"What *is* the secret?"

"There are no more secrets. We're not children anymore."

Her mind drew blanks, but her heart held answers. Even the logic of giddy adolescence—of running barefoot through backyards on a dewy summer morning, to tell a silly secret and to share a piece of toast. "Yes, we are."

"Lin, I've never gotten over you."

It was very calmly stated; she received it in perfect peace. She hadn't really been there, yet she had. The yellow house, the oak tree, the tire swing, the lawn. *Race you back to your place, on your mark, get set—*

She lowered her head, nodded—a request for verification. "Me?"

He looked at her in mild, bland amazement. He'd opened the bag and now he watched, a jeweled and snow-white feline melt into the shadows.

She blinked; this was simply hard to understand.

She repeated, simply incredulous: "With *me*?"

"I thought it was crazy, too. I mean, the implications. Since I've known you all my life, it means I've . . . always felt this way?—I mean, it just seemed nuts. But as years passed, and it wouldn't go away . . ."

"Jared . . . okay: let's work through this. I was basically, what?—your sister. So this is like an incestuous bonding. I wouldn't let you be with girls. You don't *want* to be with girls, it's like . . ."

"Very much otherwise, Linda. I've connected with women more deeply, desired them with more passion, than other men do—I'm certain of this. Because of my experience, growing up with you. Being close to you, your friend. There was nothing wrong with any of those women. They just weren't you."

"Jared . . . okay: you're in love with your childhood. I represent your childhood. I understand, since I feel the same kind of—"

"You 'represent' my childhood. My childhood was you. Lin, if there's a meaningful distinction, I am blind."

"But Jared, that's so deep. Is that normal?"

"I don't know what 'normal' is; I don't think it's *wrong*. Except that I'm confusing and upsetting you."

"I'm confused, yes. I'll tell you when I'm upset."

"I should leave."

"I'll tell you when you should leave."

They sat and looked at each other—he calm deep within, she deep in thought. She abruptly asked, softly, "When did this start?"

"In summer. Our parents were playing tennis. It was late in the day. We stood on a lawn, just looked at each other. Very much like now. Only we'd just met. 'Jared, this is Linda. She's very shy. Be nice.' That's how I learned what shy was. You were *serious*. You watched my eyes and wouldn't speak. Yet you wanted to do things. Whatever I suggested, wherever I led. You followed."

"But you said we were very young."

"We were. I don't think we'd started school, yet."

She said, "But that's so uncommon. I'm sure I've never heard of such a thing. You had a crush on me when I was *five*?"

"As we grew up, as you did things to piss me off . . . well, you were just Linda. But the basic way I felt about you was established. I never knew what it was. Since I never knew anything different."

"I suppose I should be touched." She anxiously corrected herself: "Not now. I mean, I was. Not physically. Or you did, but I mean right now, I'm emotionally flattered. Sweet of you. Nice."

He thinly said, "No problem"; he expected nothing more.

Linda asked, "What about me? Did I say things, or share the same feeling?"

"Always. Never. Lin, we were kids. We made our hearts up as we went along. We saw people kiss on TV—Ew, that's gross; you agreed. Let's go play nurfball.—Yeah. Then I'd write you a letter, asking for 'a lock of your hair'. And get a letter back, from two doors down: a little black ringlet, 'sealed with a kiss'. Then next day I'd blow it off: Girls, *ugh*. And you'd agree: Boys, *ick*."

She said, "Well, sure; we were kids. But when we were older, teens . . . I know how I was: so passive. It's hard for me to believe that nothing, you know, happened."

He assured her, "You were passive. Yet you were emotionally dynamic, like your mom. You were someone I talked with, face to face—my sister, my conscience. My peer. We shaped each other's values."

She softly asked, "You know the Lord and all, right?"

She widened her eyes, aware of who she was and what she asked—the question of a passive girl, selective of her friends.

"Linda, I've been bankrupt. Shot at. Broken-hearted. How you do that without Jesus . . . well, I'm not the one to ask."

He told her more about their youth. "All those summer days, I came over to swim in your pool. My mind was on stunts off the diving board. Playing frisbee. Mountain Dew and tunes. Though you never got me liking Joni Mitchel. Those were my conscious thoughts. Yet I remember your swimsuit, your last two summers before college. The turquoise bikini with the French-cut bottom." Linda blinked. She knew what "French-cut" was—she'd learned five days ago, at Filene's Basement. "I didn't want to ask my dad about it . . . I talked to my mom. She told me, the feelings I had about your body were all right, but I should always relate to you as a whole person. As my friend. I guess I learned to do that at a pretty early age." He shrugged, since he'd explained it all—why nothing happened then, why nothing would happen now.

Linda sat and looked at him. She gestured her hand, Look at you. He wanted nothing but to speak his heart, and that was done.

She didn't speak, and he thought that meant they were out of words. He started to get up.

She said, "No—sit." Having been treated as a dog by Shelley, she was able to put the shoe on someone else's paw.

Jared motioned, Here I stay. Linda said, "My, you're so

307

docile."

"I take that as a compliment. Since you only boss people you're very secure with. Me, your father. And Derrick, no doubt."

She said, "Oh, I ruled him completely; yes."

She fell thoughtful. Deeply thoughtful.

She realized what had happened to her, these past two weeks. She realized how strange it was, how lonely, inexplicable. She realized it was a riddle, and the answer was suddenly plain.

"Lin, I shouldn't have come. I've disturbed you. I should go."

"Jared, did you ever hit me?"

He looked at her, calm.

"Or yell? Did you ever turn cold or fierce with me? Were you ever cruel to me in any way?"

It was the question of the ages—God's reckoning with Adam, How did the woman fare. "Lin, once we met some friends of yours—some girls—at the Twin Oaks Mall. You left me to go with them."

She languidly said, "I'm sorry."

"No: they'd just bought a record you wanted to listen to. Keith Green, and you'd been waiting for it to come out. You'd had this funny religious/romantic thing for him. Whatever stage that is in a Christian woman's life, when her feelings towards Christ are that personal. That you think some man is Whom you love, clean-shaved in a silk shirt."

Linda said, "I remember," since Shelley had chided her about it. "I was seventeen."

"You ditched me, but you couldn't have been nicer about it. You explained how much it meant to you, to listen to this album. God knows, we shared that language, of all-consuming yearnings; you had every right to be understood. Your friends were calling you along, their ride was out front, it was now-or-never, so you went. You turned around to look at me; you were torn between two things. Decisions were always so hard for you, Lin."

"That doesn't excuse my behavior—not for one moment. Jared, if I didn't apologize then, I'm—"

"Well, that night you called me on the phone. You were scared, so you tried to skip over the incident. You talked about the record, how great it was, then I reminded you what you did. And over the phone, I heard—or felt—that soft intake of breath. I knew it so well, Linda. Like when I pulled sharp turns with the toboggan. And Lin, so far as punishing you, that was more than enough. But then I said, I 'wasn't interested in being your friend anymore', and hung up."

Linda frowned. "That *was* pretty mean."

"You remember."

"No, I don't. I'm *glad* I don't. You were a positive prick."

308

"Shelley called me, later that night."

Linda brightened. "Oh, wow! Were you scared?"

" 'Scared'. Lin, my mother's words—'Mrs. Bauer's on the phone, she'd like to speak with you'—are forever etched in fear on my psyche."

Linda arched her back, shook out her curls. "Cool. So then what?"

"Shelley asked me what happened, what I'd said. And I knew I was doomed—she'd graciously offered to hear my side, and I didn't have one. So I broke, I said I'd been mean to you, heartless, I was sorry as sin and it would never, ever happen again. But she just repeated"—a fair evocation of Shelley's silken arrogance: " 'What happened. What did you say', and I told her. She didn't make a sound, til I'd finished, and waited, and told her, 'That's it.' Then she just said 'Oh.—well, Linda went up to her room and cried for an hour.' "

Linda acknowledged, "That's something I would have done."

"She told me you were not to be treated this way. She asked me if I understood, and that concluded our conversation."

"Way to go, Mom."

"I was devastated. Life without your approval was meaningless. I felt empty and dark inside."

"Jared, so did I. That's why I cried in my room."

"Not to over-dramatize, but I prayed it wasn't too late. I rode my bike to Star Market—nine dark country miles, there and back. With flowers and a very-sorry card."

"No Chessman cookies?"

"Why don't you tell the story, then. Lin, you do remember."

"But I really don't."

"After thirteen years, you still hurt from it."

"Not as much as you. I have moral superiority."

"When you stood at the top of the stairs, so distant and cool, when I asked if I could come up and you said you weren't sure if I should—Lin, the bottom fell out of my world."

"I was such a wuss; I'm sure I ended up apologizing to *you*."

"That time, no. You were very strict with me. You wanted to make it clear, what I'd done to you was not allowed. You came down to the landing . . . you said you'd only forgive me if I went down on one knee."

"Oh my God."

"You told me, 'Someday you'll be married, and you'll have to obey your wife. You need to learn this, Jared.' " He tried not to laugh, recalling this now.

"And that was the worst thing you ever did to me? You never hit or yelled?"

"Linda, we grew up on Longmeadow Road. Substance abuse was eating green apples. The TV went off at seven-thirty, each and every night, unless it was *The Waltons*. 'Hitting you'. Lin,

309

you've been out in the real world too long."

"I still watch *Nick at Nite.*"

"That day, Lin, I tried to teach you something—don't leave your friend, no matter what. I was a bad teacher. But you endured my lesson. Furious, yet gentle—you took the lecture stick from my hand. You taught me something greater: never to be cruel. We raised each other, grew likeminded. Linda never yelled or hit and neither did her friend."

"But I went off on Derrick. I screamed as loud as I could, and threw my shoe at him. We'd stand and fight and I'd have my hand raised for fifteen minutes, saying, 'I'll slap you, I really will.' " In fairness to herself: "I never did, though."

Jared said, "Yeah, well; you probably got Derrick to buy the same deal you sold me: that was just 'sharing how you felt.' " He looked at the window. Steel-grey and violet of overcast dusk; the moment seemed timely, to go his way lightly. "Well kid, it's getting late . . ."

She said, "You're not leaving." She flicked a speck of lint off her knee. Black velveteen's one drawback: a lint magnet. "Don't mind that I've been blunt."

"You spoke on impulse. Girls are allowed. Your mom has my number."

"And girls are allowed to insist. Mrs. Bloom, neé Bauer, cares to have a word with you. That means, you may not leave."

"How am I supposed to answer that?"

"Oh, that's right—you've never been married. You don't know how to handle a woman. The correct response is, 'Yes dear. Anything you say.' "

Outside, some youths were shouting in the street. A bottle broke. Up towards the Gallows Hill projects, a cop car wailed its siren like the battle-cry of some unending war, Brutal Order vs. Savage Chaos. Two people from Longmeadow Road, in Merrill, sat in an upstairs apartment, in a room a gentle woman called her "parlor." They were like a diaspora—two immigrants, finding each other in a cold, unfriendly land. Like Esther and Mordecai, holding hands in the barbarous bazaar of pagan Susa: *What do you hear of your mom's arthritis . . . ?*

"It would be indecent if we didn't go to dinner."

He carefully cleared his throat. "Lin, I stopped in to let you know I'm around. If you need anything, financially or—"

"I mean right this minute. I'm starving." That was true. She hadn't eaten all day. "I'm a lady of the Nineties; I'm asking you out on a date." Emphasis on *lady*; she demured—"Telling you to ask me."

"Lin, I never met your husband. But if he loved you, and you loved him, I admire him already. I'm not about to snatch his widow."

"Jared: let me explain something to you. I'm my husband's

310

widow. I'm in charge of his affairs. Financial, spiritual and emotional. All right?—I'm qualified to make his decisions. So far as Derrick's wishes go, so far as him, him, him not approving or whatever, that is my concern, not yours. Besides, this isn't the Nineteenth Century. I don't have to wear black for the next three years. My mom even said."

"Linda, doll, you're full of grief. Life's not this dramatic."

"Linda-Doll is over her grief. She knows she is; it was real hard work. Pull her string, she says 'I want . . .' " She was ravenous, he was paying. " ' . . . steak and lobster.' "

"Do you want your childhood, Linda? Do you want your same old friend? I've spoken my heart to you, Linda. I can deliver no less than I've said."

She took an audacious guess. "Remember when we were teens—all those times we were each other's last-resort date? Did we ever tell each other, No, I'd rather go stag? Doe? Whatever?"

"I better go fix you an herb tea. Spike it with Sleepytime, so you pass out."

"Jared, I'm asking because I know: if I ever really need, if I ever really want, you never will refuse me."

"Lin, this isn't fair. I'm the one who had to return your overdue library books, because you were sure they'd arrest you. I had to pay $2.85 to hand over *Charlotte's Web* and *The Victorian Dollhouse*. I'm the one you called at one a.m. because you couldn't decide what to wear to Coleman's senior prom. I came over barefoot, half-asleep, stood under your window where you posed like Juliet. Timid as a little bird and lovelier in lilac; I said you were a vision and I went back home to bed. You 'know I won't refuse you'. What kind of loaded deck."

"So where'd you have in mind?"

Jared barely sighed, accepting the man's role—even being "told to ask," against his better judgment, he had to serve it up with all the trimmings. "Coming down Webb Street. On the wharf. On the cobbled stretch, where the scallopmen dock—"

"This travelogue isn't romantic."

"—I saw a place, Tully's. Looks nice. They say they have twin lobsters."

"Does that mean they're related?"

"No. It means they're affordable."

Linda dismissed that. "Oh, you can afford anything. Do I look all right, or should I dress?"

"It's casual, Lin. Like Fred's Folly, down at Bahre's Corner."

Dreamy-eyed, she shook her head. "Is that in Winnie-the-Pooh?"

"No, it's in Merrill."

"Oh. All right, I'll get my coat . . ."

At the foot of the stairs, she indicated the door. "Open that for me, please." Outside, the night was mild. There was a light, cold fog—Boston's March mist, scented with sea and something like mint, like the Irish City really was on Galway Bay. The neighborhood was wide awake—blue and yellow squares of light, some with curtains, some without; electric pictures on weathered walls.

As they walked up the sidewalk to his Volvo, he explained, "I had a not altogether pleasant experience, few days ago . . . opened the door for a woman, she nearly tore my lungs out. Said she wasn't my 'chattel'."

Linda watched the sidewalk. Lifting the hem of her velveteen skirt, free hand poised for balance, she minced over a fault in the cement. "Oh, she said that because she was. Your chattel." Softly, in awe: "Why do you drive a *Volvo*?"

He opened the car's door for her. Linda was moved by compassion. "Don't ask me how I know but just believe I really do: men take women way too hard."

But true or false, this insight was expressed in Linda's voice: a soft contralto murmur.

He touched the small of her back, guiding her in to sit. He asked, "How *would* you know?"

The restaurant, up close, looked a little more upscale than Jared had thought at a glance. Linda *ts*ked. "Well, I could have told you. Der and I came here a million times." In the parking lot, Jared got a sports jacket and tie out of his trunk. Linda waited in the car. This was Greater Boston: only designated street people were allowed to disrobe in public. She didn't want to see him get arrested, so she wouldn't watch.

The restaurant was an old house—circa 1800 or so, though in Salem that's hardly distinctive. It wasn't a very fancy old house, anyway. The interior was all these huge tarred oak beams and rafters; the floor was blackened brick. It felt and smelled like the lemon-polished interior of some historic factory—like a museum, Cape Anne's Oldest Bean Cannery or something. To make matters worse, the owners thought it was *haute decor* to have "antiques" perched up in the rafters. Some of these "antiques" were just obsolete household appliances. Like a wooden hand loom; specks of paint traced the ghost of *Harris & Co. of Ohio* in garish carnival letters. As if anyone wanted to sit and eat over-priced prime rib with a loom looming over them like the sword of Damocles. It was also just plain stupid, like diners of the Twenty-First Century would sit and nosh with Maytags and Hoover uprights floating over their heads. Linda shared all these impressions, and told her friend the chowder here was a must.

In contrast to the cold, hard, black decor, the table linens were sky-blue. They felt like satin. Linda liked them.

There was a fire going in a shaped-stone fireplace. It looked like part of the original house—like something people used to

312

make themselves warm, never thinking it would someday be part of some bistro's rustic ambiance.

Linda ordered a martini, asked that Jared have one too. He said he'd pass, he wasn't much of a drinker. Linda insisted, and he ordered one to please her. Barely sipped it through the meal.

Linda ordered scallops, in garlic butter. She asked, first, if garlic would bother him. Jared shook his head. They'd swapped deviled ham for Fluff in a school cafeteria. He'd eaten a sandwich he didn't like, from a Mary Poppins lunch box. "Order scallops, Lin."

Though dark outside, it was early yet; there were only two other diners, another couple. She was a snooty-looking blonde, reminded Linda of Melanie Griffin. She slipped Linda a jaded glance, Oh-who-let-you-in. The couple seemed giddy and stiff; first date, it seemed.

The food came. Linda was quiet. She listened, took small and occasional bites. Jared spoke to her calmly, softly, explaining her feelings for her. Linda felt beautiful, bathed in warmth. She smiled more than she usually did, knowing that she didn't have to.

She lay on the sofa, there in her front parlor. He sat in the chair. They'd been that way, talking, for a timeless stretch, late evening. An old, familiar pattern; teenage ennui, supine boredom. Though they were no longer teens, overwhelmed by Life's possibilities. They were both almost thirty, and were simply tired.

Linda was quiet, now—gazing at the wall, her gentle eyes unfocused.

"Lin, so quiet."

"I'm having a dream."

"I know that, dear."

She said, "I don't want to embarrass you. So I'll change a few things. This dream's about a man named . . . Jareth. That we have a sort of domestic arrangement. That I would come and live with him."

"Um . . . Lin, before you—"

"*Shh*; it's mine. I'd ask to be part of his household, and he would say, all right. But he would be proper and distant. But I would be so grateful. I'd kiss his hand, til he gently pushed me back. And told me what I should be cleaning.

"So I would clean everything always, and cook all his meals, and serve him. And of course do all his laundry.—I'm good at that, you know. At doing laundry."

"That was your chore, at home. You hated it."

"I have money coming to me from the insurance. But since he's master of the house, I'd give it all to him. He would let me sleep on the sofa. After I'd waited on him at table, he'd let me eat his table scraps. Except when I was very good—then, he'd give me a piece of cheese and bread. I'd eat it from his hand. So grateful. Then I'd say, I shouldn't get your sofa dirty. I should just have some newspapers in a corner. And he could feed me something cheap, from a big bag. Purina Cat Chow, and I'd love it. I'd kneel and watch him eagerly, while he poured it in my dish. And I shouldn't use his table. I'd ask him, Shan't I simply eat it from the floor on hands and knees, as I should also lap my milk? Shall I be so jealous of the cat, to flatter myself more deserving? He'd consider it, then tell me, it was fairer to the cat indeed and not at all unmaidenly. And I shouldn't use his bathroom, since we know I'm rather dirty—I should have a box of sand, outside. I'd change it myself."

"You're being very silly."

"No, I really would. I wouldn't expect *him* to change it. But he'd praise me, for being so neat. I'd kneel at his feet, my eyes downcast, unworthy. Then he'd stroke my hair. Then this is the real thrilling part: he'd gently lift my chin. Bid me rise, and he'd unlace my bodice, while I gazed at him in melting adoration." Jared's silence was a strong critique. "But that's not uncouth. That's the noble and uplifting end. He bares my breasts and fondles them—my womanhood, redeemed. No longer just a servant . . . oh come on, it's just a story."

"Is it slightly masochistic, do you think?"

"But that's how I am. Purely submissive. And it's spiritually pure for a woman to desire this. I mean, just in her fantasies. It involves no hurting or meanness. I'd want you to be kind.—*him* to be kind." She absently remarked, "Oh, you don't need to hear this."

After a while, he said, " 'A domestic arrangement'. I could just say, that's outrageously presumptuous on your part."

She glanced at him. Eyes wide, voice soft, she said, "You'd never."

"For years you regaled me, for hours on end, with these romantic fantasies. Everyone from Richard Gere to your English teacher at Coleman. Back then, they were PG-13; they mainly just bored the shit out of me. But I also bristled inwardly—like, what am I, your girlfriend? Not a man, just Jared? I consoled myself by thinking, while everyone else was panting after angel-food Laurie Parnell, I had the only dark, exotic beauty in our zip code, all to myself. Though now that I'm finally your *film bleu* star, I guess I shouldn't complain."

"Jared, you're right. How dare you."

He reflected, "I'm *sort* of the same . . . I always put the woman on a pedestal. My compassion is for her frailty, her vulnerability. But my passion is her strength."

Linda said, "I guess that counts me out."

He only smiled.

He looked at his watch. Linda asked, "Is it late?"

"Twelve o'clock. I turn into a pumpkin."

"Oh, okay. Good night."

Jared got his coat from the closet—the padded jacket issued for cold Arabian Desert nights, now stripped of insignia and practical, with all its pockets. He put it on, stood absently but methodically patting himself down. "Is something the matter, Jared?"

"No, I just can't find my keys."

Langorous on the sofa, Linda said, "I have them."

"Oh. Thank God. Well . . . let me see."

"No, 'cause you've been drinking."

Jared, stone sober, studied her impassively.

"Lin, I don't know how you've changed, these past six years. This childhood reunion's not without romantic aspects. But the Hollywood denouement's not on the bill. Now, madam, please: my keys."

"Jared, no. I'd rather you not. And you can have the bed. I'll be fine out here. But drinking, driving—no way. You know I'm right."

He squinted at her, curious. "Linda, why are you doing this?"

On her aster-patterned divan, she twitched her hip, ambivalent.

"I have to meet buyers, tomorrow at eight. Lin, I've got a *life*."—not the one they'd shared. He'd seen her in tantrums and tears, in cotton nightie and turquoise bikini—she was caramel, pure sweetness, from the top of her black hair to the soles of her brown feet and yet regardless, it was time for him to leave.

She got up, approached him with an insouccient roll of her hips. She held his keys—a toy she'd found. "Your life in the palm of my hand."

"All right, Lin. Thank you." He smiled, and held out his palm. She pulled them out of his reach. "Okay. Lin, I'm going to take them, now. Don't be startled, I'll just—"

She held the keys behind her back, held him at bay with her hand. She jangled the keys at him; he gently took her wrist. She took the keys with her other hand and held them out of reach. This went on for some moments. Her dark eyes gleamed with fun; she breathed small gasps of triumph and delight. It became a gentle tussle; she shoved him, playful. "Okay Lin, that was fun. Darling, I could *lose an account*. Now please."

"No!"

He took her shoulders—love, not force. "I need them. Now."

She stared, stunned and lovely, like he'd said *you* instead of *them*.

"No fair." She twirled back to the sofa, lightly bounced, lay on her side. "Linda's Safe Zone. My house, my rules."

"You know I won't get angry. But I'm not enjoying this."

"I'll give you your keys back. After I've made you breakfast. Do you still mean what you said to me, before?"

"No fade-to-bedroom,—dim-lit-body-parts; I am so sorry."

"I should slap you hard. No, what you said before: that four-letter word that rhymes with . . . *dove*" she said, with total-body luxuriance, like it was a Barry White lyric. She burst into giggles.

He leaned against the doorpost—a man who bared his soul and then did not repeat himself.

She said, "We must have been a sight. Me, at the top of the stairs. Implacable, a woman scorned. Juno despising Aeneas."

"Well, you broke my heart. You weren't exactly formidable."

"Tell me again, how you felt."

"I'll do even better—how I feel now. That childhood seems long, we look back and it was brief. The hours we had were golden and few. I can't believe I almost cut them short, by telling you I wouldn't be your friend."

Linda softly said, "But that's so sweet."

"Lin, sometimes I think: if I could just go back. Just step out my door and be seventeen again, with the summer of '82 about to unfold. If I could run barefoot through the Binette's backyard and meet you in the apple orchard . . ."

"Here we are."

Outside, some kid laid on his horn. A window opened, an old man yelled. *Hey you punks ever hear of sleeping at night*?!

She nodded, Yes: the orchard.

Then dismissed him. "I'm all set. I'll get myself a blanket."

He said, "There's a sofa or something, in the den?"

"Oh, pardon me—is there something icky about a girl's bed? I'll bet you're still a virgin."

He gave her a brooding look. The zeal of adolescence had long since been absorbed, by miles of stone walls and a perfect legion of commercial sculptures. "Sofa's fine."

"Jared, one more thing. That time I forgave you. Made you promise to be nice to me forever, evermore. Wasn't that almost like . . . ?"

" . . . when the football captain ditched you. We were upstairs in your room. You cried, and made me hold you. Said it wasn't him, you were just lonely, sick of always being lonely. That was the one and only time your mom ever knocked. 'I'd like this door to be open'—she couldn't believe it herself. Did you know what you were doing to me, Linda? Your tears, your arms around my neck? The warmth, the scent of your bosom? We were only kids, but did you know?"

"That I was claiming you?—I wasn't. I was being good. Like someone coming back to church, I knew where I belonged. I was saying 'Yes, you're Jared. You're the one for me'—obedient to who I was. Loyal to our friendship."

316

"Lin, I'll see you in the morning."

"I'll make you breakfast, anything you like. Tell me now, so I can plan."

Good-nights were already said, he went down the hall.

She waited, gave him time to get settled.

Such an inconsiderate hostess. She got a quilt and pillow from her bedroom closet, brought them to the den.

Jared was already lying on the broken-down couch. Poised for a long and lonely night; sleep was nowhere near him. He saw Linda, and stood up. "Here, I'll take those . . . nice of you, Lin."

Linda didn't give him the things. She fluffed the pillow, set it just so on the arm of the couch. Neatly spread the quilt and she folded it, just so. She smoothed her hand in circles over the staticky synthetic, fretting softly to herself. "Kind of itchy . . . to me, at least. You know I have such sensitive skin. Everything of mine is hypoallergenic. Salt-free, low sodium . . . but you work with stones all day. You wrestle with rocks, out in the sun. You probably take salt pills like correcting a poison-poor diet. Oh dear, you need someone to care for you . . ."

"Linda, you're in mourning. I feel for you, I see. But it's enough. Please go to bed."

She turned down the hem, having made a proper little bed. She faced him. This was the hard part. She knew what she intended, knew it wasn't really possible . . .

She came to him, swift and softly urgent, like a woman who wakes with a fever and he stopped her, held her from him. Soothed her as a man would calm his sister, or an aunt who wakes in the night, unwell and obsessed. "Yes, dear. Everything's okay. Everyone's all right."

"Jared, all my longing for my childhood, my grief for lost joy, I never told Derrick, I didn't know myself—Jared, it was you I missed—"

"Linda, I told *you* that. You're playing Follow Jared."

"—life had no meaning, it ended when I grew up, because I'd lost—"

He held her fingers. His lips formed words: *Calm . . . down.*

She gazed at him wetly, bit her lip, too big a girl for tizzies.

He nodded, like he'd gotten a subtle joke. "Lin, we've read this script before."

She stared at him, bewildered. Then, enlightened, sighed. "*Oh* . . . okay. When we were little, I wouldn't come out and play. But when we got older, the problem was endless good-nights. Out on that same porch, I guess. I wouldn't come off—I was stuck to you, like tape. Serves you right, for playing with girls. Big sissy."

"Aside from that last remark, there's nothing wrong with your memory."

"What were my excuses? That we'd seen a scary movie, and

317

I was upset? That my mother had been mean to me—'I won't go back in that woman's house'?—I'll bet I came up with some winners."

"Go to your room. Get in your bed, and go to sleep."

"Jared, all childishness aside—I feel badly. That you opened up, made yourself vulnerable, and I wasn't really receptive. I think we should discuss our feelings, more. I'll make some tea."

"Young lady, you will go to bed."

"Okay. Good-night kiss." She touched his chin. She kissed his lips.

When she didn't stop, he took her shoulders, to show that he would move her back. She took his hands and placed them on her hips. There, to hold the kettle of her yearning. To hold the flower pot and bless her petal lips with dew. She tried her tongue—Enough; he pushed. She offered some resistance, but of course she wasn't firm. She was only stuck on him like tape.

He held her at arm's length. If she couldn't have her way, she'd plead. "Jared, I'm so lonely."

"Linda, this is cruel."

"I agree."

"It's cruel of *you*. To try and keep the ball in play." She'd seen the ping pong table, folded and gathering dust in the Bauers' basement. "Queen of the Unending Volley. Victory through boredom. Not tonight."

"Just tell me, then."

"I love you, Lin. Good night."

"That's how I'm being cruel?"

"Sleep tight."

"You're kicking me out of your bedroom because you love me?"

"And don't let the bedbugs bite." He took her shoulders, to turn her towards the hallway.

She wouldn't budge. She lowered her head, looked thoughtfully into his eyes. Looked within her heart for faith in things she couldn't see. The solution of the riddle, *the two become one flesh.*

She kissed him deeply, thinking *Lin, remember. This is for you, for your body to remember. This is Husband, and his touch is love, your body's pride and pleasure. Remember this, and seek it again.*

She blinked. She languished, sad to death. It was finished, done. She turned and left, went toward her room.

He said "Linda" and she turned back, heart and body, to his voice. The bond was real, would hold her fast, however briefly it was to exist. As intimate and deep as any bond between daughter and father, as any between mother and son—of the essence of both, yet stronger than either. *For this reason they will leave, and cleave unto each other.* It would last until death, as it were, did them part.

She said "Yes?", blankly ready—she would do him any service, give anything he asked.

He said, "I need to get up no later than seven."

She sadly blinked; she knew that was it, all he wanted. "I've an alarm in my bedroom. I'll set it."

He said, "Thank you," and they'd finished with each other. What might have been was lost. She grieved her loss with the loss of all things, for her time was nearly over. She went to her room.

It was dark, as it ought to have been.

She undressed, and put on her blue camisole.

She fluffed her own pillow, turned down her covers, then set her alarm clock for quarter to seven. She got into bed.

She lay on her back, gazed at the ceiling. The square of light from the window, from the street lamp down below; shifting shadows from an elm's bare branches, swaying in the winter wind outside.

After a time, she smiled.

She whispered. "Lin, your things are okay. I cleaned out your car. I cleaned the apartment, really good. I didn't get to your laundry, though . . ."

She touched her hair, smiled in wonder.

"*Linda, you're okay.*"

She turned on her side, lay fetal. Soon she was asleep.

20

The alarm went off.

Linda turned it off, then lay back on her side.

She sat up. Something was different. Something was wrong.

She didn't know what it was.

She came out of the bedroom, stood in the hallway. She heard sounds from the den. A man standing, walking. Her husband—she knew the sound of his step. That calmed her, was assuring. Yet . . .

Bare shoulders and legs in the airy hall; she was cold, went back into the bedroom. She found her quilted bathrobe. Draped over the back of Derrick's chair, at his desk. Fretful, she *tsk*ed—here was something *obviously* wrong.

How would he like it if she put his shoes under her vanity?

And the more she looked around, the more things looked different, objects out of place. Her curling iron on her vanity, out of its box. Her vanity was *clean*—antique sediments of talc and blush powder, gone at a swipe of Lemon Pledge. Who would *dare*?

Then the bad news. The No-there's-not-a-simple-explanation part.

Derrick's stuff. His books. His tapes. His video games. Things he cherished, things she held sacred and never touched—

Gone.

She turned about with an anxious sigh. *Der, last night was Valentine's, not April Fools. Why would you make such drastic changes without asking or telling me? Derrick I give up, you win*—Ollie ollie oxen free.

All ye, all ye out are . . .

She went swiftly down the hall, towards the satin portiere, like a theater-goer late for curtain rise. She stopped at the curtain, didn't dare touch. "Derrick?"

The man in the den stopped moving.

He came to the portiere, moved it aside.

Linda was astonished. Her hand drifted to her mouth, then slowly dropped to her thigh.

"*Jared*?"

He, too, looked slightly amazed. Like he'd heard a woman pacing in the hall but somehow thought it wasn't she. And his words made equal sense:

"Linda, you're *okay*."

Her fear and confusion could wait. Jared was here, the friend of her youth. And what miraculous visitor ever lied when he told you, you're okay?

She came to him, swift and soft as a dove. Not holding him but making herself held—she cuddled into the trusted embrace, still as though she slept.

Jared kissed her hair. He murmured, as if awestruck: "It's you. It's *really* you."

She suddenly stepped back, held his hands—her fear and confusion wouldn't stay on hold. "Jared, *why*? You're here. Where's my husband?"

He replied to all her questions with the joyful calm of someone who grew up with someone else who's always anxious. " . . . if gangsters came and kidnapped Derrick, that's something we'll look into. Come sit with me." They sat. Holding her hand, he looked in her eyes: Was this all right?

She blinked: Of course?—she was frightened and perplexed.

"Lin, you know me. Right?"

"Jared?"

"I think so, too. What's today's date?"

"Huh?—well, isn't it the fifteenth? Jared, I want to know what's going on. Why are you asking *me* these things?" She fluttered her lashes, hapless and wronged—Why me?

"What's the last thing you remember, Lin?"

Awed, she was breathless: "*Oh God, this is getting spooky.*"

"Before just now, when you woke up. Before you went to sleep: what's the last thing that happened?"

"I got in bed . . . ?—oh. *We* went to bed. Not us; Derrick and I. Went to bed. We were sick. We drank wine that wasn't. Wine. Psychedelic nausea, we—" Jared motioned his hands, Slow down; he'd urged her to talk, now he couldn't shut her off. "—were sitting on the sofa, in the parlor. I was scared. And something happened between us, it was horrible and beautiful and frightening, we *looked too deep* into each other. Derrick and I and it was like . . ."

She was very calm. She lowered her head, her dubious, accusing look. Like Tenniel decided that Alice wasn't blonde, she was a little Brahmin princess and could tell the caterpillar things that all the hashish in his hookah wouldn't let him see.

But she couldn't describe what happened in the parlor, the night she and Derrick drank Pretty Girl wine.

" . . . it was like . . . I just . . ."

Jared helpfully offered, " ' . . . can't explain.' "

This puzzled her. "How did you know?"

"Lin, try to remember more."

She tried, and did. Her eyes shimmered with beauty, never

known on Earth. Still she was confused, afraid.

"Lin, you've had problems with your memory. You know this—right?"

"Jared, no—if I didn't remember something, I've forgotten."

"Lin, your mother told me some things. Try not to be mad. But I need to ask you the silliest question."

"Who else asked me silly questions?"

Jared paused, the second it took to figure this out: the fact that his was superlative implied there was a group. "Hon, no one. Believe me, this isn't something *I* perceived or—"

"Have I been abducted by aliens."

"No: do you think you're a man."

She calmly parted her lips—an intelligent girl who could easily answer any sensible question, utterly stumped.

Then: "Oh, obviously. Jared, yes: I'm a man. What drug is my mother *on*? Now, I want to know where Derrick is, why you're here, what this is all about and if I count to three and you don't tell me, I will scream. One. Two—"

"You've been gone. You haven't been with us."

This overwhelmed her, all at once. She softly asked, "I m-missed something?" She "missed" things by having *petit mals* and hoped it was nothing more than that.

Jared told her gently, "Hon, you missed a *lot*."

She put her hand to her mouth. That might mean a Big Bad—*grand mal*. Or a lot of Little Bads all in a row. "I missed a whole *day*?"

"Um . . . yes. You did that a number of times consecutively. Or let me put it this way—"

She grabbed his wrist. "Jared, where's my husband? I want to know this very minute—"

They froze.

She stared at him, amazed. He gazed back, lucid in his thoughts, yet watching marvels unexplained unfold.

The dark and gentle angel of the morning, her intelligent face framed by her inky curls. She read Camus and Kafka yet she couldn't understand, why she asked for her husband and grabbed Jared's wrist.

The friend of her youth, slightly shaking his head. Veteran of her childhood and, by the by, of Desert Storm—he'd cautiously come back to pay a visit, not sure it was allowed. Now he wasn't allowed to leave; he had to answer to Linda. It somehow seemed that he always would, from this moment on—that he couldn't even leave her side, except there was a reason. "I have to see who's here."

This deepened her dismay. "Why, who is it?"

"I don't know. The plumber. The burglars. I'll go see." At the satin portiere, he said, "I'll make us coffee. I'll make you some breakfast." For good measure, "I'll take care of *every*thing."

"Please do." She added, "This is really inconvenient," clutching the neck of her bathrobe as if tulip-and-iris could ward off all evil.

Jared went into the hall, met Shelley. He halted and nodded, duly impressed—he only needed his mother, now, to complete the set of dominant women in his life. "Mrs. Bauer."

Curious, she reminded him, "Shelley."—she wasn't someone's mother. "I'm on my way into town—by that I mean, Boston—to revise Conference memos. Which sounds so prestigious when really, I'm the Doughnut Girl. Bavarian cream for all deserving." She touched his hand and shared her poignant longing. "The vanilla-glazed are *so* nice.—But *voilà*, I am here. Thought I'd drop in." She peered at him closely—a lilac-scented angel in a leather coat, suspicious. "Jared, am I hopelessly old-fashioned, or is it a little early in the day for you to visit?"

Her eyes were alight, a fearless challenge: If you must be a rogue, leave my daughter out of this. Take on someone world-class.

"Dear, you're not old-fashioned, but this isn't as it seems."

"Jared, I'm . . . concerned! My God!"

"Our God is fine. I think you mean Linda."

Shelley's voice dropped to its deep and silken register. "I need to be concerned with her? Whatever did you do?" Jared glanced into the kitchen, touched Shelley's arm. She shied from a suspected seducer's touch. But he coaxed her to come sit with him at the kitchen table.

For the most part, Jared talked. Shelley stared with parted lips, like she heard a fabulous tale.

Linda appeared in the hallway, outside the kitchen door. She hovered timidly, in and out of sight, the return of a childhood inhibition—you shouldn't intrude when you're being talked about.

She glanced down at herself. Her mother's girl. *Yes, Lin, I'll admit times have changed: you may receive a close male friend—someone you've known in the home, here with us—in your bathrobe* BUT ONLY *before nine a.m. So long as the closure is buttoned* all the way. *And provided, of course, you've got something on underneath. That* doesn't *mean your blue camisole. You never understand—Lin, you're not a child. Lin, you're a beautiful woman. No, it's not an abstract thing—you're a* physically beautiful woman. *Honor yourself before men.*

She felt her hips, the camisole's silk under her quilt . . .

Oh Mother, deal with it. She came into the kitchen.

Shelley went to her. She held her daughter's shoulders, looked into her eyes.

Linda blinked, bewildered: *It's just me.*

Shelley almost wept, or laughed. Like she'd been afraid of something silly, but no man was in the closet and the moaning was the wind. Shelley hugged her daughter. Linda, squished, was wide-eyed: *What on Earth did I do?*

Jared cleared his throat. "Lin, I have to meet with buyers." Over her mother's shoulder, Linda gazed a bewildered plea. He mouthed, so Shelley wouldn't hear: *I'll call you, Lin. Tonight.*

She blinked back, perplexed: *You will?*

Jared left.

Shelley sat Linda down at the table. Rubbed her daughter's shoulder, offered to make tea. Linda said she'd cry—she wanted truth, not tea. "Mom, where's Derrick? Something's happened. You know what it is. Why won't you tell me?"

Shelley sat at her daughter's side. "Lin, sometimes I wasn't sure. I couldn't just dismiss what you were saying. Because you really believed it, Lin—that was true, for you."

"Mother, any clue will be more than welcome. I'm worried about Derrick. Is he . . . ? He is; I know. He's . . ."

Shelley gently finished, what Linda already knew. " . . . gone."

Linda covered her face with her hands. She softly wept, while Shelley stroked her hair.

At length, Shelley said, "Yes, Derrick's gone. Today is March second, Linda. Today is the second of March."

"Mom, I don't remember."

"You've been crying for two weeks. You can stop, now."

Shelley waited, then encouraged more: "Linda, you can stop crying, now."

"Mom, I can't accept this. I can't live this part of my life."

Shelley said, "He knew that, dear. That's . . ."

Shelley wondered. Her daughter asked for truth. Yet what was that, really? Scenes and events, on God's camcorder? What was truly real, and Who decided?

Do you believe in future games? Romancing the past, as it should have been lived? This isn't a question of miracles: do you believe in love?

" . . . why he lived it for you. He held you and waited until you came back. Lin, Derrick loved you so."

Shelley's eyes flashed softly, amber peace and assurance. Always the unconscious mimic, Linda flashed her own eyes, softly, back.